MW01140771

Perchance to Dream

Dr. H. John Powell

authorHOUSE®

AuthorHouse™ UK Ltd.
500 Avebury Boulevard
Central Milton Keynes, MK9 2BE
www.authorhouse.co.uk
Phone: 08001974150

First published by AuthorHouse   10/5/2011

ISBN: 978-1-4567-8155-2 (sc)

PART 1

PROLOGUE

'RIGHT', THOUGHT GORDON. 'That's it. End of five years hard grind in medicine. Join the queue tomorrow to march up to the dais and receive my Diploma. Get cards printed with M.B.Ch.B after my name. Then for my real life. A doctor.'

Why had he made such a decision? Was it because, on \account of his mother's suffering from a cancerous condition that he wished to help other folk in distress? Yes, he certainly had that basic desire. He had observed the care and attention shown to her and wished to base his life on similar lines to those of her medical attendants. Didn't the 'Dr' title identify him as a person deserving respect? Well…

Gordon refused to celebrate his last evening before graduation by joining a vodka imbibing party of rowdy students. Instead he joined his father in the sumptuous flat where they lived and contemplated quietly, sipping Earl Grey tea and remembering his years of work; work that would entitle him to drape a stethoscope over his shoulders and wear the long white coat of a qualified medical man. Thoughts came. ...

There was the anatomy dissecting room. Rows of tables bearing naked cadavers that awaited the sharpish scalpels of doctors-to-be as they carved into dead flesh to discover the internal anatomical arrangements of a human being.

There was the chemistry that revealed the secret make-up of flesh and blood. The physiology lectures instructing him about the functions of body organs. The pathology lectures that informed and showed through the microscope the appearance of diseased tissues. In the biology laboratory the foot of a live frog could be seen under the microscope. A tiny prick in a minute artery in the foot's web and he could observe the outpouring of a river of red blood cells. Gradually there would appear a build up of cells adhering to the edge of the minute wound. The river would be reduced. Suddenly it would stop. Bleeding ceased. Healing had occurred. Gordon's mind revolved around the eternal wonder of the built-in healing systems in animals and plants. As long as life was present in an individual there was also present automatic healing to correct damage. Who said miracles didn't happen?

Medical sessions often told of serious disease. The streptococcal germs that presaged not only throat infections but also possible attacks on heart valves and other organs, the tetanus that brought fearful spasms, frequently ending life unless anti-tetanus serum was available; the pneumococcus, the influenza virus, and the leprosy germ that disfigured and caused terror to millions of folk in the so-called 'third world'. And all the rest.

Surgical experience began in the anaesthetic room. Here, Gordon was allowed tentatively to push an intra-tracheal tube between the vocal chords of a patient rendered unconscious by an intravenous anaesthetic. He received the congratulations of the consultant and felt that his hands had not let him down. Invited to assist the surgeon at the operating table he felt a little shaky when requested to spread wider the instrument holding apart the abdominal wound edges.

"There's a huge aneurysm of the abdominal aorta here, laddie. I have to get my hand in. Open widely please." said the operator. Gordon squeezed the spreader opening the surgical wound wider..."That's better. Thank you" responded the great man. On another occasion he was allowed to plunge a scalpel into the depths of a quinsy thus evacuating quantities of pus. With further expertise he felt that he might, after many years of experience, attain the lofty status of a surgeon. Finally there was the examination that would determine his adequate knowledge of medicine and pass him as fit to shake the hand of the University's Chancellor and be entitled to those magic initials, M.B.Ch.B..

Gordon, a tall, well set up young man, healthy and muscular from old days on the rugby field, stretched and stood up. He said, "I've made it. Thank you, Dad, for all your help and care. I'll try to repay it by doing a really good job."

His father stood also and took him by the hand, congratulating him. He said, "You have done well, Gordon. I am very proud of you. Go out into the world and practise the business of helping people. You will find there is still a great deal to learn. I'm sure you'll be a fine doctor. Let's have a walk in the park and take some deep breaths. We have to be up early tomorrow."

A very early start next day brought them to Edinburgh in good time. Donning his graduation robes, hired for the occasion, he led his father to the McEwan hall among many other students now qualifying for their degrees, In due course he shook the Chancellor's hand His qualification was secure.

It was good to emerge from the big hall following the graduation ceremony and make their way to the open grassy slopes beneath the Salisbury Crags near the fair city of Edinburgh. The fresh air blowing gently from the east revived them and an hour later they turned their steps back to their hotel with renewed vigour and cheeks that glowed from the afternoon sun of high summer.

The next morning after stepping for the last time along Princes St. and climbing the Mound, a brisk walk took them past the New Quadrangle and the gates of the Royal Infirmary where Gordon waved goodbye to his *alma mater* ere seeking the car for the return drive to Oxenby. His father drove, not too fast, and brought them both home at last in time for a good meal and an evening's chat and bed.

Sleep for Gordon was restless. He dreamed ---

'He had promised a friend in Wakefield to assist with the choosing of nice furniture for his new home with his recently married bride. He drove there in good time and they met in a coffee shop in town, greeting each other happily as befitted the years of student fun which they had shared together in Scotland. After coffee they went from shop to shop inspecting available pieces until at last Gordon parked his car in a space fronting an emporium that boasted fine furniture and antiques.

'This was better. An hour or two spent carefully examining the pedigree of the gleaming woodwork displayed gave final satisfaction. They emerged with a precious list of excellent purchases. A double bed, a dining table with four chairs, a bow-fronted chest of drawers of ancient vintage and a tallboy that would grace their bedroom. These along with a lovely dressing table and three mirrors for the lady would provide drawer space for many years. All pieces appeared to be of good quality polished mahogany, It was a relief to return to the light of day. Not such a relief was it to find the burly figure of a police constable standing beside Gordon's little car. He waved his notebook at them and spoke sternly.

"'Is this your car, sir?"

"Yes, it is. Is there some trouble?"

"You have parked it in a no-parking area on this side of the street."

"Oh I'm sorry. But I didn't see a notice to that effect."

'The constable pointed upwards. Above him reared a tall metal post with what appeared to be a sign attached. However it was amply covered with a double layer of sacking.

"The notice isn't very visible" said Gordon.

The policeman looked upwards and grunted. "Oh. Hmm. Well, may I see your driving licence please, sir?" Gordon searched his pockets and the car's glove box.. After a minute he said,

"I'm afraid I must have left it at home".

"And your insurance policy?"

"That's at home too"

"Hmm. very careless. Let's have a look at your car licence", and he moved towards the windscreen.

"Well, well" he declared with severe emphasis. "One year out of date", and he pulled out a pencil, preparing to write.

"I got a new one for this year a few days ago. In the excitement of graduation I must have forgotten to display it."

"Are you aware, sir, that it is an offence not to display your licence?" The severity was marked.

"Yes, I know of course. I'm very sorry."

'The constable grunted and again prepared to write. "What is your name sir?" Gordon told him. "And what is your address?" Likewise. "And what is your occupation sir." Gordon told him.

"Oh, doctor eh? And just qualified of course." He laughed. A sarcastic laugh. "Of course". About to write, he paused; the memory of his little boy just sent to the hospital with bronchopneumonia came into his mind; also the clever young locum doctor who had made a swift diagnosis and arranged hospitalisation just in time to save the child's life

'He put his notebook away. "Alright you're forgiven. I won't book you this time. Just remember next time, please. And when you get home you must write to the Chief Constable here and apologise. Good afternoon, doctor. – oh and another thing. This is a one way street. Your car is facing in the wrong direction. I'll see you safely turned around. Lucky aren't you".....

"Gosh" said Gordon. to his friend after making the correction due. "I certainly am. Looking for the furniture shop I never saw the street sign. Wonder what made him change his mind".

"Sometimes police are quite kind to doctors", said his friend. "Doctors look after the police too". They returned to the friend's house and Gordon was invited to stay the night.

'Reaching home next day he searched, found, and carefully ensured the safety and whereabouts of the important car documents. Then other thoughts came to mind…Wasn't that lovely girl at the Oxford graduation ceremony, which he had attended, going to a garden party tomorrow afternoon? He smiled happily as the dream faded'

The latter part of the dream intermingled somehow with the doings of the coming day. He would gatecrash that party...

****

CHAPTER 1

THEY MEET

'OOH HE'S REALLY gorgeous' was Judith's murmur to herself when relaxing in a deck chair in the shade of an old chestnut tree. She was gazing at a tall, handsome and athletic young fellow surrounded by a bevy of smartly dressed young women in the college grounds, where students were holding their end-of-term garden party following graduation. The day was hot, the sun shone brightly and the beautiful skirts of the girls caused envy to rise in Judith's heart as she surveyed herself in the drab, uncolourful garment that was all her church-minister father could afford for her. John McFarlane was blest with only a small income. Highly intelligent, a dedicated clergyman, deprived of help from his wife on account of her severe Alzheimers condition, he was absorbed in serving the many needs of his church members Faced with those of his only child he was helpless.

The young lady, possessed of a lovely figure and

shining blonde curly hair, was very aware and appreciative of her father's predicament. She tore away her gaze from the attractive young man and tried to stop her daydreaming while noticing however that he had quietly pushed through the mob of admiring girls and sought an ice-cream van. A few minutes later she was aware of a movement beside her and a voice saying, "May I join you? My name is Gordon Jenkins. May I provide an icy counter to the day's heat?" And that same gorgeous young man handed her an ice-cream cone, pulled along a deck chair and sat down beside her. Judith opened her eyes wide in astonishment, hurriedly patted her blonde curls into place and smiled with a murmured "Thank you".

"I've been looking everywhere for you", said Gordon.. "I wanted to congratulate you on your excellent result in the Arts examination. You were the only one to pass with such a high grade and a star to boot. So, my very best congrats and good wishes. What are you planning to do with such success?"

Judith felt quite nonplussed. What an astonishing thing that this young Greek god should seek her out. It took a few seconds to regain her composure while smoothing her brown skirt tidily over her knees. Then she said, "Well thank you – and thank you too for this lovely cool present. I'm not quite sure what to do really" She licked the ice cream appreciatively. "I suppose I had thought of something in the social services line. You're doing medicine aren't you? Which branch of Hippocrates' wisdom do you plan to follow?"

"Quite a Parliamentarian, aren't you? Answer one question by posing another Jolly good. Like you I'm not certain yet. Tell you what. After this jamboree is over why not come with me and I'll treat you to a pub meal? I know quite a good little place out of town. We could talk and sort things out".

Judith thought that a lovely invitation, especially the idea of a pub meal. She knew that her wardrobe was not up to a fashionable restaurant. "That would be very nice.. Thank you" she said.

"I have a little old Princess 1300," Gordon said. "Can I pick you up? Is it the vicarage or the manse?"

He had evidently been doing some research, thought Judy, as she answered, "It's the manse. Do you know where it is? It's in Oxenby, a few miles away,"

Gordon's reply confirmed her statement. .He was well informed. On that they rose and Gordon folded and put away the deck chairs, she being quite thrilled at such an invitation, and he feeling very pleased at the prospect of so lovely a companion for the evening. With her sleek blonde hair, hazel eyes and charming figure she would turn heads in the little country pub.

The garden party ended with the singing of 'Auld Lang Syne' and all the graduates went their several ways, some of the girls being escorted attentively by their male friends.

Their peaceful departure was shattered by a sudden shouting "Dr. Jenkins, Dr.Jenkins can you come? Quickly please." A young fellow, clad in the glad rags of the graduation party, rushed madly across the grass towards Gordon as he approached the gate. "There's an emergency, please come", and the lad grasped Gordon's arm and pulled him away towards the other side of the grounds. They both hurried towards a small crowd of folk surrounding an elderly man lying in a deck chair. He was holding his hands to his chest, groaning, with sweat on his face and muttering quietly, "The pain, the pain". Gordon recognised him as one of the college tutors. Kneeling on the grass beside the chair he pulled out a stethoscope from his hip pocket; quickly undid a few buttons of the man's shirt and, with the earpieces in his ears, laid the business end of the instrument on the tutor's chest. He listened for a few moments; then, turning to the crowd he called loudly, "Has anyone got an aspirin in their handbag?" Several women began to shuffle in the depths of their fancy party handbags. One of them pulled out a pill and extended her hand to Gordon. "Will that do? " She asked.

"Perfect." he replied and, taking the tablet pushed it gently between the patient's lips, saying, "Just crunch this pill and try to swallow it; keep on crunching and swallowing until it's gone. It will do you good."

Gordon turned to find that Judith had followed him. He spoke urgently to her. "Telephone 999, tell the ambulance it's a chest pain, and please come as soon as they can. His name is Mr. Rawlinson". Judith turned and ran for the nearest gate. She knew that there was a phone box just outside. She rang, speaking clearly and urgently and giving a precise description of the patient's position within the grounds. Gordon continued to encourage the old chap to crunch his aspirin, holding the feeble pulse and listening to the heart beat. A student had thoughtfully run to the nearest building and returned with a glass of water. Judith rushed back to support his head and assist the patient to take a little drink.

"They're coming", she told Gordon. Very shortly the siren of the ambulance was heard. Competent men jumped out bringing with them a wheeled stretcher and assessed the situation; then gently lifting the patient onto the stretcher, they conveyed him to the ambulance making him as comfortable as possible. Gordon rose from the grass, dusted down his trousers, thanked the little crowd of onlookers, and told Judith, "I must go with him to the hospital and see him safely handed over to the doctor. Will you arrange to inform his people, and I'll see you later". He hopped into the vehicle rapidly and sat beside his patient. With siren sounding, the ambulance was swiftly driven off to the hospital. It was Judith's first experience of a medical emergency; feeling rather shaky she picked up her handbag, nodded to the helpful student and was given a lift home to Oxenby. Judith's home was an old-fashioned Victorian three-storey house that sported a monkey-puzzle tree in the small front garden. Her father used the rear dining room as a study. The furnishing was of a heavy, ancient vintage. The once popular antimacassars still covered the big armchairs. Electric light had replaced the gas lamps and to keep up with the times the church owning the property had installed a central heating system.

Judith sighed as she entered and greeted her father as he sat at his typewriter composing a sermon for the Sabbath. She enquired about the doctor's opinion regarding her mother. There was little change in her condition her father told her, and no word of any useful treatment.

Then, remembering Gordon's request that she should inform Mr.Rawlinson's people, she told her father of the sudden emergency. "Why I know those people," said her father, "They attend our church. They live here in Oxenby. I'll go and see his wife and tell her. I can offer her transport to the hospital. I'll go at once;" saying which he quickly strode to the garage, backed his Morris Minor out and drove off. Her father stoutly maintained that his duties were not only spiritual; he was also very mindful of his people's physical needs. Judith, knowing that he would need his evening meal retired to the old kitchen to operate the gas stove and prepare food for him and her mother. Some time later her father returned to tell his daughter that Mrs. Rawlinson had driven to the hospital in her own car.

"Oh that's good" she said; then, her mood suddenly changing to gaiety, Judith added, "Daddy I must tell you. I have an invitation to an evening meal with a nice young man."

The note of excitement was not lost on Judy's father who noted his darling daughter patting her curls into place, and whose competent brain rapidly produced a bombardment of future possibilities that might affect him and his wife. But he just replied, "That's lovely, my Darling. Have a good time. In case I'm asleep when you come in I'll leave the door open for you; we don't seem to have a spare key." She replied "OK, Daddy, I've heated up your dinner that was all ready for you, so here it is and Mummy's is on the tray for you to take up. I'll go up and get changed".

As she went upstairs she wondered how to make herself presentable for the occasion, remembering her wardrobe's limitations. A real party dress would have been welcome, but she had never possessed such a thing of beauty, and she again thought enviously of the other students with their lovely dresses. She finally chose a nice cream top and a black skirt. With a touch of make-up and a minimum of lipstick the result was simple but quite enchanting. To finish the ensemble she thought that to borrow her mother's pearl necklace and granny's rhinestone ring would not be out of place, while the charming Scottish brooch given to her last Christmas by an uncle made an attractive finishing touch…She had never possessed any nice jewellery.

Judith had just donned her 'sensible' shoes when the ancient bell that hung up in the kitchen jangled vigorously and her father left his meal and opened the door to a good-looking young man who greeted him courteously.

"Good evening, Sir, my name is Gordon Jenkins. I'm hoping to entertain Judith this evening. I expect you are her father". John MacFarlane, impressed by Gordon's polite tone, held out his hand in welcome.

"Good evening, Gordon. Come in. I am very pleased to meet you. Yes indeed, that charming girl is my daughter. I expect she is nearly ready." And he called, "Judith, you have a visitor."

"Just coming Daddy" and Judith floated down the stairs, mking a carefully staged entrance that enchanted Gordon and delighted her father.

"Well, have a nice time Gordon, and, as I told Judith, I'll leave the door open. We don't appear to have a spare key. I'll get back to my study and type my sermon for next Sunday".

The young man took the girl's arm and guided her down the front steps and out to his little car. He opened the passenger door for her and ensured that she was comfortable before starting the engine. Skilfully Gordon weaved his way through traffic, soon leaving the town behind and guiding the little car onto a quiet country road in the peaceful evening. After passing through a couple of villages Gordon said, "It's only two miles now and we'll get to the pub where I've booked a table." He went on, "It's beside a crossroads where highway-men were dealt with in the old days. The gallows have gone now of course, but there's a canal bank not far away. Would you like a walk there in the gloaming for half an hour before dinner? "

Judith thought that idea excellent and shortly, after leaving the car in the pub car park, they found the canal quite near. Its sluggish water was largely covered in waterweed with lilies here and there. A heron flapped slowly by but found nowhere to stand and moved away. Swallows curved and pirouetted through the air gobbling up mouthfuls of insects while swifts also flew at tremendous speed, twisting and turning in wonderful acrobatic agility with screams that hit the eardrums with surprise as they screeched overhead.

As they walked Judith and Gordon began to talk of the interesting subjects of their last year of study. Judith had been fascinated by the history and culture of Rome with its succession of Emperors and high officials. Stories of Rome's conquests and satellite establishments with Governors and their responsibilities to the Emperors she had always found of great interest. She related to Gordon accounts of the finding of old buildings deep underground by modern archaeologists. Imagination of the affairs relating to the Coliseum; to St. Paul and his appeal to Caesar and subsequent incarceration and ultimate fate when Nero turned on the Christian community; the building of temples in foreign lands; the subjection of the Jews and the treatment of slaves; she spoke of them all and could have gone on for hours.

Gordon was thrilled to discover what a depth of information and learning was hidden in Judith's pretty head. His education had been largely on the science side and the result had been a plenitude of brain cells packed with all kinds of scientific knowledge. When time allowed from the amassing of information about the intimate structure and working of the human body, his mind had wandered far out in space and time to think of the astonishing facts discovered concerning the universe; its amazing spaces, with unimaginable distances between stars and galaxies. Then back to earth with attempts at understanding tectonic plates, tsunamis, volcanic activity and their relation to the people and animals of the natural world in which we now live. His thoughts would stray to consider the balance of natural phenomena, plant life and animal, land and sea creatures, not forgetting the long past ages of the dinosaurs and the creatures fossilised and all ready for detailed study by modern man. They found time slipping by quite rapidly and were several minutes late when they eventually sat down at the booked table, with the conversation in abeyance but ready to start up at any time. The wine waiter approached.

"Would a glass of white wine be suitable for you? I'm not sure what your habit is about alcohol." said Gordon.

"Nor am I", replied Judith. "We don't indulge at the manse, but I have no convictions either way and I'm quite willing to experiment. You may have to carry me out of course." Gordon refrained from saying that nothing would please him more….

A discussion with the waiter resulted in the choice of a very light product and Judith found sips of this quite pleasant. With the choice of menu made they could continue to chat happily of Roman Forums, Grecian battles, Palestinian insurrections, all mixed up with the Missing Link, life on Mars, and the number of little red cells to each cubic millilitre of good red blood. By the time they had both broken into merry laughter about such illogical mixtures they found that appetites were quite enhanced. They enjoyed their meal, comparing their mixed converse with the edible mixture of melon, lamb cutlets, broccoli, beans, potatoes, laced with mint sauce, and a quite magnificent ice cream conglomeration to round it all off.

Coffee in the lounge was now the pleasurable end of this indulgence and they lingered over it, continuing to explore each other's lives and experiences in happy companion ship. Judith told Gordon of the sad discovery of her mother's brain trouble and the difficulties imposed on her father. The housekeeping was now almost entirely her responsibility for funds would only allow domestic help very rarely. Her father managed well but his parishioners needed most of his time of course and the management of church affairs rested largely on his shoulders. He often spent evenings at meetings of one sort or another and had little time for personal relaxation. There were no holidays.

Gordon quickly gained an insight into the life now led by his friend; he now began to give her an outline of his own circumstances. His father was sufficiently well heeled to send him to a good public school and to his medical course at Edinburgh University. Fortunately, as Gordon saw it, his father wisely did not inflict large amounts of pocket money on his son, believing that the young should manage their affairs sensibly with due regard to economy. He had been glad of help to buy the little second hand car, carefully chosen for quality and low running costs, and to help with fees he usually managed to hold down a job during the holidays. The family business, of which his father was the part owner and full-time managing director, was doing very creditably. However the father had told his son that he would not be passing on a fortune to him on his demise. He felt it right for a man to make his own way in the world, perhaps with a little help when required. So with that end in view Gordon had been working hard to get a good qualification.

The two young folk spent an enthralling hour or more commenting on, and dissecting the items of information that had affected their lives. After a while Gordon said,

"I don't know what you'll think of this, Judy, but I feel I must tell you. I have mentioned that my father runs a very successful business, in antiques actually. Sometimes there's a vacancy in a secretarial post. I wondered if that kind of job would appeal to you. May I mention to my father that you might be interested, do you think?"

Judy considered. Certainly her interests lay in that line of country. Thoughts of old historical people and created items of the past had always occupied a niche in her mind. While her excellent qualification might indeed enable her to fill a much more important post, such an opening could be an ideal way to making a success of her future. She could also live at home still and care for her parents. After a minute she replied, "Gordon that is very kind of you to think of it. Yes, I believe that I could be interested in that sort of work. I am pretty good on typing, letters and languages, and my spelling is reasonably good. If anything comes up I will certainly apply".

"Good then, I'll ask my father to think about it".

That seemed a suitable note on which to end their evening and Gordon looked at his watch. The time had sped by and they must be getting home. Judy slipped her wrap over her slim shoulders for the evening was becoming chilly and they smiled at each other affectionately as they settled in his little car. The drive home should have been smooth and peaceful. It was not.

While they dined and talked a heavy cloud had come across the area and a sharp shower had wetted the road. Gordon reduced speed a little and still more as he approached a bend that created a blind corner. Rounding this, a warning lamp stood on the road confronting them and a police car was stationary on the roadside. An officer was waving his hand to attract their attention. Beyond the car Gordon could see two vehicles locked in a head-on collision in the midst of the road with horns sounding madly. Other police were in close attention. At once Gordon pulled in to the roadside and stopped.

The policeman approached. Gordon said, "I see there has been an accident, officer. I am a doctor, do you need any help?"

"Yes indeed, thank you sir" was the reply. "I'm afraid someone has been badly injured. Your help would be much appreciated." Gordon jumped out of his car, shouted to Judy "Come quick," and, picking up his medical bag that he kept on the back seat, he rushed to the accident area. The driver's window of the smaller car was open, the door locked; the driver was conscious but his face was wreathed in agony. Gordon smelled petrol. He put in his hand and plucked out the ignition key. He saw that the locking button was down, pulled it up and opened the door. Leaning in over the driver he felt for the carotid artery and said "Heart's beating well, but that smell of petrol spells trouble. Let's get him out quickly. Judy, will you put your arms under his legs and lift". She did, Gordon at the same time, sliding hands and arms beneath the shoulders to lift him.. The young man shrieked and fainted. Police officers promptly came to help and between them, and with some difficulty, they extracted him, noting an increase in the smell of petrol.

They carried him back towards the ambulance which had now arrived. Rapidly they lifted him, still unconscious, into the vehicle, made him as comfortable as possible and strapped him in firmly. The woman passenger, standing beside the wrecked car, put a cigarette between her lips and flicked on he lighter.

Gordon yelled "Put that light out!" Too late. The petrol ignited. In no time the car was a mass of flames. The woman's coat caught fire. She shrieked, beating at the flames. A fireman from the fire engine that was now busy towing the other car away from the crash caught up a bucket of water and threw it quickly over the girl, dowsing the flames immediately.

"Quick," shouted Gordon to an ambulance man who, with a policeman had relieved Judith and him, "get the ambulance away. That fire will reach the petrol tank. It'll explode." He was right. It did. In a very few moments and with a tremendous roar a furious fireball enveloped the car causing it to disappear in a vast ball of flame. The girl and attending police had run for their lives and, with all the rest, were safely out of harm's way.

While fire men dealt with the blazing wreck Gordon climbed into the ambulance and examined the young man. "He's got a fractured femur, and his right ankle is dislocated" he said. "Have you got a Thomas's splint in this bus? Let's get it on him before he comes round." While the ambulance man did a quick search Gordon managed to manipulate and reduce the dislocation. His orthopaedic instruction was bearing fruit. The splint found, it was handed to Gordon. "Scissors to remove this trouser leg" was his demand. These too were found and quickly the trouser was cut from end to end and removed. Gordon now, with the ambulance man assisting, inserted the leg into the Thomas' splint which was already suitably bandaged. It was then all made fast appropriately. Elastoplast was applied to the lower leg, avoiding the ankle, a hefty string was tied to it and Gordon brought it over the splint's end attaching a heavy sandbag to provide effective traction. He then raised it up and suspended it from a gadget in the roof. The young man's eyes opened and he groaned. Gordon searched his emergency packet, always carried in the car. . Finding an ampoule of morphine he checked the dosage and quickly jabbed it into the patient's arm. "You had a bad car accident and your thigh bone is broken," Gordon said. "That injection should help a lot; you'll be off to hospital now. Try and keep still if you can and the best of luck," he said and jumped out. Turning to Judith he added, "Could you pop in and comfort that girl a bit please, Judith, while I write a note for the hospital doctor."

The girl, soaking wet from the firemen's handy bucket, had climbed into the ambulance and was sitting beside the young chap, weeping and holding his hand. "We'd just got engaged" she moaned. Judith also climbed in and put an arm around her shoulders. "That's lovely" she said. "They'll soon get him right so try not to worry. You must get off to the hospital quickly now. Bones will heal. He'll be all right. There's no time for more. But are your hands alright? I saw you beating at the flames."

"Yes" said the girl, "I had leather gloves on. I expect they'll be ruined but my hands are OK As for my coat… Oh dear! "

"Sorry about that but thank goodness your hands are OK" Judith replied. "I'll ring the ward tomorrow and find out how things are. Good bye and God bless."

She returned to Gordon and he took her hand saying, "I'm quite sure he'll make it Judy. Thank you for helping".

With one of the ambulance men inside accompanying the distressed pair, the driver closed all doors and drove off with care, the sirens shrieking. The firemen continued their task of extinguishing flames in the burning vehicle and the senior policeman approached Judith and Gordon. The latter addressed him saying, "What about the driver in the other car, is he injured?"

"I'm afraid he's dead, doctor. He must have been killed immediately. I should be very glad if you would come and confirm the death, and perhaps you would sign the appropriate form."

Gordon complied saying "That's a pity." He briefly

examined the body and sighed deeply as he signed the necessary form. Then he remarked, "I heard the chief fireman mentioning the explosion to you. I thought he said that he was curious about it; that it might not have been entirely due to petrol. That sounded rather suspicious. If that were so would it involve me in any way?"

"I cannot comment on that doctor. It has to be a confidential matter between the fire people and the police. I cannot envisage any circumstances that might cause you any concern, but if you were needed as a witness we would inform you. I must thank you for all your help, sir. It's not often we have such good professional medical assistance when we're called out to an incident like this"

Gordon replied saying, "I've been very glad to help. I have only just qualified. We celebrated at a garden party this afternoon. This was a sad end to a romantic evening for those two, and someone will be extremely sad about this other poor chap. Anyway I feel sure that lad's femur will mend in time and all will be well".

"Yes sir, I'm sure we all hope so. If you will just sign a form certifying your attendance at this incident you can then get off home." Gordon signed the form as desired, glad to end the whole sad business.

"Thank you, sir. And thank you too, Miss, you were a great help. Go carefully".

They both turned to Gordon's little car and settled themselves. They continued their journey in silence, passing through the quiet streets when entering the town until they reached the manse. They sat silently for a few minutes. Then Judith said, "Oh dear, I feel so terribly sad for them. To have such a thing happening just after the wonderful moment of becoming engaged! I expect his mind was distracted and he was driving a bit carelessly in the wet. The other driver was in the middle of the road too. Quite tragic. I 'll just have to put up a little prayer for them all."

"That's right," said Gordon, opening the car door for her. He handed his guest up the manse steps, bent and tenderly kissed her cheek, adding, "Thank you for such a lovely evening, Judy. It's a shame that it ended in that way, but it was good to be able to help. Anyway do you think we could join together again next week?"

Judith lifted her face to his, smiling. "Yes Gordon" she said, without hesitation. "That would be quite lovely. Thank you very much, it would be delightful. I'll look forward to it all the week." And, after another kiss, smilingly, they wished each other 'Goodnight.'

✳✳✳✳✳✳✳✳✳✳✳✳✳✳✳✳✳✳✳✳

Chapter 2

A FRANTIC CALL

JUDITH SLEPT SOUNDLY, waking reluctantly as her bedside telephone rang and wondering if it was her father with a worry about her mother. Looking at her watch – two o'clock - she picked up the handset.

There was a woman's voice, frightened, urgent with anxiety, blasting her ear drum.

"Judith you've got to help me. It's been going on all night. I can't bear it. Please tell me what to do."

"All right, Claudia". Judith was well used to her friend's sudden panics and took control as always. "Just tell me what's the matter? Is it Richard?"

"Yes," Claudia replied. "I'm sorry to wake you but Clive is away, out east somewhere as usual and…"

Judith cut in, demanding, "Is Richard ill?"

"Yes, I told you. He started with a bad earache three days or so ago and I took him to the doctor. He just said to put olive oil in and I did that, but it's got worse, very much worse."

"So what's the situation now?

"Well he's got a terrible headache and he's been sick. He's quite dizzy and can't stand up, and he's very hot indeed."

This is where I shout for help, thought Judith, and told Claudia to replace her phone and she would ring back very soon. She would talk to Gordon; shrugging into an old dressing gown she found his number and rang.

"Hallo. This is Dr. Jenkins. Is there trouble?"

"Gordon it's Judith. I'm sorry to wake you but I need advice about a friend's little boy."

"OK. Judy, shoot."

She quickly told the story in detail, together with the name, the child's birtrhdsy and telephone number of her friend.

"That sounds very nasty, Judith. I expect he's had some earache for quite a while and now it has flared up. He should be in hospital urgently. I'll ring the ambulance with the details and find which hospital they'll take him to. Then I'll ring your friend and warn her. I'll let you know. Bye now."

Gordon dialled 999 and relayed the story asking for very urgent attention as the case might well be a cerebral abscess. He asked to which hospital A& E department the child would be taken, and was told the Radcliffe in Oxford'. He made a note. He then rang that department and asked to speak to the doctor on duty. He was shortly connected.

"Doctor, I am sending you a child with symptoms very suggestive of a cerebral abscess. As it could be an extremely serious matter I thought I should give you advance warning." Gordon told the duty doctor all that he had heard, not forgetting to plant in that young resident's mind the thought that it might be appropriate to inform the neurosurgical registrar. He was heard patiently and thanked for his courtesy. They rang off.

Now there came the task of informing the child's mother, without causing her inordinate worry about future possibilities. *'Sufficient unto the day!'* There was no difficulty. Claudia quickly calmed down on leaning that rapid action was being taken and was thanking Gordon when she suddenly noticed the ambulance stopping outside her gate.

"Here they are" she said. "Bye." and rang off.

The ambulance crew very quickly grasped the situation and with wonderful expertise conveyed the little chap to their vehicle, wrapped him cosily and tucked him in securely. After his mother had collected her coat and handbag and jumped in beside Richard, they drove off rapidly with sirens shrieking. The hospital A&E folk received him, made a quick examination, and arranged an X-ray of the little boy's head. The young doctor agreed with Gordon's provisional diagnosis of the condition and had him transported to the neurosurgical ward. The consultant was informed, the operating theatre was alerted and the patient prepared for surgery, all in the smooth and normal routine of an efficient hospital regime.

Judith meanwhile jumped out of bed, dressed, and went downstairs intending to borrow her father's car and join Claudia at the hospital. She found the car keys, picked up her handbag, slipped on a light coat and found that the car had been left in the drive. Unlocking it she climbed in and keyed the ignition. Nothing. Repeat. No joy.

She checked all switches and discovered that the side lights had been left on. Nothing worked. The battery was quite flat. Oh dear! An emergency indeed. What to do?

Only one answer came to her distraught mind. Ring Gordon and ask if he knew the answer. This was man's work; he would know of course.

She returned to the house and for the second time that night dialled his number. The young man had fallen asleep. Waking, he just said "Yes?" Judith explained, requesting masculine know-how. Gordon understood instantly. "Has Dad got a battery charger?" he asked and laughed as Judith replied "What's that?" Feminine helplessness at its best!

"OK. Judy. I'm coming. Put the kettle on." And he put the phone down.

She switched on the electric kettle – yes they were up to date in that regard - and prepared a tea tray with ginger biscuits. In a remarkably short time the scrunch of tyres was audible and the car door slammed as Gordon hopped out and stepped to the front door. Judy opened it before he rang the bell. ."Oh Gordon, how very kind of you. I'm so sorry to do this to you after all your endeavours yesterday, you must be awfully tired."

"That's all right; always ready to help a lady in distress. Where's the garage? Let's see if Dad has a charger." Judy led the way and up on a shelf in the garage stood a useful battery charger just waiting for use. Picking it off the shelf he opened both bonnet and boot of his own small car and extracted a pair of long battery leads; opened the bonnet of Dad's car and fixed the heavy leads to connect the two batteries together. "Right", said Gordon. "Start the engine, Judy." It roared into life, to Judith's wonder and delight. "Good, let's have that tea and wait for ten minutes. Then we'll put the battery on to charge and I'll run you to the Radcliffe hospital in Oxford. Did I tell you that's where they took the little chap?"

"Oh gosh, I didn't realise", said Judith. Then you must get back and get some sleep."

Rubbish, I'm beginning to enjoy myself. I can have a snooze in the doctors' mess for an hour or two until you are ready to go home. Come on, tea first." And that was decided. After a pleasant interlude the engine was switched off and the battery charger connected. Gordon drove Judith in his own car to the city, found the hospital and conducted Judith to find and join her friend at the appropriate ward. Claudia meanwhile had established her identity, filled in forms with a shaky hand, and noted where her precious little boy was being taken. Having done all that was possible they retired to find a cup of coffee in the restaurant of the big establishment. Gordon said he would join them. This was the hard time when waiting was the sole occupation for anxious relatives. The doctor had come to see Claudia and told her of the likelihood of an operation on the child's head. There was danger of course but even so if an operation was necessary then the alternative was not to be considered.

Judith tried to settle her friend's mind to this idea and after their reviving cuppa, along with a bite to eat, she said, "Claudia, come with me to the nearby park as soon as it's light and we'll have a good brisk walk in the fresh air.. Then when shops are open we'll both need some shopping anyway. That'll take our minds off it a bit." Certainly attention to the ordinary necessities of life would help to pass the time until they could return to the hospital and inquire about Richard's condition. Judith remembered that Gordon had said, "I didn't tell you earlier Judith, but I have a friend who is a house surgeon in this hospital, so it will be easy for me to obtain information about the child and I will keep you both posted. When you have seen him in the ward it would be best for you both to go home and be busy with the usual household things. There is no point in hanging about in the hospital. Oh and Judith, it's an awfully long time until Saturday. Could we manage a dose of tea together do you think? I know a nice tea shop not far away and while we're together I can phone the hospital from the shop. I'll pick you up about 4.p.m." Afterwards he went to the doctors' quarters for a snooze telling them where to find him when they were ready.

Havng shopped and sustained themselves with a cereal and another cuppa, they called at the intensive care ward at 11.30 a.m. to catch a glimpse of little Richard, now out of the anaesthetic and fast asleep. Staff Nurse assured them that all had gone well and a good recovery was expected. With that they got the nurse to contact Gordon on the hospital phone. He met them in the car park and drove them both to the manse where they found the father's car in usable condition. Claudia begged to stay with Judith at the manse. She could not face the idea of her own empty home so, with Judith now driving her Dad's car, (having obtained his permission) they brought all Claudia's needful clothes and toilet articles' and made up a bed for her in the spare room.

It was high time to prepare a meal and they both set to with vegetables and a tin of salmon from the store cupboard and made ready. In due course Judith's father was called and a tray was prepared for her mother who was accustomed to eat in her room. While eating, they were naturally thinking of the small child trying to recover from his serious trouble. The minister offered Claudia his sympathy and said he would be praying for Richard, and so said they all.

They shared the washing up together and Judy offered her Dad a cup of tea in the study. She then told her friend that she would be going out for a while because she had an appointment with Gordon – made when driving to the hospital. "Would you mind keeping house, Claudia, and seeing to any requests or messages please?"

The idea of tea with Gordon had thrilled Judith and she quickly reviewed her finances and decided to honour Gordon with a new and pretty dress for the occasion. So it was off to the shops for an hour. Lovely! At last she would have something nice to wear.

On the dot of 4pm the little car duly arrived and announced its presence with two quiet toots on the horn. Judy danced down the steps in her new festive creation. Gordon's admiration was genuine and much appreciated.

"What have I done to deserve such lavish expenditure?"

Judy touched his hand on the steering wheel, smiled at him, saying nothing. Gordon drove her to a car park near the town centre and they walked along to a small 19th century teashop with a large bow window and a tinkling bell that announced their presence when the door opened. They were seated in the window in comfortable chairs with a little time to admire the genuine oil paintings of the town's notable events in bygone times. The lady serving them smiled and produced toasted tea-cakes with strawberry jam in a trice. She asked if Judy would be 'Mother' and settled the teapot beside her.

They chatted for a while, Gordon sympathising over the friend's concern for her kiddie and saying that he felt sure that the surgery had been well performed and should bring about a good result in time. He then told Judy that when he had spoken to his father of the matter of a job for her that good man immediately informed him that a probable vacancy was to be advertised shortly and there was no reason why Judith should not apply. He mentioned the need for a good letter of application, a C.V., and the listing of any previous jobs along with references.

Judy felt most grateful and assured Gordon that she would do her best. Then he added, "I didn't tell you yesterday, but in addition to the dinghy on the river my father and I also have a small motor-sailor moored in Lymington which is a famous yachting centre. Perhaps one day we could chase off there and try the sea. How good a sailor are you? My father taught me to crew several years ago and we sometimes go off for weekends. We sail round the Isle of Wight and up the Solent, watching some of the huge liners that go in and out at Southampton. Would that appeal sometime?"

"Gracious, I've never been on a boat. Don't people feel a bit sick sometimes? I was always pretty good at balancing in the gym at school and ride a bike proficiently, but a boat is rather different, isn't it. Can one take seasick tablets? It sounds a lovely idea as long as I can manage the waves,"

He laughed. "Yes there's a pill for every ill. I reckon we could keep you happy and I'm sure you would manage fine."

And he went on to enthuse about the joys of sailing, describing in simple terms the layout of a sailing boat, the driving force of wind, the sail adjustments and steering arrangements. Gradually Judy relaxed and began to share his obvious enthusiasm. It could be fun.

"You mentioned week-ends," she said. "Where does one sleep?"

"Oh, we tie up in a harbour, and there are plenty of B and B's". He replied. "But we'll try the river to start with. I have a fishing rod or two. You might catch a trout."

Time was passing. Judy knew it would soon be necessary to take Claudia to the hospital. The little car sped them back to the manse and they parted reluctantly after another kiss that Judy liked and, yes, wanted. She touched her cheek and held her hand there for a precious minute before entering the house.

"Hallo, Claudia, I'm back. It's time for the hospital visit. Parking Daddy's car may be difficult and it's ten miles to Oxford so come along."

"I'm all ready. I have borrowed the 'Wind in the Willows' from your bookshelf. It's his favourite. Is that all right?"

"Of course" Judith responded and fastened her seat belt. Traffic was becoming quite dense and as the hospital car park was filling up it took them a while to find a place.

It was an extensive building with many wards and other areas for patients and visitors. Staff willingly offered guidance and soon they reached the intensive care of the neurosurgical unit. The duty nurse informed them that Richard had woken up an hour earlier but was now peacefully asleep. She added that the house surgeon wished to see them and guided them to the waiting room.

After 20 minutes the doctor came and told them that Richard had done very well. There was a nasty abscess found pressing on his brain. This was drained and the wound would be kept open until the infection was gone. He was being treated with antibiotics and a saline drip to supply fluids. They could stay for a while, but the boy would probably not wake for a long time, so really they could leave him in the hospital's care and go home. They should try not to worry unduly.

Taking the doctor's advice they spent some time beside Richard's bed before finally saying Goodbye to the nurse and finding the car. Claudia said she felt that she could go home now. She added, "The nurse has my phone number and it's quite likely that my husband will ring me. I can give him the news and find out his date of return. Thank you very, very much Judith. I don't know what I should do without you!"

So after reaching the manse they collected Claudia's things and Judith ran her home.

"Goodnight, Claudia," Judith said. "You will be able to sleep now; you certainly need it. I'll tell Gordon that Richard is doing well."

They gave each other an affectionate hug and Claudia entered her home more happily.

Judith announced her return to Daddy who was still typing in his study and then curled up on the old well-worn sofa to talk on the phone to Gordon. That competent young man was pleased indeed at the way things were shaping with the child and the chat grew ever more intimate as they unburdened their souls to each other.

Have you written your application yet?" said Gordon, strike while the iron's hot, you know".

"Haven't had time, but I'll write it out in longhand tonight and type it tomorrow. I must have it as well phrased as possible. No room for errors". After a lot more talk they eventually wished each other a 'happy night's rest' with Gordon adding "Here's another kiss for you Judy." Regretfully they put down their phones.

Judith retreated to the kitchen to prepare supper for them all, singing happily. Her father joined his daughter for their meal after a tray had been prepared and he had taken it to his wife. That was a chore undertaken by him personally. He remembered her as she had previously been; a very loving, devoted and efficient woman, far from the present sorry presence in the house, helpless in mind and unable in body to perform any of her former expert household essentials. He spent a few moments looking lovingly at her and finally returned to the dining room.

"What has my darling daughter been up to today?"

It was his usual gambit after emerging from the study and making some effort to catch up with matters of everyday life and work. Judith took a forkful of pork sausage and wondered how to begin. Her father would not want a detailed account of her exciting adventures, just a little smattering of the day's events.

"Well Daddy, I have been busy with helping Claudia mostly."

"Who is Claudia lovey?"

"She is my friend of old student days. Her little boy was ill so we took him to hospital. He's getting better now."

That was enough detail to satisfy the dear man and he switched to the political affairs of the time for some minutes, afterwards reverting to church difficulties that beset his mind and always seemed clearer when he had spoken of them to his daughter. Young though Judith was she had spent so long in association with the church folk that she could often cut through the fog of their sometimes awkward problems to bring daylight where there had been darkness.

Her father ate well as usual and having helped with drying the dishes returned to the study again for further typing and contemplation.

Judith picked up their daily paper, quickly read a twenty five year old recount of the coronation of the young Queen Elizabeth and, turning to the advertisement section, looked up the advert to which Gordon had referred. She collected pencil and paper, sat at the table and studied the wording carefully. Gathering her thoughts together she assembled ideas and phrases in her mind and began to write her first application for a job. She felt that it would be needful to try to understand the inner mind of Gordon's father; not having met him this was of course difficult and must be assessed by consideration of the son's attributes and thoughts. For a couple of hours she laboured and finally wrote in long hand a letter that, she hoped, would be acceptable. She put it away until the following day when she would type it out

She then walked upstairs to check up on her mother. Finding her fast asleep in bed she kissed her gently and went down to find a book. A gentle love story would fit her mood she thought and chose one of the less lurid types on her own bookshelf. It was an old friend but still welcome to her romantic soul and conducive to a restful night. She turned to a favourite chapter and, reading idly, moved into the kitchen. Concentrating on the story she tidied up and set a breakfast tray for her father. Still reading she guided her steps into the bathroom and turned on the bath taps. To read while soaking in heated bubbly water had long been her delight and provided a feeling of warm relaxation.

To follow by sliding, refreshed and glowing, between her lavender scented sheets beneath an old fashioned eiderdown was her idea of heaven. She finished the final page, closed her book, and turned out the light. Curling up snugly, she laid her hand on her cheek to hold Gordon's kiss and a soft little smile stole onto her lips as she drifted off to sleep.

****

Chapter 3

THE INVITATION

Morning brought fresh inspiration and Judith uncovered her typewriter to create a model job application. While running her fingers through her curly hair she read through her letter once more, made a few finishing touches, and settled down to her task. Her practised touch-typing was more than equal to that little job and before long a very well presented letter was ready for posting. The matter of a C.V. took only a few minutes, involving just a very quiet life with some examination successes, an essay prize at school, success at college and the many essentials of housekeeping for her parents. Help with her father's church business was also an important part of her duties and she went into some detail on that matter before finally closing the letter.

With a shopping list for household requirements in her handbag she stepped out briskly towards town and, reaching the post office, felt a sense of adventure as she slipped the letter into the maw of the pillar box. She drew herself up to her full 5ft 6in, patted the top of the old red box and whispered 'Good luck, little letter'.

A visit to the fishmonger resulted in kippers, loved by her father, being placed in her basket along with a couple of smoked mackerel, erroneously despised by the more snooty customers who were carelessly unaware of their excellent food value. The greengrocer further along the High St. was pleased to add a good supply of apples and oranges with the much prized bananas which were now plentifully back in the shops after their deficiency during the wartime days of years long ago. Judith was easing her loaded basket from one hand to the other when a young laddie, full of mischief, came streaking along the pavement on roller skates and uncaringly crashed into her. The basket flew out of her hand and spilled its contents over the pavement. The boy regained his balance, laughed uproariously and sped on. Judith was unhurt and recovered immediately. Furious, she picked up a large hard apple and flung it with unerring aim at the back of the young sinner. Girls at her school were practised at cricket and she had been an expert fielder. The apple hit the boy between his shoulder blades with a smart thud. Surprised he turned, skidding uncontrolled into the side of a taxi temporarily halted beside the pavement in a queue of traffic. He fell, twisting his ankle and picked himself up with difficulty. Judith was horrified at what she had done, putting her hand to her mouth, saying "Oh dear, oh dear!" An aged farmer up from the country started to pick up her scattered items of fruit, saying,

"'Tis alright my dear, doant 'ee worry. T' youngster 'ad what was coming to 'im, and jolly good thing too." He added "There's a copper going to 'im, an' I reckon 'e'll tick 'im off well and truly. Taxi driver arn't too pleased with 'im either. 'E's got out and 'e's swearing like a trooper at the kid. 'E was a naughty boy all right."

Another helper comforted her also declaring, "I'm the captain of the town cricket team. We need another team member. Would you like to join us?" He seemed quite sincere. With the aid of a couple of other passers-by her basket was restored to its former glory. By this time the officer had dismissed the limping boy, confiscating his skates and obtaining his name and address. He instructed the lad to go straight home and he, the officer, would visit his parents later.

He then addressed himself to Judith, hoping she was not hurt. Reassured that she was undamaged he enquired, "Do you wish to press charges, Miss? That young fellow deserves some degree of punishment." Judith thanked him for his solicitude saying, "I really can't face a lawsuit, even a little one. The boy was certainly very naughty but I'll just forgive him." The officer made a note, thanked her for her attitude and went on his way.

About to move off Judith found another person in front of her who laid a hand on her arm to stay her departure. She was thrilled and pleased to see Gordon, also on a shopping spree.

"Well met, Judy, Pet," he said. "What has been going on and could you do with a coffee?"

"Oh Gordon, how lovely to see you. I've been having quite an adventure. There's a coffee shop over the road, come on and I'll tell you all about it." And Judy slipped her arm into Gordon's, surrendering to him her heavy basket.

Over steaming cups and while gazing happily into each other's eyes, the tale was told. Gordon broke into a gurgling laugh and complimented his companion on her accuracy at apple throwing. He added that perhaps she should accept the offer of a place on the team…

Judith made a little moue saying, "I don't really think I'd be much good. But there's something else, Gordon. I have posted off my letter replying to the advertisement for a secretarial job at the Antiques. Fingers crossed."

"That's wonderful," said Gordon, looking at his watch. "Let's celebrate with a meal to-night can we? I have a class to attend now, but there's just time to run you home; that basket's pretty heavy. The car's over in the car park."

As he assisted her out of the front seat when reaching the manse Gordon planted another kiss on her cheek. Saying gently, "7 o'clock", he quickly turned and drove off to attend his class while Judy entered the house, slightly flushed, her hand holding that kiss to her face. She liked it She liked it very much.

Punctually at 7 o'clock the little car turned up to meet Judith tripping down the steps of the manse, dressed as before in black skirt and pretty cream blouse, her hair curled attractively and features that owed very little to artificial embellishments. Her driver, clean shaven and very much in command, wore a summery open necked shirt and in the manner of an efficient chauffeur sprang out to open the car door for his guest.

The same table was ready for them and the staff of the old pub was attentive as ever Soon drinks were placed before them, an order taken and there was time for talk. Judith wanted to know how medical instruction was getting on. Gordon was plainly keen on acquiring more advanced clinical wisdom at his postgraduate class and not averse to demonstrating his knowledge. The minister's daughter began to realise something of the medical problems that confronted her father as he visited the sick of his parish. She told her host, "Listening to you explaining some of peoples' ailments causes me to appreciate Daddy's work and realise how tired he often gets when hearing about the troubles of his poorly members on doing a visiting round."

"That's good," said Gordon. "I'll bet you make him very happy. I must remember to thank him for sparing you to me for these evenings. You really make my day. It's wonderful to have the company of such a lovely girl."

Judith blushed a little and was relieved when the meal appeared. Conversation became relaxed as they did justice to an excellent dinner. They settled in the lounge over coffee and Gordon spoke again.

"I've been wondering, Judy, whether I could steal you for a week from Daddy for a little holiday together. Have you ever done any skiing?"

She wondered a little as she replied, "No never. That's something very new. What are you thinking of?"

"Well I was taught by my uncle a few years ago. It's great fun to balance on a pair of skis and swish down long snowy slopes in the French Alps. It would be much better fun with a nice girl along. I've been looking up some resorts to find who does single rooms, wondering if I could persuade you to join me." He looked at her hopefully.

Judith twisted her fingers together, thinking. Then, "It sounds wonderful", she said. "Perhaps I'd better talk to Daddy. I'd love to come and try, but there's Mummy to think of and there would be lots to arrange. When would it be anyway?"

"Well some time in the winter, of course. I would have to take advice and book soon to ensure accommodation. I wonder if my father knows of a caretaker for your Mum and Dad." He went on, "There'd be nothing to pay naturally. I had a very generous birthday present from my uncle. That would cover it nicely."

A discussion involving a small host of matters ensued. Judith remembered her hoped-for job and mentioned this.

"If I get a job I should need to negotiate time off," she said.

"If it's with my Dad's firm that wouldn't be a problem," Gordon countered.

After a long and happy discussion the evening drew to a close, and the return to Judith's home was a little overdue. Judith shyly returned the kiss when they bade each other a fond 'Good night'. With cheeks beginning to burn she looked into her father's study to explain her late return. Busily typing he had not noticed her absence. Her mother, she found, was still awake but 'away with the fairies' With her mind conjuring up thoughts of happiness to come Judith finally slid into bed, read a chapter of her book, held the kiss to her face and again smiled herself to sleep.

*

A few days passed during which Gordon, when not busy with post-graduate classes, researched the business of skiing, weather at resorts, dates, accommodation and travel possibilities. He also rang his wise uncle who displayed genuine interest and after discussion with his wife asked whether they needed a chaperone.

"We would love to come and share a holiday if you would like us", he said. Later he added that his wife knew a lady who would be very pleased indeed to take on the task of caring for the minister and his wife while Judith was absent. She would do it out of kindness of heart and would not consider payment.

Telephoning to Judith Gordon asked her to meet him for tea at a riverside café where he could tell her all. She changed into a pink crocheted creation with little rosebuds and an old blue skirt and did so joyfully, being quite thrilled to hear how much he had discovered. Gordon , entranced at the new vision before him, said, "So now you can tell Daddy all about it. Everything is fixed. Now the only thing left is for you to say is 'Yes'.

"I'll tell him tonight," said Judith and after a happy chat together she returned home, holding another kiss, to prepare the evening meal. Her father appreciated her cooking. . When replete he joined her in the kitchen and applied himself to his self-imposed task of washing up. His daughter was always glad of the help and also of the opportunity to chat with him over household problems. When all was tidy she said,

"Daddy, can you leave the typing for a bit? I have something to tell you if you can spare a few minutes."

"Always available for you my dear", he replied, and they made themselves comfortable with a cup of coffee in the lounge. Judith was not quite sure how to begin but plunged straight in saying, "I must tell you. I have a chance of a holiday. It's with Gordon. It's alright, his uncle and aunt are coming too so I'll be well chaperoned."

She told him the whole story, remembering to provide the information about a carer to come and look after her parents while she was away. Her father was quiet for a minute realising the future possibilities and how such things might affect the lives of himself and his wife in the manse. Judith felt worried at his silence. All of a sudden she began to understand the cause and gave him time to think a little and respond. At last he said, "Thank you my Darling for telling me. I'm aware that I am a quiet old bird and rather absorbed in my church matters, often to the extent of neglecting my lovely daughter. However I have realised for some time that you and Gordon are becoming quite fond of each other. I think it is a lovely idea and give it my blessing. Certainly fix it all up and enjoy the time together. We shall be all right here and the consideration for our welfare by Gordon's uncle is very kind and most acceptable. So go ahead and let me know what date the event will be The he added, "By the way I have a trustees' meeting tomorrow evening, at the church, probably a long one. Why not ask Gordon to come and have a meal here. I should like to meet him later and have a short chat. You can have the house to yourselves and watch the television!"

Judith put her arms around him and hugged him closely and silently. Still thinking he retreated to his study and began to type.

****

Chapter 4

THE RESPONSE

Judith succeeded in contacting Gordon before he commenced his appointed job in the hospital. To her invitation for him to join her for a quiet evening at the manse he said he would be delighted and she fixed a time for his arrival, provided he was free to escape from his toil.

She quickly put the house in order from top to bottom, attended to her mother and started off at a smart pace to the town for essential shopping perquisites. Her return by 11 a.m. was very necessary for there was trouble with the gas cooker and an expert had promised to arrive at that time to deal with it. The doctor would also call later in the morning to check up on her mother.

Before she left the house her father had called her to his study.

"Judith, my Darling girl" he said, "I want you to find a good dress shop in town and choose for yourself a really nice dress for an important evening with your friend. I think this cheque will cover the matter". He handed her a blank cheque duly signed.

Amazed and thrilled Judith threw her arms around his neck. "Thank you so much, Daddy." she said. "That will be quite wonderful." And she took her basket and went shopping, humming a little love song as she tripped down the street.

With grocery shopping completed Judith was back to attend to all the hassle. It went well and there was gas to cook the dinner. In the midst of it the doctor turned up and marched straight upstairs according to custom, so ensuring that he wasted no time. Judith went up to attend him and was not surprised to learn that no change had occurred. Her mother seemed entirely unaware.

Afterwards came the necessary preparations for a cosy evening with Gordon, and having dealt with her parents' needs in the food line Judith spent her afternoon with a cookbook and the gas stove, but leaving good time for the anticipated visit to the dress shop. There she was efficiently served and extremely pleased with the result. . She knew that Gordon would be very appreciative. With a hand to her face she sat down at the dining room table and did a little daydreaming....

When laying the table later she remembered her purchase of a bottle of light wine. Feeling a little guilty, for this was never seen in the manse, she found suitable glasses and made all ready. There was just time for a quick bath and to deck herself in her new finery. As she came down the stairs the bell rang.

Gordon was quite astonished and certainly most appreciative. Judith's daydreaming had indeed found life, the new dress enhancing wonderfully the appearance of the lovely young woman who opened the door to hi

So also did the welcoming refreshment lightened by the surprise of wine to complement it within the walls of the manse. The conversation was full of fun, hardly depressed by the news that Gordon would be starting work in the hospital ward next day and expected to be kept hard at it... He did full justice to Judith's culinary efforts and expressed his thanks, making her blush at the fulsome praise that he offered. The blush deepened as they busied themselves with the washing up and she shyly told Gordon that the answer about the holiday was - yes.

"Wonderful" he replied, "What a marvellous time we can have, provided of course that we don't break any bones." And they retired to the sofa with coffee and told each other stories that brought happy giggles and wonderment at the tales of student days and medical sessions in lecture and operating theatres. After a while Gordon seemed a little pensive.

"What's the matter, Gordon? You're very quiet all of a sudden. Are you all right?" Judith was concerned

"Quite all right, Judy, never better" he replied. "But I have a question to ask you. The answer is very important to me."

"Oh, really? Is there something I know that you don't? I thought doctors knew everything. They always seem so wise."

"Not quite. This is something serious."

"OK. Speak on, Gordon"

He took her hand and looked into her eyes, saying,

"I love you very much, Judy. Ever since I saw you at the garden party in that little brown dress. I'm longing for you to be my wife. Will you marry me, Judy?"

Judith slowly stood up, Gordon following. She faced him and slid her arms around his neck. She reached up, standing on tiptoe, and whispered in his ear a very definite

"Yes, I would love to marry you. I love you too. I shall adore being your wife." The kiss was firm and lasting. A promise. It was a vow of love and caring for all their time together. When at last they drew apart they smiled delightedly at each other. Each took a breath and, smiling still, broke into speech. Together they said to each other the words of the marriage service, "I will ".

It was a solemn promise of love that would bring to them both wonderful future happiness. It was followed again by an embrace that would bind each to the other for always

Warm in front of the fire and in a cosy cuddle, they talked sweet nothings that only they could share. Time seemed to stand still until interrupted by the telephone. Judith picked it up.

"Hallo, this is your father. Can I come home

"Yes surely, Daddy. Come quickly. We have some news for you"

"That was nice of him," said Gordon. "I suspect his daughter is equally thoughtful."

Judith poured wine into three glasses

"For a celebration" she said.

And in a remarkably few minutes the front door opened and banged shut again. The minister believed in giving warning of approach. He entered and extended a hand to Gordon who had a little speech ready. But Judith forestalled him with her exciting news, hugging her Dad vigorously and saying with eyes that shone like stars,

"Daddy, we're engaged! Let's celebrate!"

And, giving him no time to respond Judy raised her glass. Together they drank the toast gladly proposed by her father,

"To a very happy life together for Judith and Gordon."

When the jubilation had subsided a little Gordon made his speech requesting from the father the hand of his daughter. Daddy grasped his hand again, gladly accepting Gordon as a future son-in-law and offering warm congratulations to them both.

Then Gordon shyly drew from his pocket a little jeweller's box and presented it to his fiancée. "Hope it fits, Darling," he said.

She opened it and gasped. "It's lovely," she said and picked out the lovely gold ring set with an amethyst and two little diamonds. Gordon gently took it and slipped it onto her finger. A lingering kiss sealed the bargain.

The minister had watched with admiration. Then he too slowly put his hand into his pocket and withdrew a small jeweller's box. He had been prepared for this moment and had waited expectantly. He handed it to his daughter.

"This was my mother's engagement ring," he said. "I feel it is most fitting that you should now wear it. Please put it on."

Both rings fitted perfectly.

"Thank you ever so much, Daddy. I shall be very proud to wear it".

"There is something else," said her father again, withdrawing from his pocket another box of larger dimensions. He opened it and took from it a very lovely pearl necklace.

"My father gave this to my mother at their engagement party. Will you now wear it, please?" And he placed it around her neck and kissed his daughter.

Judith felt that heaven had come on earth as she hugged her Dad, her heart too full for words. He also felt very emotional and put a handkerchief to his eye.

She retired to the kitchen to make a cup of tea for

her father and took from the fridge sandwiches already prepared for his post-meeting homecoming. While he was eating Gordon and he conversed on numerous subjects, especially of course regarding the young doctor's future prospects. Gordon told his host that it would be necessary to work in several positions in the hospital, or even in another one, possibly, before finally deciding whether to specialise or choose general practice for his future career. They continued to talk, becoming gradually better acquainted.

Judith watched and listened for quite a while. Then noticing that the conversation was beginning to flag she said,

"I think Daddy's tired, Gordon. He's had an exhausting evening and you have a very busy day tomorrow. We must break it up".

She kissed her father "Goodnight" and took Gordon by the hand.

"Come on Darling. This has been a marvellous day. Thank you my Gordon. I shall love being married to you. This has been the most wonderful day of my life. Now you must go and get some sleep. You have a lot of work tomorrow and you'll need a jolly good rest."

Led by her hand Gordon reached his car, but it was still several minutes before they finally said 'Goodnight.' She waved both hands with tears of joy as he drove away, finally turning back to the manse and taking the cups and plates to the kitchen for washing up.

The ordinary domestic duty helped to calm her emotions and as she laid the table for breakfast her thoughts just settled to a joy that streamed through her whole being. She did not forget to express her gratitude to her father for the enchanting gift from so many years ago. The dear man was in bed, holding his handkerchief and

Judith wrapped her arms around him and hugged him closely. Visiting her mother's room she was glad to find her in bed and fast asleep. Retiring to her own bedroom she needed no stories of romance to ease her mind into dreamland. She had her own love.

Chapter 5

GETTING IT RIGHT

"Dr.Jjenkins? Good morning. I am Sister McDermid , This is my ward. I should like to talk to you for a minute; please come into my office." Sister was tall, slim and well proportioned with eyes that could both smile and flash with fire. She walked smartly in front of Gordon and seated herself at her desk..

Gordon, saying "Good morning, Sister," entered her tidy work area to stand and wait while she composed herself at her desk. She did not invite Gordon to sit down and when she spoke her words were precise and with the firmness of authority.

Sister said, "I come from a naval family, Dr Jenkins. My husband is a naval officer and like him, in naval parlance, I run a tight ship in this ward. In order that treatment of patients may be properly carried out discipline in a hospital ward is absolutely essential. My word is law and

I demand that all staff shall adhere to it exactly. I will not tolerate slackness or inefficiency. Is that understood?

"Yes, Sister, I will do my best".

"Good. You will never be late on duty. There are no precise hours after which you are at liberty. Your time off begins when the work assigned has been completed. Your off duty time will be subject to that proviso. You will always leave word where you may be contacted in case of sudden emergency. Your work here is your first priority. The patient is your immediate concern. All my nurses are aware of this attitude. Your contact with them must exist solely on clinical grounds when on duty here. If I have made myself clear you may now find the registrar who will inform you concerning your duties in my ward. I hope you will find this ward a good place in which to learn your work as a junior doctor."

Saying which, Sister rose to indicate that the interview was at an end. Gordon said "Thank you, Sister" and departed to find the registrar. He felt a little breathless.

That gentleman was waiting just round the corner and told Gordon," I always hang about to receive the battered young medico after Sister has given him his first lecture. She may seem a bit of a harridan at first, but she's not really. She is a very genuine lady. There will probably be more to come, but don't be alarmed. Her bark is worse than her bite, and the result is seen in the ward's success. Both I and the medical consultant have great respect for her, so take a deep breath and count yourself fortunate to be on her ward. I'll tell you about your work for this morning and it's all typed out on this sheet". When you've finished find me and we'll grab some food. It could be quite a while." He handed Gordon a sheaf of papers.

Such was Gordon's introduction to the art of healing. 'Phew' he thought to himself, 'What have I landed myself in?' He read his instructions with care and began work as indicated.

*

Saturday in the manse dawned bright and clear and Judith awoke to her new situation as an engaged woman but unaware of course of the strict situation in the ward where Gordon had now began his clinical work. Rapidly she took up the new challenge. She had a new responsibility; her fiancée must be supported. She knew that with his new occupation he would certainly be out of reach, so her task would involve coping with the chores of a new day as usual not forgetting that the anticipated Saturday afternoon walk with her Dad was on the menu. Apart from that delight everything was new.

Punctually at 2pm. he was ready with binoculars and a walking stick. This was a regular outing that Judith much enjoyed. Her father was a keen Nature lover when not engaged in parish duties; he always kept the day jealously for the enjoyment of his daughter's company. Shortly, they turned off the road into a field. Dad drew the girl's attention to the swallows in their twisting flight as they grabbed insects to build up strength for their autumn journey to Africa. Also speeding past their heads were several swifts, black and wonderfully streamlined, shrieking and screaming as they too gobbled insects while on the wing.. Not for the first time Judith was reminded of the amazingly hard flight that these little birds faced when returning to the warmth and insect laden air of the tropics.

On the leaves of dog roses in the hedges her father showed her a specimen of a long-horned beetle with its

46

very lengthy feelers and brilliantly bronzed wing cases. Beneath an oak tree she found the ejected gobbets from the mouth of an owl. They were formed from the undigested remains of the bird's meal of mice, or other small beasties that fell prey to that powerful beak. Overhead squawked seagulls, flown inland from the coast to become scavengers among the rubbish of the town; rubbish kindly dumped in a suitable hollow just for their benefit well away from the town's outskirts. The wind had risen and they displayed their wonderful command of the sky floating and balancing against it, then suddenly turning with a flick of their feathers and sweeping along, borne swiftly in graceful and unerring flight Gulls were a lovely sight to watch

Judith listened happily to her father's talking and explanation of such delights, wondering at his knowledge and glad that he had so absorbing an interest in the natural world and all its wonders to divert his mind from problems in the church aand home. They chatted as they went, wandering over the fields. In such excursions the daughter had the opportunity to find the real father whom she had never really known during her years of school and college. She could appreciate his learning and expertise, apart from his obvious dedication to the things of his faith and the practical side of his religion. These private walks with her father were always an eye-opener to her.

In the evening following their meal Dad betook himself to his study to complete preparation for the Sunday services. Judith fished out a pile of clothes that needed mending and went upstairs to sit with her mother. It was simply a matter of providing her with companionship, for conversation was not possible. Her mind could no longer cope with speech. She simply understood bodily needs and managed to cope fairly well with those.

There was no chance for Judith to have a talk with Gordon for he had commenced work in the hospital and was on duty for the weekend in the A & E department, having been seconded temporarily due to a doctor's illness. It was likely to be busy. But she had reckoned without her beloved's determination to find a moment for his new love. The telephone rang. Gordon had a few minutes while a nurse fetched the electrocardiogram and arranged the wiring for his patient. The delicious exchange restored equanimity for them both. They could return to hospital and domestic duties happy in their knowledge of each other's firm adoration..

Judith's habit on Sunday was to attend her father's church. While having as yet no profound religious conviction she admired her Dad's approach to the simple exposition of the gospel message with his ten-minute homily delivered with sincerity and in simple language that could be plainly understood by folk in his congregation. She felt quite strongly that the complicated trappings of ritualistic proceedings were a bar to belief and militated against the understanding of Christianity's real message. She regarded all such as 'religiosity' rather than religion. She wondered about how Gordon felt on such matters and determined to question him on the subject. Meanwhile it was simply a matter of sitting in the accustomed pew, sharing in the prayer responses, singing the old hymns and just listening to Daddy.

After the service the fellow worshipers shook his hand and broke into their accustomed gossiping and nattering.

"Have you heard how old so and so is getting on?" "I hope he's not another one at death's door". Then came the next whisper, "How about old Mrs. What's her Name? She used to be the Mission secretary; I haven't seen her for a long time." And there was much more of interest for the crowd of socially-minded people. Somehow the verbal exchanges always seemed to turn to medical matters that often involved the undertaker. However some folk greeted the minister's daughter and congratulated her on her graduation. As soon as she decently could Judith dragged her Dad away saying,

"Come on Dad, get away from all your adoring parishioners and let's take you home for your coffee and a little piece of cake."

Then, having returned to the manse and fed and watered him she said, "Now you can go and potter round the garden and water your tomatoes and what have you. While you survey the wonders of nature I'll do you a good substantial meal of roast beef and Yorkshire with potatoes and fresh veg; Rice pud. to follow. Then your inner man will be renewed."

Discovering a goodly quantity of Christmas pudding from last year in the fridge with a carton of Cornish cream, she felt it would be nice to give him a special treat.

Conversation over the meal now turned to Judith's new future.

"You will need to talk over lots of things," said her father. "As a mere male I am largely ignorant of matrimonial preparations. Dates, dresses, bridesmaids and so forth need a woman's touch. Your mother, sadly, is quite unable to help and you have no nice maiden aunts, or even married ones. You have friends of course, mostly single girls, but a more mature and experienced lady would be desirable. While I'm snoozing this afternoon I'll give it some thought."

So he dropped off to sleep and Judith picked up the phone and talked to a good friend, Gillian Garforth, married the previous year. That competent young lady invited her to go for a walk. They indulged happily in very useful 'girl chat' while toddling into the fields, leaning over gates, and watching the vast hosts of starling as they turned and twisted in their flight.. Tea followed in the friend's house where Jill's husband, Tom, was messing about with work on his dinghy's engine.

"Time I detached myself from outboard engine servicing and joined you for a cuppa. He showered congratulations on Judith. "Jolly well done love. What are you going to do with those letters after your name?" Judith said that time would have to tell and after a merry tea party she reluctantly went home to serve tea to her father. She found him busy on the telephone. Shortly he hung up saying, "That was Mrs. Angela Collins, the wife of our good doctor. She is a wise and very helpful lady and I thought she might be willing to help us in arranging a wedding. She invites you to call on her when you feel able."

"Oh, Daddy that's marvellous. Thank you for fixing that up. I'll call tomorrow morning."

She picked up her basket of mending and went up to her mother's room while the minister drove off to conduct the evening service in his church. Later they had a light supper, listened to the evening news on the radio and were going to call it a day when suddenly the phone rang and Judith was thrilled to hear the loved voice of her fiancée, thrilled too that he should find a slot in his new busy schedule to wish her 'Goodnight'. After a few minutes of chat, loving and lively, he said,

"I must go now Darling. Did I tell you? There's an urgent need for more help in A&E and I've been transferred there temporarily from my ward with the ferocious Sister.

There's a major op. in the theatre and I'm assisting. Wish me luck."

"I do", she replied, "and good luck to the patient too! I love you. Bye, Darling."

INTERVIEWS.

The morning post next day was delivered early at the manse. Picking it up from the doormat to hand to her father Judith noted a letter addressed to her personally. A good quality envelope bearing on the reverse side the title of the firm to which she had applied only a few days previously. She managed to control her excitement while doling out the glutinous porridge loved by her Dad. To keep the letter unopened any longer was impossible and she slit the envelope.

"It's from the firm's secretary" she said excitedly. "They want to see me." Promptly she passed the letter to the minister and waited for his comment. He put down his spoon, read the letter and looked at his daughter steadily. "I don't blame them," was his decided voice. "You are always a sight for sore eyes. If Gordon's father is as wise as he should be I think I'll congratulate you in advance."

The invitation for an interview gave a date and Judith wrote it in her diary with a reminder to think carefully about her apparel for such an important occasion. She became quite starry eyed and wondered when she could tell Gordon. Life was becoming very interesting indeed. On the other side of the table the minister shared her happiness while at the same time beginning to consider what changes lay in store for his wife and himself.

Then, wisely remembering the previous evening's conversation with the doctor's wife he said to Judith,

"That's wonderful my Darling. When you have replied, confirming your attendance as suggested, there is the other matter for your attention. You were going to call on the doctor's wife."

"Oh, gracious, I'd quite forgotten. That really is essential. I'll give her a ring and arrange a time. And there's quite a bit of housework to be sorted out."

"I can wash up, my dear, and I'll see to a tray for your mother and sort out beds and so on. I can even use the vacuum cleaner too. You just make ready and think out questions and answers for Mrs Collins. As you know I always have a quiet day after Sunday, so if there is anything I can do…"

A phone call to the doctor's wife produced an appointment with her for 10.30, and as their house was on the other side of town Judith unearthed her bicycle from the cluttered garage and pumped up the tyres according to long custom. With a shopping list she set forth, coping well with traffic and visiting one or two shops on her way.

The house was a huge well built structure of red brick, ser in a spacious garden well furnished with healthy large and small bushes and a Virginia creeper closely adorning the walls. A notice pointed the patients to a generous sized surgery at the side. Between pillars of the old Doric type Judith found the front door and, after hesitating a little she adjusted her hat and tucked her curls away tidily. The taking a deep breath, she rang the bell.

The solid, ageing oak door was opened by Mrs Collins herself. A lady of some fifty years, of generous proportions, erect and still with lovely brown hair charmingly curled and bearing traces of grey, she welcomed her visitor warmly and soon made her feel at home. Leading Judith to a conservatory at the rear of the house where a tray with coffee and cups awaited them, she indicated a comfortable chair and enquired about the coffee. The answer was "Yes please," and the discussion that ensued was entered into easily and without any trace of embarrassment.

"I have known about you for a long time, my dear, for my husband has often told me what a charming daughter the minister had to care for him and his unfortunate wife. Your father has told me something of your present circumstances and I must offer my loving congratulations both to you and your doctor fiancé. I hope you will be very happy together."

"Thank you, and thank your husband too for all the care and kindness that he shows to my Mum and Dad. It is very good of you to be willing to offer advice in the matters affecting my marriage and I feel most grateful. Obviously my mother is quite unable to help and I have no aunts to fill the breech."

"I am only too glad to help. Let's cut the cackle and get down to brass tacks as they say in the north. How long do you plan to be engaged and when would you like to get married? What are all the difficulties that you both face? What are your fiancé's circumstances? Has Gordon any family to consider? And there's a host of other things to think about. We shall not get answers to them all today. We'll have to meet often and iron out quite a lot of problems. The business of tying the wedding knot is quite simple. All you need is a ring and some bridesmaids! It's the other things that really matter.

And they got down to business, with their coffee.

Judith found that her adviser was indeed a most wise lady as her father had forecast. They went into these difficult questions with open minds and Judith discovered that many of them were far more complicated than she had thought. With a notebook she made a list of items that would require further elucidation from her father or fiancé, mentally stowing them away in her mind for pondering about when time allowed.

At the morning's end they said 'Goodbye' with some relief and, on Judith's part, with much gratitude. After purchasing several further essentials from the store in town she was glad to stow away her bike, put wedding palaver aside and commence the day's duties in the manse kitchen.

Having dealt with the potatoes and vegetables and popped the shepherd's pie (prepared the previous day) into the oven she suddenly thought 'the morning post?' In the flurry of going to the doctor's house she had omitted to reply to the all important invitation to an interview with her prospective employer. Hurriedly she typed out a suitable letter while waiting for the dinner to cook and took it to the pillar-box nearby.

"Well my dear, how did it go?" Such was her father's greeting when seated at the table. In the course of the meal Judith brought him up to date with all the questions that would need to be mulled over in both their minds over the next few months.

"So now you know something of what it's all about, my precious. I have to pop some of these questions often to young folk who want me to marry them. I'll help you all I can. You'll have to have intimate talks with Gordon of course."

"Thank you Daddy. I will put it all down on my machine and give him a copy. Then we can both produce answers and compare notes together. The trouble is he's a busy boy now!"

"Well he will have time off sometimes. Good thing I taught you to type. It's certainly coming in most useful for your present job. Perhaps a Christmas present of a nice portable machine would be very useful. A used machine isn't too expensive. I think you're going to be a busy girl."

The minister had always believed in 'action this day' and mentally thanked Churchill for that word. He lifted the telephone receiver on his desk and was soon engaged in talk with a typewriter expert. Judith washed up and, sitting comfortably at the dining room table, began work. After two hours she had even more questions with which to belabour her beloved man. Finding the phone free she tried to speak to him, encountering awkward receptionists and A.& E. Sisters all of whom were anxious to defend their medical expert from unsolicited calls. Explanations and persuasions eventually won the day and the two lovebirds managed to arrange a short session together that evening.

Gordon arrived in his little run-about and the meeting was rapturous. Each enquired anxiously about the other's adventures.

"What have you been doing, my darling?" was Gordon's inquisitive approach.

"Learning how to marry a man, and here's a list of items for you to think about while you consider how to marry a woman." Each was very eager to fill in accounts of their time apart. At last Judith could hand to Gordon the typed list of questions that would require definite answers not forgetting to stress that much would depend on the result of her interview with his father; both understanding that there was nothing they could do about such a momentous matter.

She had a couple of days in which to prepare for the interview and phoned to arrange a session with her hairdresser to be followed by a browse around a dress shop. There she found a wise lady who helped greatly with ideas for looking her best when the day came.

"It is far more important to look efficient than to resemble a film star," she was told. "Anyway you look pretty enough for the most fastidious employer. You do turn a nice shade of pink when you blush. You'll make a really lovely bride."

Soon additional items were added for her wardrobe that would please any discerning businessman and attract a few glances of admiration from his staff as well. She returned home feeling self-confident and well able to cope with the forthcoming trial. She could not resist arraying herself with her new apparel and quickly earned the undisguised approval of her father.

"To think that I was not aware of such a beautiful butterfly in my establishment" he said. "Gordon will need to hold you on a tight rein, not to speak of his father," for her Daddy was certain that she would gain the position which she so much desired. Judith blushed saying, "Don't be so silly, Daddy"..

During the two days wait for the interview she was able to visit the doctor's wife again and very helpful discussions ensued, some of the questions having been already answered by Gordon and her father. She began to feel that problems could be ironed out. One very important matter was the future care for her parents and this would need much thought and some compromise by both young people. Certainly her father could not be left on his own with an ailing wife.

Judith told Angela, "I am well aware that I owe much to my parents and must continue to provide them with care and a secure future. I hope that Gordon will understand and be prepared to make some small sacrifices occasionally."

Angela said, "You will need to discuss the matter with a great deal of care. Perhaps my husband could help with that." After a little further discussion they parted, having arranged for another talk.

At the weekend Gordon had a very busy duty session. There was urgent need for extra help in the A&E dept., and, as stated, he had been temporarily transferred there instead of to the ward with the redoubtable Sister McDermid. Talk with his lady love must be delayed until later. That would be after her fateful interview with his father.

During the waiting days she read up all she could from the local library about the secretarial work involved in such a firm, and used time for healthful walking exercise in the open fields where she was better able to organise her thoughts. Her father chose a text on the Sunday advising

'Give to the winds thy fears. Hope and be undismayed'

On the Monday following Judith threw fear out of the window and felt well prepared for the occasion, although maybe her excitement was slightly tinged with a little apprehension. 'Never mind the snags', she told herself, 'it's time for action'. With a kiss and a hug from her Dad she set forth bravely on her adventure in a taxi as a special luxury, a present which he had ordered as a surprise for his daughter.

****

CHAPTER 6

AM I GOOD ENOUGH?

JUDITH'S FATHER SETTLED himself comfortably at his typewriter that morning and inserted a couple of sheets with a carbon paper held between them. His trustees meeting that evening would surely demand an agenda from their minister; he was aware that they would require an accurate statement also regarding the desirability of continuing to maintain two sparsely attended chapels in the country area around their busy town. It would take a lot of thinking, typing and copying. He'd better get started.

Judith's fiancé, coping busily with a long queue of complainants in the A & E had found quite an interesting case of rheumatic fever with cardiac symptoms. He quickly asked the office to find the medical registrar. A personal word with that expert could only be most advantageous for the patient. After that would be the attention required for a young lady with a 'dinner fork' deformity of the wrist that indicated a nasty fracture. An injection of local anaesthetic would meet the case, he thought. Then he would gently manipulate and apply a plaster of Paris.

Judith's prospective employer was in a good mood. The monthly figures presented to him by the firm's accountant showed a favourable situation following his recent bout of unusual adventures in the world of antiquities; he could be well pleased with the result. His housekeeper had outdone herself in cooking him a substantial breakfast and his new B.M.W had purred satisfactorily as he drove it for the first time from his home to the reserved space opposite the polished mahogany doors of his business premises. The smoothness of the lift that conveyed him to his office on the third floor also helped to inspire in him a pleasurable glow of wellbeing. He fitted himself happily into his comfortable office chair, carefully chosen to fit his ample frame, and examined the list of his morning duties that had been laid before him. The first task seemed to be the choosing of a new secretary. He would indulge in a whisky with a little water… Good. He heaved a sigh, and pressed the bell.

Judith had enjoyed her taxi ride, composing herself nicely, and not forgetting to use her mirror to good advantage. Perhaps her heart fluttered a little as she pushed open the big double doors of the Antiques emporium and stepped onto the plush carpet leading to the receptionist's sanctum. She walked forward to the glass partition and explained,

"I am Judith Macgregor. I have an appointment to see Mr. Jenkins." The receptionist checked the time.

"Yes, his bell has just sounded. He will be ready for you. Gladys will take you up."

Gladys did so and seated Judith in a pleasant waiting room where the soft texture of the plain blue carpet and peaceful pictures of small ships and yachts on the quiet magnolia wall paper helped to create a relaxed atmosphere that she greatly appreciated. There were no other hopeful aspirants present. Gladys knocked on the door of the great man's office and, opening it, announced,

"Miss Judith Macgregor to see you, sir".

Gerald Jenkins rose as Judith entered and bowed slightly saying "Good morning Miss Macgregor." He was a tall man, straight, broad shouldered and with a kindly facial expression surmounted by a good thatch of greying hair, tidily brushed. Well dressed and courteous, he invited her to be seated, indicating the upright leather covered chair facing his desk. Judith responded with "Good morning, sir," and settled herself comfortably. She declined politely the drink that he then offered.

He shuffled a few papers on his desk, allowing her time to compose herself and then enquired, quite kindly,

"May I ask what has been your previous employment experience?"

Judith knew that such a question would be forthcoming There could only be one answer.

"This is my first job application, sir. During my last year of study my mother became ill with severe Alzheimer's and it became necessary for me to undertake the household responsibilities. Social Services are now helping us and I am free to seek other employment."

"I understand. Perhaps you would make clear to me what your duties have been in your home, apart from the usual household chores."

"Well, in a minister's house there was quite a lot of organising to be done. People would often wish to talk to my father and it was my job to arrange times in his busy schedule. They would sometimes telephone and sometimes call at the door, in which case my task would be to sort out the urgent from the less vital requests and keep everybody happy. It would have been unseemly to arrange a queue of folk on seats in the hall. I would try to give people a definite time for an interview. Apart from that I managed quite a lot of secretarial work for my father and kept his engagement calendar in order. Shopping and accounts were all normal parts of life. Church accounts also came my way and I acted for the treasurer when required."

"You seem to have been busy. How will your father manage if you're working elsewhere?"

"Oh, he's expecting to find a member of his congregation to assist him."

"Miss Macgregor, why do you think your services might be useful to this firm?

Judith smiled slightly. Her father had warned her that this might well be a pertinent question. She had prepared an answer.

"Well, sir, I majored in English when doing my B.A. and have a good grasp of the intricacies of our language, with the ability to write suitable letters to clients. I have a reasonable command of French and German and can converse and write in those languages. I am quite expert in short hand and can type rapidly and accurately.. I have a little knowledge of antiques, having become interested in such matters while at school where I read up the subject in the school library. I would be prepared to study the subject in greater depth in order to improve my usefulness. Helping my father with his church matters gives me some insight into staffing difficulties. I can sometimes assist in sorting out awkward problems."

Mr. Jenkins went on to discover how she would manage one or two particular problems that might crop up and spoke of his need for a secretary who could cope with the demands of dealers. He pointed out that she would be called upon to assist in occasionally solving staff problems, soothing ruffled feathers of staff members who felt dissatisfied, and dealing with general management of the firm's problems under his guidance. He was quite impressed with her answers. She showed confidence and ability and had obviously acquired useful training from her work in the managing of the church affairs for her father.

To his repeated question "How would your family get on without you?" she had already provided a satisfactory answer and he was pleased to learn that she could start work whenever necessary.

The interview ended on a friendly note, with the promise of a letter within a week. There were two other aspirants to be interviewed, Mr Jenkins explained. Privately he thought that he had already made his choice.

Judith exited from the building feeling that she had performed quite well and stopped in a coffee shop to settle some degree of nervous excitement. She wondered when she could meet Gordon and confide in him. That was not possible yet of course so a vigorous walk back to her father was her decision, and she found the fresh air and exercise even better than the coffee. The minister welcomed her happily with a hug and covered his typewriter for a while, prepared to learn of the interview and his daughter's hopeful prospects. He told her. "A choir member has given us two tickets for a D'Oyly Carte production of Gilbert and Sullivan's 'Pirates of Penzance'. It's a matinee, so you can relax in the theatre and still see Gordon when he comes off duty in the evening."

The opportunity sounded delightful and she promptly took up the business of preparing a meal for her Mum and Dad.

After lunch minister and daughter settled down with

their coffee to discuss the day's events. What momentous things were about to unfold themselves into the lives of them both! Judith was naturally very excited and recounted to her Dad much of the interview with her fiance's father. She was in high hopes of being accepted as his future secretary and felt that she had good reason to be so. Time would tell no doubt. Meanwhile she just asked, "What of your doings, Daddy? Have you heard of any help from the church people?"

"Yes, my precious, I have had a very satisfactory talk with a most helpful lady. She is a widow and a longstanding member of our congregation. She lost her husband from a nasty heart attack two years ago and is anxious to do something useful. She has a secretarial background and would be a great help, I'm sure. She understands our situation and would be very willing to keep an eye on your mother as well as helping with food and drinks for her. She has a private income and refuses payment. I believe that an arrangement with her would greatly benefit us both. You can take up this post, which I'm sure will be offered to you, and you can do so with an easy conscience."

"That is marvellous, Daddy," said Judith. "We'll drink to that, - with another cup of tea."

The bell rang. Judith set down her cup, rose and went to unlock the front door. Immediately it was violently flung open and an extremely untidy man burst into the house slamming the door behind him. With a scruffy, bearded face and wearing dark glasses he was only of medium build, but none the less of threatening appearance as he jutted his chin forward. His fingers were closed on the trigger of a handgun. He brought it down until it pointed at her chest.

"Yer money," he said gruffly, "and don't think of reaching fer that phone". Judith was alarmed indeed but, after a few seconds she drew herself up to her full height and in a well controlled voice, though with her heart fluttering, she replied,

"This is a clergyman's manse. We don't keep much money here, or anywhere else. I 've a £5 note though and," inspiration suddenly coming to her mind, "I can offer you a mug of tea and a rock bun, if that would help."

"Humph." was the response. "OK. The fiver first and don't you dare lift that buzzer, or else, and I mean it, see". He waved his gun threateningly

Judith led the way into the kitchen; her father, who had heard the commotion, following quietly. She switched on the kettle. The men sat down, the gunman swivelling his weapon from one to the other. Judith fetched a mug from the cupboard and put two teabags in her teapot. When the kettle was boiling she made the tea She looked at her father, who snapped his fingers. Judith remembered that during the war he had been an army chaplain and had had a lot of experience, learning many tricks of dealing with threatening enemies; he had secreted one of those tricks in their jam cupboard. She said, "I expect you like it sweet. I've run out of sugar, so can offer two sweeteners and a spoonful of honey. That do? I'll get the money afterwards".

Judith opened a cupboard door and reached for the honey. In doing so her fingers adroitly collected two small white tablets from the shelf. With a desert spoon she dropped a generous amount of honey along with the tablets and sweeteners into the mug, poured in the hot tea and added milk. She then added a teaspoon with which she stirred the tea thoroughly. Handing it to their unwelcome guest she offered also the tin of rock buns and invited him to help himself. Watching father and daughter suspiciously and holding firmly the gun, he did so and began to sip his tea.

"Humph, not too bad", he growled. "Let's 'ave the fiver now, and fergit that phone," he added. Judith opened the drawer where she kept her housekeeping and found the note which she handed to her grumpy guest

She and her Dad began to make small talk and asked the man where he lived. He told them furiously to 'shut up' and continued to drink. A few minutes later the gun slipped from relaxed hands onto the floor and the owner slumped in his seat, muttering something about 'poison'. He slowly slid off the chair following the gun to the floor and the minister rapidly snatched up a cushion to place under his head; then he turned the man into the 'recovery position' and kicked the gun well away. Judith glanced approvingly at her father, walked unhurriedly to the phone and, with steady hands, dialled 999.

After some minutes tyres screeched to a halt in the drive and two burly policemen burst through the front door, their handguns at the ready.

"You won't need those," said Judith. "A stretcher could be useful." She told the sergeant what she had done. The sergeant listened grimly, observed the prostrate figure on the kitchen floor and simply said to his subordinate,"Stretcher." The order was obeyed with alacrity, and together they lifted the unconscious man onto it and strapped him down firmly.

The sergeant got out his notebook and father and daughter related the whole story to him carefully. When they came to mentioning the tablets the officer commented that the minister needed a medical degree in order to keep such poisons about the house. The reply came fast, "My daughter is engaged to a doctor. Will that do?"

The sergeant was non-committal and simply advised that they would be needed at court the next morning. The police would keep them informed. With that and having picked up the handgun the officers departed with their catch having first collected the 'fiver' from his pocket and returned it to Judith. Peace descended upon the manse.

"Judith," said her Daddy after taking a deep breath,"I think another cup of tea would be nice, don't you? No need for honey, thank you." They had forgotten all about the Penzance Pirates. Perhaps their gun-toting 'pirate' was enough of an entertainment for the day. A long and cosy chat 'twixt Dad and his daughter was an indulgence rarely available to them and the hours of the afternoon were wiled away in heart to heart talk that brought them closer together than ever before. "Your self control was admirable Judith my darling. That was quite a frightening business for a few minutes. I'm beginning to see you in a new light." A lot of memories kept them talking but at last Judith inspected her watch saying, "Well one has to try, Daddy. Anyway I think Gordon may be free now, so if you don't mind I'll be off to tell him about our burglar. It'll be quite a change from the moans of his A & E patients anyway."

Her father agreed, wished her a happy evening and went to uncover his typewriter. A phone call came from Gordon "Hello my 'Darling Girl.' I'm off for a bit. I'll pick you up for a celebratory drink somewhere, so get into your glad rags." Judith rapidly changed into appropriate wear for the evening and adorned her face, quite unnecessarily, with lipstick, eye shadow, face cream and powder. When the bell rang and the door was opened, this time a long kiss and cuddle replaced the loaded gun to cause her heart to race happily. Hand in hand they jumped down the steps and skipped off to Gordon's little car for the enjoyment of an evening together.

A cosy corner in their favourite pub with a supply of coffee was all they required, and after exchanging sweet nothings in the manner of lovers everywhere they settled down to share accounts of their adventures. There were 'oohs' and 'ah's' with gosh and golly, interspersed with 'Whatever do you do for that?' and 'I'd have damaged his solar plexus' and a host of exclamations and astonishments with threats and admirations that left them both almost breathless. Finally, having nearly exhausted the tally of A & E moans and groans and gun-happy-piracy in the manse they reached the matter of considering their proposed skiing holiday.

Judith began. "I've got some excerpts from a travel brochure that I've borrowed from the public library. But there's such a lot of informative material; buzzing about in my brain now that I simply can't decide where we should go. Why don't we just ask your uncle for help? He is a very experienced traveller and would be sure to know."

"Yes he certainly would," said Gordon, and they composed a letter to that worthy gentleman on the spot. Having off-loaded this small but important worry from their minds it simply remained to order and enjoy a good meal together. A walk in the gloaming while it was being prepared might bring peace and contentment after an eventful day.

Darkness had fallen. There was thick cloud cover and the sky was black as they walked along the canal bank. Judith squeezed Gordon's arm saying, "It's eerie, isn't it, along here near the gallows where the highway men were hanged. I could easily feel haunted. Do you believe in ghosts, Gordon?""

Gordon held her hand tightly, pausing; then said, "I'll tell you a little story that I heard about lately, if you promise not to be alarmed. It's a true one".

"OK, Gordon. I'll be good."

"Well, here goes. On a bright, starry night with a

nearly full moon a business man was driving home at about 1a.m following a long meeting at his club. The moon cast shadows of tree branches and twiglets on the road and the driver had switched off his headlight to see the intricate patterns so displayed.

"Lovely, he thought, but for good vision he switched back the lights. The figure of an old, bent woman appeared with another shadow cast by the headlights. She was walking with a stick, obviously in some difficulty. He drew level, stopped, wound down the window saying, 'Can I help you? Do you live along here?' Getting out he opened the passenger door for her as she replied 'Thank you. Yes I live some miles along this road.' She managed, with a struggle, to seat herself in the car, .grasping her stick. He drove on.

"Five miles further on the old lady indicated a big house on the side of the road. 'Please stop here., she said. He did so and hastened to open her door. He helped her out. She tottered through the gate up a sloping path to the front door, the driver trying to assist her.

"'It's alright, I can manage' she said, taking out a big very old-fashioned key and putting it in the lock.. He wished her a very good night and, returning to his car, drove further to his home. Telling his wife about his passenger he enjoyed the cup of cocoa and biscuit she offered him.

"A couple of weeks later, passing that old house he stopped and knocked on the door. It was opened by a big, competent woman who enquired severely, "What do you want? I do not buy any items from door to door salespeople".

"It's alright madam, I am not a salesman. I just wanted to enquire about the old lady whom I brought home two weeks ago. Is she alright?"

His interrogator laughed and said, "Lots of folk in the villages around ask me that. They see her toddling around late on moonlight nights. Yes, she's alright. She used to live here. She died two years ago".

*

Judith shivered. "Let's get back inside and eat ", she said. "Then home to the bright lights".

It was a happy evening but all too short when eventually they made tracks for their homes and lovingly kissed 'Goodnight.'

*

Jack and Nancy Jenkins had completed their morning gardening stint and had settled down to coffee in the summer-house. They heard the telephone ringing in the house and Nancy went to answer it. Returning she said, "It's the hospital, Jack, somebody wants you."

Her husband heaved his bulk out of his garden chair, he was a solid man of 60 years, and stumped across the lawn to take the phone and announce his name to the operator.

"Just a moment sir," she said. After a minute or so the voice of Gordon came over the wire.

"Hallo, uncle, hope I haven't disturbed you. Sorry for the delay. I was giving an injection." "That's all right, my boy. What can I do for you?"

"Well you know this Alpine excursion we had proposed. We need your wise advice about where to go. We're quite dizzy with looking at guide books and thought it would be sensible to refer to you for guidance. We've written you a letter."

"All right, Gordon, I understand. I'll look into the matter and I'll ring you later. OK?"

"Thanks, uncle, that's a load off our minds."

Jack resumed his seat in the sunshine and told his wife. Nancy, a petite, blonde, fair-haired woman of 55, laughed happily saying, "Always ask Uncle Jack. He can do wonders."

As usual he did, after, of course, commandeering his wife to assist, and using her wisdom along with their combined knowledge and experiences of many such adventures during younger years among the snows. They finally plumped for Grosse-en-Vercors and felt sure that the young lovers would be delighted. Accommodation was soon arranged, Judith and Nancy in one room and Gordon and his uncle near by. The evening phone call to Gordon brought joy to Judith's heart when she was told of the arrangement. All was well, and Judith reassured her father that everything was under control.

Then the days dragged by as she waited for a letter that she hoped would tell her of acceptance to the staff of the antiques firm. Judith employed herself busily with all kinds of preparations for her new life and for her parents' welfare. In particular she visited the lady who would come in and look after them, finding her a most pleasant motherly soul and very well versed in the business of keeping house. Her name was Mary and she was prepared to come to the manse straight away if that was acceptable. They talked at length over a cup of tea and made arrangements that Judith felt would adequately fill the bill. Her Mum and Dad would be well cared for and she returned home to cope with domestic duties which included making ready Mary's bedroom.

The next morning Mary arrived and was settled in happily. She commenced duties immediately, relieving Judith at the cooker where she was stirring custard. After demonstrating all household arrangements to Mary, Judith felt the need for fresh air and went for a short walk. Suddenly life assumed an unusual freedom for her; she would need to think. Later her father came to take a tray up to his wife and then they sat together at the dining table. The conversation turned to church matters with sticky problems that cropped up at trustees' meetings. Often Judith could bring an atom of common sense to bear on thorny questions. Her Dad found such pearls of wisdom from his daughter quite helpful.

"Daddy why don't you try a glass of red wine?" said Judith, and she persuaded him to take a sample of it with his dinner. "It's supposed to be good for your heart, or so doctors say," she told him.

Her sleep that night was peaceful and refreshing. She awoke to the sound of the letter box rattling and dashed downstairs to seize the post.

A shriek of joy awoke the minister.

"Daddy, I've got the job!" Judith yelled and raced upstairs to show the letter to he father.

"Well, of course, I told you so" he replied mildly, but quietly very pleased indeed that his dear girl should have been chosen for what would doubtless prove quite an important position in a well established firm. Joy was unconfined as they celebrated with, of course – a cup of tea Daddy and Mary both descended in dressing gowns to celebrate by cutting the special cake baked in anticipation by Mary. Judith blew out the candle with one puff,

****

CHAPTER 7

HAPPY PROGRESS

"GOOD MORNING, MISS. Welcome to the world of antiquity. May I show you to your office, and would you like a coffee?" The senior clerk was most courteous and pleased to meet the new employee.

Judith had arrived. Celebrations at home with Dad and Gordon had been quite jubilant. Now it was time to put her theory into practice and start work. She politely declined the offer of coffee and, delighted to see her name on her office door, entered her sanctum and made a quick inspection. The room was at the rear of the building, its window looking out over a small area of parkland with grass and trees that would offer relief from work stress and were pleasing to the eye. Well carpeted, the room was furnished with a large desk with a good quality PC standing prominently upon it as well as two telephones and a few other gadgets. Several filing cabinets lined the walls; a comfortable swivelling chair at the desk and two ordinary office chairs in addition. An easy chair beside the window suggested a relaxing coffee break when needed. Adequate lighting and light green wallpaper completed the décor, the latter owing not a little to several pictures of landscapes and seascapes hung attractively about the room. Judith was very pleased and felt that it was a room designed to bring out the best that she could offer. She noted that there was no communicating door to the manager's office that was next door.

A knock on the door was followed by the entry of her employer who offered his hand in welcome. He enquired "May I use your Christian name? It's very good to see you here and I hope that you will be very happy in your work for our firm."

Judith replied, "Thank you s ir. I very much appreciate this most pleasant office and I already feel at home and will certainly do my best."

"That's good", said Mr. Jenkins "I'm glad you like it. We will get down to work straight away. Will you come into my office next door in ten minutes, please."

After ensuring that her hair was tidy Judith knocked and entered the room to find Mr. Jenkins already on the telephone with his other hand holding a small voice-recording gadget. His phone conversation was crisp and clear as was the voice used to dictate a letter for his new secretary to type. The antique business evidently owed its success to the efficient business ability displayed by its owner-manager. Judith was impressed and got down to work.

The voice with which Judith later persuaded the hospital operator to find her doctor fiancé perhaps reflected her newly acquired business acumen, and Gordon also noted the change of emphasis although that same voice very soon reverted to its more dulcet tones as they spoke together.

"How has your day been, Darling, and when can we get together and compare notes?"

"Lots to tell you my Precious, but kisses first and notes afterwards. I'm anxious to know how you got on with Dad." And a time and place for a meeting was rapidly fixed up.

A cosy corner in the usual pub found them happily sipping non-intoxicating beverages, (Gordon was still on call), and exchanging tales of clipping blood vessels on the one hand and typescript and waste paper on the other. Occasional lapses of concentration occurred when gentle caresses and loving kisses were needed to lubricate the flow of animated discussion. Judith told Gordon of her first day's work, commenting particularly on his father's courteous manner and attitude. "I thought he was lovely." said Judith. "He has a wonderful command of language and always hits the right note in his letters."

"Yes, he's a jolly nice chap, a contrast to the A & E which has been full of a mixture of heart attacks and drunken oafs with knife wounds needing vomit bowls", was Gordon's response "A lot more healthy exercise and much less beer would give doctors more time for interesting and useful work".

"What about a desert island?" said Judith.

"What about that skiing holiday?" Gordon countered..

And a couple of hours passed joyfully with much loving contact until on phoning the hospital Gordon learned of another emergency. He dropped his dearest girl at the manse and sped back to duty.

The same dearest girl routed out her father from his sermon typing and told him her story of the day, describing how the firm's owner had been polite and helpful, and the efforts of the staff to ensure that she felt at home. Judith said that she was sure that she would be competent enough to cope with the work and would do her best to learn a lot about the basics of the antique business. Her father was pleased and congratulated her all over again. He then plunged into an account of his day's proceedings, relating particularly how very helpful and understanding his new lady help was about many of the problems facing the minister of a Church. She had managed not only to display wisdom in such matters but had also been able to deal successfully with the management of the house, food and refreshments, along with the care of the sad lady upstairs. It was evident that Judith's new venture would bring a fresh outlook to their lives.

In the hospital accidents and emergencies had now become Gordon's stock in trade. Each day new problems of a medical or surgical nature presented themselves. The tonsillar abscess sent by a harassed G.P., the parents desperately worried about their little boy's phimosis, the abdominal pain that might be an appendix, gall bladder, heart attack or simply a dose of intestinal flatulence (wind to the uninitiated), were all of interest. They seemed designed by fate to educate, stimulate and challenge the young doctor as he strove to slot each one into its order of importance and arrange appropriate treatment. Gordon felt uplifted every time he made a successful diagnosis or was congratulated by a senior surgeon or physician for his effective treatment of a particularly difficult case.

'One day.' he promised himself, 'I'll be the V.I.P leading a team of juniors round the wards and sorting out the errors of some trembling young medical student.'

Meanwhile to get 'stuck in' was his sole option, and this he did, day after livelong day.

*

The new and unexpected alteration in Judith's duties meant that while her day's work was of absorbing interest, the hours of the day following her regular business occupation left her with the opportunity to indulge in activities hitherto denied to her. She had time to visit friends, mostly unmarried young women of church or old school acquaintance; some of them not contacted for months and they were delighted to renew the friendship. But feeling that this was only a partial solution of her quite pleasant problem she began to think of other possibilities. Could she perhaps take some form of exercise to enhance her health, she wondered. Maybe swimming or attendance at a gym in town might be nice, or possibly writing articles for some paper or magazine, and other ideas gradually crept into her mind.

Suddenly there came the thought that she could undertake some form of study or occupation that might be useful to a doctor's future wife, and even a help to that doctor himself.

She had no nursing qualification or experience and to acquire the necessary letters after her name would be a long and intensive business. Could she become a nurse-assistant? Were there courses of study to attend in an evening? Or what about training in ambulance work? Did the N.H.S. have openings for hopeful personnel? What about the St Johjn's Ambulance people? Yes, she thought that could be a very useful way to help her future husband. She would start enquiries.

Judith telephoned the public library; the staff were most helpful.

"We'll look out some books to provide information on these subjects," said the librarian. "Can you get along to have a look at them? You might find it very helpful to sit in our side room and find out more in detail. We have plenty of reference works."

"Yes indeed I can manage that" replied Judith. "I'll come down at once. I can cope with the encyclopaedias but I should be quite glad of some guidance as well." She changed into her cream top and a red skirt, combed and brushed her blonde curls until they shone. Then she presented herself to Mary for approval.

"You look lovely. Is all this just for messing about with encyclopaedias?" was Mary's comment.

"Well I;m hoping to find some way of helping my future husband . Maybe a bit of medical know-how might be useful.".

"A U.S. President gets by nicely with just a lovely wife. Gordon is a lucky boy," saoid Mary.

Soon Judith was seated with an encyclopaedia and began to unearth information about the St. John Ambulance people, their origin and their old history; how they began as monks who created a hospital service in Jerusalem caring for pilgrims who had fallen ill on their journey to the Church of the Holy Sepulchre. It was a long story and revealed how hospitals began. She felt sure that her Gordon had little idea of this and vowed to teach him about the origins of his work some 900 years ago. No doubt he would take her back further to the days of classical Greece when Hippocrates taught his students, and became the father of medicine. But she would insist that Christian institutions were the basis of modern medical work and would bring Gordon's history up to date. She would take him from the wars with the Muslims, the Crusades, Henry 8th and his infamous destruction of places of Christian worship to the beginning of the work of the Order of St. John, and progressing right to the present day.

So when they next met on Gordon's evening off duty, Judith had ensconced herself in his little car with a book on the St John Ambulance association in which anatomical details of the human body were carefully described. She was prepared to deliver a lecture to him and offered to do so.

"That's marvellous my Darling," said her loving fiancé, sliding a hand up her thigh from nylon covered knee. "How clever of you; I had no idea that you were interested in anatomy." His hand was removed firmly and his wrist slapped by his young lady who replied

"You have ideas beyond your station, sir. Kindly control your anatomical investigations. I am not all that available. Smilingly she added "Yet"

Gordon, repulsed gently, gave up his amorous intentions in favour of a Greek history book.

"I too have been going back in time." he said. "Would you like a medical lecture from neolithic days or shall we start with the 'father of medicine'? Hippocrates was a one time resident of the island of Kos, a Mediterranean island in the Aegean Sea. That was only about 500 years B.C."

'Here we go' thought Judith. "All right, you begin/" she said. "Then I'll bring you up to date with the exploits of the Knights Templar and the start of more modern medicine."

So they began a kind of competition involving the development of medical ideas of the ancients in the islands of the Aegean and progressing down the centuries towards more modern methods of diagnosis and treatment, assisted where necessary by the kindly help of the ambulance personnel. Hippocrates and his students of medicine with their primitive surgery vied with the equally famous Templars and monkish medics, all nicely interspersed with light-hearted banter. The names of Lister, Florence Nightingale and Simpson were not forgotten, mingling with those of contributors to Gray's Anatomy and other well known works of more recent years. They ran out of breath at last and regarded each other with shining eyes.

"Darling, what caused you to think of ambulance work?" enquired Gordon.

"Well, since starting work for your dear papa I have more time in the evenings. If I am to become the wife of a famous surgeon it is only fitting that I should possess a little medical knowledge; perhaps enough to understand his jargon and even to help his patients while they await his ministrations. Of course I've got to be careful not to have ambulance classes clashing with your times off duty. Mm, I suppose that might be a bit awkward".

"Maybe that could be arranged" said Gordon. "I believe they have doctors giving anatomy lessons to the St John's students. Perhaps I might do a session somehow. Then I should be teaching you. How about that", he said with a mischievous twinkle in his eye.

Judith gave him a playful punch in the ribs. "I guess you'll often have the last laugh," she said. "But don't count on it. I might come up with something different. You never know… "

So with much similar bantering and playful argument they emerged from the car at their favourite pub and ordered a meal to complete, with two glasses of the house wine, a very pleasant evening. Yes, Judith was becoming accustomed to imbibing small quantities of alcoholic nourishment and, while never enamoured of the stuff, pronounced it to be, as the gunman had said, 'not too bad'.

"Of course" she reminded her beloved, "You have still to arrange our journey to the French Alps, and don't forget we have to gat ourselves married. I must do another toddle to the doctor's wife and discuss mysterious details that you don't know about"

. "I'm a busy boy; I have a hospital department to run".

"No you don't, they have managers to cope with that sort of thing now".

"Huh," was Gordon's acid comment, "how far would they get without their qualified medical staff?" And the conversation rapidly descended into a dissertation on medical politics which required much of Judith's tact to control; the more so since the other customers were beginning to listen, occasionally applauding some contentious outburst from the lips of the young medico.

Judith realised things were beginning to get out of hand. She rose, saying, "I'm going to the 'ladies', then a nice walk in the fresh air willbe on the cards."

The pub was not far from the canal and thither they went to walk along the bank of the water, stopping now and then to watch a bat or two streaking past, and to listen to the weird screech of a barn owl, which, like the bat, was intent on finding its supper. The sounds of Nature were soothing to human ears. After a while Judith asked, with intent, "What's your creepy story for tonight, Darling. Any witches stirring double toil and trouble or ghosts in Dunsinane Wood?"

Gordon responded, laughing, "Well one of our registrars is a Scot from Shetland and tells a story to the mess sometimes. He was off duty one night and indulged with a few pints before hokding forth. He's an odd chap. He could be described as, perhaps, fey… He said,

"My wife and I bought an old stone built cottage on the banks of the river Trent near Epworth. A builder had restored it, for it was mentioned in the Doomsday book, so it was quite ancient. The builder didn't stay in it long and sold it to us. Very charming. Very ancient wooden beams, stone floors, solid doors, low ceilings and an old stone sink in the scullery. A coal fired oven of ancient vintage in the kitchen. The cat slept in the bottom oven when the fire went out. What with roses around the front door we reckoned we had a bargain. The funny thing was that when going upstairs at night the landing light would suddenly go out. It would stay out till next morning. We got an electrician to deal with it. He said all was well; no trouble with the wiring, but the thing still kept going out. We enquired about its history in the village. It seemed that hundreds of years ago an old lady had lived there. She was seldom seen and the locals called her a witch. She died in mysterious circumstances, sitting in her chair. A great arrow was found stuck in the back of the chair but it had not damaged her. Youngsters passing the house to go to school always crossed to the other side. The folk said it was haunted. We got quite used to the light palaver and our kids always said 'Boo' before going up to bed. We found it quite interesting and almost comforting to have a ghost living with us. We moved after three years to another job. We quite missed our ghost. Sometime afterwards the buyer rang us complaining about how his lights, all of them, kept on going in and out, even those in the new garage too. He soon moved elsewhere."

"Very ghostly Darling" said Judith. "I feel your registrar and his wife must be rather nice." And the couple, with arms entwined, soon relaxed and indulged in sweet nothings that carried them happily along to the time when duty called and return to normal routine became necessary.

A tender 'Goodnight' outside the manse was all that was needed to send them both to their respective domiciles in joyful mood thinking of all the happiness to come.

*

For some days each attended to the duties assigned to them, learning daily and acquiring experiences that would improve their education and stand them in good stead in future days.

Having written to the St. John's Ambulance people there was time, some days, to collect a different friend, Rachel, and indulge in a swim at the local baths. Rachel had been a school pal, of average height and physique, but of rather an emotional nature. She worked in an office in the town, always with a face carefully made up underneath curly brown hair, and she would flutter her eyelashes at any young male who took her fancy. Not a few were duly entrapped for temporary flirtations but for Rachel there was just one in particular. After a vigorous swim they often indulged in tea and cakes and began comparisons.

"How about your young doctor chap? Is he nice, Judith?"

"Gorgeous. Rachel. Six foot of bone and muscle with hands that love to wander over my anatomy. Of course we're engaged now. How about yours? "

"Absolutely smashing my dear. Blue eyes and flaxen hair with a gentle voice full of concealed passion. He's about to go down on his knees and ask…"

Lots more intimate detail followed.. These were most

satisfactory evenings. Each girl went home with feet treading lightly on air and hearts filled with rapturous anticipation of joys to come.

*

With the approach of autumn Judith spoke up one day. "Darling, we haven't had a holiday yet this year. Shall I contact the travel agent and see what they can do for us? Ir's getting rather late in the summer, the need is becoming urgent."

A quick phone call to the travel agent produced very soon details of a summer holiday in Cornwall. Hospital and Antiques proved most co-operative and Gordon and Judith were able to escape from work driving in Gordon's little car to view the delights of that charming county for a whole week. They were carefully ensconced in separate rooms in a quaint little fishing village and Cornwall did them proud. Atlantic storms veered north avoiding the sanctum of Merlin and King Arthur. Gordon steered his way along narrow overgrown lanes to emerge onto cliffs that gave glorious views of a far stretching coast. Rocky promontories divided the calm blue sea or, if the wind blew, enormous bursts of spray arose from the vast rolling waves that furiously pounded the rocks. They found sheltered coves where tea rooms abounded and they could view the scene peacefully while munching scones liberally plastered with thick yellow Cornish cream.

"We must have a look at Land's End" said Gordon, one day. Early next morning they set off for Penzance and, after visiting the old fishing port of Newlyn briefly - we'll come back and 'do' it properly some day, they averred - Gordon drove his small car towards Cornwall's huge granite rocks that projected westwards into the Atlantic ocean, dividing their waters between the English Channel on the south side and the Bristol Channel to the north.

They stood beside the signpost indicating the mileage to America. "Land's End" said Judith. "I never thought I should see it".

"If you look carefully you will see the Longships Lighthouse, almost on the horizon", said Gordon "When I was a little lad I read a story about that. I found it on my father's bookshelves A bit grim I thought It was in the days of the wreckers who enticed ships onto the rocks and divided the spoils between them".

"Alright, come on, give," Judith invited.

"Well it starts in Sennen village, just below here, where Owen was attending his dying wife. She heard the wreckers passing their house and, whispering, begged her husband, never to go with them again. He made a solemn promise to her before she died. That night the great light in the lighthouse never shone. A ship was wrecked on the jagged rocks. The wreckers got the cargo – casks of brandy from France - but they gave no help to the drowning sailors. After the funerals Owen stood on the shore gazing towards the Longships. He vowed that if he could help it that light would never again fail to light the way for home-bound mariners.

As he watched he spied a small dinghy coming through boisterous waves towards him. The oarsman was pulling frantically at his oars. Owen stepped forwards and helped the chap pull the dinghy up onto the beach. It was the light house keeper, only recently installed. He had survived the recent storm that wrecked the ship. He was in a state of terror, trembling, his mouth working helplessly. At last his words tumbled out. "There's devils under that rock, mister. They're coming to get me. I know they are. I'm not going back there ever again. I want to go home". He burst into tears, his chest heaving with his sobs. When able he told Owen his story. .

"It was alright at first and J lit the light every night. Then the storm began. The waves was mountains high and sprayed all over the lantern, but I wasn't feared of them. That lighthouse is strong. I helped to build it. It was the noises. The waves pounded the rocks. There's caverns under them rocks. The noise was terrible, roaring, screeching, furious. They never ended. There's devils in those caverns mister. I know there is. They's coming to get me, I thought. I went to bed and hid under all the clothes I could find. I couldn't light the lamps. I can't go back. I've got to go home. Help me, help me please" He was practically hysterical.

"Owen felt much sympathy for him. He knew about the noises when waves pounded the rocks. "Alright, you can come and have a meal with me and I'll give you a bed for the night. You can go back to your home tomorrow. I will keep those lamps burning until we find another keeper".

"Next morning the sea was much calmer. Own collected all necessary stores, loaded them into his dinghy and pulled manfully for the Longships. The light never failed again".

"Gosh, that's quite a story" said Judith. "I'm glad to see that lighthouse. Good luck to it".

"Time for a spot of grub: let's find a café". said Gordon. They drove off, thoughtfully.

"Yes my lover", said the waitress, "there's saffron buns with strawberry jam and real, yellow, thick, Cornish clotted cream. That'll do you good my lover," she repeated, rolling the 'R's in a seductive manner. And, as well as cafes, snuggling together with a Cornish pasty in a private nook near a cliff top was also often a little bit of heaven . To follow in the evenings with a well cooked meal in the village pub brought new insight as they listened to the delightful 'burr' of fisherman's voices regaling each other with tales of 'the one that got away.' It was a delightful change for the two young lovers.

But time was short and return to duty essential. Sadly, after the week, they put halcyon days, summer suns, bathing in pools and sea behind them, along with exciting sailing when their hired yacht heeled over and they hung on for dear life while trying to obey the captain's shouted commands of 'Ready about, Lee-oh,' or 'Get that anchor over the side quickly,' or 'Put out the fenders and get on with it'.

So it was into the little car and then to face the long road back home, leaving regretfully the late summer sun and Cornish walks and hidey holes. Reality must be faced. Work with its emergencies waited. It was all over too soon. Afterwards there was not enough time to spend together talking of the fun and the lovely relaxing days of holiday in an almost foreign land...

****

Chapter 8

SADNESS TIME

Plunging straight back into the business of life and work Gordon and Judith resumed duty with just occasional evenings of blissful togetherness. Rest at night after work with happy talk and cuddling sessions that gave promise of even more loving canoodling was always a welcome bonus.

One morning brought, not quiet peace, but Judith's father, urgently knocking on her bedroom door.

"Judith, will you come, please. Mummy's very ill."

"Her father sounded quite frantic with worry. Judith slipped on a dressing gown and joined him at her mother's bedside.

Her mother was breathing with quick shallow breaths and looking vaguely about her, obviously distressed. Judith felt her pulse – she knew where to find that. It was rapid and her mother's forehead was hot. Declaring, "We must ask the doctor to come and see her as soon as he can," she went to the telephone. Mary, the housekeeper, who had found the mother in this state, now brought a cup of tea and tried to administer it to her in a teaspoon. Judith and her father dressed quickly and were ready for Doctor Collins who, very shortly, arrived. The examination was brief and expert.

"She has got pneumonia I'm afraid. I think it is essential to admit her to hospital for treatment. I shall give her an injection of antibiotic straight away and then arrange an ambulance".

. He did so and while waiting for the transport wrote a letter to the hospital doctor on duty. He waited for the ambulance to arrive and then returned to his morning surgery after the ambulance team had wrapped the patient comfortably and loaded her into their vehicle. Judith and her father followed in his little car and saw her safely into the ward. They completed the usual hospital forms and waited until the doctor on duty had attended to the patient. He came to see them and confirmed the diagnosis, adding that she was certainly very ill. They would continue the antibiotic given by their own doctor and arrange a good oxygen supply. After which the outcome would depend upon her powers of resistance. She had been given a sedative that would help her to sleep.

"I think really, sir". said the registrar, "you would do better to go home and look after yourselves". They had a talk with the Sister who had just come on duty and who confirmed the doctor's words.

"We'll look after her as well as we can. You just return home and have some breakfast and try to rest. Come in this afternoon," she said.

At the manse Mary had their breakfast all ready. Judith held her father's hand and said to him, "Try and relax, Daddy. Why not take your spy-glass and have a country walk. Birds will be singing perhaps and the swallows will be sitting on the telephone wires ready to fly off to Africa. I must get ready for work. I have a lot to do today, so bye for now and I'll meet you later for that trip to the hospital

John felt that he had a very understanding daughter and was glad. He suggested to Mary that perhaps she would like to accompany him on a walk through the fields, although it was too late for the song birds now. She agreed and in due course they went off as Judith had suggested.

"The swifts have already gone," he told Mary. "Look, there's a host of swallows sitting on the wires as Judith said. They will be off soon because the supply of insects for their food is dropping rapidly with the onset of autumn." And there was more wisdom to similar effect from the man whose second love was the study of bird life.

On return the minister felt more relaxed and while Mary prepared lunch he was able to take up his unfinished typing and gather his thoughts together. A snooze in the afternoon was helpful and, later, when Judith returned home, they set off to the hospital.

Sister met them at the door of the ward. "There isn't any change to report," she said. "Your wife is still dangerously ill. We can only continue with the injections and oxygen. It will be all right for you to stay as long as you like, although she is hardly conscious. Sleep is a good medicine, anyway."

They stayed. The minister talked lovingly to his wife, although knowing that she might not be able to hear or understand. Judith just held her hand. They began to realise that there was no improvement in her condition. The duty doctor came round and examined her carefully.

"I must warn you that she is desperately ill." he said. "I fear that it seems very doubtful whether she can recover."

After returning home for supper they came again to stay beside her during the night. In the small hours her breathing became irregular. They called the nurse who informed the doctor. He attended, but told them that there was nothing more that could be done, and at 5 o'clock her breathing ceased and she was at peace. The minister and his daughter prayed together and committed her soul to God.

There followed the usual long drawn out ceremonies of certificates, funeral arrangements, church service and a reception with endless messages of sympathy. It was so long since the deceased had been in fact a real member of the household that they felt it all seemed a little hollow. Judith began to urge her father to arrange for a period of absence from the church. After that he would feel more able to resume clerical duties. She spoke to senior stewards of the church and they addressed those in higher authority who wrote to the minister advising him that he should take a 'holiday' for a couple of weeks.

He considered seriously and agreed with Judith to do so. He asked her to arrange something and she responded quickly, fixing up a coastal holiday where her Dad could pursue his ornithological leanings and find peace for his soul. At the same time she requested leave from her employer who viewed the matter with sympathy and told her to go with her father for as long as was required. He would find a temporary replacement.

"We've got a small place on the Gower Peninsula, Daddy. It's just an easy journey by car, mostly on main roads. There we could hire bicycles and take picnics and walk over the hills and valleys; climb the rocks and walk on the beaches, even paddle our feet in the briny. It will still be fairly warm and there's a lot of bird life." A few days afterwards, with the car packed, they moved off to the Gower.

While driving he ransacked his memory and told Judith of his early days with her mother. He told her "We used to have lovely holidays in between sessions of church work, getting away to the Lake District and climbing the hills to view the shining waters of Grassmere and Derwentwater, Ullswater and the rest . Your mother was wonderfully helpful looking after our church members too, always spotting when someone was absent, ill, and needing a visit. She was a very lovely person."

Many stories came to his mind and the telling of them seemed to ease his tensions. They hired bicycles and cycled the roads to the isolated bays of the Gower peninsula, finding beauty in the rocky coastline, the breaking waves and white foam as it swished up sandy beaches. To the north they lifted their eyes to the rolling, misty hills of Wales. They visited the almost hidden Mewslade bay and Rhossilli with its four miles of extensive sandy beach. A walk to the end of the promontory of Worm's head gave good exercise and provided a wide view of the sea with its vast array of waves ever pushing towards the shore, then crashing with a mighty roar upon the rocks and shooting great clouds of spray high up against the cliffs. Evenings were spent with books beside a lighted fire as the temperature dropped, or sometimes a game of Chess or Scrabble kept their brains alert until sleep took over, bringing quietness of mind and body. A fortnight found them relaxed and with minds at peace and ready to face the problems of their lives at home. Driving back they stopped at Caerleon to bring to mind the old tales of Arthur and Guinevere presiding over the Knights of the Round Table. Finally, when home at the manse, they thrilled to find that Mary had performed miracles in ordering the house and its needs, while at the hospital Gordon was overjoyed to have his sweetheart back in his arms. His father was only too happy to welcome his secretary back at her desk.

Judith settled in with her usual expertise and rapidly caught up with her in-tray to the relief of all the staff at Antiques. They had become accustomed to her efficiency; all appreciated her return to their midst.

While away in the Gower Judith had remembered her idea of possibly writing short stories. She had sometimes busied herself making notes of ideas that came to her mind. One evening when all was quiet she brought out her notebook and began to make notes of how such a story might be composed. Structure was important. She began to enjoy herself. Settling at her new typewriter which her father had acquired she thought of a title and typed it out. After a few minutes an idea came and she put the days of sadness behind her and began to transcribe thoughts into print. Suddenly she realised that it was late and of course she must sleep and then attend to duty. She would return to her story later. But although work and concentration was now the order, with minds refreshed this became just routine and easy to accomplish.******************

CHAPTER 9

SOMETHING DIFFERENT

ONE EVENING OVER a lime and lemon Gordon said, "I'm doing a ward round on my own tomorrow. Would you like to come and have a dekko? Only Sister and a nurse will be with me and they are very decent folk. I'm sure they would agree. It would be an eye-opener for you to look at life from the standpoint of the medics". So to the Oxenby hospital next day Judith duly went.

At the hospital reception desk she was directed to the relevant ward and Gordon met her at the nurses' station, introducing her to the Sister. Together with the staff nurse they entered a six-bed ward. The hospital was fairly new and the old fashioned 20 bed wards had been replaced by smaller wards of more modern type, light and airy with three beds on each side. Between the beds were lockers for the patients' essentials and jugs of water available. A gadget with switches for light and an emergency call button were provided, but in so small a hospital they still waited for radios for each bed, and a ward telephone.

The little team visited each bed in turn, the Sister giving Gordon a short resume of the troubles of each occupant with the G.P's letter and the story of the complaint.. Gordon's task was to examine and come to a diagnosis, if possible, or to order further tests, x-rays or laboratory investigations that would enable a diagnosis to be made. If that had been done and treatment commenced, it was a matter of assessing how the patient was responding and the ordering of further care as necessary. Judith found it all very interesting and was occasionally shown x-rays of a patient's anatomy; she found that fascinating and wished she knew more about the human condition. She was told a little about intravenous drips and their uses. She noted that one patient was in a very serious state, being unconscious and in a coma. Another was bright and restless and obviously very anxious to be discharged to her home. After some 40 minutes the round ended and all retired to Sister's office for a cup of coffee and a chat about the state of the ward and its occupants. Judith understood that the staff were busy and shortly stood up and after graciously thanking Sister and her staff Judith took her leave.

Gordon saw her to the ward door. "Enough for today, my Darling? That should give you pause to think."

"Yes I fancy you're right my Gordon. That was a real eye-opener for me and very different from delving into age old antiquities. The human body is certainly an antique, but modern methods of healing are most instructive. I'd better think hard so back to work. Good night, my love".

Judith Writes For Fun.

Judith returned home with a bewildering multitude of thoughts engendered by her hospital experience streaming into her mind and demanding action. Allowing them to develop she remembered that her hospital visit could provide an interesting way to begin a story..

As a youngster she had always enjoyed essays and the composing of gentle adventures that entertained her teacher. 'Why not' she thought, 'produce a little medical story to amuse her beloved and give him a good night's sleep'. She brought out the neglected notebook for making notes of how such a story might be composed. It could bring in quiet adventures to remind him of the sea and sun which they had left behind with their little holiday. She might base it in the Med. A travel brochure could help. There was one at the receptionist's desk; also an encyclopaedia . She would bring hospital wards and its patients to life in print. This could be great fun. She begged typing paper from her father, sat down and typed -

ESCAPISM.
A Story to Relieve the Mind from Modern Mayhem.

Bed six in ward 27 of the county hospital had been given the name Jessica by her parents of yesteryear. She had now been hidden away from civilisation, as she put it, for a good three weeks, and was becoming thoroughly fed up with the ward regimentation and was determined not to be a hospital 'case'. She had gladly parted company with her gall bladder on the operating table and knew that the operation had been successful; she was now taking full diet. For some reason the professor of surgery wanted to keep her for a few more days, perhaps to use her 'case' for demonstration to his class of students; these kindly intentions of the professor did not appeal to her She would escape from this public display of her anatomy and get home to her cosy flat and friends Thoughts streamed through her brain. Her wits began to work.

Jessica knew that the comatose patient in bed three, whose name was Ruth, was desperately ill and not expected to live. It was just a matter of time. She also knew that the nurse coming on the evening shift was new to the ward and did not yet know the patients or their state of health. The young doctor was also new to the ward and could not be expected to remember yet which patient was in which bed. Quickly she made up her mind. The nurses' shift changed. The new staff nurse entered the ward.

"Nurse, can I speak to you please?" said Jessica.

"Yes, what can I do for you?"

"Well I have been here in bed six for three weeks and would very much like to be beside the window. I know the lady in bed three is in a coma and unlikely to live. Do you think our beds could be changed round? She would then be nearer the nurse's station and easier to keep an eye on".

Staff nurse thought quickly. Why not?

"Yes, all right. I'll arrange it for you." She told her junior to fetch one of the male attendants to effect the change. Shortly afterwards this was done; bedside lockers were also changed to their new positions. However nurses were busy with an emergency and the business of altering the change of bed positions on the board beside the nurses' station was overlooked. Bed three was still recorded as comatose.

Jessica, now in bed three, was anything but! She pulled the curtains around her bed and having returned from a toilet session she sat and thought. She would dress, pack her essentials in a small bag, stay in bed until all was very quiet and then sneak out unnoticed by any of the staff. Could it be done? Yes, she thought so. She would borrow a nurse's cape that would hide her luggage and pretend she was going for a walk along the corridor.

And that was precisely what she did after drawing back the curtain. She snoozed for an hour or two, and then woke up to observe carefully the staff movements. When both nurses had been called to attend a patient in the next ward she arose, pulled the curtains again around her bed, looked cautiously round the ward and, observing that the nurses' station was not manned, she quietly and swiftly moved out. Jessica picked up and donned a nurse's cape to provide disguise and left the ward. Leaving the cape in the visitors' room she entered the corridor and marched nonchalantly along towards the hospital exit. Twice a ward orderly offered her a cheery 'Goodnight' to which she responded in good spirit. Finding a telephone near the main entrance of the hospital she ordered a taxi and sat reading a magazine until a taxi driver appeared.

She was free! Free from her pesky gall-bladder, free from hospital regimentation, free to enjoy her life and do what she liked. Hurrah! She directed the driver to take her to a small hotel, took a deep breath and could hardly refrain from bursting into song. She paid the driver, signed in at the hotel desk, found her room and climbed under the eiderdown, clothes and all. Sleep, with the peace that comes after stress, was a quick and most welcome release.

In the ward nurses were busy with a new patient. They noted the quietness in bed three where the supposed comatose patient was unmoving save for her shallow breathing, and, as the light was on behind the curtains of bed six they assumed that the patient there was reading, as usual, far into the night. The nurses were too busy to be concerned about that. When morning came the incoming staff, also new to the ward, had not realised the change of beds and thought they now had two comatose patients. They examined the lady in bed six, found an extremely feeble and erratic pulse, assumed that death was near and, unknowingly, informed Jessica's uncle, the supposed next of kin and, of course, the doctor on duty. The uncle of our errant friend, Jessica, her next of kin, was an elderly, grumpy fellow, not unduly concerned about the imminent demise of a younger woman who had never been close to him, and much more bothered about his worritable arthritis. He told the staff to send for the undertaker when it happened. Nature took its course, the doctor certified the cause of death; the undertaker took charge and the hospital's responsibility was ended. When someone drew back the curtains around bed three, astonishment gave way to recriminations and an investigation was paramount. With the results this story is not concerned.

Jessica had enjoyed her uninterrupted sleep in her hotel bed, free from the clatter of early morning tea from laden trolleys. She took a hot bath and dressed at leisure. She found the breakfast excellent and savoured each mouthful. Replete and happy she phoned the hospital reception desk; she explained and offered apologies and asked for her remaining possessions to be sent to reception where she would collect them or send someone on her behalf. She took a bus to her flat, let herself in and switched on the heating and the kettle. With a cup of tea she sat in her accustomed easy chair, opened a stack of mail and began to deal with correspondence.

The phone rang.

"Jessica, where have you been? I have been trying to find you for weeks." It was the voice of a good friend with whom she had long shared jjoys and troubles, as well as holidays and weekend breaks. Explanations were obviously essential and would take quite a while.

"I've been on the operating table getting rid of my gall bladder." said Jessica. "Let's meet for a coffee in town and we can have a good natter." At their favourite coffee shop they found a secluded spot with a table for two. There, beginning with the emergency of a gall-bladder colic Jessica took her friend Monica through the whole gamut of medical emergencies and investigations and treatments until both were tired of the recital of woe. She stopped for breath.

"Coo, you have had a real adventure," said Monica, brushing aside the extravagant curls of red-gold hair that adorned her blonde features. She was a tall, well made and vigorous woman, living on her own and something of a know-all. The two women were very fond of each other.

"I've been wishing to suggest to you a different kind of fun," she continued. "What about an ocean cruise to banish the fumes of ether or whatever? They tell me the Med. is rather nice in October. I've booked a cabin and there might still be a cabin for two on a higher deck. I rang the office this morning. Want a change of scene? View the sleek and graceful dolphins instead of harassed nurses and medicos? What about it?"

"Done," said our heroine. "Just the job. Romance on the high seas with flying fish dropping in through the window. Lovely idea."

"I think mariners call windows by a different name, portholes, I believe. Let's go and book straight away." This from her friend. After paying their bill they bounced out of the shop and crossed the street to the travel agent. They were going to have fun.

"Good morning Madam, you were the lady who enquired about a possible two berth cabin on the Mediterranean cruise?"

"Yes that's right, is it still available?"

"Yes you're in luck; it's on one of the higher decks but with no passage way outside the window. You are looking straight out to sea. The porthole can be opened so the flying fish can hop in for breakfast!" And the attendant demonstrated the position on the big liner to them both in a brochure revealing pictures of the accommodation, dining areas, decks and playing facilities, not forgetting the swimming bath and the lifeboats. She told them the ports of call and mentioned that lectures would be given the evening prior to docking at a new port. Most of the sailing would be done at night, including evenings. Lots of questions and lots of answers and explanations filled a happy hour.

"First class," .said Jessica, "let's go for it." Excitedly, they signed the forms, paid their deposits, collected brochures and departed to a favourite restaurant for a celebratory lunch. While chatting over roast pork and apple sauce, with raspberries and cream to follow, Jessica remembered her gear in the hospital and was glad to have Monica's offer of company to drive over to collect it. The idea that Jessica was supposed to have crossed the river Jordan to bend her way heavenwards had not yet percolated to the reception desk. She escaped any interrogation about such difficult matters.

Doubtless some bright young medico would pick up the trail and begin enquiries, but she hoped to be on the high seas by then An undertaker arranging her funeral was not amused when told of the mistake. Corrections were in order, profuse apologies offered to distressed relatives and proper arrangements were made. Jessica's uncle just fumed about his arthritis. There were red faces in ward 27. But the hospital was busy and two empty beds were welcomed by the medical staff. " Just what we need," said the registrar. The professor would find another subject for demonstration to his students.

There were only a few days in which to collect clothes for the cruise and on a fine dry day they popped off to join the coach for their destination. Comfortably settled, Jessica was happy to admire the passing landscape, the green trees, some now yellowing, and the docile beasts in the fields. After a while she remarked to her friend

"We don't seem to be on the right road for Southampton. Do you think the driver knows the way?"

"The plane leaves from Gatwick, Jess. This is all right. Don't worry, we'll get there."

"What plane?" said Jessica. "I thought we were going sailing."

"That's right, but the ship is in Venice. We fly over Europe to join it."

"Good gracious," came the astonished reply. "What fun, I've never flown before. Shouldn't I be frightened or make my will or something?"

"Rubbish. It's as safe as houses. You'll enjoy it."

The conversation became animated as Monica enthused over the trip and Jessica interrupted with interminable questions, excited at the prospect now revealed.

The coach drew up at the airport. They found their guide and reported to the desk, to the Passport and Customs folk, and finally found seats in the appropriate lounge. A cup of tea, a comfort session and the queue at the gate as their flight was announced. Greeted on board the plane by a smiling air hostess, they found their seats and belted up. A safety demonstration followed and the engines commenced producing a gentle vibration. Slowly, then faster, they moved to the start of the runway and the engines were tested. Then with a tremendous roar the plane moved off, gathering speed at an astounding rate until suddenly the feel of wheels on the runway vanished; the plane rose with the ground falling away below them. Jessica hung on to her seat, relaxing as they returned to normal level flight.

"Coo, that was marvellous," she said. "How long till we get there?" She was answered by the captain's voice with the reassuring tones and helpful information of an expert professional.

"If you look outside you'll see the English channel in a minute," said Monica. "The next thing will be lunch brought on a tray. Aren't you lucky!"

Drinks were brought, the channel merged with France, and the French countryside faded away as the plane rose through and above the clouds. Now Jessica was thrilled to see a vast level expanse of white cloud beneath them, the sun shining brilliantly upon it. This was a new and wonderful experience and it filled her with a great sense of awe and peace.

The plane droned on steadily; lunch arrived on a tray and the newness and thrill of it all brought to her a delightful sleepiness. She drowsed off, woken eventually by a sudden change of the engine note as it quietened when the plane began to drop gently down to a lower altitude... Jessica looked out to see the mountains of Austria, some still with traces of the last winter's snow

They had passed through cloud and the woods and fields of the countryside were visible. The 'Seatbelt' sign appeared and they dropped further to see roads and traffic followed by the airport runway and buildings whizzing swiftly past the windows. There was a bump and immediately the tremendous roar of the reverse thrust of the plane's engines. Jessica hung on to her seat tightly, but everybody seemed quite calm and very shortly the plane slowed to a gentle pace as it moved around the runway towards its station.

"Phew" said Jessica, "that was an excitement. What happens now?"

"Just follow the rest of the mob," said her friend.

She soon cottoned on, as passengers stood up to grab their possessions from the luggage rack and formed a queue for leaving the plane. Our ladies joined in the exodus to find a bus waiting to convey them all to the baggage hall, and after collecting their suitcases from the circulating carousel, they quickly found their guide who directed them to the appropriate coach that would take them to the age old-city of Venice. There lay their cruise ship, waiting to reveal to them the classical and eastern world, so wonderfully different from the modern world of their birth. The guide checked that all his passengers were present and the coach set off smoothly.

Driver and guide conversed together and shortly the guide's voice came over the loud speaker.

"It seems that we are too early for the ship. We are going to drive through the country for a while and then stop at a nice restaurant where you can obtain refreshments. I hope this is satisfactory."

All signified their agreement. They journeyed through fields and past crops new to them all, but recognised the extensive fields of vines with men and women tending them. Their guide kept up a running commentary explaining the treatment of these vineyards and the way in which grapes were finally transformed into bottles of wine to titillate the palate. The afternoon was very warm and the stop at an excellent restaurant equipped with a cooling system and circulating fans was most welcome. Here they could sample an enchanting variety of sugary sweetmeats and have a taste of the local wines at the expense of the shipping company. At a time appointed they gladly filed into their coach and, chatting happily to each other, they headed for the city and the waiting liner.

Venice at last, so old in story, so famed for its military history, its ancient buildings and waterways. Through its streets, over its canals they progressed until, reaching the Grand Canal, they espied their ship lying n the water. There also lay a medley of small boats, gondolas in fact, many tied up opposite St Mark's Square with their gondoliers waiting for custom. Conversation became excited as the old stagers pointed out the famous features of Venice now visible to the newcomers. St Marks, of course; the Doge's palace, the Bridge of Sighs, were all to be admired when passing down the Grand Canal and the company took note while preparing to board. Then to the ship, up the gangway, greet the officers, splendidly attired, and obey the directions to their staterooms. All went like clockwork; there was hasty inspection of the cabin facilities, the usual non-reading of the printed notices regarding action advised in the event of an emergency, and then all the passengers lined the ship's rails intent on watching for the moment when, with all ropes untied and hawsers flung into the water, the vessel would imperceptibly move quietly away from the land and consign herself to the waves. And so it was. After a warning blast from the ship's siren all the 12000 tons of the rather lovely floating hotel became detached from *terra firma* and a gap appeared between the ship's side and the wharf, gradually widening. They were off.

"Here we go," said Monica. "We'll get an announcement

about lifeboat drill very soon. Did you read the little chit telling you where to find your lifebelt and lifeboat station."

"Good gracious, no I didn't. Ought we to pop along and find out about it?"

"No, wait till the alarm sounds. Then we'll get them, probably under the bunks in the cabin." Monica was very calm and much more interested in the idea of the exciting food that would greet them in the dining saloon. Meanwhile they would watch their progress down the Grand Canal and out into the waters of the Adriatic. The sea was calm, the ship rising and falling to the gentle swell; the clouds of evening appeared in a purple line above the western horizon and the sun seemed to be going down to its night's rest more rapidly than at home.

"Let's go down and sort out our things," said Monica. We'll have to change into our glad rags for dinner. Hope you have plenty of diamonds to flash about to impress the rest of the female mob."

"I have some paste glitters, if that's what you mean. I don't intend to compete with anybody, so artificial pearls can be my standby."

So down the companionway they trod cheerily – "They don't have stairs on a ship" said Monica, - and made their way to their cabin. They found the steward had turned down the beds and everything was spick and span. Quickly they unpacked, filling drawers and the single cupboard, and could then attend to the business of glamorizing themselves. The creams, powder, paint, shadow, eyelashes, and the lipstick, all were used to good effect, perhaps a little overdone, but who would bother? Dinner was announced over the Tannoy and they joined Monica's 'mob' of other overdone females competing for masculine attention. Expecting to find themselves at the

Captain's table, they were disappointed. Other V.I.P.'s had beaten them to it; they were shown to more humble positions, oh dear. Of the meal it suffices to say that the chef had made it a dinner to remember. With the gay chatter and inevitable efforts to outdo each other the whole effect made a charming introduction to life on board ship. They were well satisfied and afterwards walked the deck in the gloaming of a summer's evening happy in anticipation of the 'holiday of a lifetime'.

Monica steered her friend towards the ship's bows. They leaned against the rail and watched as the 'sharp end' pushed vigorously though the water creating a curling wave, falling over, white against the 'wine dark sea,' and with a white line of broken foam running along the side of the vessel towards the stern. Jessica was fascinated. She could have stared at it for ever.

. The night sky glittered with stars and Monica, a fount of knowledge, pointed out the 'Bear' and the Pole Star for her friend's edification, along with such constellations as were visible at that season of the year. Bed called after their eventful day; they turned towards their cabin, glad to change into pyjamas. Jessica climbed up the sturdy little ladder to occupy the top bunk with Monica below; then the quiet humming and vibration of the vessel's mighty power house along with the gentle movement created a soporific element that soon brought sleep to relax their weary bodies.

Morning brought a change. Movement was apparent. Their cabin was fairly far forward. Suddenly the bows rose sharply, leaving their stomachs to feel as if falling. Then a violent fall and stomachs rose into their chests; all mixed with a side-to-side leaning that caused them to stagger and hold urgently onto ladder or washbasin It went on and on. Queasiness was afflicting both of them and quickly they sat down on the bottom bunk; they laid down as well as possible with heads at opposite ends.

"Not much hope of breakfast today, I think," said Monica..

"Couldn't care less," was the reply.

The voice of the chief officer came over the Tannoy. "I am sorry about the weather, folks", he said. "We were warned last night of the approach of a low-pressure-system and of rough seas. We have been making as much speed as possible and will now be docking in port at Corfu, on the west side of the island an about an hour's time. The ship will tie up and breakfast will be served in the dining saloon. For any people who would prefer a little nourishment in their cabins they should make a request to their steward who will bring sandwiches and a flask of tea or coffee. Thank you for your patience".

"Shall we see how we feel when we've docked? " said Monica. "I expect we'll stay in port for the rest of the day and the worst of the storm will have passed before we put to sea again."

"Good idea, I couldn't eat a thing at the moment. Maybe we could go ashore and view the town. The travel agent said it was quite picturesque." So they waited hopefully, and in due course, as promised, the ship slowed, the movement lessened, and they rose to venture on deck to watch the docking procedure with a few other hardy souls all anxious to miss nothing.

Lines were thrown, hawsers pulled ashore and fastened around bollards and all was snug and 'ship-safe and Bristol fashion' at last. The engines stopped and vibration disappeared.

"What ho for brekker?" was the word from Monica, and they made their way along with those brave enough to accompany them. There was a significant number of absentees at the tables.

But the stewards were cheerful and obviously well accustomed to the conditions as they announced triumphantly that a full English breakfast was available. Our ladies opted for cereals and toast with coffee.

Refreshed, they were invited to join a guide who would show them Corfu town. Macs were advised and at an appointed time they stepped ashore to join the company of folk who wished to view the newness offered in Corfu. They walked along the quay into town, glad of the exercise and chance to stretch their legs. Arriving in the street opposite the harbour they were immediately plunged into the atmosphere of the place by the sight of donkey-drawn carriages, all open and of ancient vintage. The donkeys, patient beasties, were garlanded with flowers of bougainvillea and poinsettia thrown around their necks. The two lassies elected to share with a few others a ride up to the temple of Achilles. A long trail along an earth road through olive groves, ancient trees, gnarled with time, dry as dust but still bearing a few olives as yet unpicked. They reached the quite imposing palace, white and immaculate, standing on a high cliff where it dominated the surrounding area. The interior was impressive and they industriously snapped photos of the paintings on the walls with their cameras. Outside, looking down over the cliff, they could see the little Mouse Island with its nunnery, floating seemingly on the water, quiet and serene, but with spray from the vigorous waves still rising high and white above the rocks. Their donkeys bore them back to town, passing a number of black-gowned elderly women who were employed in gathering late fruit from orange trees. A charming small town with coffee shops invited customers, with neat tables and chairs arrayed on pavements in the sunshine. Enjoying a walk through the streets they spent time admiring shops and their contents before returning to the ship. Their trip had been all new, clean and well worth the modest outlay and the time and trouble.

"All quite lovely, isn't it? That was a fascinating ride in the donkey carriage, and the palace, the Mouse Island, the old trees, all quite different from home. The narrow streets, tables and chairs on pavements. Wouldn't you like to stay for ever? But I'm afraid we'll just have to climb aboard again. Never mind there'll be a nice buffet lunch on the deck. Come on, pal, come and eat." Monica waxed almost lyrical with delight and led the way back to the ship's gangway.

They felt well satisfied to leave behind them the old narrow streets of the town, the donkeys garlanded with flowers as they wended their way along the quay to climb up the gangway and attend the buffet lunch as described. The former furious wind of the early morning had dropped and looking out to sea there were less white horses visible. The tour would doubtless proceed as planned. So they happily chatted with fellow passengers and viewed the attractive viands set out on the tables all decked with sparkling white cloths and vases of fresh flowers. They tucked in with gusto and, with tummies well sated, found books in their cabins, returned to the deck, settled cosily in the generous seating provided, read for a while, and fell asleep.

The evening's entertainment included a talk about the wonders of ancient Greece that they would see the next day. The lecturer spoke of the fingers of the Peloponnese, the approach to Athens, the far-off view of the Parthenon with its mighty pillars, the Bay of Salamis and the long-ago-defeat of the fleet of Darius the Persian king. The speech of St. Paul to the men of Athens who worshipped the *unknown god* was mentioned along with some of the impressive wonders of Athenian culture that they could visit on the following day, after landing at the Piraeus.

The docking next morning - a fine sunny day- was followed by a coach ride from the Piraeus to Athens and they began to absorb the 'culture' as described. They found it all quite enchanting..

The famous Parthenon, the Elgin Marbles, minus those taken by Lord Elgin for preservation supposedly to our own country, the Temple of Apollo, the Areopagus and the view of the whole city of Athens laid out before their eyes made a wonderfully new and exciting experience. Their return to the ship, followed that evening by a further talk concerning the morrow's expedition to Ephesus, well supplied them with excellent material for postcards for their friends, and, with a good dinner inside them, they gave way to a somnolence that promised a satisfying and relaxing sleep. .

The next day dawned fair and sunny, now lacking all trace of the gale that had plagued them in the Adriatic, and a calm voyage across the Aegean brought them to the port of Kusadasi where they observed another cruise ship anchored in the harbour. But to detail all their further adventures in their cruise is outside the scope of this story. Let it suffice that they wondered at the sole mighty pillar that remained from the Temple of Diana, visited the huge amphitheatre where St Paul addressed *the men of Ephesus,* examined the supposed house of St John and the room where Mary, the mother of Jesus, spent her latter days; then sailing on to Haifa they were transported to the sea of Galilee, bathed joyfully in that sea at Tiberias, visited old Capernaum, and inspected Nazareth and the underground 'workshop' within the Church there which was thought to be that of Joseph. They were rather thrilled to stop on the road leading to Damascus, perhaps near the spot where Saul suddenly lost his sight and noted the hill where the Transfiguration occurred. Finally they returned, thinking, to their cosy cabin.

"Oh dear," said Monica. "I forgot. We should have brought a bottle of water from the river Jordan when we paddled there. That was where John the Baptist baptised Jesus with that water. Oh, well next time perhaps". . *

Voyaging westwards their vessel put in at Rhodes where a dose of cold virus hampered them so that a sea bathe was denied. Later they managed an amble around the mighty walls followed in the evening by a very interesting *'Sound and Light'* show in the city when deeds of the Knights Templar entertained them: the old story of the Colossus of Rhodes bestriding the harbour entrance made them gasp with astonishment.

A visit to the slightly restored Palace of King Minos rewarded them on their way back when stopping for some hours in Crete. The reconstructed pillars at Knossos gave a reminder of the vast destruction caused by the volcanic explosion of the nearby island of Santorini with the resulting Tsunami occurring many years B.C. They admired the Queen's bathroom with its wall painting of dolphins; they thrilled when the lecturer mentioned the story of Theseus and Ariadne and the long thread used to bring him back to her after his battle with the Minotaur. Then back to the Adriatic and a visit to Split on the Yugoslav coast, where stormy weather upset their planned trip to Dubrovnik. The ship was obliged to up-anchor and move further away from the rocky coast so making their return to it in a small boat a very wetting experience. But they were well satisfied with the eventful cruise, and enjoyed, on their return to Venice, a swift motorboat adventure among the canals and under the bridges, photographing St Marks and all the gondolas waiting for custom. The gondoliers merrily blew kisses to the ladies as they finally disembarked to transfer by coach to the plane for home.

Another streak along the runway, another lift into the air and, wonderfully soon afterwards Jessica was saying, "How lovely to see the green fields of dear old England. It's a welcome change from the dry, dusty lands around the Med."

"Yes," said Monica. "That does make you think. No wonder we have an immigration problem".

Another heavy 'bump', another reverse thrust roar, and the two friends gladly acknowledged that they were home, not as immigrants but as folk who truly belonged to those lovely green fields of their own dear country.

Many were the hours that Jessica and Monica enjoyed visiting each other and recounting again the fun and excitements of their Mediterranean holiday that enlivened the dull days of the following winter,

****

Judith sat back and took a deep breath. Then she reread her story, correcting where necessary, and laughed a little at the way memories, school lessons and books with travel brochures had all come together to make a creation for her fingertips.

'All right,' she said to herself. 'Perhaps I can sell it and make Daddy some money for his favourite charity.' And with a satisfied smirk she tidied up for the night and went to bed.

****

CHAPTER 10

KIDNAPPED

ON WAKING A few mornings later Judith felt pleased that she had managed to write a little story and realised that there could be many times when, with her future husband busy in hospital she could turn to writing, possibly with some monetary gain involved, she hoped.

She sped off jauntily to work prepared to do justice to her employer's secretarial tasks. Seated at her desk she took up the first of the pile of letters and began to type.

Gradually a collection of replies mounted up until by coffee time she was quite ready for a few minutes of relaxation. She prepared the coffee and took it with the letters to her employer's room.

"Ah, hallo Judith how nice to see you. I'm ready for a cuppa too. And is all that correspondence ready for me to sign?"

"Yes, sir, it's all yours." And she mentioned one or two problems that were involved with some of the letters.

Among them was a matter of a reply to some museum curator in Cairo.

Mr. Jenkins demolished a biscuit and sipped his coffee. After a pause he said,

"Judith, I have a little proposal to put to you. You have become quite expert in producing ideas about dealing with some of my customers. I wonder if you would like a change from the mundane work of the office. I have been wishing to buy two rather special icons from the museum in Cairo. They would require collection personally and bringing home carefully in someone's luggage. Would you like to be that someone? It would involve a plane flight to Cairo and a few days in a nice hotel there. A little holiday in fact; you might have time to look at the Pyramids. Have a day or two to think it over, and perhaps discuss the matter with your father."

Judith smoothed her hair adjusting a curl or two and repled,

"Good gracious, sir, this is a surprise. Do you really think that I could cope with that kind of business, and all on my own?"

"Yes, I'm quite sure of your competence, and I wondered if I could persuade the hospital authorities to allow my son to accompany you. Would that appeal?"

"It sounds wonderful, sir, and to have Gordon with me would be a marvellous treat. May I talk to Daddy and let you know in a day or two?" And with the thought simmering in Judith's mind all day, she brought the subject to the minister that evening. He considered carefully.

"It sounds a very interesting offer, Judith. I know something about Cairo; it is an extremely busy city and of course customs are different. You would be well cared for in a good hotel and transport would be by taxi everywhere. With Gordon to look after you all should be well. It could be a very nice change for you and a chance for you both to get better acquainted too. I would agree as long as you are happy about it."

"I'm so glad you agree, Daddy. I'm quite thrilled about it. I'll tell Mr Jenkins and hope he can fix things for Gordon."

The decision made, she told her employer and ten days afterwards he was able to tell Judith that her fiancé had been released from the hospital for the jaunt. He gave his secretary a few days leave to do some essential shopping along with a generous cheque to acquire adequate clothing and luggage for the trip. The following week a car bearing Gordon and a driver drew up at the manse door to collect Judith and take them both to Heathrow. Tickets and emergency passports were all up to date, provided by the firm.

It was Judith's first plane experience and she clung to Gordon's arm as the aircraft roared along the runway and lifted steeply into the shy. The rumbling of the wheels had ceased and as she viewed the ground falling away beneath them she felt a wonderful sense of exhilaration. "Marvellous" she said. "What fun!"

Judith thought back to the story that she had written and was thrilled to realise that she was now experiencing the same thrills; the waves of the English Channel; the fields of France, the plane roaring upwards through the misty cloud cover into the brilliant sky with the white cloud surface reflecting glorious sunlight. As the plane levelled and the seatbelt sign was turned off the two sweethearts held hands and gazed into each others eyes with looks that spoke of enduring love and trust.

Their flight time was not wasted. Gordon, accustomed to travel with father or uncle, was actively pointing out geographical features. He used his knowledge, culled from study of the earth's history to describe areas of Europe as they passed over them. He mentioned the ancient violent upheavals that changed the landscape and seascape; the rise of the Alps, the retreat of Ephesus from its importance as a seaport to becoming entirely landlocked, the other changes in the Mediterranean over thousands of years. He enthused about it all.

Judith, with her brain attuned to the arts and especially to the history of old classical days of Greece and Rome, followed his words with interest, questioning, interjecting comments, revealing yet more of her quickness of thought and her ability to understand and absorb new facts and ideas hitherto unknown to her. While they chatted drinks were served and later meals on little trays, all neatly arranged and very edible. Looking through the ports they could see the sharp peaks of mountains protruding through the cloud. Was it the Matterhorn? Could that be Mont Blanc? The speculation was an absorbing interest. Over the Mediterranean cloud occasionally gave way to a view of the sea far below, but by this time they were tired and sleepy, gladly missing the film show of western gun battles between cowboys or Colonel Blank's lusty warriors defying the Indians. The plane droned on and they snoozed peacefully together until eventually the engines' note changed and their ears began to tell them of the descent towards Africa.

The sea came into view and the white line of breaking foam on the coastline. Egypt was drawing near. Suddenly Judith cried "Look at that huge harbour. Is it Alexandria where Cleopatra landed to meet Mark Anthony?"

"Or from where Nelson sailed to give the French a drubbing?" said Gordon.

"And this must be the bit of Africa which Rommel

tried to take over after chasing our army out of Libya," she added

"Only Monty turned on him and drove the Nazis out of Africa altogether."

They grinned at each other and to Judith's question "Shall we see the Pyramids?" Gordon replied that it would depend on which way the plane turned to approach the landing strip for Cairo's airport. A few minutes later after the seatbelts warning sign had appeared and the stewardesses were checking that all passengers were wearing their seatbelts the plane tipped over to make for Cairo.

"I'm afraid the Pyramids will remain unseen, Darling. The plane tipped over the other way. It all depends on wind direction; I'll explain later. Anyway you can see the spread of Cairo if you look through the port. Pretty big isn't it."

Rapidly they descended, buildings flying past the port until there was a firm bump followed by the furious roar of reverse thrust. The plane slowed markedly and spent some minutes rolling along the runway to its destination ere it stopped.

"All right, Darling?" enquired Gordon. "Absolutely wonderful." she replied. "Now all I need is a camel to ride off into the sunset with my beloved. Or maybe just a little trot to see the Sphinx".

"What you're going to get is a taxi to the hotel, once we've rescued our luggage from the carousel."

"What's a carousel?" she enquired. "Oh yes, of course", and she remembered that she had written of it in her story; when it shortly appeared she enthused once again. After completing the needful immigration arrangements they were glad to find a representative from the hotel holding up a placard displaying their names. He led them to a taxi and very soon they were being driven through the crowded streets of Cairo past shops and open stalls, pushcarts and even an occasional camel, to find a most civilised hotel with pleasant attendants anxious to care for their needs.

After inspecting their sleeping quarters and doing a little unpacking they indulged in a long drink of ice cold fruit juice and asked if there was a park where they might walk prior to the evening meal. Learning that such existed not far away Gordon and Judith walked along, resisting the pleas for backsheesh from importunate begging folk until they reached the park gates. Suddenly the idyll ended, violently.

A car drew up behind them. It stopped with a screech of tyres. Three men jumped out, one of them striking Gordon's head with a heavy sandbag, one applied a cloth soaked in chloroform over Judith's face and the other dragged her to the car. They roughly pulled her onto the back seat. Gordon fell, unconscious, while Judith was rapidly reduced to a similar state from the anaesthetic. The car sped away, rounded a corner and quietly joined the dense traffic of the city as it sped homewards for the night.

Pedestrians and onlookers hurried away. When Gordon gradually recovered from the blow to his head he found himself alone and, sadly, without his darling Judith. It was useless to shout for help, there was no one to hear. All he could do was to rise with difficulty, hold to the railings and wait for his vision and dizziness to clear. Tenderly he held a hand to his bruised and painful head. Gradually he regained a sense of balance; then dragged himself unsteadily back to the hotel. He asked for a chair and, haltingly, reported to the management what had happened. . The management were sympathetic and prompt to telephone the police who promised to attend to the matter. The hotel doctor stitched up Gordon's head, bleeding from striking the ground, and gave him tablets for the headache. The police, shortly arriving, made the usual enquiries. There was little to tell them, but Gordon begged that a report should go to the consul immediately and all possible action be taken to apprehend the kidnappers. They gloomily said that it happened all the time but they would try to help. They recorded such details as they could from Gordon's statement.

Gordon was in despair, utterly shattered. He sat with head in hands His precious love had been captured and taken who knows where. His head ached. He felt sick He longed for someone to take charge and help. What on earth could he do in a foreign land with foreign customs, foreign language? He asked the manager, "What will happen? Why should they take her?"

"It is probably a kidnap for money." The manager told him. "They will not harm her. All they want is money. If you have a father at home you should phone him at once."

He telephoned his father; he was lucky, the call coming through quite quickly.

"Dad, we're here in Cairo. Something dreadful has happened. We went out for a walk. I was knocked unconscious and Judith has been abducted. It's a kidnap. They must have known we were coming. I don't know what to do...."

Gerald Jenkins was extremely concerned, realising how dreadfully upset Gordon must be and blaming himself for sending Judith to Egypt.

"That's terrible, Gordon. I will fly out straight away and join you. I'll set things in motion with the Chief Constable of our home region at once. It is vital that you go to attend the consul's office yourself, late though it is. Telephone them at once and take a taxi. I am driving down to Heathrow immediately." Gordon promptly put through a call to that office and was eventually connected to an official who invited him to come along in person. The hotel provided transport and he was finally admitted to the Consul's department.

"Good evening, sir, how may I help you?" said the official

"My friend and I were attacked outside a park. I was knocked unconscious and she must have been bundled into a car and taken off somewhere. We had only just arrived in the city by plane. May I beg for urgent action to find her and capture the kidnappers please."

"Yes we'll do all that we can, but it is extremely difficult. This sort of trouble is a very frequent occurrence."

"I have telephoned my father who employs my girl friend. He is hoping to catch a plane for Cairo as soon as possible."

"That's good. We shall be pleased to see him and, I repeat we will certainly do all we can. Will you now describe your young lady with as much detail as possible please. Then you may leave things in our hands and with the police of course."

With that assurance Gordon was obliged to be reasonably satisfied. After giving the required description as well as he could manage he returned to the hotel to take more headache tablets and await events, but feeling desperately upset. But there was something else to do, urgently. He must phone Judith's father.

He put the call through. He sat, despairing, waiting. He was wondering how to tell the minister about the kidnapping when the phone rang. His future father-in-law said, "It's alright Gordon don't worry about how to tell me. Your father has rung me and I know he's coming to join you tomorrow. Don't worry old chap, everything will turn out OK." There were more words of consolation. The minister was a past master of such understanding and wise counsel and, while privately very concerned, he knew that the emotions of the younger man must be considered and allayed as far as possible. It was a long phone call.

At last Gordon went to bed. Sleep was a long time coming.

Slowly; very slowly, Judith began to be aware; she moved her hands, her feet, arms and legs. She rolled her head a little. She opened her eyes. She was in a bright room, lying on a fairly comfortable bed. She felt her clothing, a nightdress. A sheet and a light blanket covered her body and there was a pillow beneath her head. She raised her head and looked around. A window, protected outside with iron bars, gave a good light. The room was not large but adequate. A bedside table with three drawers, two easy chairs, a cupboard and a small whitewood table covered with a tablecloth completed the furniture. In one of the chairs was seated a woman, a Muslim, her age not apparent. She turned her head, noticing that Judith was awake and asked in tolerable English if she would like some tea.

"Yes, please, and where am I? What has happened? I don't understand," Judith replied.

"I not talk, I bring tea" said the woman and she departed from the room locking the door behind her.

Judith realised that she had been kidnapped, remembered the chloroform and tried to imagine why and for what purpose. Her minder returned with a tray bearing a pot of tea and a few biscuits and set it on the whitewood table.

"But why, what is it all about?" said Judith.

"I not talk" said the woman again. There would be no explanation.

"It must be a kidnap. Is there a ransom? My friend and I do not have money. My father is a minister of the church. He only has a very small income. They must let me go; I am no use to them" And she went on talking between sips of the hot sweet tea but to no avail. Her companion obviously had instructions to say nothing.

Judith rose from the bed and looked in the cupboard. No clothes, only a light cardigan. She put it on and demanded her clothes. There was no reply.

The woman enquired if Judith would like some breakfast – the question showing Judith that she had been unconscious all night. She could bring fruit and cereal, also a glass of orange juice. She added that her name was Shari and departed on her errand, again locking the door.

Understanding dawned. Judith realised that she was a prisoner, though kindly treated. A look through the window showed that her room was on the third floor of a large house in a long street of similar houses. Escape seemed impossible. Her food arrived and she ate it reluctantly and sadly. A copy of a Reader's Digest accompanied the meal. Judith thanked her minder and said she would like a Bible. Shari said she would try to find one.

*

In Gordon's hotel the waiter came to his breakfast table where Gordon sat miserably, toying with a piece of toast. "There is a telephone call for you, sir. "

"Hallo laddie," said his father. "I have got a flight to Cairo and I'm in Heathrow about to board the plane".

He gave the flight number. "See you this evening at the consul's office".

His son was impressed thinking 'That's quick work; Dad's put the skids on; he's taking this very seriously and quite right too. He can be a wonderworker when he tries.' He felt a little better and managed a cereal.

Gordon spent his day thinking and trying to devise some scheme to find and rescue his beloved. It was going to need tact and wisdom. True he was young, but he had received a good training in dealing with the evil enemies of the human framework. Perhaps Dad would have some ideas.

Having found the time of his father's expected arrival in the airport, Gordon was there well in advance to meet him.

"Thought it would be good to get together urgently and have a chat before meeting the high-ups," he told his Dad. The latter appreciated the thought and hugged his son tightly.

"Don't worry too much, son," he said. "We'll sort this out, so keep your chin up. They won't hurt her. All they want is money. The Chief of Police will be with the Consul. It has all been arranged. through our Chief Constable at home. Things will begin to happen very soon."

*

Arriving at the Consul's office they found matters as stated. The two officers were most solicitous and went into matters very thoroughly. Mr. Jenkins' Chief Constable had phoned the Consul's office to ensure that the utmost consideration be given to the problem. The Chief of Police in Cairo would be, they felt, extremely efficient. He told them that such things went on all the time, but his force were well experienced and would pull out all the stops.

Gordon's father thanked him, saying that the thought had occurred to him that plain clothes men might be posted in many wine bars to listen to people overloaded with alcohol and thereby more loquacious. There might be one of the criminal's team more likely than others to boast about expected riches after ransom payment was paid. Such a person might be plied with increasingly strong wine until he let out information that would lead to the whereabouts of their captive. This idea was approved and to his further thought that perhaps he might employ a private detective the Chief was quite receptive, as long as that person would work with the official force. The Consul went so far as to suggest a man well known to him who had sometimes been very helpful and offered his phone for contacting the person, known to them as Mr. Ali Mohammed. Shortly that gentleman spoke to Gordon's father and arranged to meet them next day.

The meeting broke up and father and son went to their hotel feeling more hopeful. They chatted further over their evening meal and retired to bed early, but only following a further talk with Mohammed who gave them instructions by telephone as follows.-

"You will be under close supervision by the kidnappers. We must not meet openly. To-morrow, prepare yourselves for a sail on the river. Take a taxi to a certain wharf, (he told them which one). You will find a boat there named 'Tec'. Go to it and step on board. The sailor will receive you without speaking; he is both deaf and dumb. I shall join you there and we will move away on the water, far from any possibility of being overheard. I shall be disguised like an Arab, selling perfumes. Goodnight and sweet dreams."

The next morning they took a taxi to the Nile and found the wharf and boat as nstructed. They stepped on board and the sailor who had obviously been expecting them provided comfortable cushions. They waited. Half an hour later a small car drew up on the wharf and from it stepped an Arab, poorly dressed, limping a little, and with an old attaché case in one hand. He too reached the boat and, after making signs to the sailor, sat down opposite the visitors. When well away from the riverbank he greeted them, offering a handshake that was firm and promising.

The sailor adjusted the sail and steered for the middle of the river. When sufficiently away from any human contact Mohammed said "Now we can talk." And talk they did. Upstream and down they sailed, glad of a breeze to counter the heat. . More and more river traffic moved blithely along in a steady wind from the Med. Their sailor, unable to communicate by sound or speech, knew well the signs of wind and wave, tweaking his single sail dexterously to give that extra half-knot that brought him a happy gleam of pleasure. At last Mohammed was satisfied that he could make plans and made signs for return to base.

He stressed the utmost importance of keeping their relationship secret, insisting that any phone conversation originating from father or son must be from an outside telephone and never the same one. When the kidnappers left their ransom message he was to be informed immediately. Meanwhile they were to behave like tourists.

"Go and see the museums" he said, "the ancient ruins, even the Pyramids, but keep looking in at the hotel in case of messages from the kidnappers." Them, on parting separately from Mohammed, they left a good time interval before they too stepped out of the boat.

Judith spent a very boring rime. She read her book and asked for more. Her meals were well presented but she longed for exercise. After two days she spoke vehemently about the need for her clothes and demanded that her minder should ask again from her employers. The request was granted this time as also was her further request that she should be allowed to walk in the corridor for exercise. All the windows were barred and there was a guard on the stairs so an escape was impossible anyway. That made things a little better but she felt very alone and longed for Gordon.

Apart from reading she felt it would be good to maintain her good health and several times daily she did a work out with physical exercises, learnt from old days in the college gym. This rather surprised her companion who commentated unfavourably about it as being somewhat unfeminine for a lady. Judith found it difficult to keep up conversation with her but assured her that the English were quite accustomed to keep-fit regimes and she would continue to maintain her strength in this way. Trying to start a chat, Judith asked why Shari did this kind of work She replied

"If I not work I not get pay. Was nothing else so I work for them".

"But who are they. Why did they take me?" And the answer came as before,

"I not speak. If I speak they will beat me.". That ended the discussion.

During the journey back to the hotel Gordon was silent, thinking. Arrived back they enquired for messages and learnt that none had come. They decided to follow the advice and visit museums and so forth, enduring the busy traffic of the city and trying to show an interest in the ancient icons and signs of long years ago which filled many rooms of the museums, wiling away their hours of waiting for ransom messages. While the father was naturally quite interested in these curios of antiquity, Gordon's mind was otherwise engaged. He was unceasingly trying to work out how his darling girl could be rescued once her whereabouts was known.

For three days no messages reached them. Then while at lunch one day a waiter brought them a missive handed in, he said, by a small urchin of no fixed abode. Was it the long awaited demand?

The printed note consisted of characters from a daily paper making words as follows:

"You want buy icons for £250,000. You want daughter back. You not buy icons. You pay money for daughter. When we get money, you get daughter. We tell you when and how. Do not fail. Or else…Wait for more message."

"That seems plain common sense," said Dad. "Now we can get things moving. Firstly we'll tell Mohammed".

At that moment the waiter came with the message that there was a phone call for Gordon. It was their detective himself saying that he had news and he gave them an address where they could meet. He added that they would find a car outside the hotel bearing the name of a Painter and Decorator. "Get in quickly, and the driver will ensure that you are not followed. He will bring you to this house and we can discuss the next steps."

They admired the driver's dexterity as he twisted and turned amidst the busy traffic of Cairo's streets. At a small house in a back street they found Mohammed who welcomed them, supplied a large jug of fruit juice and got down to business at once.

Mr. Jenkins showed him the printed message and added that he had made arrangements for that amount of money to be lodged in an account in his name in a Cairo bank. "Good", said Mohammed. "Let's try to ensure that it will not be needed."

He continued saying, "We have been very successful with the alcoholic nourishment that you suggested. The proprietor of the wine bar hopes you will reimburse him for rather a lot of wine. One boastful gentleman was in a generous mood and treated all the customers liberally. He is expecting a goodly share of your money and told everybody how clever the kidnappers had been. More to the point he indicated quite clearly where their prisoner is being housed. She is quire safe and well cared for. I have informed the Chief of Police and am to meet him in an hour's time."

"That's excellent, Mr Mohammed. Now we just need to get the criminals out of that house. That could be a problem" said the father.

Gordon chipped in. "That is where I might offer a bit of help, Mr. Mohammed. May I tell you what I have in mind?"

"Yes of course, please go ahead".

"Well it is likely, isn't it, that the baddies have guns and would use them in an emergency. Our problem is to persuade them to leave the house peacefully so that no one gets hurt. The last thing we need is blood and injury, or even worse. You agree?"

"Certainly, it will take some thought I'm afraid".

"Well let me give you my idea. As you know I'm a doctor. Medical training has a great deal to do with the treatment of baddies. In our experience the baddies are germs; deadly ones very often. We attack them with antibiotics. I personally give double the recommended dose immediately. Hit them hard and pull no punches. There's nothing like a good syringe and a long needle to plant the medicine just where it's needed. In this case you need to immobilise these criminals so that they can't fight back. Am I right?"

"Go on, doctor."

"You will need a supply of gas masks, say half a dozen; then a couple of dozen polythene bags. Load each bag with half a pound of sulphur. Surround the house with men. Break all the downstairs windows and throw in a couple of bags of sulphur, already lit and burning. Sulphur dioxide is an extremely unpleasant gas. Poisonous. The lungs can't stand it. If they're thrown out send in more. Very soon your kidnappers will be streaming out of the house with cloths over their faces, gasping and spluttering and quite unable to use their guns. To make assurance doubly sure have a pair of ropes in front of the doors back and front. When the men emerge, pull the ropes tight and trip them up. Men and guns will be scattered on the ground, an easy prey to the police. How does that strike you?"

"Thank you, Gordon. That is a most interesting idea. I'll tell the Police Chief at once. I'll ring to tell you what he says". With that Mohammed shook hands with them both, said 'Goodbye' and drove off to police headquarters.

"I can see my money was not wasted sending you to university for a medical course. Where did you learn that trick?" asked his father, quite impressed

"I got it from a story in a book that mentioned slaughtering white ants in Africa, Dad. I'll tell you all about it sometime." Returning by taxi to their hotel for their evening meal, they then awaited news from Mohammed. Two hours later the call came through.

"The Chief is quite interested and agrees to try your plan. The gas masks are ready for use and the house is being surrounded. We'll tell you when it's all over."

"Not a bit of it", replied Gordon vehemently. "I'm coming to get my girl. Tell them to wait for me."

. In the dark night he and his father climbed into a taxi that drove rapidly through much quieter streets to the scene of operations. There they were supplied with gas masks and all was ready with the house surrounded.

At the sound of a police whistle the house was floodlit; bricks smashed every window on the gound floor and burning sulphur was thrown in as instructed. Shouts and curses were heard and two sulphur bags were thrown out but were at once replaced. Less than a minute afterwards the criminals rushed out, coughing and gasping, faces covered with cloths. Each tripped over the ropes as they were pulled tight; guns were scattered. Police with handcuffs had no problem in securing the whole gang of half a dozen men.

Gordon, ready for action, had his mask on. "Come on", he shouted to two policemen, and he rushed forward into the house and up the stairs carrying two masks. The guard at the top was helpless with coughing and gasping.

Gordon shouted loudly, "Judith, don't open your door. DO NOT OPEN YOUR DOOR. WAIT UNTIL I FIND YOU". A door slammed shut and, reaching it, he shouted instructions.

"There is very strong gas out here. I will throw gas masks in through the door. Put them on. When they are tightly fixed, open the door and come out quickly".

Immediately he opened their door, threw the masks in and closed it smartly. He could hear the ladies talking as they tried to fasten the unaccustomed masks. At length Judith shouted, "OK. We're coming".

They emerged. Gordon took Judith's hand and one of the men grasped Shari's hand. They sped down the stairs and out into the fresh air at last.

To tear off their masks was the work of seconds only. Their embrace lasted much, much longer. The delight of the police and their helpers as the spotlights illuminated the loving couple was tangible. The despair of the spluttering criminals brought a grin to the face of the Chief of Police who was in attendance

"All right you two. Break it up and let's go home" said Dad.

"I've not seen these baddies yet" said Judith. "Let's just watch them being loaded into the Black Maria for their little journey to a very safe house. Please," she added. And the wheels of justice began slowly to grind, to the intense satisfaction of them all.

As they were leaving the Chief came and extended his hand to Gordon saying, "Thank you, sir, for showing the police how to catch criminals. We'll remember. And may we all offer you, young lady, our sincere felicitations on your safe release from the hands of these unpleasant people."

The journey back to the hotel found father and son commenting on their gracious treatment by the Chief of Police; how he might well have been a little irritated by outside ideas of ordering police affairs. Said his father, "I think, Gordon, that you may have provided a solution to many similar problems that would normally be settled by a gunfight,with blood and injury. Perhaps the idea will seep through to other authorities. Well done my boy. Now let's put through a call to Judith's father". This was promptly arranged and they waited for the call impatiently.

*

In the manse the minister was sleeping fitfully as was his housekeeper; it had been a harrowing day. An old member of the congregation had died after a long illness and there was no further news of Judith to encourage him. Suddenly at 1 a.m. the telephone shrilled. He leapt out of bed and picked up the receiver. To his delight the voice of his daughter came over loud and clear. "Hallo, Daddy darling. I'm out safe and sound and very thankful. So stop worrying and we'll see you very soon. Everything went well. We hope to get a plane flight tomorrow. We'll tell you all about it later. So go, dance a jig and have a celebratory cup of tea with Mary. Lots of love and 'bye' for now".

What a wonderful surprise. He promptly knocked on Mary's door and shouted the good news to her. "Mary, it's marvellous, she's rescued. She's coming home. I'll boil a kettle. It's a miracle. Come and give thanks". Shortly Mary appeared in her dressing gown and took over the celebration, adding a piece of a newly baked sponge cake to settle their excitements. An hour's chat over the cups was essential to provide the basis for relaxation; eventually they settled off to sleep.. In the morning their faces were radiant. Mary began to cook furiously and Judith's Dad gave up sermonising and blew up balloons, writing on them the message, 'Welcome Home My Darling".

****

CHAPTER 11

HOME AND HAPPINESS

NOT EVEN THE Israelites fleeing from Pharoah, could have matched the delight of the young lovebirds when they mo longer felt the rumble of the aircraft's wheels on the runway as their plane lifted off away from Egypt towards home. Leave behind the Pyramids, the Sphinx, the museums and the mummies; the fateful harbour. Turn towards their 'green and pleasant land' with the lovely future of their union that came nearer with every mile of travel.

The flight found them blissfully happy, holding hands as they gazed adoringly at each other. Judith's voice was firm and certain.

"It's wonderful to be free and back with you, Darling", she ,said . "I have to confess I had doubts sometimes but I knew you would rescue me eventually. So I made sure of exercising to keep my strength up, and I didn't forget a Bible passage sometimes. The old prophets were experts at encouraging the Israelites when captive in Babylon. I'm sorry that you and Daddy had such a worrying time though. It will be good to see him again."

The plane droned on. To rest with her head on Gordon' shoulder was Judith's idea of heaven. To have a vision of the dear green fields of her homeland caused her to exclaim with delight. To feel the bump as they landed at Heathrow was a glorious moment for the ending of their Egyptian Odyssey.

There came the car ride home with luggage in the boot and Gerald Jenkins at the wheel. Then, "Daddy I'm here," was her excited shout as she flung open the door of her home and in no time at all came the longed-for pressure of her father's arms around her.

"This is lovely Daddy. I was beginning to wonder if I should ever see you again". And a few tears slowly trickled down her face. .Gradually emotion subsided as Mary, competent as ever, brought in the tea and cakes Gordon was persuaded to give a brief account of their adventure, after which he and his father tactfully withdrew. Judith and her Dad could enjoy their time contentedly together.

To say that Judith received an enthusiastic welcome from the folk at her workplace would be an understatement. The staff of 'Jenkins Antiques' were ecstatic in their greetings to her. Kisses and flowers, specially crafted cards and a party thrown in her honour quite interfered with the company's business. The boss was very understanding and made a speech at the party which, while lauding the heroine of the hour, also served to remind his staff that Christmas trading was now a most essential part of their duties and he hoped that once the champagne had been liberally poured out and consumed it would be nice for them all to get down to work. He added,

"Thank you all for the way you have kept the firm

going while I have been in Cairo's museums. It is extremely good to leave behind the skulduggery of Cairo and return to indulge in the delightful civilisation of England's 'green and pleasant land'. Of course I must mention the contribution made by my son in effecting Judith's rescue. Naturally I now assume that Gordon will be awarded a knighthood in the New Year's honours list. We can all apply for tickets to attend the Palace". Loud cheers greeted his humour, while Gordon, who was of course present at the party, cheered and applauded vigorously. He and Judith promptly rose, embracing with kisses and hugging, to the delight of all who happily cheered and stamped their feet.

The weekend was coming up for them to spend sweetly together, after which the hospital would claim Gordon and the Antiques would load Judith with work. And so it was, with Gordon returning to the hospital routine while Judith settled to work with her usual expertise on the little mountain of work that had accumulated on her desk. She rapidly caught up with her in-tray, to the relief of all the staff who had become accustomed to her efficiency and appreciated her return to their midst. They were enthusiastic in demonstrating schemes for the advertising of their wares, having Christmas sales in mind. A different shop window was filled with huge paintings of Santa with his reindeer streaking around the chimney pots distributing largesse in the form of four-penny pieces, unheard of for many decades; little figures in ancient Egyptian style depicting a Pharaoh with Cleopatra; others lauding the figure of King Robert the Bruce with his spider and Boudicca in her chariot brandishing a whip. On the snow-laden ground the figures of child singers waved hymnbooks and merrily sang of 'Good Kind Wenceslas' and 'Thou and I will see him dine'. For folk venturing into the shop a bar with stools had been set up with sherry and coffee facilities as an encouragement. The dear old Christmas music soothed their souls, ruffled by the noise of heavy traffic and the chatter of pedestrians seeking to accomplish in a few days what would normally have taken months. What a hectic time!

The employer busied himself arranging the icon deal with the Cairo museum and another with the post office, keeping his secretary hard at it typing messages, while others of the staff wrapped parcels and insured them to reach their destination by Christmas Day.

*

At the hospital some of the young nurses devoted occasional minutes trying to flirt with Gordon, nudging him with demands to know what he had been up to among the harems of Tutankhamun. Male members, when not engaged in medical or surgical affairs, queried him about adventures amidst the museum mummies, but Gordon fended them off with comments concerning pressure of work. He was determined to keep secret, as far as possible the real reason for the long delay caused by their hair-raising adventures with Cairo criminals. There was quite enough to keep him occupied with the grim results of traffic indiscretions and heart problems due to injudicious use of fatty food, little veg. and even less exercise. In such spare time as the young lovers could snatch they revelled in each others company and managed to send off joint greeting cards to many friends all of whom were anxious to know when the wedding would take place.

Judith's father found much relief from the recent anxiety and typed vigorously on his old machine, hoping earnestly to touch folks' hearts with an extra special Christmas Day message.

With the days speeding by Judith resumed her visits to the doctor's wife who remained most helpful in suggesting wedding ideas that would both please and prove quite economical. Angela also enquired, "Why not advance the date? Do you really have to wait until midsummer? You don't want some adventurous and glamorous young nurse snapping him up while you spend time collecting more pennies for a wedding breakfast. I think you should go in for a little bit of subtle seduction, very gently of course. Perhaps you might try being 'hard to get'."

"Oh, I hadn't thought of that," was the reply. "Maybe I'm too easily obtainable?"

"Well, he's only male, you know, and there's a whole hospital full of charming females, all eager to find a nice young doctor to appreciate their wares! You may have competition. Be realistic. Be prepared. Life can be quite predatory you know."

"I realise that." said Judith. "But I assure you that Gordon and I are very sure of each other and I am mot at all concerned about possible seduction by the charming female staff of the hospital. That's not on at all. Anyway I will talk to Daddy about an earlier date."

So they spent time working around that idea and how to arrange an earlier wedding, perhaps in the New Year before their planned skiing excursion. Adventures seemed to be descending on them thick and fast, thought Judith. What a busy life it was. First, find a minute to chase Daddy.

That gentleman was busy preparing for the Christmas events, sermons in the pulpit and coffee parties in the hall, being at pains to ensure that as many folk as possible were given a little job to do; none should be left on the sidelines, willing to help but not invited. However he found time to listen to his beloved Judith as she tried, delicately, to suggest the idea of nuptial arrangements being advanced, even injecting the idea of a definite date towards the end of January.

"Oh, that's an interesting idea my darling", he said, "But what about bedrooms? I know the manse is quite spacious but there are limits you know."

"Come off it, Daddy. We are going to be married you know. Married people only need one bedroom. Get with it Daddy!"

"Oh well, what about bathrooms then? We only have one."

"Yes, that's a bit of a snag. I suppose that Mummy's room couldn't be made 'en suite' could it? Would church funds run to that? It's a nice big room, very adequate for two. But anyway there's no time or hurry for that at the moment."

Her father paused, thinking. Then he said, "Well a kind person, a church member, left in his will last year a useful sum of money for upkeep of the manse premises. It might be possible to use some of that perhaps. I should need to refer this to the stewards and a management committee of course. It would certainly solve the problem."

"That's lovely", replied Judith. Sure that all problems were now solved she went dancing off to the hospital to find Gordon and announce to him that he was to be married in the New Year, so he'd better 'get his skids on'. He, poor chap, was busy trying to make head or tail of an extremely abusive woman who loudly berated the medical profession for its incompetence when they couldn't decide whether she had a gall bladder problem, a heart attack or a dose of pleurisy. In view of her vehement protests Gordon was convinced that 'heart attack' was out of the question, pleurisy was unlikely, so a gallstone was the likely diagnosis. Since the lady was fair, fat and forty, this seemed to fit in with his medical teaching. He turned away from her to be assailed by his intended with the alarming news that he was to be married very much earlier than he had thought. This extra sudden announcement caused him to turn to Sister for support. "What about a cuppa, Sister" he said. "Unless you have some brandy in the cupboard - for medicinal purposes only of course…."

Judith left the hospital to cope with its own emergencies and, instead, began thinking of the wearisome business of Christmas shopping that had been delayed by her sudden seclusion in the 'safe house' of the Egyptian kidnappers. There was food, a turkey, and all the rest along with decorations and, of course, a tree, all to be arranged, all to be bought and conveyed to make ready the manse for the lovely festival of the New Born Babe. She was greatly relieved to find that Mary, the housekeeper, had thought of nearly all these things.

"It's all right, Judith, you can just leave all that lot to me and concentrate on the wonderful delight of getting married. Why don't you go along and see Mrs Collins? She's sure to have some enchanting ideas to tickle your fancy and make you stir your stumps."

Nothing loath Judith duly went. Angela Collins mentioned 'bridesmaids' and that became a problem. With no nieces or nephews Judith straightaway thought of her two rather special friends, Claudia and Gillian. She telephoned to both of them and fixed a coffee date when she could pose her problem to them. Meeting in the coffee shop the next day after work the subject was hesitantly brought up. The friends looked at each other with wide-opening eyes and cries, nay shrieks of delight.

"Darling, yes of course, we'll do it. What fun! Lovely

to be bridesmaids again, well, matrons of honour anyway. Whoopee!"

And, laughing and giggling, they swept into the nitty-gritty of the solemnity of marriage and bridal gear and matrons of honour. They quickly relieved all Judith's anxieties.

"And we'll help with the reception and all the foodstuffs at the manse as well. Nothing for you to worry about The manse is plenty big enough; the whole church congregation will be able to cram into it. Don't worry about a thing, (as the anaesthetist said when he shoved his needle into the vein of the Caesarean section lassie.)"

"And Judith, precious, you'll need a wedding dress. We are just the right people for that. We'll do it for you. We really are experts, and we can always get help from a friend who is a professional dressmaker. Leave it all to us." And like the true friends that they were, both zoomed off to raid their P.O. Savings books and visit a shop in the town for dress materials and all the needful.

Judith felt quite overwhelmed and very happy to have so much taken off her hands. Her father too was much relieved to have such willing help for his darling daughter. Mary assured him that all would be taken care of and he could just concentrate on his own business. The question of wedding invitations was now uppermost and quickly dealt with when, at lunchtime Judith dropped into an appropriate printer's and arranged matters. She called on the doctor's wife again to inform her about the wedding dress arrangement and discussed a few more essentials with her. Angela told her that she would be glad to send off the wedding invitations if she could have a list of names and addresses.

One morning the tree arrived before breakfast and her friends rang up before she left for work to give her a date for a fitting of the dress. It would be quite ready by Dec. 23rd they told her. What a wonderful relief. Now there was only the tree to be decorated, holly to be procured, lights to be fitted on the tree and Christmas stockings to be filled. Other presents she had coped with already.

*

For Gordon things were easier. A cheque from his uncle would more than cover the honeymoon that he was planning. A visit to a travel agent when he was off duty provided a couple of holiday brochures for the lovebirds to browse over. A choice, a cheque, inspection of their passports, and all would be 'in the bag'.

Oh really, what about that all-important item, the ring? On a Saturday morning the two set off to the jewellers, (having told the hospital where he was going), and made that most essential bargain, with careful fitting of the little piece of gold, followed by a kiss and cuddle in the shop and a coffee in town, interrupted naturally by an urgent message saying that the doctor was wanted to advise about a patient's condition. The staff wanted to be certain that a male patient was fit for his proposed hernia operation.

"I'm sorry my Darling. Here we go again. Bye for now Sweetheart."

The days were romping along and the 23rd saw Judith being subjected to the all-important 'fitting'. .An inch off here, a little tuck there and the inevitable tweaking and adjustments until the experts were satisfied that perfection was within grasp. They'd go and display their art to the doctor's wife and earn her approbation. Then hang the wedding dress in the clothes cupboard until the 'Great Day'. And so it was.

Christmas Eve duly arrived with all the wedding matters settled and Judith now gave her attention to the preparations in the kitchen. Here Mary reigned supreme and was adept at making tactful suggestions that were firm orders, disguised suitably for her assistant's benefit. The pastry making, the mincemeat, the pudding to be stirred, the preparation of the 'bird', and all the fuss and palaver of fun and festivities kept them both very busy. When 'Carols from Kings' finally came up on the 'box' they sank gratefully into chairs with teacups and freshly baked mince pies. Dad was routed out from his typing to share the feast of music and mincemeat. The culmination of Christmas preparations was quite exhausting!

After a game of Scrabble they each retired to their rooms to prepare stockings, as from Santa Claus, for the morning fun. Finally Judith, determined to wish Gordon a Happy Christmas in advance, rang the hospital.

"Sorry, he's not on the ward. We think he may be in the theatre," was the message from Staff nurse. Judith, about to hang up, thinking 'poor old chap, an emergency on Christmas Eve, how typical', just asked staff nurse to send him her love and kisses; then she set stockings outside Mary's and her father's rooms and curled up cosily in bed thinking of the happy cuddles to come minus nighties, minus pyjamas, just cuddling closely, stroking each others' smooth skins and making love…

In the morning the sound of 'Christians awake' blaring forth from the old gramophone downstairs told Judith of her Dad's early rising. She found a stocking outside her own room and visited her father's bedroom to share the fun of opening them.

The telephone rang. Hooray, it would be Gordon, of course. It wasn't.

"Hallo is that Judith?" sounded a sleepy voice. "This

is the registrar from the hospital. "Gordon says to tell you a 'Happy Christmas.' He says he'll ring you when he wakes up."

"Oh, dear!. The poor man. Has he had a busy night in the operating theatre?" Judith enquired.

"Well he's in the theatre now, sleeping under an anaesthetic, having his appendix out on the operating table".

"Oh, dea!!. My Darling Gordon! When did that happen? No wonder I couldn't find him last night. That's terrible. Is he going to be all right?"

"Yes, quite all right. The consultant surgeon himself is doing the op. Don't worry at all. Come and see him at lunch time. I've been up half the night. I'm going to sleep." And the registrar rang off.

Judith felt much distressed and told her father. That wise man comforted her saying, "It will be quite all right my darling. It's all a very standard procedure now-a-days. Don't be in a hurry to see him; let him sleep it off. Come to the morning service. That will help to take your mind off it. Then you can pop in and see him afterwards. Drop in this afternoon."

However Judith decided on 'duty first'...She was determined to see him before then. Remembering that Gordon's father was invited to their Christmas dinner, she asked her Dad to excuse her. She would take a sandwich to the hospital and stay beside her beloved. She might arrive home for a bite of the plum pudding and Cornish clotted cream, if Gordon wanted to sleep. So, with a slice of the turkey wrapped up in a piece of French loaf she hurried to the hospital, found the ward and begged Sister for permission to wait beside him until he woke up.

An hour later staff nurse entered with her tray of goodies, tapped her patient on the shoulder saying "Wakey

wakey" and slipped a thermometer into his mouth. Taking his wrist she counted his pulse. "Hmm, doing nicely" she said. Gordon murmured sleepily and caught hold of her hand, cuddling it closely to his cheek saying, "Just what I need." Staff nurse was well accustomed to the amorous approaches of male patients and said firmly, "I want that hand, have the other one." She extracted it as he released the pressure, collected the thermometer, picked up Judith's hand and quickly dropped it into Gordon's clutch." With a conspirator's wink at Judith she marched on her way.

Placing an arm round his shoulders and with a firm kiss on his lips Judith told him to wake up and come back to life. Surprised, he opened his eyes and said, "Hallo Darling, where am I?" She told him and gradually his memory returned; he tried to sit up, said "Ouch" and slid down again. Junior nurse entered with a cup of tea that Judith helped him to drink. Later the dietician came to enquire about what food he would like. He remembered that it was Christmas Day and demanded turkey and all the trimmings. But he had reckoned without his minder. Judith responded for him," Just a little custard and a couple of biscuits please", and while he was waiting she very firmly laid down the law as regards hospital rules, telling him that he was now a patient and must do exactly as he was told.

"That's very right indeed, Judith" said the registrar, entering behind her. "Gordon will now obey with no argument."

He briefly examined his patient, pronounced that all was well and advised rest and peace with small meals only. It was not long ere Gordon became very sleepy and settled down for a nap. His ladylove recognised the need for sleep and, bidding the staff, 'Farewell and Happy Christmas' she departed to find her way on foot to the church.

But time had moved on and the morning Service in the church was beginning. She was a little late but slipped quietly into the back pew. She enjoyed the Christmas hymns, the story of the Birth and found the children's enactment of the three wise men bringing presents as enchanting as ever. Her father's Christmas chat - she couldn't call it a sermon - was as helpful as always and the organist created a medley of music that rounded off the occasion with a lovely feeling of 'peace and goodwill'.

Judith found, while greeting the worshippers afterwards, that Gordon's father was present. He said he was just going to the hospital to see his son, having learnt from the surgeon of his calamity, but he would try to be in time for the dinner to which they had invited him. He gave her a lift to the hospital. She told him that she would stay beside Gordon and join them later for a spot of Christmas pudding.

Gerald Jenkins, having greeted his son in the hospital and commiserated with him, left him in Judith's care and arrived in good time at the manse for his Christmas celebration. He had lost his wife to a cancerous condition five years previously and, after the lonely years, had been very pleased to accept the minister's invitation. The festival had usually been rather a quiet and uninspiring celebration without her, but this year it promised to be quite gay, although the festivities would be different without his son's presence.

"Gerald", said the guest, as the minister greeted him at the door. "John" was the reply, and they immediately felt at home with each other. They commiserated with each other for a few minutes about Gordon's sudden surgical trouble; John then found his new friend a drink, after carefully enquiring about his preference.

"Something soft please, I'm driving, and anyway I

would prefer to join you in that line". And they fell into pleasing converse after John had mentioned that the ancient relics of Greece and Rome were of considerable interest to him.

"I have other interests beside ornithology and composing sermons," he said and mentioned icons, the poetry of Homer, the philosophy of Plato, and the Roman collapse in the face of the Gallic invasion; such ancient stuff kept them going until dinner was announced by Mary.

"Since you are the father of a young surgical aspirant", she said to Gerald, "perhaps you would like to wield the knife?" He accepted the invitation to good effect. Having made good inroads into the 'bird' they declared themselves to be well pleased with Mary's efforts and helped to clear the table for the advent of the plum pudding, lighted with brandy for the occasion. No sooner had it graced the table than Judith burst in bidding them, "Stop! Wait a minute for me. Gordon's going to be awake and kissed by all the nurses so I've rushed back to see the plum pudding lighted and help you to behave yourselves".

Delighted to see Judith, they were happy to learn of Gordon's progress. The tasty offering was much appreciated and approved to Mary's pleasure while crackers, puzzles and fancy paper hats all added to the jollity. A few presents were found under the tree, including some for the absent Gordon, and a happy hour was spent digesting their dinner and relieving Mary of the washing up Then at her suggestion of a brisk walk in the fresh, crisp air of late December they reluctantly ventured out, returning later with rosy cheeks and ready for the customary roasting of chestnuts in front of the hot fire. Judith, of course had excused herself to go and cheer the victim of the morning's operating theatre, only to find him still entertaining other 'angels'. She was not entirely pleased…

*

In the manse John and Gerald discussed with Mary the proposal for an earlier wedding. What effect would the operation have on such an arrangement? This was a matter for the surgeon in charge. No doubt the couple concerned would query him about it Both men enthused about all the wedding arrangements and were very happy about it all. John would arrange for a clerical friend to assist in the ceremony. Before leaving to go to the hospital Gerald said to his host, "Please allow me to arrange for all the transport required. It will give me great pleasure to hire the wedding car and see to its decoration for such a lovely occasion. There may be other cars needed too. Please leave it all to me. There is nearly a month to fix everything."

John was most grateful and accepted the offer saying, "Thank you indeed Gerald. That will be a wonderfully big load off my back". He felt that he had surely made a valuable friend for future days.

*

In the side ward Gordon was impatient, speaking his mind without reserve to his dearest girl when she visited in the evenings. "Honestly," he said, "fancy spending Christmas in bed with an appendix!"

"Without it", corrected Judith. "I saw the consultant who said to tell you that he had sent the thing to pathology and when it returns you can have it for posterity in a bottle of alcohol."

"I'll make its storage priority No.!" was the comment.

"As long as it doesn't sit on my pantry shelf for me to feast my eyes on every time I open the door," countered Judith. "You can hide it away among the tools in the garage."

"When you have yours out we'll put them together with a piece of wedding cake and label the bottle "Married Bliss," said Gordon.

"By the way," he added, "I forgot to tell you. I've spoken to uncle on the phone. We've got to cancel our skiing holiday of course and he will attend to that Sad, but maybe some day in the future. I then asked him to help in finding a good spot for a honeymoon. He was very helpful and it's all fixed up. We can canoodle together in a charming villa in the Canaries with swimming pool and maid service all laid on."

"Marvellous" said Judith, "what about the cost?"

"All met by wedding present cheques. Aren't we lucky?"

The time passed with Judith busy during the daytime at the office, leaving Gordon to the tender ministrations of nurses who delightedly occupied spare minutes in teasing him. He became increasingly restive. Feeling well he begged to be allowed gentle exercise and this was granted, encouraged in fact. Then naturally he demanded to know the date of his discharge. "I must be out for the New Year", he told the registrar. That medical adviser consulted the surgeon who agreed to the request, provided Gordon promised to do nothing to strain the scar or the muscles underneath. He emphasised that there must be no possible chance of a hernia occurring under the scar. "Understood and promise given", said Gordon and he told his beloved the good news on her evening visit..

"That's marvellous, but what about our wedding date?" she demanded. "Does the surgeon know about that and can it go ahead as planned?"

They were both present when that gentleman paid his last visit and put the all-important question to him. "Perfectly all right", he replied. "as long as you obey the rules with gentle exercise only". Winking at Gordon, he added "anyway you've got five more weeks, so best of luck."

The discharge day arrived with Gordon up and dressed, packed and ready for off. Two bigger stitches had been removed, making for comfort that was appreciated. The subcuticular stitch would come out easily in a few days time. It would leave a very neat scar that would almost disappear. To Judith's disapproval his nurses all dropped in for 'goodbye' kisses and they all waved happily as the two walked away down the corridor. His father had brought the car to the door and the return home was marked as they entered the manse by a mad cheer from the patient and happy tears from his betrothed. After lunch Gerald took his son home for a rest.

*

It was New Year's Eve and again the celebration took place at the manse. Mary and Judith had created a sumptuous dinner and even the minister joined in the toast to the next year with a glass of light wine for the occasion. Gordon, having a head of dark hair was persuaded to take a piece of coal and bring the New Year in according to the established old-fashioned custom. All felt that justice had been done. They all joined in the good old Scottish songs and dancing that made merry folk of all regions both north and south. Gordon held Judith pressed closely to him saying, "Your body can give my scar all the support it needs!"

To Judith and Gordon it would be their special year of solemn union in marriage and as they kissed again under the mistletoe a very meaningful and loving gaze quickly stole into their eyes.

The midnight moment passed quickly and amidst the singing on the T.V. the oldsters of the party indulged in the telling of old time stories while the young folk just sat and held hands happily. Nobody rose very early that morning, except perhaps the chaps who prepared the horses and dogs for the fox hunting. A light frost adorned the grass and stimulated them all to take a vigorous morning walk ere making for coffee in their favourite pub near the canal. The minister pronounced it, to his surprise, as quite civilised.

January brought snow in small driblets at times, work to be attended and fresh sermons to be typed while Gordon, being unemployed, summoned up his courage to take the gentle exercise prescribed by his surgeon. Borrowing a neighbour's red setter he took it for a long walk, admiring its tremendous vigour and promising himself that such must be his own aim. Wedding preparations proceeded apace with final fittings, a new suit for the groom and a showing off of the matrons of honour in their new finery. Extra decorations cheered up the old manse; balloons were blown up and realistic 'snow' scattered on the holly and the mistletoe. At last all was ready.

The night before their wedding was traditionally an evening for male and female parties to get together separately and make 'whoopee'. Gordon and Judith vetoed the idea, spending the preparatory hours with a light meal together and helping each other to pack the essentials for their coming honeymoon. At last they separated, each to their own beds.

The Day of their Lives dawned fair and bright, again with a wide covering of frost. A light breakfast helped to subdue a rather nervous feeling in them both. Then came the final packing, the worries lest anything had been overlooked and, separately, last walks with their Dads before they made their final separation from their families. For each a taste of lunch was downed somehow followed by the all-important donning of bridal robes and suits. Gordon polished his shoes once again while his father adjusted his attire and fussed unnecessarily. Judith tweaked her curls incessantly into place and her helpers enjoyed tedious minutes arranging and altering and ensuring perfection of her shimmering white bridal dress. Similarly her matrons of honour were duly attired and all was at the peak of readiness when the doorbell rang.

A liveried chauffeur greeted them, announcing, "Your wedding car, sir." Dad took his daughter's arm and they walked sedately to the gleaming Roll-Royce that awaited them. The others followed in another car and many were the bystanders who noted the occasion and waved and clapped their hands shouting fancy messages to cheer them on.

Their entry to the church was marked by peals from the organ and, slowly, father and daughter progressed up the aisle between smiling friends and relatives to reach the spot where Gordon stood awaiting his bride. She released her arm from her father's and slipped her hand into Gordon's waiting arm with a radiant smile; their eyes twinkling as they gazed at each other. John, her father, went forward to stand beside the other clergyman.

The service commenced with the happy yet serious

hymns and equally serious phrases of the printed service sheets. All progressed well. The reasons for marriage were read solemnly and brought grins and blushes - not only from the happy couple - and the best man remembered not to drop the ring. The promises were read out carefully and Gordon and Judith looked into each others eyes lovingly as he slipped the ring onto her finger and each said, remembering the first time, "I will."

Judith's father declared that they were man and wife.

The impressive silence was suddenly broken by a single handclap. It was taken up, slowly at first, then with verve and enthusiasm by the whole congregation, with glad calls to the bridal pair and merry conversation broke out throughout the church as the couple retired to sign the register. As they took their places at the head of the little queue the organ sounded mightily, thundering out the glorious. Bridal March of Mendelssohn

The procession down the centre aisle was slow but firm with Judith and Gordon, arm in arm, smiling and bowing right and left. A pause occurred at the door for grouping of the wedding party and photography, quickly because a breeze had sprung up, and all gladly entered their cars to the merry ringing of the church bells when returning to the manse where a warm drink and nourishment were waiting.

The hand shaking, greetings, chatter with old friends, high tea, cake cutting, speeches with cards and humour; all brought great fun. Then the change to going-away-clothing and final farewells and departure in the little car, carrying, unknown to them, a smoked mackerel fixed with wire onto the hottest part of the exhaust pipe. They were truly married and confetti showered them liberally as they waved goodbye and entered the car.

Leaving behind the town of their birth they speeded

up on the motorway towards their chosen airport. Not many miles from home there wafted into the vehicle gentle airs of smoking mackerel and Gordon guessed what his friends had been playing at during the solemn church service.

"Can you put up with it until the airport, my darling?" he asked his bride. "Then I'll don an old coat that I keep in the boot and crawl under the car or lift the bonnet to unload the fishy offering that is probably wired onto the exhaust-pipe".

"OK, I'll endure the pesky stink," she said.. "All part of the fun of married life."

And in due course the mackerel found the waste bin, the baggage was surrendered at the reception desk and the pair flew off happily to their honeymoon *Shangri--la*

****

CHAPTER 12

NEW LIFE, NEW LOVE

WE TAKE LEAVE of our newly weds as they commence together their journey of married life. The details of their honeymoon both as regards place and intimacies of discovering each other shall be their own secret. It is certainly not our prerogative to enquire or consider where they went, how they reached their proposed destination or any details of their wedded bliss. Such must be their own private business and is to be respected Let it be enough to know that in the warmth of a subtropical island, in a seaside villa with a swimming pool and maid service they found great joy during the two weeks of a delightful honeymoon.

They found out more and more of their mental and physical similarities and differences. They found these things intriguing and fun. They found interest with much delight in their new sexual adventure and great satisfaction. In their daily life there were naturally occasions when ideas differed. Seeking understanding of each other's points of view they learnt to hold them in respect. Investigation of their surroundings; enjoyment of foreign food, foreign customs and language, learning gradually to understand strange ways of doings things were intriguing.. There were journeys by bus or train around new coastal areas, through tunnels in mountains, sometimes venturing into huge caverns with new forms of entertainment, occasionally joining a sailing boat and eating barbecued fish or crab alongside other cheery holiday makers, all adding colour to other experiences. The newness, the strangeness and the wholesome differences of such an unusual life brought to them a glowing satisfaction that greatly helped to cement their union.

"Isn't it wonderful, Darling", said Judith "to come to such a vastly different life and feel as if you'd belonged here for ever. I love it. Honeymoon is really marvellous." It was their last night on the island. Back to the airport tomorrow.

"Yes, it's been very precious, my Sweetie. I'm glad I married you. Did you know how nervous I was when I proposed?"

"No, you were very serious indeed. No trace of nerves. Are you like that when you wield a scalpel?"

"That's different. Come on let's go to bed."

Together with arms around each other they mounted the stairs.

Showered, teeth brushed and hair, curly and straight, all brushed and shiny, they regarded their nightie and pyjamas.. He grinned happily saying, "A bit later, my Lovely?"

"Gordon, I'm glad I married you. You're so tender and gentle, even if as strong as an ox." And they curled arms around each other.

"You should see me on a rugger pitch my Pet."

"How can you play such a murderous game, Gordon? It's wicked. They all seem bent on destroying each other."

Oh, it's good fun, especially in the middle of the scrum when you go heads down, arms wrapped around your big chums on either side and then just push like mad. I remember one chap at school who had just started playing rugger. He hadn't played before – some tale of a bad heart - all a lot of rubbish when you saw him racing up the steepest hill in the town on his old bike. Bad heart my foot. So he was put in the scrum, being eleven stone. He could certainly push. Great asset he was. Trouble was, out of the scrum he couldn't tell which end of the field was which without his glasses. Heigh ho!"

Judith released herself and hopped onto the bed. "Darling," she said, "you 're adorable".

"Sweetest, want a dose of sleeping medicine?"

"Mm", she murmured. She fluttered her eyelashes at him and lay back, as a dreamy smile spread over her face.

*

The return to dear old England to face whatever would be their future was based on a time together that would give solid unity in body and spirit, each relying fully on the other .There would be difficulties, awkward times, new experiences and lots of new contacts and thoughts to be encountered, but the recent grounding of their time together would be sufficient to meet these things, and they were determined to surmount obstacles and make a really united front in their new lives

Most importantly Judith's firm Christian faith and principles had often been the subject of their discussions, and Gordon was becoming quite prepared to understand what it could mean to their joint future.

Full of energy, hope and love they returned to renew their acquaintance with the mundane things of ordinary existence. Judith, given an enthusiastic welcome by the Antiques staff, took up the cudgels and tackled her in-tray of correspondence with a will. Gordon, with a week to go before commencing work back in the urgent department of the A & E, concentrated on acquiring muscular fitness with vigorous walking and other exercises and, when the minister could spare time, made a point of discussing with him the basic principles of the Christian faith. He was anxious to discard all the non-essentials such as symbolism, silly garments and so forth and discover for himself what it was really all about. Judith's father, being a practical man, heartily sympathised with this view and entered into talks with Gordon in a truly sensible manner. He approved thoroughly of Albert Schweitzer's opinion , namely that there was too much symbolism, candles, incense, bowing and scraping, and insufficient consideration of the main essentials of the teaching of Jesus, with simple exposition of its meaning as affected the ordinary lives of His followers.

John, having persuaded Gordon to address him thus, made it clear that he was something of a rebel as regards a lot of the ideas and beliefs of the 'church'. John wished Gordon to understand that as far as he was concerned the word 'church' referred to the great company of people who were true followers of Christ, trying to accept and obey His commands and basing their lives on them. Gordon felt that he was in contact with a kindred spirit at last and determined to have further discussions with John during the future days. Since he and Judith were to be resident at the manse that would not be too difficult.

Concerning that residence, division of the manse's living space was settled quite amicably between them all. The large reception room with the minister's study attached would always be available for John and visiting parishioners, and he would take his meals with Mary in the big, comfortable kitchen. The dining room behind it would become a lounge-diner for the young folk, providing them with privacy, the minister's study, next to the kitchen would remain i.s.q., while bedrooms and bathing facilities upstairs were quite adequate for them all. An en-suite bedroom for the young folk would be nice but there was no urgency for such luxury.

On each evening of that week Gordon met Judith when she finished work, greeting her with a loving kiss and a cuddle as they snuggled together in his small car. A short shopping spree for provisions and they were soon back in the comfort of their erstwhile home. Mary was careful to complete her culinary tasks in advance leaving the cooking facilities for Judith. They took care not to tread on each other's toes. After the meal the happy couple organised furniture, hung a few pictures of old favourite times and places and cosied themselves on a large settee to talk and, in a close embrace, to plan their future lives.

"What about children, Gordon? We'll have to think about reproduction won't we, but not just yet I fancy. Let's get ourselves settled first, but not wait too long of course."

"That's a big question", said Gordon. "I shall need two more 'house' jobs before seeking a general practice position. A job as assistant with a view to partnership is my aim. Then we can bed ourselves down in a house and think about increasing the population. That would take about a couple of years I should think, plus nine months naturally."

"I should be happy with that, I think. We certainly don't want a little nipper chasing around the manse and getting under Daddy's feet, although no doubt Mary would be in her element."

"Are we alright so far, Judy? I haven't been very careful I'm afraid".

"Yes all is well. A woman knows what to do, and I've taken precautions".

"Yummy, I'm tired. Let's go to bed."

"Nice idea," said Judith. "You get breakfast ready while I tidy up and chase a bath If you're a good boy you can scrub my back".

*

The week soon sped by and next Monday found them leaving together for work. They kissed good-bye outside the Antiques emporium, Gordon hurrying on to the hospital. He was given a rousing welcome by the staff of A & E but told to seek work elsewhere. They had a new doctor now and Gordon was posted, he found, back to the medical ward. He marched off sprightly to meet the Sister and registrar of the ward to which he had been assigned again. Sister once again took him into her office and she and the registrar quickly gave him an outline of his duties. "You will gradually learn", she said. "There are many more details that you'll discover while applying yourself to the new routine, and of course emergencies will inevitably occur. I am pleased to learn that reports of your work in A&E have been very satisfactory. Your Sister there revealed that you had done well. Now is your chance to prove yourself further" She added, regarding him severely. "Do not imagine that a medical ward is a pushover. . It is by no means a holiday after the fun and games of the very busy A&E. We all work very hard. Come on, let's see the patients".

Sister's ward round was a useful eye-opener for him as she introduced him to each patient in turn, giving a brief summary of the diagnosis and treatment prescribed by the consultant. That gentleman Gordon would meet later when he came to do his round. It was necessary for the houseman to have the details of each patient in his mind for that occasion. The registrar got him to examine several of the more seriously ill patients and have their details ready for the consultant when he arrived.

In due course the great man came along, greeted the staff and saying separately to Gordon, "Welcome to our wards, Dr. Jenkins. I sincerely hope that you will be very happy with us and I can assure you that you will be kept extremely busy." His team having assembled, a full ward round now took place. Gordon found his brain being tested to the uttermost to absorb and retain all the wisdom now being flung at him. He realised the urgent need to keep abreast of the latest knowledge in medical matters and vowed that he would work as never before

After rushing to the hospital restaurant for a hurried lunch, it was Gordon's duty then to continue with a host of routine tasks until his day's work was complete. Finally he discovered that, while able to return home for his evening meal, he would later be on duty for emergencies during the night and it would be necessary to sleep at the hospital; while on call. He reflected that the life of a doctor was not the hoped-for-paradise that some people imagined.

By the time Gordon left the hospital Judith was long gone from her day's work and he found her in their kitchen busily creating a nutritious dinner for them. She was rather dismayed to hear that he would be required to sleep in the hospital.

"Oh dear," she cried, "Is this what I've let myself in for?"

"Sorry, Darling, but there will be nights off when other chaps will take calls".

"Mm, I guess there's more to this medical lark than I had supposed. Well, people needing urgent attention must come first I suppose, so doctors and their wives have to accept and behave accordingly. When will you be able to sleep at home I wonder?."

"I'm not sure yet. I shall have to find out. Anyway what have you been doing, and have the icons from Tutankamun's tomb arrived yet?"

"No icons are yet to hand and certainly not from the tomb of that gentleman. I've just been doing secretarial work all day, typing and taking notes of further letters. Rather dull at present. I expect it will present more fun and games later".

The conversation continued with cut and thrust as they probed each other's minds during the meal for more detail. Washing up was followed by a good cuddle while watching the dreary news programme that related its usual tales of horror and vice. They switched off the set as John knocked on the door and entered saying, "I've done enough typing for to-night. It would be nice to chat up you two lovebirds for a change. I'm sure you have stories that could match the aggro of Nebuchadnezzar and all his invasions of Israel to deal with their recalcitrant kings and prophets".

The telephone rang and he reached for it commenting that it was probably his trustees meeting in trouble again. It wasn't. He handed the phone to Gordon.saying,

"Somebody wants to know if there's a doctor in the house. Over to you laddie".

Gordon took the instrument and listened. After a few moments he put it down.

"Oh dear, that's the end of our evening cosiness, Darling. My colleague has had an accident and there's a medical emergency needing help. So it's 'Good night' I'm afraid. Sorry my Sweetie. All my love. See you to-morrow for breakfast – hopefully."

Gordon stood up, stretched, bade his father-in-law 'Goodnight' and took his wife in his arms for a brief kiss and cuddle. Donning his coat he sallied forth into the night reminding himself of the treatment for an acute myocardial infarct. He drove fast but carefully.

****

Chapter 12

ANOTHER COUPLING?

Judith said sadly, "Well Dad, that seems to be what medical life is all about. I'll make you a coffee and you can tell me all about your doings while we were away. . How did you get on with Mary?"

Her father thought quietly to himself while the coffee brewed. Then "Judith, I think I must tell you. I am becoming rather fond of that lady."

"Really Daddy? How long has this been going on?"

"Mm, well for a month or two. I expect that seeing you and Gordon being such a pair of love-birds may have stirred the emotions a bit. After all I'm not exactly an old chap yet. Not quite over the hill. What do you think I ought to do?"

"Daddy, why not ask her to marry you? She is very fond of you too I know. We should have had a double wedding. I think this is marvellous. It seems so right. I'm sure Mummy would approve."

. "But what would the church people say? It's only a short while since we lost your mother".

"Daddy, she has been lost to you for a very long time. She has been only a shadow in the house for years and never a wife in any sense of the word. I think the folk would understand and sympathise. I feel sure that most of them would thoroughly approve. Mary is a lovely person and is already a great help to you in running church affairs. Why not go and talk to a few of the senior members and sound them out. Perhaps I could help too. I know them all very well and a word from me could well save you from embarrassment."

"Judith my Darling girl thank you so much. I felt sure you would understand. I really have become very fond of Mary and I am very glad to know that you are not offended".

. And they talked long into the night.

The next morning brought the minister down to breakfast holding a hand to his face that was quite swollen. He sat with a slight groan saying, "I think I'll forgo breakfast, Judith dear. I've had bother with a tooth for a week or two and in the middle of the night it became very troublesome. I think I must see the dentist".

"Oh, I'm so sorry, Daddy. Why didn't you tell us".

"Well, my dear I didn't want to spoil your return to life after that lovely honeymoon. I'll just ring the dental surgeon". He did so and was given an appointment at 11a.m. He added, "You get off to work, dear. I shall be alright, and I'll report to you later when you come home".

That evening he was much happier and relished the meal that Mary had cooked. To Judith's enquiry he told her news of a successful extraction of the offending molar. The pain had gone.

Judith said, hesitantly, "I have a little story that might

interest you. I heard it on the radio one day. It's all about a naughty tooth that plagued an old chap in Scotland. Would you like to hear it?"

"Yes certainly, my Pet. It might make a children's address one day".

"I doubt it, Daddy. I wrote for a copy. Here it is.-"Judith searched her bag and passed an envelope to the minister. He opened it and, calling Mary to come, he read with interest -

A DENTAL JOB.

It was a cold, grey, mirthless morning. The doctor's waiting room in an old Scottish city had filled with weary, poorly folk, desperate for help. One by one they entered the doctor's room, later to drift off hopefully to find a chemist.

The doctor, a strapping young fellow with shoulders and arms that would have graced a pack of rugby forwards in Murrayfield rang his bell for the next patient.

In obvious pain and holding his hand to his face an ill clad man of middle age stumbled into the room. Closing the door behind him he blurted out, "I canna bear the pain, doctor. Wull ye no tak it oot, as soon as ye can, please".

The young doctor looked at him with sympathy. The man's face was swollen on one side; his forehead was hot despite the weather. Plainly he needed urgent relief. The doctor had no dental degree. When asked, the patient told him he could not get a dental appointment until the next day.

Thoughtfully the memory of some dental instruction

during his training came into the young doctor's mind. He made a decision.

"Alright I'll take it out. I'll just give you an injection first".

Lifting a small syringe he was about to draw up a suitable dose of local anaesthetic when his patient cried out, "I dinna want ony needle, doctor. Juist tak it oot".

Surprised and shrugging his shoulders, the operator laid aside his syringe but took another saying, "You must have a dose of penicillin first anyway". The patient submitted. Then the doctor took up a Guy's forceps designed for extraction of teeth from the lower jaw. He instructed the patient to open his mouth as wide as possible and inserted a mouth gag.

Saying "Bite on that, hard," he deftly placed his forceps on the suspected cause of the pain and, fixing it firmly, began the extraction. The man howled, nay, shrieked with pain, but the doctor's muscles were well used to difficulties and he waggled and wiggled, to and fro, side to side, until the big molar, accompanied by it's owners shrieks and yells, was freed from its cosy bed. The doctor held it up in triumph, pleased with his success. So pleased that he opened the waiting room door and held up the tooth, still in the grasp of his forceps for all to behold. The waiting folk had heard the agonised sounds and quietly applauded, although some looked apprehensive. The young man grinned and returned to his room. As soon as he could speak his patient, between groans, said, "Doctor, ye've got the wrong tooth; it's the wrong tooth" Still holding his face tenderly he went away.

*

"Good gracious, poor chap", said her father. "I'm glad you didn't show me that before my appointment. I might still be moaning in fear and trepidation. Very kind of you my dear, maybe I could make a sermon from it. Thank you for that plateful, Mary. Most welcome. Now I can go and type, but not that story for a children's address I think."

Pressure of work kept Judith busy for several days after that. Then after careful thought she decided to visit her helpful mentor, the doctor's wife, and phoned her to arrange a time. Angela met her at the door and welcomed her with open arms, enquiring how married life was suiting her. Judith replied that it was just right for her and added that it seemed to be an infectious commodity.

"Oh really? What do you mean my dear?"

"Well it looks as if the manse is becoming a matrimonial agency. My father has fallen for his housekeeper. I think they should get married."

"Really Judith? How lovely, dear. She is a delightful person and will make a splendid wife for a parson. When will it be? Before Easter I would think; then they could go off on honeymoon. This is simply rapturous, Judith. What gorgeous fun!"

And the pair went into the details of question and answer for a couple of hours. By then both were quite tired; they decided to call it a day and resume their conversation in a few days time.

John was well aware that he should refer the whole matter to the authorities of his church and made an appointment for an interview with their appropriate committee. A week later he told Judith that all was well and his wedding was approved. He and Mary had decided on a date and a weekend was spent busily sending notices to many friends. John's Anglican colleague stated, "I shall be supremely happy to tie another knot."

"I will make the wedding cake" said Mary and mixed and cooked all the ingredients with her customary aplomb, not forgetting a lot of muscular exertion. Judith's dressmaking friends laughed happily and demanded to be involved with both decorations and loads of fancy cooking. Gerald took care of transport as before while his brother, Gordon's uncle, was very pleased to play the good fairy once more. He booked a honeymoon retreat for the happy pair in a cosy hotel in the semi-tropical regions of which he was quite a connoisseur.

Mary produced a civil servant relative from the treasury who averred that he would gladly give her away, and John rediscovered an old friend in the form of a Scottish laird. That worthy extricated himself from the glens to travel south, hiding a bottle of whisky in his rear pocket, to perform the honours of acting as best man to one of his hereditary enemies. He and the civil servant were booked into the same hotel and, having realised that they were officially political opponents, they promptly joined forces to demolish the laird's hidden bottle and made inroads into a second one, thus becoming the best of friends by midnight before the wedding day.

On the date arranged, with the late February day bringing bright sunshine to grace the occasion, Mary, in a lovely dark blue gown specially chosen from a specialist dressmaker, took her place in the Rolls-Royce beside her treasury official who beamed with pride and whose alcoholic fumes had been suitably drowned with strong coffee. John, resplendent in his attire of bow tie and tails of former vintage, looked a most proud and slightly nervous groom. With his Scottish laird from the northern glens he had already reached the church and waited gladly for his bride. The news of their impending union had spread far and wide resulting in a large number of folk lining the streets to the church, and filling the pews of that fine old building full to overflowing.

The bride and escort followed by Judith's two friends, again press-ganged to act as matrons of honour, entered the doors to the swell of the bridal march of Wagner. Mary joined John to slip her hand into his waiting arm, returning his nervous grin with a smile most radiant and loving.

Again the lovely words, the solemn promises, the ring and the pronouncement that declared them to be man and wife; again the single handclap and the following loud acclaim; followed by the official signing of the register. Once again the organ blazed forth with Mendenssohn's triumphant declaration of matrimony to accompany that most important walk, where John and Mary walked arm in arm down the aisle of the minister's own church, between the rows of happy and lovingly smiling people whom they both served.

It was a wonderfully crowded manse with folk occupying every room and even the stairs as a huge crowd assembled there to do honour to their beloved minister. Bride and groom joined their hands together on the knife blade for the cake cutting, and the sonorous voice from Scotland boomed out the messages by telegram and letter making good use of such spicy little comments as added to the joyful occasion. Some bright spark rounded off the affair with a loud voice declaring that 'he's a jolly good fellow,' and the whole crowd of merrymakers agreed with him with loud voiced enthusiasm. Eventually it was with some relief that bride and groom escaped to slide into the comfortable car with a chauffeur arranged thoughtfully by Gerald for their journey to the chosen airport. There were no humorous or odorous articles attached to the vehicle, nor any funny messages wishing them wedded bliss, but the crowd all waved and cheered as the happy couple raised their hands in a 'Farewell' salute.

"Gosh" said Gordon as soon as his voice could be heard above the cheering din. "Now you know who really loves whom. Dad has fixed up a dinner for us with the honourable matrons and the best men, so when we've recovered we'll all get together at his appointed restaurant and make 'whoopee' Your friends, Judith, know to bring their husbands. I wonder if Dad has hired a piper with kilt and bagpipe".

And the merry evening continued with a haggis being piped in by a kilted Scottish piper, topped by a selection of luscious sweetmeats along with speeches in honour of the minister and his delightful bride. Finally came the lusty singing of 'Auld Lang Syne.'

The Sunday service next day, taken by a friendly lay preacher, was well attended and the coffee crowd in the church hall afterwards chattered very appreciatively of their minister and his new lady. Judith felt very thrilled that her father was so highly regarded. She resolved to write a small article in the monthly magazine thanking them all for their good wishes and kindness. Meanwhile it was lovely to have Gordon home for the weekend, especially with the manse all to themselves, so they snuggled down together in wedded happiness.

****

Chapter 13

TOGETHER

"If honeymoon brings to them the sort of happiness that it's given us it will be quite a new life for them both", said Judith, one evening after the day's work.

"Well it can't quite", replied Gordon. "There's age and physiology to consider, you know."

"That's rubbish. Not everything can be measured by medical science, my lad. There's such a thing as the spiritual dimension you know, if I may use a common political expression."

"You're getting too deep for me after a day spent vetting likely subjects for our new research bod. What's for grub tonight?"

"Huh, men!" said Judith vehemently. "One track mind as usual. What about roast beef and Yorkshire, would that keep you happy?"

"Marvellous," replied the hungry young medico.

"Judith I love you." His arms encircled her waist, squeezing until she begged for breath.

They had enjoyed their two weeks in the big manse, making free of the spaciousness but quite looking forward to the imminent return of John and Mary when there would be a pleasantly different feel to the place. Life would be more complete they felt. It would be good to find the manse occupied and in good working order when they returned home from their day's work, and with the pleasant feeling of loved ones present and a very warm welcome at the end of the day.

Work in Antiques and medical wards was interesting and often complicated with emergencies, so that return to normality in the solid old house of good Yorkshire brick supervised by the united, mature couple, would bring relaxation and ease of mind on entering the door.

Gordon downed his beef and pudding with relish and then told Judith, "Dad has laid on a car to collect them from the airport, so if they're due in around six o'clock tomorrow they could be back here by eight. Will that be OK. for an evening meal, Darling?"

"Excellent. It'll be lamb chops and roast 'tatties with mint sauce and veg. That do?"

"First class. You're a wonderful girl. Glad I married you."

"Good. In that case you can wash up. I've a letter to type. Join me later."

And the evening continued with chat, repartee, and laughter as they reported to each other some of the events of the day. An icon had disappeared and was found later in the dustbin. The boss was not pleased. A nurse had dropped a bedpan. Sister vented her fury on the helpless girl until Gordon had managed to calm her down and let the poor kid escape. The consultant had lost his glasses; a senior nurse ventured to suggest that he look on the end of his nose. He shot venomous glances all around. Judith couldn't start her car and needed a push; the car park attendant was sarcastic.

The 10 p.m. news was as wretchedly full of horror and vice as ever. Turn it off and settle for bath and bed. Much nicer.

And in the morning it was back to the grindstone for them both. The day threatened rain and the blackbird sang his contralto greeting from the branch of an apple tree that was thinking of bursting into leaf (but not just yet.) Winter jasmine was glorying in lovely yellow florets that lined the garden walls. Celandines were lifting bright golden faces to the sky and all nature was urging winter to depart and allow the loveliness of springtime to shed radiance over field and garden. John and Mary were due to return from their honeymoon. Gordon had a few hours off duty.

"Darling, what about an early dinner at our favourite pub? " They telephoned and quickly arranged as desired. A last meal on their own was a delight and the staff excelled themselves to make it memorable. In good time they left to be home for John and Mary returning

In the early evening Gordon rounded the corner of his previous encounter with catastrophy. In the distance an ambulance was approaching, its siren sounding loudly. In the foreground a man of middle age was leading a sprightly horse towards a gate into a field. Suddenly as the noisy vehicle drew near the horse, a big 16 hands beauty, took fright and jumped sideways from the edge of the road into the path of the ambulance. The violence of the driver's horn made things worse. The horse owner struggled to return the animal to safety, but in vain. He let go of the bridle and jumped back to save himself.. The vehicle braked hard with tyres screeching and swerved to avoid the animal hoping to be clear of its owner. The man fell, his lower leg struck by the bumper as the ambulance stopped. He yelled. The driver and Gordon jumped out to attend to him. Judith emerged and walked quietly to the horse, now shivering with fright on the other side of the road. Gently she caught the bridle and stroked the frightened animal, speaking quietly and trying to reassure it.

The horse's owner sat up, cringing with pain in his leg but more concerned for the horse. "Can you catch him and put him in that field please. Here are the keys to the padlock". He fished out a bunch of keys from his trouser pocket. "It's alright, my wife has got him", .said Gordon. "She's very good with horses. I'm a doctor so let's have a look at your leg". He passed the keys to the driver who crossed the road to Judith. Together they encouraged the animal to pass through the gate and enter the field. They replaced the padlock.

While carefully feeling the man's leg Gordon enquired of the driver, "What is your emergency trouble?" He replied "We have a chap with a strangulated hernia. He's not very happy."

"I should think not. I'm a doctor so I can tell you that you have a very good reason to get away as fast as possible.. I'll attend to this gentleman. I think he has a cracked fibula. If you will phone the police from the ambulance and give them all the details I expect they will take this chap to the hospital It wasn't your fault. You're in the clear, so better get off. Bye bye."

After checking his patient's condition and conferring with his assistant the driver hurriedly mounted his vehicle and drove off, only sounding his siren when well away from the field.

Gordon then chatted to the disabled horse owner, finding him to be a local farmer who hoped to race the splendid animal. He was profoundly thankful to the ambulance driver for avoiding the horse. "A bony break in my leg will mend easily enough" he said. "That could have been a death warrant for my racing beauty. She has an excellent pedigree and was left to me in the will of a friendly racing enthusiast." Gordon told him the fibula was fractured and with help from Judith they made an emergency splint from a few daily papers kept for just such a purpose, wrapped it around the leg with a couple of four inch crepe bandages. They helped him into their car and Gordon supplied codeine tablets to ease the pain.

Shortly afterwards the police appeared and the matter was related to them in detail. The farmer assured them that it was a pure accident and there was no question of legal action. With Gordon's assurances regarding the need for the patient in the ambulance to be hurried to hospital the police were satisfied and offered to convey the farmer there also if he agreed. They could then speak to the ambulance driver. With satisfaction all around, finishing with the information that the farmer was a patient of Dr. Collins the incident was closed. Gordon and Judith expected to reach home in time to welcome John and Mary back to their own front door. It had been an eventful day once again.

*

The plane landed in good time, and, as Gordon had reckoned, the chauffeur swiftly deposited John and Mary at the manse doors when they entered to the feel of a warm house, polished and tidy with a bright fire in their sitting room and the smell of a hot meal wafting through from the kitchen.

"We're here!" was their cry, and young and not so young joyfully hugged each other as Judith and Gordon responded with a loving welcome. John and Mary shortly hastened up stairs to change and unpack a few items of luggage followed by Judith's voice telling of food in twenty minutes.

Then the question and answer session. A good flight? Nice weather? A first for the hotel? Plenty of sun? Have you learnt the language? Retiring there? And all the other queries that made them still feel on holiday. In the middle of it all Judith entered with the dinner and all the trimmings; minds took a different slant, conversation lending sauce to an excellent repast…The men washed up afterwards while the ladies nattered gently over the more feminine things of honeymoon bliss. All gathered for coffee and talk of what had been happening at home and of future matters of church and state. The medical side of the equation was neglected until Gordon piped up saying that he regretted the need to return for night duty. He had walked from the hospital and was glad of Judith's offer to drive him back, leaving the returned honeymoon couple to savour more of their first evening at home as man and wife. There was time for the younger pair to drop into the hospital restaurant for another cuppa and chat for a while.

"They look quite radiant", said Judith. "That has done them a lot of good. It seems almost a pity that we are going to dilute their occupation of the manse with our presence".

"Yes they fit together nicely" said Gordon. "But we don't have any option for some time, I fear. Can we try things for a year, I wonder. That would give me two more six-month hospital jobs, maybe not all in this hospital, of course. Then I could try for general practice."

"Oh dear", said Judith. "Does that mean you would be living away in some other town? I hadn't thought of that possibility. I can't leave my job here or I would take digs to be near you. Life has complications."

And they talked over the complications for another hour until Judith concluded that she must return to the manse and prepare for work next day. In the car before she drove off they embraced tenderly with many good night kisses and vows of affection. The future they would face when it came. Meanwhile to work. The next morning they all awoke to a dull grey day and to the sound of the telephone. The minister answered. The voice was not from the hospital. One of his church stewards had a problem. Work had returned for John too.

For several days routine work of manse, church, hospital and antiques proceeded with the every-day and mundane matters inextricably mixed with emergencies as they occurred. There was quite sufficient to keep all our characters on their toes; seldom was there time to relax until the ends of the dreary March days came to offer rest and warmth beside the fires in the solid old building that housed them. But snowdrops had peeped up, and daffodils were revealing their golden blooms. Crocuses were appearing in clusters beneath the bare trees where a robin trilled his clear, liquid soprano; thrush repeated his merry song and blackbird sang his husky, fluty notes to remind humans that spring was chasing away the dark days of winter past and would bring its promise of new radiance into all life.

In the house Mary had instituted a campaign to clean for spring every available surface and many hidden crevices rarely accessible without shifting the solid old furniture. That needed polishing too, she said. Curtains were unmercifully removed, sometimes with difficulty and sent off to the laundry; items long forgotten were unearthed and cleaned and polished. Mary's silver plate shone with a fresh glitter and the dust and sooty deposits of winter vanished under her busy and competent hand. The minister sorted out the church problems with his stewards and insistently declared "There must be not be the slightest interference with my papers and books; I shall attend to them all in due course." Between them, and assisted by Judith when available in the evenings, the whole place shone and reflected the urgency of preparation for brighter days.

In the business of antiques Gerald kept a tight rein on the efficiency of his staff, leading the way with necessary reform where needed. In the hospital medical superintendent and matron were adept at demanding better ways of attending to patients' needs in every department. Spring was about to come.at last.

****

CHAPTER 14

SEPARATE BUT UNITED

As the year advanced Gordon began to consider what further hospital job would be desirable. The advertisement pages of the medical journals were often in his hands when time allowed. .Talking to senior medical men finally convinced him that orthopaedic experience would be an essential for his career advancement. He found an advert requiring a junior houseman in the orthopaedic department of the Northern General Hospital in Sheffield. He replied immediately and a few days later he was urging his small car northwards toward that city for an interview. He gave a good account of himself, and his references were very satisfactory. The job was his as soon as he had finished his present stint.

Gordon took his wife in his arms and told her gently.

"Darling, I've nearly finished my stint and orthopaedics will have to be next. A job in Sheffield came up and I drove up for an interview. I've got the job". There were tears but

Judith was prepared for the new kind of life that she had envisaged. She bore up bravely. There was no option. "OK my love. It will be different but needs must. I suppose. We'd better get ready"..

In due course the day of separation arrived. A special 'going-away-party' had been held the previous night. Gordon was all packed up and ready for off, sad to be leaving his beloved, but also excited. They stood together beside his car. Judith gave him last minute instructions, holding her emotions firmly in check. "I've got all your clothes in good order," she said. "Every article of wear is labelled with your name ready for the hospital laundry, so no mistakes can be made. I've packed a basket of useful eatables for you and there's a letter for you to find in your suitcase. So Goodbye my Darling and God bless and keep you safe." While firmly stifling her anxieties their leave-taking was most loving. She waved until his car had turned the corner; then hurried to her bedroom and sobbed and sobbed

A different chapter in all their lives would now commence where each would attend earnestly to their different spheres of work, but always sought to be together whenever opportunity allowed. There were would be times when Judith could catch a train for Sheffield and spend a pleasant weekend with her beloved, and on other occasions Gordon would drive down to join her at the manse and savour Mary's cooking. But such times were dependent on hospital routine and its various emergencies; these always took pride of place and were strictly observed.

However a notable event had occurred that was to make a big difference in the smooth equanimity of their lives. When Gordon began his new job Judith had been aware of some unusual symptoms. After a couple of weeks she had felt it advisable to visit her doctor to report the missing of two monthly periods and occasional morning sickly bouts. There was only one verdict open to him…

Next day Gordon arrived with a few days off duty. They booked a candle-light dinner at their favourite pub. Judith dressed with care, applying eye shadow and lipstick quite needlessly but most attractively. The eyes of diners were drawn towards her in appreciation. The loving pair found their table. They sat, sipping cocktails of tropical fruit.

Hesitantly, stumbling over her words, unsure of Gordon's reaction, Judith told him.

He listened, mouth opening wide, not quite taking it in. Suddenly the message reached him. He leaped up, reached for her, drew her towards him saying loudly for all to hear, "We're going to have a baby." Then with eyes lighting up and a huge grin spreading over his face he enfolded her in his arms, saying, "Judy my Darling, that's wonderful, absolutely wonderful."

Immensely relieved and barely able to speak, Judith hugged and hugged him. Guests throughout the dining area smiled, grinned, laughed and applause broke out with the ladies clapping happily and the men stamping their feet. It was quite a while ere normality returned.

Gordon's visit only lasted two days but both he and Judith were radiantly happy and spent the time nattering over all kinds of future joys and possibilities. With John and Mary they celebrated and stuck up lists of needed items of apparel, nappies, vests, cardigans and a host of other necessities all over the house. At last, the weekend over, they returned to work thrilled and deeply satisfied.

During the early days of pregnancy, after the morning sickness had passed, Judith's employer would request her company on some of his visits to a foreign land for the purpose of looking at or purchasing antiques or desirable icons. These jaunts were precious to her, both for their interest and for bringing useful education and experience for her future work. Flights to St Petersburg/Leningrad and to Florence occurred, and even Iceland was not neglected. Judith enjoyed them and found that such excursions provided plenty of interesting discussions with Gordon when they met. Later as her pregnancy advanced it was considered inadvisable to undertake such journeys and then the meetings of man and wife depended on Gordon's freedom for driving to the manse.

For him, while Judith was all the time improving her knowledge of the business, there was a huge storehouse of new experiences being built up. New conditions of orthopaedic interest constantly came within his purview and were carefully explained to him by his consultant. He wrote up such talks and stored many items of information in his brain. Modern treatments replaced the old standbys and fresh equipment was needed to undertake fresh methods. All required understanding and careful handling.

For Gordon the operating theatre provided new interest and needed new expertise. Instead of carving into a strangulated hernia, chopping off bits of gangrenous gut and stitching together the ends of healthy intestine, (then hoping for return of function), there was a matter of chiselling away at a piece of bone. Traction for a fracture, the setting of broken bones, the investigation of bony growths and decisions regarding benign or cancerous growths now occupied his thoughts. The difference between bony breaks and strains or rupture of ligament fibres needed much thought. The need to explain to patients and their relatives about their diagnoses and treatments was just as important in orthopaedics as in surgery or medicine or obstetrics. Such required much care and not a little time, very often, in order to provide satisfactory understanding. All of this added together to create the basis of good medical education, ensuring that Gordon would be aware of a patient's vital need for explanation.

He found the practical operating theatre experience quite fascinating and his senior colleagues were adept at demonstrating and assisting him to perform well. The registrar impressed upon him "When you are dealing with a compound fracture of a large bone there could be found damage to a nerve or major blood vessel lying in the depths of the wound. You need to search carefully for that kind of possibility. If you find either of them you must then call for the expert assistance of a senior surgeon without hesitation. " Gordon listened, took careful note and remembered.

While normally his work was confined to the N.H.S. hospitals, other interesting opportunities sometimes came his way. On one occasion the consultant needed an assistant at a nursing home where he was operating to relieve bony pressure on a protruding lumbar disk. "Gordon", he said, "I need an assistant at an operation in a Nursing Home; would you like to come and give a hand?" The invitation was joyfully accepted. "This laddie has suffered awful back pain for weeks", said the consultant as he carefully carved an incision into the lower lumbar region of his patient. "Yesterday he had a frightful spasm of pain on getting out of bed He only just had time to throw himself back on the bed before he fainted" He dissected further. "Now you can see where the central part of the disc – the nucleus – is pressing on a branch of the nerve coming out from the spinal cord". It was pushing the nerve against bone. Muscle paralysis had already occurred so immediate relief was essential. "We'll need to do a laminectomy", he said, adding, "that means chopping away the little bit of bone against which the nerve is being squeezed", and he proceeded to instruct Gordon in the delicate task of removing the small disc responsible for the trouble, together with a little piece of bone. Great care was needed to avoid any damage to the affected branch of the spinal cord. The young man was glad of the interesting experience and later happily recounted it to Judith in great detail. They shared a happy glow of satisfaction when Gordon produced the generous cheque given by the surgeon in payment for his services.

"Just look at this, Judy. Isn't your husband a clever boy. That'll swell the bank balance and keep them happy."

There were times when, if his hands were not actually needed at an operation, the anaesthetist would offer to teach him how to insert an intra-tracheal tube. All good experience. Useful too.

So week after week and month after month the young lovers continued to equip themselves As often as possible they joined together; if in Sheffield, an outing to the Playhouse or the famous Crucible theatre would be quite a thrill. Nearer to Christmas an evening when Handel's Messiah was performed at the City Hall would be a wonderful occasion when one of the famous conductors, perhaps Malcolm Sergeant or a successor would draw the glorious music from the willing and expert performers in the orchestra. Judith's father needed no persuasion to join the party with Mary and all felt uplifted in spirit, joining with fervour in the tremendous applause that followed the rendering of that famous work.

*

One morning Gordon's registrar received a message from

the appointment's department. He spent a few minutes thinking and, when the consultant arrived for the morning theatre work, put his problem to him.

"I learn, sir, that our next houseman following Dr Jenkins has been obliged to 'give back word' on account of illness in his family. Do you think we could ask Gordon Jenkins if he would do another three months until a replacement can be found?"

The consultant considered. "Yes I think that's an excellent idea. We'll ask him after this session." And when changing out of their theatre togs, they did. Gordon felt a bit shaken. "That's rather a shock. My wife expects her first during that time. May I talk to her and let you know later?"

"Yes of course. She must be considered. We have some time yet. Go and see her this weekend, we can manage here alright," aid the consultant. And it was arranged.

It was rather an emotional time for both of them when Gordon told his dear wife of the hospital's proposal. Judith was naturally shocked to find that her husband would be absent when her baby was expected to arrive. She was most upset and very displeased that the hospital should demand such a sacrifice from her. Gordon did nothing to argue the case or to persuade her to accept the situation. After a time of weeping and clinging to him, emotions gradually settled and she began to think carefully. "I suppose other people's needs must be considered. Operations would be put off and folk would be very disappointed. I guess I'd better agree, Darling. I did marry you for better or worse. It's not so very much worse. Alright they can have you." Her smile came through the tears and she hugged her husband tightly.

Preparations for Christmas and the New Year were as joyful as ever, and, although Gordon's duty involved several hours during the Great Day, he still managed to streak in his little car to join his beloved wife and the family for a brief hour or two in the afternoon. His father joined the party also and Mary and Judith produced a culinary creation as tasty as the occasion demanded. Judith, seven months pregnant, was reluctant later to let her dear one go, but duty came first and she wiped a tear away as Gordon sped away to brave the hours of night calls, operating theatre or whatever. At the Manse they borrowed the registrar from their own hospital, Gordon being absent, and the New Year was brought in by that dark-haired gentleman bearing the accustomed offering. He commented that appendices were a bit scarce that year. Gerald kindly bore a gift to John and Mary of a reproduction of the 'Praying Hands' that, he knew, the minister so greatly admired.

Judith proclaimed to the little company, "this year", and gently patted her protruding tummy. The incumbent responded with a kick or two that was acknowledged by its mother's quiet giggle. Mary watched the little pantomime and added her own merry smile of happiness, squeezing Judith's arm affectionately. Her father presented her with two pairs of waterproof pants saying, "These are to be worn, when the wee nipper commences his peripatetic adventures on the manse carpets."

Judith replied , "I know the shop attendants where you bought those pants; they also deal with the coffee and biscuits in the church hall". She further commented, "I'll bet they had a good giggle. I wonder if they knew of the possibility of twins in my tummy. Midwives tend to gossip sometimes. Or perhaps they thought too, Daddy, that you're not quite over the hill yet either. How about it"?

Her father had the grace to blush, while Mary cackled heartily saying, "He's got a hope!"

Seven weeks later John surprised his daughter one morning holding her bulge and wearing an apprehensive expression. "Are things happening? Shall I go and fetch the car my Darling?"

"Yes, please Daddy. It's been going on since six o'clock. Time to get to the hospital. I have my case all ready in the hall."

"OK. Do we warn Gordon now, Judith?"

"No, I don't think so, Daddy. We'll tell him when it's all over. If he rings tell him I'm having a day with friends. I'll ring him to-morrow."

After a careful drive through the morning traffic Judith was given a warm welcome by the Sister of the maternity ward. Booking in, given a bed, examination, blood checks and all the normal routine of hospital admission followed, with Judith trying to cope with pains as they occurred. Her father was naturally given leave to absent himself and the business of labour was all established under the competent organisation of Sister and her staff

Very late that night in his Sheffield hospital Gordon emerged from the operating theatre to hear a voice on the Tannoy saying, 'Dr. Jenkins to the telephone please'. He removed his mask and found an instrument, wondering what new emergency awaited him. "Hallo, Dr. Jenkins speaking, what can I do for you?"

The positive voice of Judith's Sister-on-duty replied, "Congratulations to a new father. You have a fine little daughter. Would you like to speak to her mother?"

Gordon nearly dropped his instrument and hopped from one foot to the other until the much loved voice of his dearest wife restored equanimity telling him, "I've done it, Darling. We have a lovely little girl. Seven pounds, eight ounces. Both of us are fine. When can you come and see us?"

"Judy my Darling girl, that's wonderful. Are you sure you're all right? I'll try for to-morrow. I'll have to ask management if duties can be switched. You're a marvellous girl. I love you."

The greetings and conversation that ensued kept the phone busy for some time until the Sister intervened, insisting that Judith was tired and must be allowed to rest. A tender 'Good bye' ended their very loving talk.

Gordon promptly ran to the office to discover whether he would be able to take the next day off to visit Judith and his new-born daughter. The office was closed of course. He was in quite a tizzy, being congratulated by all staff still awake and felt in need of support, both moral and physical. Somebody found him a 'restorative," while a hefty slice of fruit cake was donated from another's locker. He sat and slowly returned to normal. After a while he realised that decision about his journey must wait until morning when he must approach the hospital authority. Sleep was imperative, so after packing a bag he lay down between the sheets and hoped for a quiet night. He was still on duty.

He was lucky and swallowed a hurried breakfast before chasing to the hospital office and stating his case. Packing his little car hopefully he endured a half hour wait while arrangements were made. Yes, he could go, but only for two days. Hospitals were busy places.

The February morning was chilly and wet with a drizzle driven by a westerly wind. Getting out of Sheffield was a bind with clouds of spray whipped up onto his windscreen from heavy traffic, but never mind - he was on his way to see his lovely wife and baby. He whistled, sang and drove as fast as he dared. He improvised love songs searching for hopeless rhymes, he emulated a blackbird cheering up a sitting hen bird, a thrush that 'repeats his song twice over lest he forget that first fine careless rapture.' By midday the 'dreaming spires' of the old town, (but not Oxford) were within his sight and soon he was parked and rushing to the reception desk of the hospital for information The receptionist smiled and congratulated him, directing him to 'Maternity' and recognising in the urgent voice the excitement of a young husband becoming a new father.

"Can I see my wife please? I've just arrived from Sheffield."

"You'll need to wait for a few minutes sir, she's on the toilet." It was ever thus. He waited. After an interminable time staff nurse appeared and told him, "You can go in now, sir."

Tenderly and lovingly he greeted Judith, and only when quite satisfied concerning her good health after the birth experience did he turn to the nurse and accepted from her the seven pond scrap of humanity that was now rightfully his baby girl.

It was not the first time he had held a baby, but his own was different. Judith was delighted to see the look of wonder on her husband's face as he gazed at the tiny child and settled her comfortably in the crook of his arm. "Welcome, our Jilly", said Gordon, for that was the name decided on several months before. "May your years with us be wonderfully happy."

Little Jilly snuggled cosily into her father's arms. Shortly she turned her face towards his shirt-front and began to search with her lips. Judith spotted the baby's intention and instructed her husband, "You haven't got the right apparatus, my lad. Better pass the wee mite to her Mum".

The transition effected, Gordon watched as his wife

undid her maternity bra and provided her newborn with a little nourishment, and her husband with a lesson on the naturalness of breast-feeding. Gordon sat down to admire. The baby sucked strongly. Judith smiled a smug little maternal smile. The staff-nurse entered saying to Judith, "Your father is here, Mrs. Jenkins. . Shall I tell him to wait?"

"No, tell him to come in and enjoy the show!"

John, accompanied by Mary, was promptly admitted and they joyfully greeted Judith and Gordon. They enthused over the sight of baby Jilly, with Mary declaring that she was the split image of Judith. John apologised for his intrusion, saying that it was a long time since he had witnessed such matters and should he be blushing.

"Don't bother, Daddy, there's a lot more to come, especially with Gordon around". It was the turn of that young man to go scarlet, while staff nurse giggled in the back ground, before edging out into the corridor. The party became quite merry with laughter when Gordon was told to take the infant and get its wind up.. "You may as well start to be a father right now", said his wife. "I've told Daddy that there'll be lots more of that too, so practice now and make perfect".

After some time Judith began to show signs of weariness and her guests excused themselves.

Mary invited Gordon to lunch and he promised to return after his wife's afternoon rest when they could have a proper chat. His father had been invited to the meal and the conversation became quite vigorous with the discussion swinging from maternity and its problems to troubles with bones and their attachments both in and out of the operating theatre.

Gerald was naturally anxious to learn how long his capable assistant would be absent from the Antiques business. Mary took it upon herself to assure him that Judith would surely be longing to return to her desk, but it was essential that she should first acquire a very real bonding with her baby. She thought that would take three months or so but felt certain that Judith would intend to accept secretarial work to undertake at home and thus relieve the pressure on a temporary typist. After that she, Mary, would be only too happy to care for the little lady during his mother's absence from home. She hoped that Gordon, when able to spend a day or two, would also act up as father-in–waiting, so to speak, and would be able to spare time to cuddle his daughter in one arm while his wife occupied the other.

The lunch session became very happy, covering many points until Gordon spoke of his need to visit his wife. Then a good sleep would be advisable before taking the road back to work. So it was back to the ward for the young father; there precious time together being occupied with mutual assurances of their love for each other.

Next morning on Gordon's final hospital visit Judith took the opportunity to reassure her beloved, saying -

"I must obviously give our wee poppet a lot of my time, my Darling, "but you will never need to feel that you're in the back seat. I will divide my love between you both but you will always be the man in my life."

Their tears mingled together as they kissed goodbye.

As Gordon left the hospital, listening to the fluty contralto notes of a blackbird on a cherry tree still bare of leaf on its branches, he was aware of that genuine reassurance and joined the bird with a merry whistle.

Wending his way through the Sunday afternoon traffic with the rain reduced to a trickle and the wind lessening he felt happy and secure in the realisation of his new fatherhood. On the open road cars full of people were returning from their visits to friends and family and all was peaceful with no need for ruining a happy day by furiously tearing along life's highway to the security of home.

But half way to Sheffield somebody had felt such a need and, in streaking round a corner had misjudged a distance and slammed his car violently into another vehicle coming from the opposite direction. The road was partly blocked, but two police cars had already arrived and traffic was being directed around the accident. As Gordon drew level with a policeman he opened his window saying, "I'm a doctor, can I help at all?" The officer was pleased and directed Gordon to a safe position near the accident site. Then, with stethoscope in his pocket and medical bag in his hand, Gordon hastened to the scene to find one casualty, a woman, sitting in a police car, sobbing and holding one arm very tenderly. He gently enquired how the injury had happened, and was told that the woman had been reaching round to the back seat to give her dog a biscuit when her car was violently struck. There had been a horrible pain striking through her shoulder and she could not move the arm. A gentle examination convinced Gordon that he was faced with a dislocation of the left shoulder joint. She was a passenger in the car and had not been driving. Rapidly he remembered a similar case that he had dealt with in the hospital. "If you can keep still and let me put it right your pain will soon go away." he said.

The patient agreed. "Alright doctor, anything you can do. I'll give you the arm and hold onto the seat."

She did so. Gordon knelt on the ground beside the police car, carefully took the wrist in his hand, manipulated the arm as described in his textbook and with a sudden jerk the joint clicked into place, accompanied by a loud shriek from the woman. "Oh, that was awful", she shouted.

Gordon at once agreed. "Yes it certainly must have hurt, but is it better now?" he asked.

"It's pretty sore but better than it was and I can move the arm," she replied, when she could speak again. "Good, but don't try moving it any more. You'll need a triangular bandage and a big crepe bandage to rest it and keep it still." He looked at the policeman who had watched in admiration and asked if there was a First Aid box that might have such articles. The man promptly produced a nicely painted box bearing the appropriate inscription, and bandages were quickly found and applied. Gordon felt in his pocket and found a couple of painkiller tablets. "These will help. They simply contain paracetamol and codeine. It relieves pain quite a lot. Here are two more for tonight. Try and see y our doctor tomorrow".

By the time she had wallowed them, aided by a cup of tea from the policeman's flask, the ambulance had arrived and two paramedics hurried to see what help they could render. They expressed themselves as very pleased to find a doctor had already dealt with the casualty, but of course they said, "We have to examine her and ensure that she is all right to go home. We will probably wish to take her to the hospital for a further check". They found that the other driver had sustained only bruises, so they took over the responsibility for completing forms and making further arrangements as needed, the police assisting.

Gordon was thanked suitably by all concerned and he continued on his way, feeling that medicine was just the right job for him; nothing like a simple emergency successfully treated to give him a profound feeling of satisfaction and self reliance. Negotiating Sheffield's busy streets he was glad to find the hospital gates open and a space available in its overfull car park. Shortly after checking in he was not quite so pleased when he was called to the phone and informed that since a colleague had been struck down with the 'flu' he would be on call for the night. A doctor's life indeed

Opportunities for further visits to his wife and baby were few but he succeeded in dropping in a day or two after Judith returned home. All was going according to plan with baby feeding well and nappies being filled, while Judith had rapidly regained her energy and looked quite radiant. Her breasts full, her stance erect, her eyes glowing, the baby in her arms and looking like a real woman. Gordon spent a night on one occasion when he slept through the infant's lusty crying for a feed. Judith awoke and did her duty, looking sympathetically at her dear man who was obviously tired after nights up and miles on the road. Baby business produced problems all round she reckoned. On waking Gordon discovered that fathers had responsibilities beyond the mere matter of earning money to feed a bank account. However, cuddling a baby, though new to him, was fast becoming a very pleasant chore, even when moisture seeped through the nappy onto his nicely creased trousers.

"It's best to wear old things when visiting your new infant, my love; shall I get you a pair of old bags from the Salvation Army shop?"

"Jolly good idea, Sweetie. I'll have one at the hospital for car repairs and one here for infantile urinary incompetence. My consultant would approve your idea because he's got a small menagerie of young nippers. I think he rushes in to emergencies to get away from household duties. Some of the jobs could easily be done by the registrar".

And they enjoyed a weekend of story swapping as well as cuddling on the couch when the days' responsibilities were finished. Gordon found that the minister also was quite enjoying getting used to infant needs and often offered a useful shoulder for the baby's comfort and burping. He took suitable precautions against infantile tiddles, accepting gladly his wife's wise advice; she reckoned to be very experienced. The other grandpa joined them for an evening meal and merry converse kept them all rocking with laughter as stories from each came to mind and were vividly told until bedtime claimed their weary bodies.

One weekend Gordon had an extra day and joined Judith for morning coffee at the Antique shop, performing shopping duties for her before finally hitting the road back to Sheffield.

"That's been a lovely time", she said, "How many more months of drudgery have you got on this stint?"

"Only two to go, and anyway it's all very useful learning experience. I'm quite enjoying the surgery and still get the occasional private session, although the registrar normally is given those lucrative options. We'll have to think hard about the future after this job is finished". And it was a long 'good bye' session with much hugging and kissing to sustain them until the next visit.

It was time to go. They parted reluctantly and Judith waved with the baby in one arm and a tear trickling down her cheek. Mary took the baby from her and offered a handkerchief. "Come on, duck, let's have a cup of tea" she said, and with her other arm around Judith she guided her into the manse. Rain was beginning to fall; Gordon would have an unpleasant drive; Judith put up a little prayer for him.

The weeks went by, with Judith becoming expert at the business of baby palaver and she began to introduce more solid food into Jilly's diet. She attended the postnatal and infant welfare sessions at the hospital and faithfully carried out suggestions from the staff. The little girl flourished.

Judith's father, inspired by the child's progress made up children's stories for the youngsters of his congregation, pointing out that Jesus had instructed his disciples to allow the children to be brought to Him 'For of such is the Kingdom of Heaven.' Mary too, in her place as the leader of the 'Womens' Own,' used children's stories to illustrate her talks on biblical matters. Gordon, when able to visit, was always enchanted by his charming baby, but often his look seemed far away. "Thinking of what's coming next, Darling?" asked his wife. Gordon nodded.

Whenever time allowed they would chat thoughtfully about the possibilities. The orthopaedic work was certainly very attractive and extremely interesting. One morning in the hospital the consultant called Gordon to examine a man complaining of a very painful back with numbness of one leg and some degree of weakness in the other. The x-ray was not sufficiently clear and the more modern MMR was arranged. It involved introducing a long needle into the space around the spinal cord and injecting a radio-opaque fluid. The resulting picture, when read by the radiologist, revealed very definite pressure on the spinal cord by a prolapsed disc in the lumbar region.

"I am not at all happy about this," said the consultant. "I propose to ask our neurosurgeon expert to have a look at him." This was done and the two senior men went into a huddle and discussed the case out of the patient's earshot. They called the registrar and Gordon and told them the upshot of their findings and their decision. "We think this difficulty can only be relieved by an operation to ease the pressure on the spinal cord, and we will tell the patient. If he and his family agree we will perform this as soon as possible. He is heading for paralysis of that leg and the sooner we do it the better."

Two days later all was ready in the theatre and both

the junior doctors were invited to be present at the operation when both surgeons would share the very tricky procedure. They were invited to look at the difficult situation when the nerves were exposed in the depths of the wound. They could observe how the nucleus of the disk had prolapsed and was pressing against nerve tissue of the spinal cord. The disk nucleus had in fact by then actually split in two. The pieces were removed with great care. after a laminectomy had been performed. The area was meticulously inspected for any other abnormality and the whole wound was closed.

Gordon felt most impressed again and had long conversations with the registrar who told him that he was certainly intending to move further on in orthopaedics hoping one day to obtain a consultant's position. This seemed to make it all the more urgent for Gordon to decide which way his future career should now bend. He had gained quite a lot of knowledge and experience in surgery, medicine, obstetrics and gynaecology and now orthopaedics. Should he choose one of them in preference to another or would it be a more holistic approach to opt for general practice where he could well be involved in any or all of these various branches of medical work and experience.

He would talk to Judith. It was not a matter for one person to decide separately. It must be a united decision. Having reached that conclusion he retired to bed after the long day and slept soundly.

****

CHAPTER 15

LOOKING FORWARD

THE DAYS WERE beginning to lengthen but with curtains still drawn early and a warm fire in the grate to banish the threat of March's wet and wind-swept days. Evening surgery had finished and Dr. Donald Collins was relaxing and dozing before the flames. His wife steadily clicked her needles, knitting woolly squares to make blankets for babies in Malawi. She waited for him to awake, refreshed and ready for supper and a game of Scrabble. He stirred and stretched, opening his eyes. Angela thought she might express her ideas and addressed him "Donald, you know old George who had dinner with us last night? Isn't he getting on a bit? I thought he looked rather tired. Has he had a holiday this last year?"

"No dear, I don't think he's been away since Whitsun when he had a few days in Scarborough. What's on your mind?"

"Well I know you plan to join the two practices

together when he retires. He's now 62, so he has three years of hard slog to go. Well, you remember Judith and Gordon and their baby girl."

"I should certainly never forget them, a very lovely trio. That's a little family that's very worth while."

"Yes indeed. I hear that Gordon's orthopaedic job is coming to completion before long. The end of this month I think."

"Oh, yes, I think that's right. So what are you thinking?"

"What if George offered him an assistantship for the next three years. That would qualify him as an excellent choice for assistant with view to partnership for some enterprising and hard working G.P".

Donald was quiet for a minute or two. Then he said,

"I've always thought there's more in your lovely head than ideas about clicking needles for blankets in Africa. That sounds an excellent idea. It would make life very much easier for George in his last few years; it would be a first class introduction to G.P for young Gordon too. I'll talk to George about it. I'll have to introduce the idea very carefully. He can be rather obstinate and might worry about the monetary side of things. But his health is far more important. Thank you for that dose of your wisdom, my Darling."

"Good, I'm glad you agree. If George agrees too I'll mention it to Judith; she can think about it and broach the subject to Gordon. Come on let's eat and exercise our brain power on the Scrabble board."

Angela made arrangements and invited George to dine with them two days later when she laid on his favourite lamb chops with all the trimmings. After a delightful sherry trifle she whisked away the dishes and made coffee while the men retired to enjoy their port over the sitting room fire. Donald gently introduced the subject of an assistant to his friend, Angela meanwhile dawdling over her duties in the kitchen. It was also an opportunity to commence a letter to Judith. After some time she judged it was about right to take in the coffee and she placed it in front of the men in the sitting room. George addressed her. "You've been exercising your little grey cells on my behalf, Angela, so Donald tells me. He has put an interesting idea into my head. I must think it over for a couple of days. I'll tell you at the weekend what I think about it. Anyway thank you for being so concerned."

"We're rather fond of you, George, and we think you deserve some help to ease your responsibilities during your later years in G.P. Young Gordon has worked hard at his hospital jobs and would be a real help to you. You could teach him a lot, so it would certainly be to his advantage as well."

"Thank you, Angela. I will look into it carefully, and I'm very grateful to you both".

. And the conversation moved on to the eternally prickly subject of medical politics.

After another hour of discussion and argument that even politicians would have admired, both men began to yawn. It had been a busy day. Angela rose to fetch George's coat and 'Goodnights' were said sleepily. After George had gone Donald rose and stretched, his wife telling him to get off to bed while she finished her letter.

While general practice for Donald occupied his days with the bronchitis of his patients during the dull dark days of November, Judith found herself busy in persuading her little lambkin that new feeds were just as nice as her accustomed ones. One morning Judith, having heard from Angela about her idea, was opening the mail, and found a letter from their fellow G.P. Dr. George wrote,

"I have thought around all the pros and cons of the idea about Gordon as an assistant to me during the next three years and have decided firmly in favour of it. I am sure it would give me a lot of relief, and I hope that it could prove advantageous to your husband. If you would like to sound him out on the matter and tell me what he feels I would then be very pleased to write to him with an offer."

Cuddling little Jilly in one arm and waving the letter happily with the other hand Judith burst excitedly into her father's study saying, "Daddy, old Dr. George agrees to Angela's idea. Isn't that wonderful? It will be a marvellous chance for Gordon to get to grips with general practice, because George is quite highly regarded in the profession. I'll ring Gordon as soon as I can find out when he will be off duty and able to talk."

Two hours elapsed before she could make contact with Gordon. During that time he had been busily engaged in theatre work with his surgeon who was endeavouring to recreate a useful bone when a compound fracture of a femur had resulted from an horrific motor accident during heavy rain. There was the business of stainless steel screws and other inserts to ensure healing of the bone in a reasonably straight line and the use of antibiotics in the wound to prevent infection. Gordon certainly learnt much about repair work. Would he really take to such tasks himself? It gave him much to think about. Removing his mask, gown and boots he retired to the doctors' mess for a cuppa. Shortly the phone rang, answered by another young colleague.

"It's for you Gordon," said the latter

"Hallo, oh hallo Darling, how lovely to hear you. What's the news? How is our little cherub?"

The reply came in no uncertain terms that left him gasping in astonishment.

. "Good gracious", he said. "That means I could go straight from here to a G.P. job all laid on; and be able to live at home. That sounds marvellous. I think I had already reached the conclusion that G.P. is my best bet. I have a weekend off here so I'll join you for breakfast tomorrow."

"That will be quite delightful, Darling. You'll be in time to deal with nappy palaver while I get off to work. You are clever! Anyway I'll fix an appointment with George, probably at coffee time when he has finished morning surgery. Jilly's calling so bye-bye for now."

Gordon could not refrain from enthusing over his stroke of good fortune with a couple of other men in the mess, who congratulated him on such good luck Then came the morning outpatients session with the registrar in command. Later, after lunch he would check on duty times and do a ward round with the consultant. Somewhere in his schedule there might be time to pack a bag and check on petrol and water and brake-fluid in the car, remembering that he was also on duty for calls that night. Such was the life of a young medico during his early years in hospital.

At 6a.m. next morning night duty operating theatre staff was busy. The Sister picked up the phone.

"Page Dr. Jenkins please." she said. Gordon, about to pick up his bag and make for the car, replied. "This is theatre." said Sister. "The registrar is asking for you to assist at an accident case, as soon as possible please." Gordon sighed. "I'm on my way." he said.

At 8a.m. he rang his wife to tell her that he would be late for the nappy session. "Sorry, and all that Darling, but I'm afraid she will need your attention this time."

"Pig", said his wife. Gordon grinned and once again picked up his bag.

Morning traffic was quite ferocious that day but he succeeded in reaching the manse in time for a very late breakfast, kindly cooked for him by Mary. He greeted his sleepy daughter and John who came from the study to talk while he ate and relayed a message from George that the doctor would be very pleased to see him at about 11.45.a.m. At that hour precisely Gordon rang the bell of the doctor's house.

They greeted each other politely, George hoping that his visitor was not too tired after his busy theatre session and hectic drive. He added that he sometimes did an anaesthetic session for a dentist on a Saturday morning, and there was a case to be dealt with that morning. Would Gordon like to attend and view the procedure? The invitation was accepted with pleasure. 'More grist to the mill' thought Gordon. The dentist's surgery was five miles away in a little village that morning, and the two men were able to chat usefully during the drive.

The dental surgery was set back from the road amidst a charming arrangement of small bushes and cherry trees that flowered beautifully in the spring but whose leaves were now falling, leaving bare branches with the building outlined behind them. The place was well lit and looked welcoming. The dental surgeon gripped Gordon's hand with strong slim fingers and welcomed him gladly telling George, "We have two sufferers for today and all is ready for the fray, so out with your needles and let's have a go".

The dentist's chair was occupied by a nervous lady patient with the nicely attired receptionist gently holding her hand. George took charge and prepared rapidly. He greeted the patient and soothed her fears, enquiring about her health and asking permission to listen to her heart. The surgeon assured him that her health record was satisfactory. "I always like to listen myself", George told

Gordon. Satisfied, he took the patient's hand and, telling her not to worry about a thing, gently pushed the little needle of his syringe into a vein in the arm. "Just count for me, dear, please", he said. The lady's voice tailed off after the count of four. The doctor looked at the operator, nodding. The latter grasped his murderous forceps and began to extract teeth, one after another. .

The operation finished, and the new teeth happily fitting into her mouth, the lady, awake and mumbling her thanks, was assisted back to the waiting room.

"So that's what it's all about, Gordon." said George. "If it's all right with our forceps wizard would you like to perform on the next patient?" The dentist assenting, Gordon accepted the challenge, hoping that he wouldn't disgrace himself. All went well and he felt that he had been given a very pleasant introduction to the assistantship that he had already decided to accept if offered. During the drive George told him that he had written an invitation to him, offering him the position, but now that Gordon had arrived he could save the stamp and deliver it in person. On the drive back the acceptance was also delivered in person and George stopped the car and offered his hand. Gordon gripped the offered hand sealing the bargain.

"It's all settled, Darling", said Gordon flinging his arms round his wife who met him excitedly at the door. "I've quite decided now. I'm going to be a G.P. and live at home with you and our little sweetie."

"That will be wonderful. What a relief to think somebody else can attend to the nappy business sometimes. Thank you my valiant knight. I shall have to learn to cook lots of new dishes on the Aga."

"We haven't got an Aga." replied her husband. "Yet", said his wife, with a meaningful look in her eye.

John and Mary emerged from the study where she had been typing out John's new sermon intended for enlivening his parishioners next morning.

"How did you get on," said John. "Did you take to the doctor and assist the dentist to draw teeth?" When Gordon replied that everything had gone well, Judith added excitedly, "And he's going to become a G.P. and stay at home and wash nappies."

"Don't be too sure about that," said Mary. "His job may conflict with such an entrancing idea. Conveniently for him sometimes I guess. Anyway we thought you two might like to have the day off and we'll look after Jilly. Away you go and enjoy yourselves. I might teach John how to wash nappies."

And off went the two lovebirds while John retreated to his study murmuring something about preparing the order of service. Mary shrugged resignedly and faced the kitchen with a pile of washing and a joint to pop into the oven. Very soon Gordon and Judith kissed their sleeping infant 'bye bye' and settled into the little car for a jaunt into the country, hoping to reach Stratford on Avon and find a meal and perhaps attend a performance of 'Hamlet' at the Theatre. All went well. They reached the famous old town and admired Shakespeare's house; joined numerous Americans for lunch in a pub and found good seats in the lovely new theatre. The afternoon matinee was a rendering of the Merchant of Venice so they cuddled closely together and listened to old Shylock soliloquising about 'Monies' and 'Venting Rheum upon my Beard'. Portia pronounced her dictum in no uncertain terms as usual and they came away feeling that the 'Quality of Mercy' had not been strained. The 'Gentle Rain from Heaven' was falling as they left the theatre but shelter was available in another charming old pub, where they absorbed more sustenance by candlelight ere taking to the road for a happy journey home. There all was peaceful with lights in the hall and kitchen where cocoa and biscuits awaited them. Jilly was obviously asleep in the grandparents' room. Her mum and dad settled into their bed for a loving end to an eventful day.

Returning next day to the big Sheffield hospital, Gordon realised that this might well be the last time he would need to bid farewell to his wife and baby girl. Just three weeks lay before him; then to the wider world of general practice. Life threatened him with experiences as yet unmet and far from the ordered ways of hospital regimentation. He must search and discover all he could about it.

*

"Time to titivate yourselves, girls, aren't you coming to the party?" Thus the Sister of Gordon's ward addressed her junior nurses off duty, reminding them that it was time to bid farewell to Dr. Jenkins. Gordon had become quite a hero among the staff, being quite a personable chap as well as a budding surgeon in the theatre. Having a wife and baby daughter and the fame of newspaper mention when he reduced a dislocation at the roadside all helped to identify him as a person of renown. Now that he had landed a job in G.P. even before his orthopaedic stint was finished he was marked out as being a doctor of note. All members of the nursing staff were determined to kiss him 'goodbye'.

So when Gordon entered the dining room for the evening meal, he found balloons and crackers with lovely girls all dolled out in party dresses and greeting him with merry shouts and a welter of kisses from those who could reach him amid the throng. To identify these fairy-like creatures when normally he only saw demure females in hospital uniform was quite beyond him. But he loved it even though sorry that Judith could not be there to share the fun. Sister and some of her staff had made special fare for the occasion. The residents had coughed up with bottles of cheap bubbly, and the consultant had condescended to come in and propose Gordon's health with a merry speech. Other speeches, witty and humorous added to the general hilarity. Somebody called "Speech from Gordon Jenkins", and the whole party broke into vigorous clamour demanding that Gordon respond.

He rose rather reluctantly, looked at the merry throng, loving the lot of them, and took a deep breath.

"Thank you everybody," he began. "I have had a wonderful six months, being looked after by such a delightful bevy of glamorous ladies. You have taught me lots of new tricks, not only medical. Thank you too to our Consultant for putting up with such a raw recruit and to you, Mr. Registrar for all the teaching that both of you have given me in the art of orthopaedics. I feel that I am now on the way to deserving the stethoscope that is the doctor's wand of office. Now it's off to the outer world of trying to solve patients' troubles, maybe, in general practice. Thank you again for all your help. Some day I'll come and tell you if I've made a fortune. It just remains to say a tearful farewell and assure you all of my very best wishes."

Gordon was cheered to the echo and as he finally rose to leave, the girls scrambled to kiss him goodbye, some, in their happiness, even wetting his face with affectionate tears. Dishevelled, and with tie awry Gordon staggered to his room and finished his packing. Quite exhausted he made it into bed and slept his last night, thankfully off duty The stint was over, but he had learnt a lot about the troubles that affected human anatomy with its bones and joints and the bits holding them together.

About to drive through the hospital gates next morning he waited while a couple of ambulances and a police car entered and drew up outside the A& E department. 'How nice that I'm off duty' he thought. But instead of treading on the accelerator he braked hard and stopped. He remembered that his replacement had not yet arrived at the hospital. He entered A&E to find a sorry collection of casualties, two of them looking serious. He found Sister and asked if they had enough medical staff to cope. If not perhaps he could help. Sister replied that she would be very thankful for help. Gordon parked his car out of the way and got down to work, asking that the hospital should ring his wife and explain why he would be late. It was well over two hours before he finally left the hospital gates and his vigorous orthopaedic job behind and thinking, 'can general practice really provide more excitements than that?'

Judith greeted him with fervent kisses. She said, "I rang Dr George and told him the score, and he replied, 'Good, that shows he's a real doctor. That's what we want in our profession'".

****

CHAPTER 16

A G.P. IN THE MAKING

THE BABY'S CRYING woke Gordon from a deep sleep following his busy day with travel and happy hours of talking with Judith. Beside him his sleeping wife stirred but did not show any desire to wake. 'Oh well, I'd better try to settle her', he thought. He rose quietly and lifted Jilly from her cot laying her against his shoulder and hoping that the relief of 'wind up' would occur to ease her internal economy. It didn't…More vigorous measures were needed. He found her bath and filled it with warm water from the tap. He removed her nappy, (clean, thank goodness) and laid the little poppet gently in the water. He was rewarded by a gurgle of delight. After laving the water over her tummy for some minutes while she kicked away with pleasure he finally found a warm towel and rescued the happy child for a drying session. There was a warm feed in a thermos and he settled down to give this to her. .'Better than sleeping medicine', he thought She was asleep in two minutes, laying her head on Gordon's shoulder. After returning the little lady to her cot her father slid into bed and quietly curved an arm around his wife.

"Jolly good, Darling" aid she. "What a clever boy you are".

"Good gracious, were you awake all the time?" he asked.

"Of course, you don't think I could sleep through that, do you?"

"Huh. Trying to teach me the art of general practice, were you?"

"Well, practice anyway. What about a cup of tea? It's all ready in that other thermos". Gordon grumbled but hopped out of bed and obliged, taking a cup to his wife who put an arm around his neck and kissed him saying, "That's a nice hubby. Do it again sometime. I've been missing out on this while you've had nurses holding your hands". The 'nice hubby' responded with a less sleepy hug and both soon roused into a long needed loving session with a midnight passion that surprised both of them. Afterwards sleepiness readily stole over them as they subsided into each other's arms.

Judith woke him late with a cup of tea, telling him that Dr. George had said he would not be needed until Monday. "Mary says she will do nursemaid today if we would like a day together. So what about having another day at Stratford?"

"Marvellous. And do I get morning tea in bed every day in G.P.?"

"No, you do not. Your breakfast will be on the table in ten minutes. Rise and shine."

Gordon said "Humph", andswallowed his cooling tea while applying the razor to his stubble. "OK Darling, Stratford it shall be," he said.

The Americans had left two seats in the front row of the theatre and Gordon and Judith cuddled into them and enjoyed Shakespeare's Macbeth with its 'Out out Damned Spot' and 'Great Birnam wood to high Dunsinane hill'. Later a candlelight dinner in a cosy café rounded off their day and Judith fell asleep during the drive home. Her husband felt very satisfied thinking that if this was a foretaste of general practice it was going to be a little bit of heaven.

It wasn't a foretaste and heaven would be something attained only after much drudgery. He discovered that later. One morning a pair of miners from far-away Yorkshire waited impatiently in his surgery.

"Orl roight Bert. Wot yer goin' to tell 'im then?"

"Mm well, Kevin, Ah thowt ah'd do a moan about me bad back. It's worked before. an 'e's a new boy, ain't 'e?"

"E'd soon scupper that one. E'd drop a pun note on the floor an tha'd bend dawn an pick it oop. Bang goes tha' certificate. Ah'm goin' ter tell 'im ah've got the diarrhoea. There's nowt 'e can do abaht that. Tha'd better think again".

Thus went the conversation in the doctor's waiting room on the first day of Gordon's installation in his little consulting room. It would be quite a while before he discovered the various tricks that 'patients' got up to in order to oblige doctors to sign for them certificates of incapacity. He found eventually that Doncaster Races and Cardiff Arms Park with Wimbledon in the summer and Murrayfield for those of the Scottish persuasion were all occasions when he should be wary of 'note' seekers. Fans of such sporting regions could present themselves in small droves besieging the surgery. Genuine sufferers tended to be crowded out. Gordon learnt slowly, with some annoyance naturally, that there was more to G.P.

than met the eye and was glad of advice given by his senior colleague. After morning surgeries ended they were able to spend a little time together with a coffee and talk over the subtleties and workings of their chosen profession. These were valuable sessions. Often patients and their symptoms were discussed and many difficult diagnostic points were made clear. Gordon felt glad indeed that he was able to learn from such a knowledgeable man, long versed in the business of medical practice, often involving the matter of sorting out the sick from the not-so-sick.

A couple of months passed while the young doctor was slowly introduced by his patients to the quirks of the practice and the mental diversification of his patients. Many were the eye openers for him. From the squalling infant with its tummy full of wind and the helpless young mother unable to understand that the child needed raising up vertically to obtain relief, to the midlife man or woman with problems peculiar to middle age, and the ancient old chap hobbling with two sticks to the shops, he gradually came to realise what life was all about. He would never cease to learn, by day when the geography of the district teased his mind, and during night calls when, with a night's sleep ruined, he needed to make a diagnosis between a gall-bladder colic and a severe blockage of a coronary artery. In the first instance there would be recourse to his medical bag while the second demanded both instant pain relief and a highly urgent phone call to the nearest ambulance, probably also an equally urgent conversation with the doctor on call in the hospital. It was useful, he found, that the hospital staff knew him to be a man who would not waste their time and energies.

Gordon had found his tiny consulting room was part of a building purposely built next to his colleague's house. There was a waiting room with reasonably easy chairs having a receptionist's desk and rotating drums of patients' records efficiently positioned. Two doors led from the waiting room directly to the two consulting rooms so that there was little time lost between the exit of one patient and the entry of the next.

A small laboratory between the two surgery rooms provided facilities for the testing of urine and blood specimens, while blood pressures and antenatal assessments could also be properly conducted. For more advanced investigations such as radiography or heart monitoring with electrocardiography the services of the hospital outpatient staff were needed away back in the 50-60s. Should the doctor feel that urgent help from a consultant was desirable it was possible to arrange a domiciliary visit from the desired expert at the patient's home, usually with the G.P. also in attendance. The consultant's services would be paid for by the N,H.S. Prescriptions were written in the patient's presence and instructions given verbally. Taken straight to the chemist there was little delay ere the needed medicine was dispensed. But of course the fifties, sixties, seventies and eighties have passed into history. Computers have supplanted old fashioned notions. Expensive pills replace cheap lotions. Opinions regarding such benefits vary.

Gordon's mind got a distinct impression that some people were devising symptoms in order to meet and assess the new doctor. Little could be done about it and only satisfaction with that doctor's approach to his patients and adequate attention to their complaints, whether real or imaginary, would eventually produce satisfaction on both sides. All these matters were gradually assimilated by Gordon, as well as the complicated business of finding patients' homes in the mysterious back streets of the area. A detailed street map was useful and the advice of George was found very helpful on many occasions. One of his problems was the provision of a medical bag that would contain emergency drugs and injections adequate for treating serious emergencies that might crop up. Again George proved most helpful. One item that was probably an unusual inhabitant of a doctor's bag was the provision of a couple of bottles of plasma; just in case an accident presented with blood loss needing rapid fluid replacement. A giving set, all sterilised and ready for use was included. The time would perhaps come when Gordon and his patient would be thankful for that thoughtful addition to a G.P.'s armamentarium.

Transport for himself must be efficient and without breakdown. It must be reliable day and night. Here arose the question of whether his little car could be regarded as fit for the job. Consultation with his father and George brought matters to a head and Gordon decided that he should contemplate a change to a larger run-of-the-mill motor car. Serious talks with Judith and reading of adverts and consultations with 'Which' magazine in the local library enabled them to make a choice. One morning he collected a year old used model of a well-known marque from the garage, providing much satisfaction for them all.

"But what bout your precious Princess, Gordon? Are you trading that in?" Gordon's eyes twinkled as he replied,

"All three of my Princesses are precious, Darling. The one with wheels is for your own use. Have fun!"

Judith's face was radiant as she flung her arms around her spouse and thanked him with kisses galore.

It remained for Gordon to establish himself as a good doctor among the general practitioners of the district. Such could only be done by genuine hard work and to this he applied himself by day, evening and night. Between practice sessions he managed to squeeze in happy times for family life, when not interrupted by emergencies. Judith and their baby girl were of the utmost importance and it was not easy to ensure that they received proper attention when the affairs of practice made conflicting demands.

Judith meanwhile was daily discovering how to manage her baby's affairs along with her own to fit smoothly into Gordon's preoccupation with his medical work. She came to realise that while it was one thing to look after a small child with her husband far away in his own sphere, it was a very different matter when they were together, somehow adjusting to the practice demands, the baby's requirements, and needs of husband and wife. Add to that the complication of her work at the Antique business, now that she had commenced her secretarial job again, and her brain was often in a whirl trying to cope with the unending demands and duties that landed in her lap.

However manage she did by resolutely timing herself to fit baby's feeds, husband's needs, shopping requirements, and household arrangements in a proper order of importance. It was fortunate that Mary was so willing to co-operate and was extremely efficient in household management, enabling Judith to devote the necessary attention to other demands made upon her by her employer and the staff at her workplace. It was not easy. The medical call before breakfast demanding an urgent visit to a patient's home before morning surgery, the late call after evening surgery when some man, returning from work, found his wife in trouble and rang up frantically saying 'I don't like the look of her', all needed care and consideration even with a baby howling in her arms. Many times Judith found the more orderly matters of the office and her typewriter to be a relaxation from the hectic life of a G.P.'s wife.

Health wise the pair managed well, each trying to ensure a good spot of exercise during the day. Gordon would often leave his car some distance from a patient's house, if there was time, to give himself a quick walk, while Judith would get off her bus well before it reached her work place for the same reason. At weekends when off duty they would usually find a country walk most enjoyable, taking a picnic to sustain themselves and of course very adequate feedstuffs for their small poppet. A Saturday afternoon might find them setting forth for the nearest zoo, hoping to entertain their infant with the vision of exotic creatures other than the cats and dogs that had become familiar to her. They were rather tickled to observe that the mighty trunk of an elephant or the huge fangs of a multi-striped tiger marching around his cage were far less of an interest than the chirpy little sparrows that hopped around their picnic table pecking away at crumbs dropped for them. Jilly would watch them lovingly, clapping her hands and squealing with delight when one hopped onto the table, quite unafraid, and flew off with a larger piece of bread to demolish it at leisure. Great fun, far better that the mighty beasts of Africa, the gorillas of the Congo or the crocodiles of the Zambesi. Mum and Dad learnt something too. What, not 'tiger, tiger, burning bight in the forests of the night', --no. no, rather 'little sparrow hopping sweetly, picking breadcrumbs up so neatly.' And the small girlie was quite entranced.

So the days and weeks passed, speeding into months. By the time her first birthday arrived general practice had provided Gordon with a good dose of reality, coping with the lives of ordinary folk in their daily round of health and illnesses, while Judith massaged her many duties into good order, admittedly with the invaluable help of Mary, and had also been taught more of the antique business by her employer. She had travelled with him again to Venice, to Prague, and to Florence, on each occasion finding more and more of interest to make her an ever more valuable ally in the now flourishing business.

Fortunately their days were not entirely working stints. True, Gordon did most of the night work while George often employed a locum to take night calls for him. Alternate weekends off helped, and then there were holidays. They took a week each at Easter and arranged for two weeks holiday in the summer, trying to avoid the school holidays. For the first year or two they remained at home making excursions to nearby beauty spots; this was easier than taking a baby off to the coast with all the hassle of its feeds, nappies and so forth. But occasionally they would arrange a couple of nights away, perhaps at Llandudno or maybe on the Gower coast where the lovely beaches are washed by water from a branch of the Gulf Stream that raised its temperature slightly. Little Jilly was encouraged to enter the water and splash happily in the tiny waves or try swimming with arm bands for support in the deep pools left by the receding tide.. Gordon and Judith would lie on beach towels and watch the gulls riding high against the wind, their outstretched wings balancing them with precision, floating with no discernable movement of their feathers or, twitching a feather or two, they would turn and, borne with wind behind them, streak with tremendous speed down the length of the beach and around the headland. Watching those masters of the air in their effortless flight brought them endless interest; they could watch for hours, but squeaks of joy from their little one as she found a new shell or a crab's claw or a defunct starfish would bring them back solidly to earth. On the beach the kiddie found plenty of entertainment and for parental exercise what better than to have Dad demonstrate his ability to build a bigger sandcastle than their neighbour's. A picnic and a shady snooze for Jilly under their large sun umbrella would be followed later by tea and bath time and bed with a made-up-bedtime-story from Daddy while his beloved prepared a nutritious supper. Then would come a quiet relaxing evening, perhaps with a book and a cosy night for parents as they cuddled closely and cast off the burdens of responsibility. These simple things of life became wonderfully satisfactory, and if a landlady offered to baby-sit while they spent an evening at the theatre or in a cinema, holding hands, what could be better! Return to the more mundane things of life was always easier after shaking off dull care in a different setting. Holidays were precious, bringing lovely memories for the dull days of winter, as did photographs of their little girl as she planted a tiny sandcastle on top of her Daddy's big one, o'er topping it with a defunct starfish..

Thus year succeeded year. General practice became interesting, epidemics almost *a la carte*, child growth and development ordered by the book and injections for their little one properly observed. They considered that a mother's care and that of the father, when available, was of greater importance than pre-school attempted instruction and believed that parental teaching should if possible take precedence.

Jilly would be four years old ere she was introduced to the educational system. Her parents felt that she had benefited from home care, instruction and example, rather than from what she might have picked up during the kind of lessons that were the norm in infant school. Certainly she was becoming a well behaved and an intelligent child and was well loved by all. Opportunities for intercourse with children of her own age came as she met with the children of her parents' friends in their various social contacts that were frequently arranged by the mums and dads. They learnt to behave nicely, disagree without fighting overmuch and to enjoy fun together. Gordon and Judith considered that their little one was progressing well and felt very satisfied. However it would be good to enjoy a proper holiday together before she began her schooling '

****

Chapter 17

FUN ON THE WAVES

A LARGE APPLE rustled through the leaves over Gordon's head and thudded onto the sun-baked ground behind their rented Roseland cottage. He looked up at the autumn harvest in the tree and wisely shifted his deck chair to a safer spot. Judith, his wife, emerged from the kitchen with their small girl of four years dancing happily beside her. Their summer holiday looked quite promising; it was going to be lovely she thought.

"Have a cup of coffee, Darling," she said, and placed it on the little table, gladly subsiding onto another chair beside him. While Jilly, their precious offspring, picked up the apple and inspected it, Gordon regarded his wife thoughtfully. After a while he said "How would you like to have a look at the sea, and perhaps venture onto it in a little boat? It's a lovely day. It's warm, slight breeze, calm sea, just the job perhaps?"

Judith considered. They had decided on a Cornish

holiday hoping for warmth and refreshing days with a sandy beach for their small poppet to make sandcastles, with coastal walks for themselves while a minder would care for their sleeping daughter. It was their summer holiday time and they'd rented a cottage in the Cornish village of Gerrans near Portscatho in the Roseland peninsula. The rear garden looked over green fields while the front of the house faced the road from which a branch led round Gerrans church and steeply down to the pretty harbour where small dinghies and motor boats made a lovely picture floating quietly on the sheltered water. Beyond, the curving skyline melded into the headlands on either side of a wide bay. It made a peaceful scene and one that they would come to love and value in future years. The idea of actually hopping into a small rocking boat and navigating over the waves in Cornish seas had never occurred to Judith. Cautiously she replied,

"Well, it sounds pretty adventurous. Where would we find calm water? Would we have a proper sailor on board or would we have to do all the work ourselves?"

"That's easy. I'm only thinking of a dinghy with an outboard motor and a pair of oars. All the work amounts to is pushing the boat into the water, stepping in, pushing off with a stroke or two of an oar and starting the outboard motor. I would only have to pull a string and the motor starts. If it has a gear you simply push the gear handle and off you go. Simple."

"How about the steering?" asked his wife, feeling only half convinced.

"That's very easy. The motor has a big handle and you steer by moving the handle just a bit one way or the other."

The discussion continued for a while, covering such things as when and where, whether they would really be on the sea or might it be on a lake or a river, and if they would need life jackets.

Their rented accommodation consisted of a double storey house on the one main road through the Gerrans village from which, as mentioned, a steep road led down to Portscatho. This was situated on the east coast of the Roseland peninsula- a triangle of land pointing across Carrick Rhodes towards Falmouth and separated from the mainland of the county by the river Fal. Another river, the Percuil, flowed down through the area towards the village of St Mawes, a well known beauty spot in that part of Cornwall. In that smaller river estuary and at the entrance to St. Mawes bay were moored a great variety of lovely yachts. From their gleaming sides the sunlight reflected radiantly; the tintinabulation of the halliards striking in the wind against their masts delighted the ears.

The rear aspect of the house faced west looking over a steep slope leading down to a creek, an offshoot of the river mentioned. It was not visible from the house on account of the thick bushes that grew in the fields below. From the rear garden could be seen the fields beyond the river rising to the skyline and dotted with white blobs that told of sheep while the larger brown ones were cows, all of which found plentiful grazing on the fertile expanse of grass.

Such was the charming view that Judith found most relaxing, but she realised that they could not stay around quietly in the garden all day. Some kind of exercise and adventure were essential components of a real holiday.

"Right ho" she said. "I'm game. Let's give it a go. I'll get some food ready." Suiting action to words she entered the kitchen and commenced preparations for a picnic. She buttered sandwiches, spread them with tinned salmon, added tomatoes and slapped all the provisions into a capacous basket. Her husband was left to capture the imagination of his lovely daughter with visions of life on the rolling waves.

When all was ready they drove off carrying light macs, towels and a basket of goodies. The road led back out of the village in an ever-decreasing width and they were lucky to scrape past without damage when meeting an oncoming van. Stones in the hedge could jut out sometimes with disastrous consequences. At crossroads they had the option of going forward, the long way round to St. Mawes, or taking a short cut to the left. There was a warning sign that indicated 6ft.6 in would be the minimum width to be encountered. Gordon took a deep breath and swung his wheel to the left. High banks with trees overhead created a welcome shade from the brilliant morning sun. At a sharp bend the road suddenly narrowed revealing between those high banks and lofty overhanging hedges a veritable 'tunnel of green gloom'. Gordon wisely blew his horn, proceeding cautiously. It was just as well for a large farm tractor emerged from the narrow entrance which had been enlarged since the erection of the notice. Both vehicles braked and Gordon was obliged to reverse until the tractor could pass safely. Then it was back to the dark narrow entrance where headlights revealed the sides of the road and warned any possible on-coming traffic of their presence. The green and gloomy passage was a small revelation of the charming and sometimes difficult passageways of Cornwall. They felt relieved when moving after 100 yards onto a wider section of road. Judith remembered the comments of some American friends who had found the area some years previously. They told her that they were both excited and terrified in that same gloomy tunnel, but so fascinated that they were obliged to return to their digs by the same route when evening created even more of a 'black hole'. The huge highways of the States were dull by comparison. Cornwall was frightening, but fun.

Another four miles, passing the attractive village of St. Just, and St Mawes came in sight. Suddenly there was a glimpse of water on their left between rather lovely private houses shaded by huge fir trees. A little further and, after passing several large pines that had survived a minor hurricane in previous years, the road ran along the frontage of St Mawes, providing a view of a wide beach and a great expanse of blue water that extended right and left. To the right were the houses, shops and hotels of the village, with houses that gleamed white in the sun, spreading far up the steep hillside. To the left the bay gave into the mouth of the Percuil River which rounded a small low headland jutting into the water. Many white painted yachts with tall masts were moored there creating a most lovely picture as they gleamed brilliantly in the sunshine. Behind the moored yachts they caught a glimpse of a small inlet. At its head stood an old building, Place Manor by name, with the ancient chapel of St Anthony closely attached to it. Henry the eighth was believed to have married one of his ill-fated wives within its aged walls. Before them, across a wide stretch of calm water bright in the morning sun, lay the quayside where the Falmouth ferry was discharging its passengers. A crowd of folk leaving St Mawes waited to board it for their ride across Carrick roads to that famous old town. The quay created something of a protected harbour for small boats of which several lay waiting for custom. Gordon stopped the car and they gazed in delight at the enchanting scene. Below the road a sandy beach extended on both sides, bordering the advancing tide.

"Just the place for a swim after the boating expedition"

said Judith, and so said Jilly and Gordon. The car moved on to find a vast car park in the village centre. Then with their little girlie they walked on towards the quay and found notice boards inviting hopeful sailors to risk life and limb in a small boat equipped with a little vibrating engine and sail romantically to the islands of the sea, or maybe just to Place Manor and the old church.

The owner quickly recognised novices to the water frolic and was disposed to be helpful in good Cornish fashion. He chose a well cared for dinghy, clean and fairly spacious and gave all the needful instruction about engine operation as well as advice regarding tides and the avoidance of larger vessels (of which there were very few anyway). The dinghy had an anchor and a good coil of rope in the prow with an outboard engine firmly fixed on the stern. Adults' and a child's life jackets were supplied, together with a whistle in case of difficulty. While the owner held the dinghy firmly the family stepped in, one by one, and seated themselves, Gordon beside the engine and Judith on the centre seat holding their darling daughter. Ensuring that they were seated properly to balance the dinghy well the owner, having instructed Gordon in the operation of the engine, then wished them 'happy sailing' and gently pushed the boat into deeper water.

The sun shone. The sky was blue. The breeze was gentle. The water hardly moved. The ferry had gone. The sea in the harbour was flat and no waves threatened. Gordon took a deep breath, checked that Judith was cuddling Jilly closely, and pulled the small rope attached to the outboard engine.

The little engine roared gently into life. Gordon pressed the gear handle into service. The dinghy responded. They moved forward while Judith placed one hand firmly on the gunwale and her husband held the steering handle, moving it slightly to and fro to test the steering response. He soon noticed that they were heading for the opposite shore and moved the handle appropriately. Over the flat water they proceeded and Gordon felt able to increase the speed a little. Moving towards a large yacht Gordon began to take steering seriously, heading away from it towards the open water of St. Mawes bay, with Falmouth in the far distance.

Judith noticed the change in direction and asked anxiously, "We're not going to Falmouth surely?" An immediate reply reassured her- "No my love, it's too far, and there's a big oil tanker in the way. Perhaps we might just move along the coast a little way. We'll keep close to the shore."

They continued out towards the point of land opposite the castle built to guard with its guns the port of St.Mawes and the waters of Carrick roads. They began to feel the lift of the rounded waves that were always present, even if very small and gentle.

"Nice, Mummy," .said Jilly as, settled on her mother's lap, she felt the quiet motion and rocked herself to and fro. Gordon noted her happy face saying firmly "We have a little girl, Judy, who is going to make a good sailor." Satisfaction produced smiles all round as Judith relaxed. The engine purred, the boat glided forwards over the little wavelets and Gordon changed his course to port, (left to the uninitiated) heading around the point of the bay towards St. Anthony's head with its lighthouse in the distance. Yachts and a merchant ship passed by well away on their starboard side, (right side of course) and on their port side a little foam broke white on the rocks while sunlight bathed the grassy shores behind them. A seagull wheeled overhead inspecting the family for possible food. Suddenly a dark smooth head popped out of the water thirty yards away, its big eyes watching them intently. It was spotted instantly by the wee girl who shouted "What's that Daddy?"

Gordon looked where she pointed, slowed his engine and put it out of gear. The boat stopped.

"Good gracious it must be a seal," he replied. ."Do you see it Judith?" Of course their daughter wanted to know all about seals and, with her father telling her quietly about them, it was some time ere they were able to move

on, the animal watching them, unafraid and curious. The minutes passed busily with question and answer, Jilly's parents trying to explain to her the difference between seals and fish. All the time they were approaching the lighthouse, but before reaching the rocks on which it stood a pleasant sandy beach appeared on their port side, and Gordon steered towards it.

"Just the place for a picnic, how about it Judith?"

"Lovely," she replied. "Sun, sand and sea. . What could be better?"

Gordon ran the dinghy peacefully into the shallow water of the shore and switched off the engine All hopped out, Jilly splashing delightedly in the tiny breaking wavelets and Judith lugging her basket of provender ashore while Gordon pulled up the engine to protect the propeller and took the anchor up the beach to dug it into the sand.

"It wouldn't do for the dinghy to sail off without us", he remarked. Above the high tide line they found a rock to lean against and relaxed on towels spread on the sand. Jilly collected her bucket and spade from her mother's basket and commenced to build a sandcastle in the damper sand nearer the water. It was time for lunch and then a snooze, maybe. When comfortably settled Judith brought out sandwiches and a flask of coffee. They finished with an apple and while each downed a cup of Decaf, they gave their little one a fruity drink to refresh her. She then returned to her self-imposed task of building the biggest castle she could manage. Her parents, having cleared up the picnic, lay in the sun, taking turns to cast an eye on their daughter. Off and on they snoozed, fed, warmed and happy.

Time passed. Suddenly there came a shriek,

"Mummy, the wave's drowning my castle. Come quick."

Jilly had been kneeling beside her fine creation, unmindful of the approaching tide behind her as she decorated the walls with little shells from the beach. A large merchant ship had passed going into Falmouth; the wave from its passing had broken on the shore swishing up water and foam to wet the little lady's legs and bottom while smashing over the castle and reducing it to sandy mush. Parents comforted her and promised to help build another above the reach of the tide. Daddy tried to explain about tides and the need to watch the sea's advance. "I should have told you, Darling," he said. "The sea comes in and out twice a day. Just now it's coming in so you have to watch how far it is coming. Anyway it's only water, you'll soon dry off."

Jilly was rubbed with a towel and told to race up the beach to help the drying off process. An enthusiastic red setter from a picnicking yacht party ran with her vigorously with Gordon and Judith joining the fun. They greeted the other folk, thanking them for the help of their dog that was ready for plenty more of such exertion and returned to build another castle. With the adults' help this was soon accomplished. Eventually after a further snooze and afternoon tea from Judith's basket it was time to pack up and sail back to base.

Rescue the anchor, pull the dinghy inshore, step on

board and push off. Pull the little rope and their motor purred into action again and took them safely back into the waters of St. Mawes bay. Jilly was asleep on her mother's lap by the time they rounded the harbour mole and returned the boat to its owner.

"Hope you all enjoyed your trip" said he, as Gordon paid the fee and expressed thanks for the lovely ride. . "It all went well." he said. "Our kiddie will make a good sailor. Maybe we'll want to try a yacht next time," added Gordon.

"I could fix that too sir, just let me know when you want to try. The weather is all right for the next few days. Here's my card with a phone number. Give me a ring and we'll have a chat about it". After the old salt had tied up with a bowline he offered a huge hand to his customer.

And with that the family boarded their car and made for home. Jilly with a substantial supper of scrambled egg and apple pie and cream subsided gladly into her little bed and slept. Parents put their feet up and after cooking and demolishing a good meal chose books from a selection in the handy shelves; not too long afterwards they closed their books to follow their little daughter into dreamland. The waves had done a good jo

*

Two days followed to give their little girl more fun on the beach. More castles were built, Moats were made around them, care being taken to ensure that the tide could just reach and fill the moats. Bridges were essential to satisfy Gordon's aspirations naturally, and pieces of driftwood proved adequate. Jilly danced and shrieked happily every time a small wave finally demolished the whole structures.

Paddling and bathing in the water when it had been warmed by the heated sand, was a necessary discipline followed by vigorous runs on the beach and picnics to follow. Judith, rather like the dear mother of 'Swiss Family Robinson', always seemed to have the necessary supplies in her capacious basket. How delightful it was to find the ice-cream man never far away with his useful van. Holidays were lovely and with such a charming little daughter both parents felt relaxed and refreshed as they returned for a while to their youth and made friends with her.

One afternoon Judith reminded her husband that his yachting trip needed attention. She knew that Gordon urgently needed a complete rest and change after his strenuous tasks in the hospital. She would ensure that his needs received priority.

"Yes indeed. I wonder how the Atlantic weather is progressing. Is this fine spell going to continue much longer? Have you heard any weather news, Darling?"

Judith cottoned on quickly to her husband's thoughts.

"Why don't you just phone that sailor man and ask him? Perhaps you could fix a sailing lesson while you're on the phone."

Gordon smiled at having his mind read and, producing the phone number from his breast pocket waved the little card happily, saying, "What an excellent idea, Darling".

He was soon in conversation with the marine expert and after learning that there were likely to be two more days suitable for amateur sailing sessions, he arranged a time next morning for them to be introduced to the mysteries of riding the waves in a sailing vessel. So there was a valuable evening spent with a Yachting magazine where a mariner of repute offered advice and hints for the novice.

The next morning dawned clear and bright with only a few pockets of mist that soon cleared away in the bright sun. Complete with necessary gear they proceeded to St Mawes to find Harry, the vessel's master and owner, ready and waiting. The same dinghy would take them to the 30 ft. yacht that lay at her mooring across the bay and they climbed aboard willingly. Harry soon had the motor purring and said he would explain a few things as they motored across.

He did. The yacht, he explained, is attached to a chain that goes down to a very heavy stone on the bottom of the river. The chain is attached to a large floating buoy and a branch of the chain has a loop which travels over the bows to slip over a large cleat on the foredeck. That branch is supported by a little buoy with a rope. That, when the boat is moored, sits on the foredeck and is thrown over into the water when the yacht is going to move away from the mooring. On returning after sailing the little buoy is picked up by its loop and the chain can then be pulled up and fastened.

On reaching the yacht Harry demonstrated the mooring arrangement and then moved to the stern to show the rudder and a ladder by which they could climb onto the boat. He tied the dinghy to cleats at each side of the transom and invited them to climb aboard. Gordon went first and assisted his wife and Jilly, settling them on cushioned seating in the cockpit.

Then the sailing instructions. Having taken Gordon down into the cabin and shown him the engine in its separate compartment, Harry demonstrated the controls situated near the steersman's position next to the tiller. There was a starter button and another to stop the motor.

The gear lever had a forward and reverse position. The accelerator was beside it.

"Use that gently," said Harry. He then invited Judith to enter the cabin by climbing down the 'companionway' and showed her the little stove, gas fired and with a button that lighted the gas very reliably first time. The kettle was supplied with drinking water from a tap over the sink. There were cupboards for food supplies and comfortable cushions on the seats. The latter were used as beds if the crew wished to remain overnight. Lights in the cabin were supplied with power from the big 12 volt batteries concealed beneath seats adjacent to the engine compartment. Four adults could sleep if required. A door led forward to the 'heads'. Here a useful toilet was situated with water flushing available controlled by a long handle. Above, in the roof, was a hinged skylight, well secured to keep everything preserved from spray coming over the bows. There was space for an anchor with plenty of rope in case of need. Back in the cabin Harry demonstrated a card table, also a clock, barometer, compass and thermometer. Maps of the locality were stowed away handily for use

"Now," said Harry, "let's talk about sailing because that is what you're here for, right?" Gordon and Judith nodded their heads, impressed by all the technology and not quite ready to speak.

Gordon did not intend to disclose that his father had instructed him in the sailing art. Judith said she felt quite dizzy after all the information, but there was more to come.

"OK. Here we go. A yacht is driven by wind blowing on sails. No wind, no go. No sails no go. There are different forms of rigging, i.e. different sails and different ways of arranging them. Here you have a mainsail, the big one at the back, and a jib sail, smaller in front. The mainsail is attached to the top of the mast and all the way down it to the boom; then along the boom to the far end. When the wind moves it you must mind your heads, the boom may swing across the boat, so - duck or grouse! The jib stretches from the masthead to the bows. Both are controlled by ropes which we call sheets. Got it? At present the mainsail is all tied up on the boom and the jib is wrapped around the forward stay. We can bring them into use later, but first we'll get used to moving on the engine and steering with the tiller.

"When the wind blows the ship leans over. That causes the ship's keel to push against the water, the other way. Water cannot be compressed so, in effect it pushes back. In order to escape these two forces the ship moves forward. As the forces continue the forward movement also continues until the skipper decides to steer out of the wind. Then the movement stops. Right? Both his scholars nodded again, Judith again feeling rather mystified. Life jackets were then donned on Harry's orders.

"I know, it's all a bit new," said Harry. "Let's get going. We'll start the engine; then throw off the little buoy and the loop of chain. We put the gear lever into forward and the propeller moves us forward. Then we have the business of steering with the tiller moving the rudder. That is different from the little engine on the dinghy with its handle but the effect is the same".

He pressed the start button. There was a rumble below the deck as the engine revved into life. Judith placed her arm protectively around the little girl who clapped her hands saying "What is it Mummy?"

"Now to work. May I use Christian names? Gordon will you kindly go forward and pull the chain loop off that big cleat on the deck. Throw it overboard along with the little buoy and its rope. Throw them under the guardrail please, the same way that the loop came in. I'll find a job for you, Judith, a bit later. Looking after Jilly is most important. If she wants to stand on the seat, please hold her firmly".

"Chain away," shouted Gordon and Harry looked all around to note any moving boats. None moved so he pushed the gear lever into the driving position. The engine note changed and the boat moved forward. Gordon returned to his seat and was promptly pressed into service.

"She's all yours, just take the tiller and practice steering. There's plenty of room in St Mawes bay and we are well away from other craft. The ferry has just gone. Keep over to the port side and you'll have no difficulty." He released the tiller to Gordon who gripped it tightly, looking round quickly to make sure of space around them.

The yacht moved along smoothly, gently rising and falling over the small undulations when little waves from a far-off merchant vessel reached her as she proceeded towards the point of the bay on the port side.

"Isn't she lovely?" said Gordon to his wife, smiling happily.

"Which she?" Judith enquired. "You've got three now".

"Hah," said Gordon. "I guess you'll all qualify."

Progressing round the point and keeping well clear of the rocks Gordon steered towards the St. Anthony's lighthouse, wave movement becoming more pronounced as he approached open water.

"What about a halt at that little cove this side of the lighthouse?" asked Judith

"Yes, all right." said Harry. "Judith will you go forward into the front compartment, grab the anchor and put it up on the foredeck. The lid over the loo is open I think. You might notice that the other end of the anchor rope is firmly attached to a hefty ring in that part of the boat. When we reach a nice position Gordon will stop the engine. The boat will slow down, 'lose way' we call it, and it will stop. Then I will throw the anchor over the side underneath the rail."

Judith managed very competently. Gordon stopped the engine at an appropriate spot. Harry threw over the anchor, and Judith quickly returned for their lovely daughter firmly to hold her Mummy's hand. Soon Gordon brought the dinghy, which they had towed behind them, to the stern of the yacht and tied its ropes to the stern cleats. Judith climbed down the short ladder first, and received from her husband the picnic basket and towels, not forgetting bucket and spade for Jilly. Gordon assisted his small daughter to climb down the little ladder to his wife's arms and he quickly followed. Harry said he would stay on board, ensure that the anchor was holding, eat his sandwiches and snooze while they disported themselves on the beach. When all were comfortably seated in the dinghy it simply remained to untie the ropes from the stern cleats on the yacht and take up the oars for the short row to the beach. After securing the little boat Gordon handed over the party, picnic and commissariat to his wife. He settled for a snooze on his towel, his back against the same rock.

Jilly took her bucket and spade and after making half a dozen little castles demanded her parents' assistance to make a 'really big one.' So Gordon was routed out and Judith covered her prepared lunch with a towel to join with him in busily digging up damp sand to construct the mightiest castle that Jilly had ever seen. The red setter was again in evidence and, after chasing all the gulls off the beach came to join the fun. Tiring of spade work Jilly was soon romping with her and raced her to the end of the beach where the other family were ensconced, enjoying a rest in the sunshine while their yacht lazily swung to and fro with the tide. Judith paddled along with Gordon to introduce themselves to the other party which consisted of a husband and his wife, Jeremy and April, with their eight-year-old son. The husband's widowed mother, Jessie, was also one of the party and was busily preparing lunch while the parents relaxed. Roger, their son, was happily practising swimming with his new flippers, racing back and forth to their boat, climbing aboard and diving off it to swim back to the shore. As much of this exercise was performed underwater, holding his breath, he hoped to beat his class mates in the long-dive competition at his school's water sports next term.

During conversation it soon transpired that the family lived near Swindon, not so many miles from their home. They all got on well together and, with their obvious delight in sailing, were not long in arranging not only to sail their yachts together, but, when at home, to visit and prolong their contact into more permanent friendship. After lunch at opposite ends of the beach the adults joined together to talk of mutual interests while Granny composed herself for a snooze under a large beach umbrella. Roger invited JIlly to join him for a little climb among the rocks investigating the denizens of the shaded pools, and off they went together, the youngster being adjured by his parents to take good care of the little girl and not to go out of sight.

Gordon discovered that Jeremy was on the staff of a pharmaceutical firm, so the two men were soon deep in discussion of the pros and cons of drugs of one sort or another. His wife, April, proved to be a teacher and interested in ancient history. The two women therefore found much in common, and talk would obviously go on round the clock. However Jilly came running along to interrupt with a bucket full of water wherein swam shrimps and tiny fish, minute crabs, and even a blenny filched from the rock pools that had absorbed her interest. She looked tired however, and was persuaded to opt for a little snooze near Granny, sharing the shade of the umbrella. A rolled up pullover was used for a pillow and she was soon fast asleep, leaving Roger free to continue his swimming or practise rowing in the other family's dinghy from the beach towards the lighthouse. Noting this, his father called him to return and keep nearer inshore

The two men gave up discussion of medical and pharmaceutical matters after a while, finding more relaxing the talk of sailing and all its ramifications. Jeremy naturally asked Gordon how long he had been a sailor. The latter was unwilling as yet to divulge his sailing sessions with his father so Jeremy, assuming this to be his first experience, began to help him with many useful points some of which, during his years of hospital work, Gordon had forgotten. They talked about the 'rules of the road,' particularly questions pertaining to methods of meeting and avoiding other boats. Harry, owner of Gordon's yacht, had already drawn his attention to this and Jeremy made sure that he understood the importance of his advice. He said, "It's like driving on the continent; you have to keep to the right, not the left. So if a boat is approaching you and you're on a collision course, you must turn right, not left, as in a car in our country. At the same time you must be aware that not all people at the helm of a yacht are aware of the rules, and if they make a mistake and turn left you will still be on a collision course. Then if you can you must turn strongly left to avoid them. If you are under sail there may not be time for that so just steer the boat right round and go back the way you've come. It's easier if your engine is doing the work of course."

"That sounds good sense", said Gordon. "Avoid damage first and argue afterwards if needs be."

"That's right," said his friend, and they continued to discuss points and questions raised by Gordon while walking to and fro along the little beach. The ladies made merry with lots of 'girl talk' finding a host of interests common to them both. April was quite envious of Judith's journeys to seek arty subjects in continental cities saying, "Majorca is the only place we've been to. We have bought a 'time-share' there, and feel we must get value from it so we return each year".

"Nice," said Judith. "You'll be sure of sunshine there".

"Well, not always you know," said April, "it can rain there too. But really we like the Cornish holiday better with the sailing and exercise. We always feel better for it and able to face the autumn gales and winter. We love it here. Do you think you'll come again?" Judith glanced away to where the two men were earnestly nattering about the fine points of sailing. "I think my Gordon is well hooked." she said, "I'm sure we shall be back."

****

CHAPTER 18

BACK TO THE JOB

RELAXING DAYS AND nights in their delightful Cornish village had given them refreshment of body and mind, but such enchantments could not long continue and the day came when, after packing up, the little family of three journeyed away from their charming *Shnagri-la* to return to their more mundane duties at home. They passed the great 'mountains of the moon' as some called the huge piles of whitish soil cleared away from St. Austell's china clay pits, and couldn't resist the desire to visit them. High up at the top of them they looked down to view the furious jets of water that washed out the white clay from far below. It settled into tanks, the white powder being later transferred to a special type of merchant boat designed for the purpose of conveying it far and wide to purchasers in our own land and in others who used it mostly to help in the manufacture of paper. Gordon remembered that it was also a constituent of a mixture used for tummy upsets with a small dose of morphine or codeine. China clay, or kaolin, was well known to the medical profession for absorbing the toxins produced by various germs. It was very useful material.

Proceeding further they came to grim old Bodmin moor with the dire prison that housed so many infamous and dangerous characters. The Princetown prison was known to them from the tale of Sherlock Holmes by A.J.Cronin. There are few who are ignorant of the story of the Baskerville hound of death baying in the night in the wilds of the moor; a bleak and desolate place in the dark days of winter. The Jamaica Inn, also widely famed in the annals of literature, appealed to them for sustenance. JIlly was glad of a rest from the car, enjoying a drink and a biscuit while parents indulged in quoting to each other grim and age-old tales of the moor culled from memories of school books when they read by torchlight under the bedclothes, avidly turning the pages when they should have been asleep..

They dragged themselves away from the huge empty hills surmounted by craggy tors and, after crossing the River Tamar, said 'goodbye' to Cornwall and began to savour the lovely green fields and wooded landscape of 'glorious Devon'. The road was faster now and full of traffic returning, like them, from holidays. They had also used up journey time and, when nearing the Glastonbury region decided that a B&B for the night would help to ease the journey and give them a chance next day to enjoy the shaded lanes and lush hedges of Somerset. Leaving the motorway they found a room in a guesthouse at the top of a hill in Street, vowing to visit the well-known Clarks' shoe-making-factory and sample its offerings. The old Abbey on Glastonbury Tor was a 'must' of course and thither, after a late meal in a café, they bent their steps.

Wandering around the ruins old stories again came to mind as did memories of the devastation wrought by King Henry when he caused the destruction of so many fine churches throughout the land.

"What a foolish man he was" said Judith. "He thought he was displaying his power when all the time he was simply destroying because his mind was too weak to appreciate goodness when it was practised in front of him."

"How do you make that out?" said Gordon. "Surely he possessed the power and authority to banish the influence of the church at that time when he believed it was evil."

"But the gospel of love that was preached by the church has lasted and grown while the power of Henry's armed men has caused only trouble and destruction. It is not force that is powerful, Gordon, it is the power of loving-kindness. Wasn't it the monks who started the hospitals, and everything that has grown from that kind of work? So I believe strongly that force is simply an excuse for weakness. It is used instead of good plain commonsense. Isn't there a saying, 'Derbyshire born and Derbyshire bred, strong in the arm and weak in the head?' Force is very often an excuse for weakness of intellect and laziness of mind; people who should know better taking a sword or gun when they should be talking and persuading and offering help and friendship. Daddy has rather a good sermon on that subject. Apologies to Derbyshire of course".

Thinking carefully Gordon felt that he should admit that she was right.

The guesthouse was at the top of the hill in Street, far removed from the smell of the leather preparation in the village. Now a youth hostel, it was then situated in a splendid position overlooking the area of Sedgemoor where was fought the 'last battle on English soil', so it was said. After a pleasant meal they left their lovely daughter in the care of the housekeeper and walked along the country lanes to experience the quality of the Somerset countryside, the peace and the quiet after miles of noisy traffic and fume filled air. As dusk fell Judith perceived a tiny light in the hedgerow and bent to examine it. The light was promptly extinguished.

"Did you see it, Gordon? It's a glow-worm. I haven't seen one for years. Probably the insecticides used by farmers has killed them off. Pity".

"What's a glow-worm anyway?"

"You poor uneducated chap. It's a beetle. The light is used by the female beetle to attract her mate".

"Now I know where you get it from. You certainly light up at times".

Judith blushed in the darkness of the evening, and put her arms around his neck, whispering, "It must be infectious, my Pet.". And the evening and the morning led to another day.

The well sprung beds of the country guest house had provided a good night's sleep and Jilly bounced into their room in the morning radiating happiness. She had already been in the garden with their hostess and they had gathered around the 'butterfly tree' revelling in the beauty of the peacock, red admiral and tortoiseshell butterflies that were sipping nectar from the luxuriant flowers of the buddleia. She jumped onto their bed describing joyfully those lovely little creatures that she now called her friends. They were 'having their breakfast' she said, and would soon be 'spreading their wings and sunbathing'. Parents commented as they dressed on the charming way in which her mental development was advancing

Rather sadly they left the loveliness of flowers and field

and hedgerow to hit the motorway for home. They noted Weston-super-Mare to the west on their map, skirted Bristol to join the M4 traffic as Gordon pointed the car's nose towards Swindon and Oxenby.

"Back to people's miseries." said Gordon.

"Return to mysterious icons." replied his wife.

But despite the prospect of work awaiting them both felt refreshed and full of energy for facing any interesting experiences or frantic emergencies in the coming months. Eventually they stopped at the gates of the manse.

Jilly jumped from the car and rushed into Mary's arms on arrival and Judith was hugged happily by her father. After a quick unpacking and phoning his father, Gordon decided to give George a ring and announce that he was back. George was obviously tired and glad to know of his assistant's return.

"I'm extremely glad to hear that you're back," he said, "especially because there is a maternity case in the offing. Just your cup of tea old chap, can you cope, do you think?"

'Was this the first emergency?' Gordon thought. He could only say that he would be pleased to take up the cudgels and get stuck in. This was general practice and he had set his hand to the plough. He helped himself to a hurried cup of tea and found his 'midwifery bag' in the cupboard under the stairs, (his normal bag was always in the car) he checked that the car was all unloaded and bade his family 'goodbye, see you sometime'.

Within only seconds following his arrival at the house of the 'case' he realised that an emergency was indeed threatening. The midwife attending the woman hurried to meet him in the kitchen, telling him "I am most concerned at the amount of haemorrhage. The baby arrived alright and seems quite healthy, but I don't think that the placenta is quite complete." Gordon took a quick look at it and agreed. After assessing the patient's condition he said,

"I think this is something we have to settle here and now. No waiting for an ambulance. If I start the anaesthetic can you continue it while I collect the remaining piece of placenta?"

"Yes, I think so, but what about the hospital, doctor?"

"No time for such luxury. We must cope with this right away."

Arrangements were rapidly made, with explanations to patient and the anxious husband. Very soon Gordon had put her under the anaesthetic and handed the mask over to the midwife while he dinned sterile gloves and proceeded to 'collect' the offending and reluctant piece of afterbirth whose continued presence in the womb was causing the bleeding. It didn't take long and the operator was thankful for the experience he had obtained in the maternity department of the hospital.

"Right, Sister, off with the mask please". As he felt the patient's pulse again, he was immediately more concerned. It was more rapid than ever and could hardly be felt at the wrist. He quickly filled a syringe and administered a dose of ergometrine, at the same time rubbing the uterine swelling to stimulate contractions that would stop the bleeding. Then, opening his bag, he told the midwife,

"This is the time to bring out that plasma that I have long carried in my bag for just such an emergency.". The giving set emerged as well and plasma and set were quickly connected, the needle inserted into a vein in the arm, not without difficulty owing to the low blood pressure, and the infusion begun with drops merging together at first into a steady stream. The patient's knees were drawn up and pushed towards her tummy to further help in raising the blood pressure. After some time the breathing gradually eased and a faint pulse could be felt at the wrist. Later the patient's eyes opened. The rate of drops was slowed a little. The woman's conscious thought began to take over and she moved her head and asked haltingly, "Where's my baby, is he all right?"

"Here he is, darling, he's fine" said the midwife, taking the child from the patient's mother who had been anxious to help. "Can I give him to her, doctor?"

"Yes, I think so; it will help to encourage uterine contractions and will certainly be a very useful comfort to her."

The baby was carefully given to the mother, placing him on her chest where she held him as well as she could. Gradually strength seemed to return to her and the attendants' began to relax. "That's lovely," said the midwife. "Cuddle him close, my dear." Weakly the young mother responded and managed a little smile.

The drip of plasma was reaching the end of the bottle and Gordon, assessing matters, thought that more might well be helpful. He waited for the right moment and swiftly changed bottles. Then leaving her for a minute, he went outside to where the anxious husband was pacing to and fro and gave him the good news that his wife was much improved and he could come in and see her for a minute or two as soon as the midwife had everything ready. Most expeditiously the bed was dealt with, the baby bathed and wrapped up suitably and the young father invited to come in and see his wife. He hesitantly entered the room, stood aghast for a moment or two at the sight of the drip bottle and tubing, and then went to greet and kiss his wife, murmuring words of encouragement. He was persuaded to hold his baby and very gently picked up the tiny morsel from his wife's arms.

"Cuddle him tight," said the midwife, "and be careful, don't drop him"

*

A successful confinement is always a happy occasion for the medical attendants and Gordon entered his surgery next morning, after his holiday, feeling joyful and ready for everything that could be thrown at him Perhaps the first greeting came from his colleague who entered, clapped Gordon on his shoulder and congratulated him on a job well done. He said, "News travels fast around here. The townsfolk are all agog to see the new doctor who has brought up-to-date-hospital-medicine to the back streets of their town. Be prepared to blush becomingly, laddie, you're quite a hero."

By coffee time with morning surgery over, Gordon was a little red in the face and glad to escape from the good wishes of the patients, many of whom were well informed about the event of the previous evening. George was well into his second cup of coffee and remarked that his morning surgery had been nice and quiet for a change, with everyone wanting to see the new doctor. He handed Gordon the list of morning visits, commenting, "You're going to have a busy day; I hope your new found energy will last out". Indeed by the end of the day, after being called out of evening surgery to relieve an asthmatic of her breathing difficulty, he felt that being a hero was not all that might be desired. It was a pleasure to return home and find his little girl waiting for her bedtime story, so he continued the adventures of John and Mary while Judith prepared his favourite macaroni and cheese with apricots and Cornish cream to follow.

"You're an important member of the hierarchy in this town now", said his wife "I've been getting greetings from all and sundry in the store this morning. I hope it won't go to your head. Will you still be the gentle medical genius prepared to comfort a tiny child and whisper encouragement to an anxious mum and dad?"

There was a pause, then Gordon said "I think I can take it with a pinch of salt, Darling girl. I'm only glad that it all went well and the lady has recovered nicely. We've got to get her blood back to normal now. I shall be just as keen to learn more about George's practice and patients. I'm sure he'll continue to educate me."

Much of the evening was spent discussing the coming days of their small daughter, now four years old with the school year fast approaching. They both felt that the time spent at home under parental and grandparents' influence had been most valuable for her, but it was now time to introduce her to the regime of school with its contacts with other children and the influence of teachers. Judith would enquire about the best way to find out all she could about the local infant school and when to make the approach to the Head teacher. She would start tomorrow while Gordon was in surgery. There were still a few days before she would return to her secretarial work. She sighed. Life was going to change.

*

"What's the matter, little boy?" Jilly had emerged from the morning lesson into the playground nibbling her small sweet cake and instantly recognised the distress of the child, not much smaller than herself, who had tucked himself away in a corner and was sobbing bitterly. While all the others were playing tag or catch or some such he was quite alone and obviously needed comfort. Jilly, always alert to a soul in trouble, had threaded her way between the noisy, rushing crowd of kids and stood beside him, taking his hand. "What's your name?" she asked. "Mine is Jilly. I've got an extra cake in my paper bag, here, would you like it? "

The little chap stopped crying and mopped his eyes. Dressed nicely with a blue and pink tie neatly tied at the neck of an immaculate white shirt and with polished shoes, short grey trousers, and knee length stockings, he politely thanked Jilly for the cake. . "My name's Ronald," he said. "My Mummy calls me Ronnie, and she's gone away and nobody wants me to play with them." And he began to cry again.

"Oh, but she'll be coming to collect you after school, won't she? " Jilly said.

"No, only an old granny, and I don't think she likes me anyway. Mummy and Daddy have gone off on holiday."

The little girl felt unable to cope with this and produced a large soft ball from her school bag. "Let's have a game," she said, and very soon throwing, catching, running and jumping with happy laughter were replacing the tears of the morning break. It was the beginning of a friendship that would last for years.

Judith had taken her daughter to interview the teacher of the infant school and felt happy to have Jilly accepted into what appeared to be a well-organised institution with kindly, sympathetic staff. She was sure that the child would be happy there and so it proved. Judith could take her to the school and Mary would go and check on her after the morning session. Later would come an afternoon session following lunch at school and a rest period. Judith was satisfied that she could resume her job with no worries about her little girl.

Even on her first morning at the school her daughter had begun to make her presence felt in comforting the lonely child. . Judith heard about that episode from Jilly later; and she felt both happy and proud of their small darling.

The antique business continued to provide satisfaction from the customers and good relations amongst the staff. Judith's father-in-law had again planned an expedition, and once again she was pressed into service as a most competent assistant when she and Gerald flew off, this time to Athens on another icon–hunting tour of the city. He understood that it was unlikely that the Greek authorities would be willing to allow their old treasures to leave the country, but at least it served as a little holiday and an opportunity to view the old temples and other priceless assets from classical times. Judith greatly appreciated the opportunity to further expand her education in those matters. Gordon would cope with the family having the help of their baby sitter who had agreed to camp in their spare room for the few nights while Judith was away.

Thus several future years of the family's progress were assured. Gordon was well settled into general practice. Judith also was very satisfied in her quite important work for his father's business, and their adored girlie seemed to be nicely adjusted to the beginning of the years of education. Relations with John and Mary were on a firm footing and they could so continue until the day of George's retirement, when Gordon would then be well qualified to find a good opening in his future life as a general practitioner.

How to record the intervening time between Jilly's

starting at infant school and her upgrading to the junior school branch of education? Most importantly the record should first take cognisance of a conversation between husband and wife one evening in the autumn term. Gordon was talking of his day's work with his patient contacts and doing a gentle moan concerning the vagaries of general practice.

"Anyway, Darling, that's enough about my bothers and my patients' complaints; how have you been doing in the antique trade and how will the next two years turn out while my colleague completes his forty years?"

Judith took a little time to consider. She then spoke about her job in the office, her employer's vigorous essays into finding more and more valuable articles to appeal to collectors, and the occasional squabbles among the staff that were hers to manage, smooth over and deal with in a satisfactory manner for all concerned. She paused; then she said, "Our little girl seems to be enjoying her time in the infant school and is very happy playing with other kids. Wouldn't it be fun for her to have a little sister of her own to play with? What name would we give to a sister for Jilly? How about Jemima?"

"Puddleduck, you mean of course. Anyway that idea is not in our sights at present".

"Well, no celebrations at the moment certainly", said Judith slowly, "but would you be interested in a little lady called Grace, say, in about seven months time?"

"Have you been visiting an Adoption Society or something?"

Suddenly Gordon sat up straight and looked seriously at his wife. "Judith have you been holding out on me? Do you mean we might have one of our own?" And he jumped up and put his arms tenderly around her. She nodded, clasping him around the neck and hugging tightly.

"I've only just found out. I went to see our doctor this afternoon. Are you pleased?"

"My Darling Girl, that's wonderful. You know I'll be absolutely delighted".

And for a while speech was quite superfluous. Hugging was all. Breathing was in abeyance until Judith reminded her excited husband -

"I have two to breathe for now, Darling, let's sit down and talk it over". The talking and discussion continued for the rest of the evening until bed called and they could unwind in each other's arms. Life, they agreed, was marvellous.

The weeks and months that followed passed in joyous expectation. John and Mary were informed and knitting began in earnest with the two ladies happily clicking their needles every evening. Gordon informed his father and Gerald ensured that there was no undue strain put upon Judith, doing some of the secretarial work himself so that it was not necessary for her to take work home.

Half term with its little holiday brought further happiness with Jilly to share the family doings and the November fireworks were celebrated as usual. Jilly's eyes sparkled to the bright explosions in the dark sky; the usual garden bonfire and hot sausages and ginger drinks all added to more adventures of the dark nights of coming yuletide. Again came the annual fun of Christmas shopping, the decorations, the cards and letters, the tree and dear little silver and golden balls; tiny bells tinkled when its branches were touched and sharp needles pricked bare toes on the carpet; the carols and girls and boys singing at the door, the ginger drinks and Christmas cake to encourage them. At the church the crib and candles, the plays and the wise men kneeling; the happy greetings, the party at home with crackers, the plum pudding and the digging for shiny sixpences, not forgetting the watching for Santa Claus. It was a magical time to bring fun and happiness to Jilly and all her family. 'Why can't it continue all the year' was the thought in Judith's mind; she would write to the papers about such an idea. But the age-old gladness quickly passed giving way to the New Year with its chills, colds and coughs and long frosty nights. What a pity, thought Judith, that the fun of Christmas parties should be so often followed by the attacks of viruses distributed in the course of such happy times. Doctors should do something about it, as she told Gordon in no uncertain terms. He just acquiesced. What advantage was there in arguing with a woman whose mind was already made up?

All this time her pregnancy continued as planned, her girth increasing steadily, accompanied by a feeling of great wellbeing. Was it true that the immune system acquires a boost during the months of pregnancy? Certainly Judith suffered no ill effects from contacts with all the respiratory troubles of her family and neighbours, and at her doctor's appointments she was declared normal in all respects. The midwife hung her gold wedding ring on a length of cotton and it swung round over Judith's bulging tummy to reveal that a girl was on the way. A 50% chance of being right was always good odds anyway. Jilly learnt all about the expected arrival of a baby for her to play with and demanded a go with the stethoscope to hear the foetal heart in her mummy's tummy. Her excitement quite infected the rest of the family and even grandpa lent his ear, when not attuned to his typing, to listen to the faint *lubb-dupp* that penetrated the muscular walls of the womb and the anatomical layers of Judith's abdominal wall

Jilly was entranced and poured out questions that were sometimes rather embarrassing to answer. How to tell a small child where 'it' came from, or how did 'it' get there stumped them all. They hurriedly found some other attraction to divert her mind, a game of Happy Family or Rummy perhaps?

The weeks rolled on, a bag was packed and in due course a hurried chase to the hospital maternity department resulted in the entry to this world of a charming curly-topped baby girl; a little poppet eager to join in the business of sucking anything in front of her and holding tightly to offered fingers, as is the wont of babies everywhere.

Judith made a rapid recovery, imbued with the wonderful maternal joy of a mother for the second time. She loved the delicious feel of the child at her breast and was thrilled again as she watched her husband's face as he too felt the wonder of new parenthood.

Jilly rejoiced in her baby sister and soon grasped her name. Grace 2 and Grace 3 became the names of her dollies, and she was often at hand to entertain and comfort the baby when her mother was busy, or, later, back at work. What fun she found it to hold her in her arms and even push the pram when walking with Judith in the park. She learnt how to pick up the baby safely, how to assist in bathing her, testing the water temperature and, later, when breast feeding had finished, how to help in making up feeds and offer the bottle to her little sister. The business of 'winding' the child wasn't forgotten either. Needless to say the wonder of breast-feeding was an eye opener to Jilly and she wanted to know if milk from the bottle was the same. There were plenty of questions and parents' brains were teased often.

As for Gordon, he was 'over the moon' and thrilled to see his baby girl, pick her up and 'wind' her, hurrying home from evening surgery to oversee bathing sessions and bedtime palaver. When doing his rounds he would make a point of passing his house as often as possible to drop in and admire his new treasure. The amazing advent of new life was always a little bit of heaven.

*

The months and a couple of years went by with new experiences being absorbed into their routines; the coping with colds and chicken pox, the injections to avoid the horror of measles, whooping cough, diphtheria and tetanus, all were normal parts of life and taken in their stride. Other concerns such as the approaching junior school for Jilly and the ending of Gordon's five-year stint with his .colleague were now on the horizon. Why five years? Well George had felt so much relieved by the help from his colleague that he had decided to continue two more years. It would all help his pension income..

*

George retired in June with a farewell party given in hiss honour when Gordon was also thanked amidst the jubilation of celebrating the many years spent by George in caring for the health of his patients. Presents and good wishes for George abounded. He found it most embarrassing to bid a somewhat sad 'Goodbye' to all the staff who so kindly wished him well. He fought to control his emotions.

Concluding his 'Thank you' speech he said, "I want to make it clear that my patients will now be under the medical care of Dr. Collins and his partner. With this conclusion to my practise of medicine in the town and district I can now be very happy. I can put my feet up and cease to overload a physique that for some time has been under considerable strain; a strain that has been much relieved by taking Dr. Jenkins into the practice as an assistant. Now of course his employment will terminate and he will be free to seek other work. So to you, Gordon, my sincere thanks for all your valuable help over the last few years and, to all of you dear colleagues and friends, my thanks and loving good wishes for your future prosperity".

Dr.Collins then made a farewell speech to his friend, quoting and lauding his faithful work along with the many improvements that he had delivered in the practise of medicine in the district. He ended, "Dr George we all desire that you should know of our very deep appreciation of all your wonderful service to the people of this town and district. But we remember that behind a successful man there is usually a fine supporting woman. To you Geraldine we offer the thanks of the community for all your wonderful support in your husbands work among the people of this town.

As we bid you 'goodbye' we wish you and your dear wife a long, happy and healthy retirement". The company rose to applaud loudly and long in recognition of their appreciation of Dr. George.

Then Dr. Collins had a surprise to deliver; two surprises in fact. After a short consultation with his colleague he saw no reason to withhold the good news and would do so now in public. He rose and said, "I have something of interest to announce to Dr. Jenkins who has so admirably supported Dr. George for the past years. You are now out of a job, Gordon. But do not be dismayed. Doctor King in a town nearby is in need of a locum while he takes a very much-needed holiday. He talked to me about his problem and wishes to offer you the position of holiday locum in his practice for the month while he is absent. I hope that the idea may be acceptable to you".

Gordon rose to his feet feeling quite overwhelmed. He replied, "That's wonderful, sir, I feel that it is most acceptable and I am sure that Judith will be very pleased too. Thank you very much for your help".

"That's just what I wanted to hear", said Dr. Collins. . "I have something else for you to consider. My partner and I have been discussing for several months the future of our practice. It will now be a good deal larger. We have decided to offer to you, after your locum finishes, the post of assistantship with view to partnership in our practice. Now this is something that you will need to consider carefully, and not feel pressed to make a decision about it. Certainly not until you have completed the locum job with Dr. King. During the coming weeks you may find something that appeals to you more and the whole matter will require much discussion with your wife and family, so do not respond to this offer at present. It is something that you will have behind you for the future".

Again Gordon rose to stand, rather shakily, uncertain what to say. But speak he must. He said, "That is very, very kind of you, sir. It is a marvellous offer and I don't know what to say. I shall have to think about it very seriously and talk it over with Judith and the family. Thank you most awfully".

"That is the right response," said Dr. Collins. "Now, before you all begin to dance the 'Gay Gordons,' may I suggest we conclude this happy party with singing for George the song he so well deserves, 'For he's a jolly good fellow, and so say all of us'".

And having made the rafters ring with their salutation the nurses and female staff of George's practice gathered round him and smothered him with hugs and kisses. They loved him, and, as the fiddlers fiddled vigorously, they gathered him happily into the Gay Gordons dance. The men swung their ladies around almost off their feet; then stood still, tapping with one foot as the music changed. The ladies, reaching up to entwine fingers, twirled around, twinkle-toed,, swirling their lovely floral skirts with gay abandon as the fiddlers played the dear old songs of Scotland. At long last, exhausted, as also were the fiddlers, all formed a big circle holding hands, ending the evening with a happy rendering of 'Auld Lang Syne'. It was the end of an era, an era of devoted service by a dedicated doctor. It was the beginning of service by a young doctor whose devotion would be tested time after time during the years to come.

****

PART 2

Chapter 1

MUDLARK

"Good gracious Darling Jilly, whatever have you been up t o? You're all covered in mud, and who is this poor little fellow?" Judith exclaimed in horror and astonishment as she surveyed her six year old daughter approaching, leading a little chap of four years who clung tightly to her hand. Tears were trickling down his cheeks. Both were dripping wet, with tousled hair sadly muddied, as were their faces and hands. Clothes were similarly garnished and knees, legs and feet were plastered with quantities of wet mud. Their sandals were missing. The children had obviously come across the field adjacent to the back garden of the house.

"His name's Tommy, Mummy. He'd fallen in the big pond and couldn't get out so I jumped in and rescued him. It was awfully wet and muddy."

"That was very brave of you.my treasure. Anyway strip off those wet clothes and come for a nice warm bath. Good job it's a warm day. What pond anyhow? First a good bath and later you can tell me all about it."

Having disposed of their clothes in the washing machine she led the way upstairs and turned on the bath taps.

"Mummy, what's that funny thing that David's got?" inquired Jilly, pointing to the nether regions of the small boy. "Oh that's easy" said her mother. "That's what makes a boy a boy. When he wants to do a wee he just stands at the toilet and the water comes out of it. Neat isn't it. Girls have to push panties down and sit. Boys just undo the zip."

"That's real cute, wish I was a boy," Jilly commented. So both hopped into the bath and enjoyed the warmth and the generous soapy bubbles. Later came the warm towels and fresh clothes.

"Tommy, I'm sorry I haven't any boys' shirts and trousers". 'Yet'- she added to herself with a glimmer of a blush. "You'll have to make do with panties and a dress, OK? By the way where do you live, Tommy? Because we must tell your mummy that you are here. I expect she will be very anxious."

The little chap took Judith's hand, led her to a window and pointed to the house next door. It was a little distance away due to the size of the huge gardens. Judith further inquired regarding the mother's surname and looked up the telephone number. She promptly dialled the number and a short conversation ensued with a woman's frantic voice at the other end becoming relieved and most grateful for the kind services rendered by her new neighbour. Return of the straying truant was soon arranged with his rescuer and her mother being invited to tea. Judith wrote a note for her husband explaining their absence, picked up her two year old, Grace, and off they went.

Meanwhile another little drama was occurring.. Further down river from the site of the accident / rescue an angler had established his perch and was still waiting for a bite. He noticed two pairs of children's sandals slowly floating towards his line. They were within reach of his fishing net and very quickly he secured them both. Then he began to wonder how they had been lost. There was certainly no sign of drowned bodies in the water so he walked slowly along the bank of the river, (for that was the real nature of Jilly's 'pond') and discovered the place where plainly someone had stumbled at the edge of the bank. There the edge had given way and he could see where slithering down the bank had occurred. A few yards further down river beside a fallen tree there was a place where obviously traces of a scramble up the bank were visible. . It had left signs of muddy handholds on a branch and footmarks sliding and digging into the steep river bank. From the size of the shoes he knew that two children had been involved. They had clearly escaped from a dangerous situation. There was no indication of where they might have gone. He quickly put two and two together and realised that a useful rescue had taken place, with an older child plucking a younger one from a probably tragic end.

There were at least two fields between his site and the nearest houses of the village. He concluded that his best course would be to pack up the fishing expedition and take the nice leather sandals to the village shop. There the owners would be likely to call and would be able to identify their property. So this he did

The shop was almost a mini-supermarket, supplying most articles needed for the ordinary use of the local folk besides functioning as a sub-post office, and was presided over by a matronly, bosomy lady with a merry smile and a twinkle in her eyes. The angler had known and admired her for years and related to her the circumstances of his find. "Well, just fancy", said the lady. "I will see that the story gets around and I'll ensure that these sandals are treated and polished for the owners. My young assistant would love to do a tidy job on them I am quite sure. She is quite a competent girl. Did you catch any fish?" she added. The contact developed into a pleasant chat with the angler inviting the shopkeeper to an evening dinner and seats at the theatre where 'My Fair Lady' was on show for the umpteenth time in Oxenby. Might some romantic attachment one day be the sequel for these two, - the lady widowed for seven years and the fisherman a bachelor, perhaps both willing to change their lonesome existence? Time alone would tell.

*

The tea party was going well, with Judith getting to know her neighbour, named Sally, who had been resident there for some ten years. "My husband is a bank manager in the town" said Sally, "and we have an older boy of eight years named Jason as well as Tommy. Both attend local schools nearby, and I drive them there each morning". The village atmosphere and that at the schools was quite lovely, Sally told her visitor. She hoped that Judith and her family would be happy among them.

Explanations were due, Judith saying," My husband is a doctor considering the offer of an assistantship with a view to partnership in a practice in Oxenby.. He is a named Gordon, trained in Edinburgh with four hospital jobs to his credit and now feels that general practice will be best suited to him. The practice where he has been working has been joined to another practice following the retirement of its elderly doctor. Gordon has been offered an assistantship with view to partnership in the combined practice. Meanwhile he's working as a locum here for Dr. King who's on holiday, while thinking it over. We have taken the house next door pending the outcome of this arrangement. We like it very much here and as the house is up for sale and only a few miles from the town, perhaps we could be your new neighbours, Sally".

The two women rose and stood together looking out of the rear window over the fields. They were uncut meadows and lit by the afternoon sun shining on long grasses intermingled with a charming variety of colourful flowers. "It really is lovely," said Judith, "and with a nice pond over there my husband would delight in investigating pond life. He is something of a naturalist, you see."

"Pond?" said Sally. "That's no pond my dear, that's a big river!" Judith's eyes and mouth opened wide and she sagged at the knees. Sally caught her and hastily sat her in the nearest chair. Judith put her hand to her mouth saying faintly, "Oh, my God".

"Yes indeed", said Sally. "They had a very narrow escape. Your little girl deserves a medal. It was extremely brave of her. I had been calling Tommy for a long time. He usually goes and curls up in the summerhouse, but I never thought he would go off all the way to the river, over two long fields. That's something to watch out for in future. I love the sight of Tommy in a girl's outfit. That makes me wonder a bit… At that moment the bell rang.

"Shall I answer it?" said Jilly. "I think it might be Daddy. I can see his car in our drive". Off she went, without waiting for a reply, her sister Grace following faithfully.

"Hallo Daddy, we're having a party," she cried, as

her father took her hand and picked up little Grace for a cuddle.

"Good afternoon doctor, welcome to the feast, and how do you do?" said Sally with a delightful smile. "Judith and I are just indulging in girl chat; I guess you get a lot of that."

"All the time," he replied. "The local ladies were unloading their moans and groans on me all morning. And my name is Gordon," he added. I got Judith's note and thought it was a good opportunity to meet the neighbours as well as fortifying myself with a cuppa before evening surgery. Hallo, Judy, Darling. You look rather pale. Is something the matter?"

Judith told him in no uncertain terms. Gordon's attitude changed instantly and, putting down Grace, he sat beside his wife with an arm around her, feeling her pulse. He was relieved to find it steady and of good volume.

"Well, no wonder you felt faint. We'll have to think about that river. I knew there was one somewhere near but didn't think it was quite so close. Anyway you are all right now and we can talk later. Thank you for the cuppa, Sally. I have had a call to see someone in the village shop before surgery, so I must move along very shortly if you'll excuse me."

Sally gave him a warm invitation to come and talk to her husband, Roland, saying that the latter would be free the next evening. He had a Rotary meeting this evening. Gordon thanked her and said that he would be very pleased to meet her husband. Then he gave his daughters each a kiss and a cuddle and said he would tell them a bedtime story when surgery was finished. He added that Jilly was a wonderful girl and he was very proud of her. While donning his coat preparatory to leaving, Sally's young son, Jason, entered. A fair-haired youngster of eight years, he was introduced by his mother and politely suffered a kiss on both cheeks from Judith followed by a solemn handshake with Gordon. He then said "Excuse me," and vanished quickly towards the kitchen. Judith helped Sally to prepare an evening meal and shared it with the children, including the eight year old who had kindly detached himself from his friends to come and say 'Hallo' to Jilly. Computer games were not really Jason's favourites so they unearthed the old-fashioned 'Snakes and Ladders' and all enjoyed the fun, even Grace and Tommy happily shaking the dice and turning them out, until the younger boy confessed to feeling tired. He'd had a stressful day

At the shop Gordon found himself again the object of female curiosity, but managed to identify the sandals after suffering a long account of an impending tragedy, narrowly averted. He took and promised to restore the sandals to their owners, then retreating to his evening surgery.

He pressed the bell and the first patient came in. It was late before he finished. A crowd of folk were avid to see the new doctor, and he just had to be polite and satisfy their desires. On reaching home his little girls were sleepy and Jilly said the story would keep until tomorrow. She contented herself with holding her Daddy's hand and very soon she joined Grace in dreamland.

At last Judith and Gordon could unburden their souls to each other her, and he poured a couple of glasses of red wine to help them relax after the day's events. They discussed the news, the village and, of course, their new neighbours. After a while Gordon said to his wife,

"What was all that faintness about, Judy? I know it must have been a bit of a shock to hear abut the river, but you don't shock easily, so why? "

She thought for a few seconds and then said, "Did you like those little boys, Jason and Tommy, Gordon?"

"Certainly, lovely little chaps. Why?"

"Would you like a little boy of your own then?"

"Judith! You know I would. Wait a bit. What do you mean?"

"Well, I seem to have missed a couple…."

"Darling! My Precious! Judy! Do you really mean we might have…?"

And there was much passionate embracing and kissing. The clock stood still. When at last they had time to think again Gordon declared, "Tomorrow I'll go straight down to town and buy two pairs of boys' trousers."

Said his wife,"I saw a baby-shop in town. I looked yesterday. They have a good stock of nappies; first things first my Darling".

****

CHAPTER 2

A HAPPY DAY

THE MORNING PORRIDGE was thick and glutinous. Gordon congratulated his wife, enquiring how she managed it.

"Oh" said she, "I think this Aga is wonderful. I just popped a cup of oats into a saucepan last night, with salt and water naturally, and slung it into the bottom oven and this is the result.

"Marvellous. Vantage number one for staying on here, - if I'm given the chance of course." Her husband finished his plateful and gulped down his morning tea while fondling his two year old playing on a rug on the kitchen floor. Jilly had already gone to school with Sally and Jason.

"Darling," said his wife. "I heard you answering the phone a few minutes ago. Was it something…?"

"Yes I'm afraid so; needs a visit before surgery, so I'll defer my toast until later." Saying which he collected gloves and stethoscope, coat and car keys, kissed his concerned wife and vanished towards the garage. As he opened the door Judith answered another phone call. "Gordon," she shouted, the receptionist says that it's Mrs Bledstone with another acute asthma attack, so take your medical bleeper." He acknowledged, slammed that useful instrument onto the car roof, where it adhered by means of a powerful magnet, switched it on and made haste with headlights blazing and horn sounding when needed.

Other vehicles gave way appropriately and in three quick minutes he braked to a stop outside his patient's well-remembered house. Medical case in hand he rapidly rushed upstairs and found the poor lady in the throes of a nasty attack, able to breathe air in but having extreme difficulty in expelling it. He quickly opened the case and took from it a sterile syringe and an ampoule of the old fashioned aminophylline, thinking how good it was to have no vicious little Jack Russell dog guarding his mistress with bared fangs and furious bark – as was the custom with another similar case. Here he could quietly locate a vein in the arm and slowly, very, very slowly, inject the drug that would ease the tight bronchial muscles to bring breathing back to normal. Gradually relief ensued and his patient began to breathe normally. She expressed her thanks to her doctor for yet another life-saving venture. He issued instructions, hoping that she would now be able to get some refreshing sleep and took his leave. The return journey was by a more circuitous route, avoiding the traffic build-up on the more direct main road, and, reaching home, he indulged in a marmalade sandwich and another cup of tea ere facing the oncoming battle of the morning surgery.

Sitting in his consulting room he pressed the bell. He was prepared for the scrimshanking work-shy types who wanted notes to enable them to attend their favourite football match and had developed tricks to catch them out. To the genuine folk with real problems he had time to listen, examine, search records and ensure, as far as possible, that adequate treatment was offered. For any who plainly required specialist care he would use the telephone to make sure of the earliest appointment available. If that needed a little extra time, well, the patient's life was in the balance. It was time well spent, he considered.

So the morning surgery proceeded apace. Occasionally some light relief was interspersed among the tally of sore throats and backache problems when one or two sporting types discovered that Gordon was a keen follower of rugby and football struggles, both amateur and professional. Invitations to be introduced to the local clubs resulted and even a keen racing dog owner tried to entertain his doctor with accounts of the local races on a nearby racetrack. He was however pleased to accept the invitation of a coal mine official to take a voyage down to the bottom of a coal mine and see for himself the conditions of work that enhanced the morning surgery's appointment list with genuine grumblers.

Coffee time came at last with the cheerful voice of the receptionist announcing;

"That's it, time to put your feet up with a cuppa. And here's a dose of the visiting list to encourage you."

This was a welcome break when Gordon and his employing G.P., now returned from holiday, spent a few minutes reviving themselves and divided the list of home visits between them. They would sometimes discuss, briefly, the local work situation with its quota of troubles, strikes and dole queues. A map of the area had been supplied to Gordon for ease of finding roads and patients' houses, and, armed with this, and recovered from the long stint in the consulting room, he would set forth on a round of home visiting, with all the problems involved. In this exercise a big concern was to discover new addresses in extensive new housing schemes where no map had yet been issued. To find a house and especially to find his way out of the estate could be a problem. The sight of a lorry delivering supplies would be welcome and the driver would usually be helpful.

"Lost, are yer, mate? I'm moving out in a minute. Just you follow me and we'll have you out of this maze in no time."

That could be a godsend that would bring Gordon back home in time for a late lunch. His wife never worried. He always made it, eventually.

"Come on, Darling. It's keeping hot in the Aga. Sit down and make yourself at home, at last."

"Thank you my Pet. I've just a couple of phone calls to the hospital to make, and then I'll be with you."

And so the day continued with the rest of the visits and evening surgery to complete his schedule. Finally at home and putting his feet up with a welcome cuppa he could relax as Judith reminded him,

"You have another call to make, Gordon. Our neighbours, Roland and Sally, have invited us to dine with them this evening. That should be good fun."

"Oh how very kind. I'd forgotten. That's lovely. It will certainly be nice to make their better acquaintance. Meantime a wee snooze should revive me."

Judith found her elder daughter in their dining room, busily engaged with some homework problems. An offer of help was declined so she began to prepare for the evening's entertainment. The telephone rang and Judith picked it up holding Grace with her other hand.

"Hallo, it's Sally. Look, we have an excellent baby-sitter. I wonder if you would let Jilly and Grace sleep here in a spare bed while we hit the high spots this evening. Georgina is the lady's name and I know she would be delighted to arrange bath and bed for your little charmers, if you and she agree. What do you think?"

"That sounds a wonderful idea." Judith replied. "We could bring them in the car and pick them up with it afterwards. They wouldn't even wake up. They are pretty sound sleepers. Thank you for the thought. See you soon."

Jilly, consulted, agreed with enthusiasm and later when dressing for the occasion Gordon was told of the arrangement and agreed also. In due course they all drove around to their neighbour's house, rang the bell and were happily received. The baby-sitter had arrived and was found to be most agreeable and appeared most competent. The girls soon made friends with her.

"My husband is longing to meet you." Sally now told them and led the way to the lounge where a tall, well muscled man with an open face, well tanned by the summer sun, rose to greet them.

Judith offered her cheek to his kiss and Gordon found his handshake firm and most friendly.

"Welcome to this haven for odd bods," said Roland. "Sally tells me that you will be our port of call for medical emergencies. We'll hope not to meet too often at that port".

"That sounds good to me," replied the young doctor. "In return I trust that you won't need to call me in too often to chase me about the overdraft. My last bank manager sent me letters of protest if I strayed over the very minute limit set by his bank. He wanted to know how many private school fees I had to cope with. He even conceded a small, rather smug comment, saying, 'Of course you have to live too, haven't you?'"

On that basis they soon discovered points of contact and felt that companionship could easily lead to a pleasant and lasting friendship. Roland guided them to his car and drove them to a pleasant restaurant a few miles out into the country. It was approached through an avenue of tall elm trees, still free from the prevalent disease that affected the species. The car slowed and quietened, allowing the soft cooing of doves to sound a welcome as they moved forward between the trees. The restaurant stood alone surrounded by a small host of cherry trees that, with large grassy lawns on front and sides, provided a lovely ambience for the imposing building with its generous covering of Virginia creeper..

"It's an old manor house." remarked their host. "The upper two stories provide excellent accommodation for guests wishing to spend weekends or more in a peaceful retreat. You'll find its service within matches the fine appearance of the exterior. It has some dubious reputation of having sheltered the Young Pretender at one time, although nothing is certain about that. However it really is quite good. We have our Rotary meetings here. Are you a member by any chance?"

"No, I haven't progressed to that illustrious height as yet," replied Gordon. "Whether membership would go with general practice I'm not at all sure."

Discussion of that subject was inconclusive so they all settled with drinks and began to search out each other's favourite occupations apart from their professional lives. The ladies quickly found points of common interest and chatted happily, laughing and giggling as they touched on their earlier years of girlhood and student fun. Gordon mentioned that he was something of a naturalist in spare time with interests in insect and bird life. He had roamed the fields and glens of Scotland and even climbed the sombre mountains of Skye to seek out the habitat of the golden eagle. Now however, having noted that the river passed through the nearby town, he wondered whether some kind of watery frolic might become a future pastime.

"Now that is interesting indeed," said his companion. "I should tell you that fun on the water has been the mainstay of my existence for years. I keep a motorboat on the river, moored to a jetty near the town and we often detach ourselves from the hurly burly of business life to spend afternoons or even weekends meandering up and down the river. A rod and line is relaxing too even though the fish are not too keen. What about you and Judith joining us one Saturday? I know a good pub near the river bank a few miles upstream."

"That sounds quite delightful." replied Gordon. May I mention the idea to Judith? Perhaps I could bring my little net and add specimens to my home aquarium. Of course such future fun depends to a large extent on my employment which is not yet settled."

The waiter announced that their meal was ready and over general talk an outing was arranged for the following weekend. Naturally they assumed the acquiescence of their four children.

Gradually they discovered a host of other points of mutual likes or dislikes that could offer variegated colour to their lives.

. There was music, classical and even mildly modern if not too garish. Gilbert and Sullivan was a favourite for them all, but most of the 'rock and pop' with its noisy drumming they found unsuitable to their tastes. There was art, painting and sculpture by the great masters. They spoke of poetry and literature, mentioning the poets and writers both ancient and modern; of the philosophers and men of science, not omitting churchmen and folk both distinguished and humble who had added to the welfare and humane development of mankind. Time alone would limit their discussion Their final accolade went to Shakespeare and his wisdom. That they found fascinating and vowed to spend evenings together at the theatre during the winter. The talk went on and on.

Coffee was served outside after dinner. Occasionally a bat would flitter past, and a barn owl swooped over their heads on silent wing, just a faint gleam of white in the gloaming of a summer's eve. A short walk in the extensive grounds made a pleasant way to end the day. By then Gordon and Judith felt that a basis for an enduring friendship had been established, and the short drive home promised to be happy and satisfying. The offer of a 'nightcap' was declined since Gordon would be taking on night calls after midnight, so it simply remained to collect their sleepy daughters and, with many expressions of thanks, they said 'Goodnight' to their generous hosts and returned to their own comfortable abode next door..

After depositing Jilly and Grace in their cosy beds they chatted happily for half an hour, by which time Gordon judged it safe to make tracks for bed, hoping for a quiet night without emergencies to disturb the peace. They downed a mug of cocoa each as they slowly made their way upstairs. With an arm wrapped around his wife as they drowsily drifted off towards sleep Gordon yawned and quietly asked, "Judy, have you found out the probable date of our son's arrival, Darling?"

"Of course," was the sleepy reply; "I can still do arithmetic to the 11 plus standard, and," yawning, "I can still remember appropriate lines from dear old Shakespeare." She paused. "How would the 'Ides of March' suit you?" But answer came there none. Gordon had already slipped into dreamland.

*

Some days afterwards, evening surgery having been completed, the two doctors were relaxing over their coffee. Dr. King, Gordon's employer, cleared his throat and addressed his young colleague. --

"We doctors meet together monthly for a dinner and lecture on some abstruse subject and, of course, we discuss the state of medicine and our own positions in the N.H.S. I know that your old friend, Dr. Collins, who recommended me to offer you this locum job, has made an offer to you of an assistantship in his practice. He is a fine man and well worth joining. He also knows that I have been considering finding a young doctor to join me in the practice here. You have come here with excellent experience in hospital and in G.P. with Dr. George. His patients have got to know and like you and so have mine during these last few weeks. I'm aware that you wish to continue in general practice, so after some thought I have decided to offer you an assistantship with view to partnership. This places you in the enviable position of being able to choose between two offers. Be assured that either of us will be very pleased to have you to work with us, and you are entirely free to make a choice that is suitable to you and your family. Take a week or two to think it over. Your old doctor and I are good friends and neither of us will take it amiss when you accept one offer and decline the other. Now run away and talk to your wife about your success."

After Gordon had made a suitable reply to Dr. King's most interesting offer, he and Judith found a great deal to discuss when he reported to her the thrilling news of yet another offer. They spent an extremely happy and interesting evening. They discussed the options from many points of view and followed it all with a good night's sleep.

****

CHAPTER 3

SETTLING IN PEACEFULLY?

JUDITH WAS INDEED thrilled to learn of the new offer that Gordon had received. She began at once to set down on paper the pros and cons of each offer and had many of these ready to discuss with him when he returned home at the end of every busy day. He gladly accepted her efforts and congratulated her on the concise method of approaching the problem. Being what she was he could have expected nothing less. They both realised that there was a lot at stake and much thought and realism would be needed in coming to a decision.

Evenings and weekends were going to be busy. Consultations with John and Mary would be essential. So would arrange an interview with their bank manager. How nice that they had become friendly with one already.

"So let's examine the situation properly" said Judith, one evening.

"Yes, it's high time we made our minds up. There's a

lot at stake. To begin with you're pregnant. We've got to remember that."

"You can leave that out of it," she said. "I can have a baby anywhere and I shall always cope. If we're there we'd have Mary to help when needed; if here well, we have met a very good baby sitter".

"And what about schools, that's rather an important issue."

"Well we know about the infant school here. We have yet to enquire about the junior school. Sally says they are very happy with Jason's school."

"Your father seems quite content to have us in his domain, but one wonders whether he would prefer to remain on his own with Mary. Maybe it is time we left the nest and struck out on our own. We shouldn't live in their pockets too long."

"That is very true. Older people require freedom from howling kids. They are all right for a short time but however much grannies and grandpas say they love their young offspring such little bodies can be quite trying and older folk need freedom to do their own thing."

"We have made very nice friends in both areas of course. Here it's useful having a good relationship with the bank manager. They would introduce us to other folk. I feel sure we could make a very happy life here. It's a nice house too, and you've made friends with the Aga, my Darling. The porridge is always good."

"That's a great way of choosing where to establish a medical practice, I don't think. What about working with the other doctors?"

"I should get on well with our old doc and although I don't know his partner I feel sure we could rub along quite well. As for the doctor in this practice, well I have come to know him very well and I'm sure we should work successfully together."

"And, finally, what about the patients?" said Judith.

"I don't think we have any problem there. In Oxenby I have got to know many of them, either through the hospital work or in George's practice. We do well together. Working as a locum for a month has given me a fair knowledge of the folk here in Bifford."

They mulled over the problem for a couple of weeks, being careful to have discussions with John and Mary and not omitting a talk with Judith's old doctor who had made the first offer to Gordon. Banking was carefully discussed and a day on the river with Sally and Roland helped further to cement their friendship, and probably also to reach a decision. Gordon would accept the second offer from his new colleague, Dr. King in Bifford, and wrote a carefully worded latter of acceptance, appreciating his kindness. Another letter couched in similar terms, but declining his offer politely, went to Dr. Collins.

The work awaited them. Solicitors drew up a legal agreement. The house next to Sally and Roland was available. A mortgage was arranged. An interview with the head teacher of the junior school was satisfactory and packing began,

The moving day came. A Friday saw them with all their belongings tucked into a van, their car packed and John and Mary waving them off. An easy, quiet journey of ten miles and they were opening the door of their own house with a firm hug and tender kisses to record this first adventure on their own. What a thrill to feel that it was all theirs. How wonderful to make a home for themselves, and their small daughters who danced with joy and helped to extract parcels and goodies from the van and car, stowing them away as indicated. What matter if items were temporarily mislaid? They were bound to turn up sometime and it was nothing to worry about. Settling in to the first house of their own was a wonderful new adventure that the little family of four found a delightful experience. Shopping for beds and furniture, arranging it and fitting in all their belongings; Jilly helped, unloading whatever she could manage and advising her Mum and Dad was just part of the fun.

"I hope I've put everything where you want it, Mum. But don't ask me where everything is, 'cos I've no idea," said Jilly."

"Thank you my Pet. I guess all the bits will turn up as along as Dad's instruments are safely placed. Perhaps it might be better to put them on his bed. He's bound to find them there.".

"OK Mum, but why not put them in his car along with his medical bag. Then he won't need to search for them".

Judith agreed willingly. Her little daughter was becoming a wise young lady, she thought.

A quick meal on the Aga, a short rest, a walk in the fields and evening was upon them quickly. Time for two excited little girls to try their new beds A bit later Mum and Dad celebrated happily in theirs...The night of sound sleep was followed by a morning of brilliant sunshine that reflected the bright and happy feelings in the whole family. Judith tried the new shower, enthused over its useful equipment and dressed. Gordon followed.

Judith ran up the stairs and knocked on the bathroom door. "Gordon, that's the telephone".

"Oh dear, can you take it Love. I'm in the middle of a shave, face covered with soap".

"Yes, all right, but you're not on duty till tomorrow are you? I'll see what it's all about". And she picked up the phone.

"This is the police station, Miss. Sergeant Williams speaking I understand you have just moved in and I wanted to know if you are actually there because we need to come and talk to you".

"Can't you tell me over the phone?"

"It's rather difficult Miss. We'll be with you in a very few minutes",

"It was the police, Gordon", called Judith. "They're coming straight away".

"OK Darling. Whatever do they want? I'm ready now. .I'll be with you in two ticks". And he rapidly pulled on a shirt, donned his trousers and brushed his hair.

The front door bell rang. Two policemen stood at the door, tall and with grave faces.

"Sergeant Williams Mrs Jenkins; and this is Constable James. May we come in and sit down for a minute please". Judith ushered them into the front room.

"Mrs Jenkins, this is rather a shock I'm afraid. There has been a car accident and your father and his wife are in hospital in Bristol. They are both rather poorly".

"Oh, dear, they were both going off after we left yesterday, for a holiday. Are they seriously hurt?"

"Well they were both unconscious and it was some time before we could identify them. They are still in the operating theatre, but we don't have any details yet".

"That's dreadful", said Judith, and her eyes filled with tears. She unearthed a handkerchief. "Could you get the hospital on the phone, Gordon? They'll speak to you I'm sure".

The police supplied the hospital's phone number and Gordon was soon connected. After some minutes he was put through to the Sister in the Acute Admissions department, and spent some time on the phone. At last he thanked Sister and disconnected.

"It seems there was a nasty head-on collision. Both have head injuries and the neurosurgeon has been called in to operate. Dad also has a fractured femur, and Mary has suffered lacerations of the arm and shoulder. We are to ring again in an hour".

Judith wept copiously. The sergeant said, "I'm extremely sorry to be the bearer of such bad news on your first day here, Mrs Jenkins. If there is anything we can do to help please let us know". Saying which, he and the constable rose to leave.

"Thank you Sergeant," said Gordon. "I'm sure that we shall cope. We shall be making ready to go and see them at once of course". At the door the Sergeant revealed a few details saying,

"We learnt that it happened on a straight stretch of the M.5. A big lorry strayed across the road. They could not have avoided it. The traffic police suspect that the driver had been drinking and had fallen asleep at the wheel. A helicopter was called and they were very rapidly transferred to the hospital. I'm very sorry; we know that they are a very fine pair of people". The policemen said 'Goodbye' and returned to their station.

Gordon sat beside his wife and cuddled her closely. "I'm so sorry my Treasure," he said. "Just when they were off on a lovely relaxing holiday; it's really tragic. I'll tell my father. I know he will be upset too. And I'll ring Sally and see if she will look after Jilly and Grace for a few days while we go off to Bristol."

Judith nodded, still weeping. She mumbled, "Good thing Jilly and Grace are still asleep. I don't know what to say to Jilly. She'll be very upset; she's very fond of her grandpa and Mary." and she sobbed afresh.

Gordon kissed her and supplied a fresh handkerchief. He rose and went off to beg for help from their neighbour.

Sally quickly understood and willingly agreed to look after the children. She would come at once and comfort Judith and help her to pack a few things. She did so and prepared breakfast for them all, waking Jilly and Grace and asking if they would like to stay with her and Jason and Tommy for a few days because her Mummy and Daddy had a sudden emergency to go to. Jilly was delighted and didn't ask too many awkward questions. Grace just clung to her sister. By the time they were ready to leave it was nearly time to ring the hospital.

Gordon's father had expressed sympathy and said Judith must take as long as was necessary; the firm would cope and he would get a temp. to come in and work in the office. He would also inform the church stewards.

The surgical registrar came on the phone and gave encouraging news saying, "Both patients have suffered depressed fractures of the skull, but there was no intracranial bleeding of any consequence and it's expected that they will recover well. The gentleman's femur needed an operation with pinning to secure the bone ends and he had stood that and the operation on his fractured skull went well. His wife has also had her skull attended to and all nasty deep lacerations sutured. She too is in reasonable condition. I'm very glad you can come and I'll enquire about possible hospital accommodation for you. Bye for now."

Judith dried her eyes; Sally wished them 'Godspeed' and took the hands of the little girls who had wrapped their arms around their Mummy and told her to come back soon. In the car Gordon checked the fuel gauge and let in the clutch. It had all been very sudden. No time for prolonged farewells. It was quite a long drive to Bristol.

*

When they called at the hospital's reception desk Judith could not help remembering the fateful occasion when she visited her mother whose condition was stated to have worsened. *'Please God, keep them safe for us,'* was her urgent prayer now as they went to find the ward. The staff nurse in the intensive care ward met them and confirmed that both patients were as satisfactory as could be expected and holding their own well. There was as yet no sign of consciousness but all vital signs were quite good. After waiting beside them for half an hour Gordon persuaded his wife to go to the restaurant for a meal and refreshment. He managed to have a word with the registrar who reported to him in medical terms and also said that a room had been found for them in the nurses' quarters.

The next morning dawned bright and sunny. They made their way to the intensive care ward, meeting many hurrying staff en route. The hospital seemed to be full of uniformed people moving smartly in all directions. It was all most impressive. Sister called them into her office.

"Good morning, Dr and Mrs Jenkins. I'm glad to tell you that your parents have recovered consciousness and all their vital signs are good. We are quite pleased with them. It will be alright for you to go in and talk, but for a few minutes only." They did so, careful not to appear over anxious or harassed, and assured John and Mary that they were both in good hands, well loved and cherished; also that Judith would stay near by until they were fit to be back in the general ward. The car business would be attended to. The other driver was in police care. The patients could just relax and concentrate on getting better. With minds of the damaged pair now at rest Gordon and Judith could settle their own problems. He said, "I shall have to return to-day for starting my job tomorrow my Darling. The girls will probably need a few things and I'll be there to attend to them. It's Sunday today and I'm sure Sally will be able to look after them until Wednesday when the term begins. After that we shall be able to work out a satisfactory arrangement until you return home."

"Yes, OK Gordon, my Darling. Life can be difficult at times, but thank goodness for the efficiency of a good hospital. Can we just do a shopping trip in Bristol before you go"?

After a short shopping expedition in the city involving, among other things, rental of a hire car for Judith, it was time to part. A loving embrace, farewell advice and good wishes, and Gordon turned towards home leaving his wife with an emptiness in her heart and still a lot of concern in her mind. Several days passed during which she walked rather aimlessly in the streets of Bristol, pottered in a few shops, ate small meals with a book on her lap and worried considerably about her father's future. Only a few minutes daily were allowed for visiting John and Mary, but their condition continued to improve and there were no untoward signs of trouble. She attended to telephone messages to and from the church stewards who wished to assure her parents of the love and concern of his congregation and were adamant that he should have a very adequate convalescence, however long it took. The church authorities had been advised and were making arrangements for a supply minister to take charge pending John's return.

Feeling a need for personal refreshment Judith decided to drive to the coast and investigate the possibilities of taking a holiday somewhere in the region of Weston-super-Mare. Setting the wheels of her hired car on the A38 she enjoyed the undulating road to the southwest, later deviating towards Weston and passing through the town to reach the sea front. The tide was out, very far out, and a vast expanse of sandy beach was exposed, giving onto extensive mudflats. Further out to sea the islands of Steepholme and Flatholme were descried with the mountains of Wales as a backdrop to the scene. Judith visualised the beach with an incoming tide over warm sand and a host of bathers having fun disporting themselves; she thought it might indeed be an ideal place for her little daughters to enjoy a seaside holiday. She noted the large boating pool on the beach and considered that Gordon could well teach his little girls the fun of sailing a small yacht in the gentle breeze. Perhaps there was one that he could hire? Dreaming was fun. Exercise was needed too and having found a means of reaching Brean Down she parked the car, sought out her bag of sandwiches, crossed the river Axe by a small ferry and commenced walking. It was a good hour's walk and the view from the top of the Down over the Bristol Channel was impressive with the Welsh coast seen as it extended westwards for many miles. Could she see the isle of Lundy? Well, perhaps not quite. At the end of the promontory she found a comfortable spot out of the wind that was now rising and relaxed with her picnic and book. After a while drowsiness overtook her and she dropped asleep on the grassy headland.

She awoke refreshed, looked at her watch and realised that time had passed on, leaving her a long way to walk and travel in order to reach the hospital for her visit to the invalids. Walking vigorously Judith enjoyed the feel of wind in her face and hair. Her day off had been a success. Back in the car she noted that the tide had quickly come in and little waves were breaking on the beach in a long line of white foam. Reluctantly she turned her back on the idyllic scene and headed for the city.

John and Mary were doing well and would be moved to the general ward tomorrow, she was told. They were in good spirits, wishing that they could be together, but the days of male and female patients in the same ward had not yet come to that hospital, so messages were needed to be passed from one to the other. She learned that a minister of their church in Bristol had visited her parents and had asked to talk to her on the phone.

That evening she rang him up on the number he had given. He told her that his name was Richard Eddison and that he was the hospital chaplain. Learning of the presence of a fellow minister he had visited her parents and been informed of the situation and of her continued presence in Bristol. He assured her that if he could help by ensuring a regular visiting rota by members of is own congregation, and of course by himself, thus enabling her to return to her family and her work, he would be glad to do so. It seemed that it might be several weeks before the pair would be considered fit to return home. He felt that the family would like to discuss this. Would Judith care to think it over and let him know?

Judith thanked him, saying that she was most grateful for the offer and she would reply as soon as she had consulted her husband and her parents. She rang Gordon straight away. There was little she could do in a practical manner in Bristol and she felt that her parents would approve the scheme. He replied that he would be delighted and knew that their precious daughters would be quite over the moon. His father would be pleased to have Judith back in harness too.

Next morning the Sister arranged for a consultation with the hospital registrar and Judith was allowed to go in and discuss the matter with her parents. They both thought the idea was excellent and felt most grateful to the chaplain for his kindly thought. By lunchtime the doctor had given his approval too and Judith managed to see the chaplain and personally thank him for his helpful suggestion.

"It is most kind of you and your members to undertake this visiting scheme." she told him. "My father has only been married to Mary for a short while, following the death of my mother who suffered from Alzheimers. He is very highly regarded in his church and the stewards and church authorities have made arrangements for a supply minister to take charge. I shall be glad indeed to get back to the family and, of course o get stuck into my job too. Thank you very much Mr. Eddison." It only remained for her to attend to a few shopping requirements for her parents and spend time visiting them that evening. The chaplain's arrangements would begin next day and she would drive home to Gordon, Jilly, .and Grace.

*

"Mummy, are you really coming home tomorrow?" Jilly managed her 'r's well. Her parents had been quite good teachers. She was quite competent on the 'phone too.

"Yes my Darling Jilly, I am, really and truly. Gran.and grandpa have been rather ill and I have had to stay for a long time I'm afraid. But they are ever so much better now and kind folk here are going to visit them, so I can come home and look after you. Have you had a nice time with Jason and is Grace quite happy?"

"Oh yes, Mummy, and school is fun too, and Auntie Sally has been lovely.

The phone call was a long one with Sally joining in as well so that her husband complained that his calls to Rotarian friends were so few that they hardly recognised his voice. Gordon noticed that Judith's vocal cords seemed to be a little strained and enquired if she was all right.

The morning saw Judith gladly pointing her hired car towards home. She dropped in en route to have a look at Bath and had coffee in the Pump Room, taking the opportunity to potter round the edge of the Roman baths and taste the water. Ugh! Here was antiquity indeed. She would report to her boss and suggest that his arthritis might benefit from immersion in the waters of that famous spa.

Embracing Sally happily in the warmth of her own home she found that her friend had prepared a meal for her and Gordon and left it ready in the Aga's bottom oven. That dear man rushed through his visiting round and entered the house flinging wide the door and throwing his arms around his wife in a hug that made her ribs creak and caused her to beg for breath. Question and answer started and continued between mouthfuls of steak and kidney pie with apple pie and cream to follow, until Gordon broke off to attend the afternoon children's surgery and continue his visiting round thereafter.

Judith felt wonderfully welcomed and she relaxed for a while until it was time to stir her stumps and meet her little darling at the school gates. Grace was sleeping in Sally's house. That became a meeting long to be remembered. It was the first time that mother and daughters had been separated

"This time I've just brought you a bunch of your favourite bananas, Jilly. Next time I go away to a hospital I'll come back with a baby for you to play with."

"Ooh lovely, Mummy. Will it be a girl or a boy?"

"Well, we shall have to wait and see, so you'll need to be patient".

And a long session of question and answer occupied them for hours until teatime had given way to a game of 'snakes and ladders,' followed by bath and bed with Daddy home from evening surgery and ready with a story about a different John and Mary and their little dog Pip. How delightful to be home again without the ambulance sirens of the big city, now replaced by thoughts of two sleepy little girls back in their own room and a cosy cuddle for two loving parents in the comfort of the home that they had made together.

Judith was not quite adjusted to the idea of leaving her precious child at the gates of a new school, but Jilly seemed very happy and went off next morning talking merrily to the other children. Grace seemed unconcerned; she was only too glad to hold her Mummy's hand. Only two days were left in this week and after the weekend Judith would be returning to her work at the antique shop.

She would be using Gordon's old car, kept for her own transport Her hired car would be collected by the owners. Would Gordon then be able to take the children to school? It all depended on the possible emergencies in the practice. But Sally had already envisaged this difficulty and promised that she would be willing to see Jilly and Jason and Tommy to school if Gordon was held up, and her husband had mentioned that he could also be called on if necessary. Meanwhile it was back to the cooking on the Aga, back to the washing machine, drying and ironing, followed by lunch and off to collect the wee girlie in the afternoon. Then the peaceful family times together, the country walks, the telephone calls to Bristol with good reports of their dear ones in the hospital there On the Sunday Judith spoke of going to her old church to meet the folk and reassure them of her father's good progress. Gordon told her that he would gladly go too and Jilly declined an invitation to stay with Sally and Jason, saying that she and Grace wished to be with her Mummy.

The church visit was a great success, many folk

expressing their concern and sending good wishes to their minister and his wife. They were both well loved. The new young locum in the pulpit was 'all right' but, well, he didn't choose the right hymns, he used set prayers from the C of E lot, he didn't have a story for the kids, and his sermons were like set pieces from a textbook, and he didn't come to shake hands after the service, and so on. Criticisms from some churchgoers could be rather unkind sometimes. Judith sought him out and, finding that he was only just out of theological college, felt rather sorry for him. It would take him time to settle down. Perhaps an older minister could be found to help him. She mentioned the thought to the stewards who said they would look into it. Then home to dinner from the Aga and a cosy afternoon.

*

A great welcome awaited Judith at her work place, Gordon's father being especially kind and the staff presenting her with a gorgeous bunch of flowers. Judith reported to him the good progress of her father and Mary and mentioned her visit to the famous Roman baths. She wondered if Gerald had ever visited them. Gerald enthused, "Yes indeed, I know them well and some pieces on our display shelves come from dear old Bath. That city is always worth investigating. Maybe we could go together one day, if your family can spare you. For that matter they could come too. Let's make it a weekend visit from Friday to Sunday. Bath Abbey is a fine old piece of architecture and well worth seeing. Meanwhile I have a few letters that would be glad of your attention."

CHAPTER 4

ON THE FOLLOWING Saturday Judith was not needed at work and was present when letters and other mail dropped through the letterbox. She sorted it into two small piles. A letter from her old town looked interesting; it was from the family solicitor. It read as follows. –

'Dear Judith, it was a great pleasure to find you in your usual seat in the church on Sunday last. Like all the rest of the congregation I heard your glowing report of the good progress being made by your father and Mary. We were all most pleased about that. I should like to bring to your notice a point of which your father is probably not aware. It seems very likely that compensation may be available to him for the injuries that he and Mary sustained in this accident. It may be quite a substantial amount and could very well help them to indulge in some little luxury when recovering their energy in the coming months. Will you mention this to him? If he would like me to discover more

I should be glad to help in this matter. There would be no charge for such services I assure you. Your father is very dear to us all. With kindest regards, etc.'

"Gordon", shouted Judith. "Listen to this". And she read the letter to him while he was spooning in his glutinous porridge from the ever co-operative Aga..

"That's marvellous, and it's very good of your friendly solicitor to write so kindly", said Gordon, happily spooning in his generous ration of lovely warm grub. "You must ring up Dad as soon as possible and I'll get a copy of the letter and post it to him. It could bring them a lot of joy. What about a world cruise, or maybe the Mediterranean and Egypt? I don't imagine they would be subject to a kidnapping foray." And they indulged in happy laughter together, remembering Judith's kidnapping and Gordon's method to secure her release.

Saturday proved a good tine to phone her father and he was brought to the phone at the nurse's station. It could only be a short chat but Judith ensured that he got the message, and he was very pleased, saying he would write to the solicitor.

Jilly had been given a little homework and was persuaded to do it right away and then join her parents for a picnic as the day looked warm and sunny. She set to with a will and, with crayons and a little elbow grease, produced a fair likeness of her teacher brandishing a piece of chalk. Well, the long hair and the skirt and the chalk were passable anyway. The family picnic was the first for a long time. Having found that Toad of Toad Hall was being shown at a Stratford matinee they drove over and introduced their daughters to another dose of 'Toady' magic from the 'Wind in the Willows'. Afterwards they succeeded in finding accommodation for the night at a guesthouse - one not filled with visitors from the U.S.A.

The children enjoyed looking at the swans on the river and throwing them bits of bread and cake, wondering at the way they buried their heads deep in the water. They thrilled with excitement when joining Mum and Dad for the candle-lit dinner before bedtime called. Ever such fun! It had been a lovely time for them all.

On a Saturday morning three weeks later Gordon was doing a morning emergency surgery when Judith answered the phone. She almost squeaked with delight. Her father's voice came over loud and clear.

"We're being discharged next weekend" he said, "coming home at last," and Mary joined in the jubilation.

"That's wonderful, Daddy, just what we've been waiting for." And she called Jilly to the phone to speak to her Gran. and Grandpa. Joy new no bounds as the child jumped up and down with excitement.

"I think Gordon may be on duty, but anyway Jilly and I will come and collect you. We'll have a celebration party if you feel strong enough." They nattered merrily until the hospital cut them off At lunchtime she told her husband, his morning round finished, and he too was very pleased. However he thought they should be prepared for the possibility that other arrangements might be made.

"They've had a very severe shaking up and may not be up to car travel with all the twists and turns, braking and traffic signals. We'll ring in a couple of days and find out."

When they did the story had altered. John told them that the hospital had arranged with the Red Cross to collect them, put them on a train and accompany them all the way by train and taxi to their home. It was felt that such a journey would be much less traumatic with first class travel all the way.

"OK. I'll go down the weekend before and take clothes or whatever," said Judith. They may want some things and I can collect some of their luggage and bring it back; do washing and so forth. I'm sure Gerald will excuse me for a day if necessary; then I could go on the Friday."

"I'll see if I can get a day off, perhaps hire a locum for a day. Then I can drive you" said her husband. "You have to take life a little more easily you know. You're a bit energetic at times; slow down a bit."

However the hospital office phoned to confirm the altered arrangements. The Red Cross had been contacted and they would provide transport to Bristol Railway Station where first class travel tickets would be waiting for John and Mary. There would be a guide to accompany them and attend to all their needs, and to arrange a taxi from Oxford to the manse. The journey would be quiet and easy. There would be no need for visiting them in advance. All washing would be done by the hospital laundry.

The Red Cross telephoned to announce the probable time of arrival and the manse shone with spit and polish and welcoming flowers and warm fires. The family all stood at the gate in the autumn sunshine to form a guard of honour. Neighbours had been told and came out to cheer. The homecoming was indeed a wonderful occasion. It was a heroes' welcome. After the enthusiasm with all the hugs and kisses John and Mary were told to relax and rest for an hour with a warm drink. When rested lunch would be awaiting them and having told their story and eaten their fill they were encouraged to indulge in an afternoon sleep in a warm bedroom. There were to be no untoward reactions to their long journey. Obediently they obeyed instructions, determined to be fit enough for meeting their faithful congregation at the morning service next day.

That also proved to be a most happy occasion with many expressions of goodwill. They felt glad that Judith and the family were at hand to rescue them from all the attention and once again insist on rest and gentle recuperation. Sally took over the children for a couple of days. Judith was able to introduce her father and Mary to a relaxed form of living on the Monday with their cleaner coming in to provide care until the social services had arranged regular supervision. Coping with the build up of mail became a heroic task and they dealt with it in small doses. Gentle exercise was an essential part of recuperation. Letters would have to wait.

A letter from their solicitor awaited them and this they opened with interest. Expressing his pleasure at their return to health he told them the gist of his adventures with the insurance company. The lorry was properly insured and the hospital bill and injury compensation was covered. He was making a substantial claim and felt certain that it would be met. He was sure that their doctor would insist on a long and beneficial holiday and he wished them a pleasant time and 'God speed'.

"How kind," said Mary. "Are we going to the Serengeti or the catacombs or just an amble down the darkened passages of the Pyramids? Personally I feel like being wafted to sleep on the gentle billows of the Med. But it's your Sabbatical so over to you my dear."

"Well, I'm inclined to agree with you", replied John "I feel that gentle rolling over the sea to Greece could prove very relaxing, and I should love to visit Athens and see the·Parthenon and visit the Areopagus. It would be interesting to see where Paul addressed the 'men of Athens' and perceived that they were 'a mite superstitious.' After that why not give the Pyramids a miss and fly to the parklands of Africa and view the beasties of that continent in their natural habitat?"

"That sounds a very good way of using compensation monies. I hope you are not allergic to malarial parasites or mosquitoes. I've met them in the past of course. (Mary had lived in Africa for years with her first husband.) We need to be very careful indeed about that little difficulty."

They spoke to Gordon about 'allergy' to malaria parasites. They were firmly corrected and referred to their doctor for suitable anti-malarial tablets. After that they enjoyed days of anticipation and preparation for a jolly good holiday in warm tropical lands. Gordon offered to make all necessary arrangements and commenced work with the telephone in one hand and a travel brochure in the other.

*

Judith, now back to housekeeping with breakfast for husband and her important young schoolgirl, strictly laid down proper rules for keeping her house in order while at the same time ensuring that she reached her workplace on time. There her employer invariably found his secretary seated at her desk with letters for reply neatly assembled and herself tidily and attractively attired and looking very competent. He depended upon efficiency and often congratulated himself on so fortunate a choice of staff, especially in the person of Judith. He mentioned to her that if they needed any help in organising her parents' trip to foreign parts he would be glad to be of service. First of course would be the receipt of the insurance cheque. That might take a little time. Gerald thought he might stimulate matters in that direction. He would try.

Meanwhile the returned patients exercised and employed all their strength in getting themselves back to normal. A physiotherapist from the hospital called regularly and was most attentive. Gordon checked up on her advice and was interested to find that she could teach him a thing or two. He made a mental note of some of her advice for use with his own patients.

Thus with school, home work and small children palaver the family continued for a couple of weeks until, one pleasant morning, there fell on the doormat a letter from the insurance company containing the long awaited cheque. It was quite a big one and John and Mary hugged each other with delight. Their planned excursion would be more than covered. They phoned Gerald and asked him to tell Judith

"Yes, I'll do that", he replied. "Also perhaps I could relieve Gordon of some responsibility over this travel business. If he agrees I will speak to the travel agent and check that all the planned arrangements are in order. If so I will instruct them to go ahead".

****

CHAPTER 5

RENEWAL

"Mummy, Gran and Grandpa are getting very excited and look ever so happy. What's happened Mummy?" Little Jilly was obviously sharing their happiness but anxious to know why. Judith told her, explaining about the voyage through the Med and the trip to Africa.

"Mummy, what's the Med? Teacher was talking about it today in geography and I wasn't listening properly." So her parents took up the tale and explained about the big sea that separated Africa from Europe. This stepped up their daughter's knowledge of her own country too, because Gran and Grandpa would have to drive to the English Channel and cross it before proceeding further. All good fun and all an extra bit of information to be tucked away into a brain wide open for knowledge.

"But Mummy, Daddy, how do they get across the channel? Is there a boat?" And that was where her father showed her the map of Europe and its surrounding seas and countries and really 'went to town'. He taught his little girl about the seas, the land, the mountains and lakes and showed how her much loved Grandparents would fly to Venice, the city amidst the waters. Then they would board a ship to sail on a voyage through the Mediterranean to Athens, Turkey and Egypt before flying on to the very far plains of the Serengeti National Park, beside Lake Victoriza in Tanzania, away south in middle Africa. She began to droop with sleepiness and her Mum decided, "Enough is quite enough for the time being and bed is a much better idea for a little girl than a clever lecture, so come on Jilly".

Next morning she remembered enough of the lecture from her Daddy to tell him, "When teacher asked the form to write about an adventure in their summer holidays I asked, Daddy, if she would let me write about an expected adventure for my Gran and Grandpa in mighty Africa. Teacher said that would be quite all right, so can I borrow some paper please and I'll have a happy time telling her about it."

Meanwhile those two expectant folk were making urgent preparations for their visit to that land of sunshine and exotic animals. Cool clothing, sun defying headgear, anti-insect cream, anti-malarial drugs and lots of little necessities that each thought might be needed. One morning they opened with excitement a letter from the travel agent to find that a date had been fixed for their travel. They danced a jig round the study, or at least as good a jig as John's repaired femur would allow. He would need to use a stick for some time. At last it was really going to happen. Urgently they made final checks on their luggage. They must phone Gerald and tell him, and did so. "It's going to be wonderful, John. You'll enjoy Africa" said Mary

"With you, Dearest, I'll enjoy all that life throws at us", he replied. The fun was about to start.

That evening while, with Jilly and Grace, the family were busily checking on their preparations, the front door bell rang. It was Gerald, come to offer his felicitations and also offering transport to Heathrow to catch their plane to Venice. Being well accustomed to such matters he knew that he could facilitate their passage through that fearsome hive of aeroplane industry. They accepted most gratefully. With Judith going along as well their transition to the right plane would be smooth and easy.

The following week, with luggage checked over for the last time, they hugged the little girls, hugged Judith and Gordon too, loaded everything in Gerald's car and they were off to the airport. All systems GO.

What a wonderful feeling, suddenly to feel the ending of rumbling wheels on the tarmac and rise, floating in the air, with a view of the airport, the grass, the trees, houses, roads, and traffic, and then the clouds all falling behind and underneath them. It was their first time for a plane flight and they were determined to enjoy every minute of it. They hugged each other. The air-hostess noticed the middle aged couple so obviously thrilled by it all and solicitously said, "Nice to see folk so happy. Would you like a cup of tea?"

"A lovely idea" they both said at once. The plane levelled, the seat belts were loosened and they wondered at the view of the enormous expanse of brilliant white cloud floating below them. They began to relax sipping their tea and nibbling biscuits. After a while they slept.

A meal time greeted them on awakening and they found delight in the tray of food presented. Soon after finishing their meal there came a lessening of engine sound as the plane commenced to lose height. They were able to see the mountains and snow covered summits of some of them. Fields and valleys appeared, then a town or two and the seatbelt sign indicating that they were shortly to approach and land at the airport near Venice. Buildings flashed by, a bump spoke of a safe landing followed by the mighty roar of reverse thrust of which Gerald had warned them. Polite thanks to the airline crew, pass through the customs and then to board the coach that would swiftly take them past canals and over bridges, bringing its passengers to the dockside where lay their expected white ship, brilliantly reflecting the late afternoon sun. They had a little climb up the gangway, a smartly clad officer to welcome them, and a crew member to show them to their cabin. Relief, a hug, and they gave thanks for a happy landing. They were very thrilled with the two-bunk cabin and after stowing away some of their possessions, were ready to investigate their new abode. They found and greeted the cabin steward and instructions followed for finding the restaurant, the lounges, and the decks. From the ship's rail John and Mary revelled in the view of Venice, the Grand Canal, St. Marks and the Square, the collection of gondolas with their gondoliers who waved to them merrily, blowing kisses to the lady. They walked the decks, fascinated by the view of the city, the shipping, and the preparations for departure. Suddenly the decks began to vibrate and they realised that ships' engines had started. A loud blast from the ship's siren nearly deafened them. Huge mooring ropes were thrown from the bollards on the dockside and slowly a gap appeared between the ship and the quay. They were off. With other passengers they watched the buildings of the city slide slowly past and listened to the voice on the Tannoy describing the view and naming important buildings as they passed. As in Judith's story, St Mark's, the Doge's palace, the Bridge of Sighs, all appeared to remind them of history long forgotten. A walk round the deck restored their circulation. It was John's first cruising adventure and he was quite thrilled with all the new technology and facilities for their journey and entertainment.

The light began to fade. It was time to prepare for the evening repast. Finding their cabin they made short work of donning a long dress and amber-like beads for Mary with a charming Scottish brooch, and a suit for John who forsook his dog collar and went attired wearing an old school tie. With the rest of the folk they presented themselves to the chief steward to be given their appointed table. To their surprise the chief steward addressed them most respectfully, saying, "The captain has directed me to place you at his table, sir. Here is a list of the other guests who will be seated there". He summoned another steward to guide them to their places. Looking at the list they found that there were several eminent persons, such as professors, a senior doctor and well known authors with their ladies among the company. Some of them were already seated and they introduced themselves to each other. The steward told them, "The captain presents his compliments but regrets that he cannot be present until the ship leaves the Grand Canal and is in open water. Please enjoy yourselves."

As he left them he handed a sealed envelope to the minister, saying that he would come for a reply later. John excused himself to the guests while he opened the envelope and read the short message. It was an invitation to him to take the morning service the next day, being a Sunday. This made an interesting start to the holiday. He felt that he must accept this; he was always prepared for such an eventuality. He passed the note to Mary murmuring "Got a job already". She smiled tolerantly.

A query from an elderly, bearded man of obvious substance - a banker perhaps - who humorously enquired, "Is the captain inviting you to steer the vessel for him?"

John replied in similar vein. "Not quite; he seems to think I might like to steer the minds of the passengers at the Sunday service tomorrow".

"But shouldn't you be flaunting a dog collar?" pursued his questioner.

"I sometimes leave it behind on occasions such as this. It seems to make conversation rather stilted. How many of you leave your stethoscopes behind?"

"Good point. But we've only one medico among us. Where do you keep your hearing aid, doctor?" he said, addressing the senior medicine man.

"Would you like to undo a button or two?" said that gentleman, rapidly pulling his stethoscope from his hip pocket. "Let's see if you have an aortic whoosh to the left of your sternum." A chuckle from the questioner and a merry laugh from the ladies brought a flavour of happiness to the small community and conversation became general.

The meal was excellent, the steward collected a reply from John affirming that he would be pleased to accept the invitation, and the company finally broke up to walk the decks and enjoy the fresh air before retiring to rest. Mary took John's arm as the ship rose and fell with the onset of wave motion in the open sea. After a couple of rounds of the deck they stopped to lean against the rail and watch the bow wave curling with .its white crest ever breaking as the ship plunged on into the waters of the Adriatic. A mesmerising feeling stole over both as they watched the water sliding by peacefully to turn into the boiling wake at the ship's stern. For quite a while they stayed by the rail watching. Gentle rocking by the quiet waves was a pleasant inducement to sleep. Reluctantly they turned their steps towards their cabin.

*

"They'll be on the high seas now, Darling." said Judith to her elder daughter. "Did you hear the weather report for the Mediterranean region?"

"I saw the weather map last night, Mummy. It showed a high pressure area over Greece and Italy. Doesn't that mean nice weather with plenty of sunshine?" The young lady had showed considerable interest in her father's geography lecture and was pleased to air her knowledge. She and her mother struggled into their coats to beat the rain, collecting, respectively, school satchel and handbag with sheets of office memorabilia in Judith's tidy black document case. They sallied forth into a November shower, Judith driving Jilly to her school. Then hurriedly they said goodbye and went their separate ways. Gordon would leave for the surgery by car shortly afterwards.

On her morning journey to the office Judith found it interesting to note how the summer's work and holiday routine had now been reversed, with the young family now fully engaged in their daily work while the older folk were relaxing in enjoyment of a well deserved change of environment. It would be several weeks ere they could relate to each other the fun enjoyed and new experiences encountered. Meanwhile they must get 'stuck in'.

They did, all three entering earnestly into their allotted tasks while not forgetting the care of little Grace, whose baby-sitter found her an easy and loving little companion. The sweet child's great delight was happy caring for the baby dollies now in her charge. She fed them with make-believe bottles; she changed their nappies, she combed their golden locks, told them a bedtime story and put them to sleep. When they woke crying she winded and fed them again until their 'mother' was quite ready to fall asleep herself, tired by her faithful guardianship of the very young. A busy little girl was Grace.

*

The weekend arrived with welcoming relief from duty and all were quite ready for a country walk, well clothed and insulated from the increasingly wintry weather. It was good to return to the fireside, pile on an extra log and use a toasting fork to toast muffins for their tea. Sally, with Jason and Tommy, came in to join in a game and, while Gordon and Sally's husband, Roland, retired to the study room for a chat, the young fry contented themselves with the ever popular Ladders with Snakes going up and sliding down. Later the baby-sitter came to help with bedtime for the young and further care while the four parents, with the children properly bedded and supervised, prepared to enjoy an evening at their favourite restaurant deep in the country.

The private room, the quiet ambience with lighted candles and the tablecloth of Irish linen adorned with sparkling silvery cutlery all combined to make for relaxation after the week of concentrated work. They talked of children, banking, antiques and the wondrous ruins to be seen by Mary and John, reminding them of classical Greece and Rome, all mixed with the moans and oddities of a doctor's day as he sorted out the sick and the not-so-sick. They found laughter in the fun and frolic of housekeeping happenings to wile away the time until the arrival of an excellent meal claimed their attention. Thoughts of their loved ones surviving the waves and sailing into the future came to occupy their minds as did visions of their camp fires in the plains of the great African continent. They told each other tales of returned travellers, who had listened with apprehension to the talking drums of Africa, blended with others of intrepid adventurers who had barely escaped with their lives from stampeding elephants or the rush of a poorly sighted rhinoceros. It was all good fun and cheered the dark night of approaching winter. Perhaps they could all, one day, live in tents in the vast plains of the Serengeti, just for a holiday of course.

The good food, the happy chatting, fun stories of their early days, medical mayhem merrily regaled, all combined to ease the tensions of the working week past. At last, leaving once again their ever welcoming host and his staff, they returned to their waiting firesides, wished each other a happy night's rest and found delight in the comfort of their homes where the night brought peace to them all.

****

Chapter 6

HOLIDAY AND HOME

"Mary, we're free, come and look", cried John. He had jumped down from his bunk and was gazing in rapture through his porthole at the vast blue expanse of the Adriatic. How quite marvellous to awake free at last from all responsibility and be able to enjoy the glory of sunshine and the smooth gliding of their ship on the waters of the Med. Mary joined him and they gave thanks together for life and all its wonder.

The captain attended breakfast and made pleasant conversation with all the passengers, not omitting to express thanks to John for agreeing to take the morning service. A couple of John's companions, including his interrogator of the previous night, said they would come and hear what guidance he had to offer.

The service went off well with John reading the account of St. Paul's adventurous, stormy sail to Malta, and his remarks on another occasion to King Agrippa.

The doctor said it made them think. Mary thought it was probably about time too.

The days passed very pleasantly; a little lecture being given the evening before landing at a new port. The visit to Corfu was interesting, with the palace of Achilles, Mouse Island and the donkeys' garlands of flowers just as related in Judith's story, which they had read. John revelled later in the visit to Athens and the accounts of its ancient fame, finding a book in the ship's library that dealt with Greek history. The victory over the Persian fleet at Salamis, the old story of Sparta and the messenger who ran the first marathon, the politics of Pericles and the mysterious oracle of Delphi, all made John feel quite invigorated to be back among his classical studies, far from the demands of the normal work of his church that often tired him.

Crossing the Aegean to Kusadisi he was thrilled to indulge in a coach trip to the famed theatre at Ephesus where he remembered the words of St` Paul when he addressed the Ephesians. . Was it all recorded in Judith's story? She must have taken in more from his sermons than he had realised.

The visit to the Holy Land was, again, a unique feature of the tour. Walking the Via Dolorosa, swimming in the Sea of Galilee, paddling in Jordan River and with old Capernaum, Nazareth and Damascus thrown in quite made John's day. Mary had been on a similar excursion with her former husband, so they had plenty to share and discuss.

Sailing further, Turkey's capital was not included in the tour but Rhodes and memories of the Knights Templar added interest to their evenings with a 'Sound and Light' programme within the walls of the old city. Knossos in the island of Crete was a must, demonstrating the ancient Minoan civilisation with its heating and bathing facilities and even the painting of the dolphin on the wall of the Queen's bathroom. John and Mary took it all in with wonder and delight. The tales of Theseus and Ariadne, the Minotaur and the thread to bring the hero back safely to her, all stimulated John's mind with memories of his classical studies in school days. He felt happy and relaxed and Mary was glad of his obvious wellbeing.

Finally there came the diversion to Cairo. A day out visiting the Pyramids, the Sphinx and the great Museum in Cairo introduced a plethora of further wonders to their minds. There was no time for flying to Luxor or cruising up the Nile; they had a booking on a plane to convey them across Africa to Mombasa..

South across Egypt, almost following the Nile in its huge meanderings and high above the mountains of Ethiopia they flew to come down into the hot, steamy land of tropical Africa. They were very glad to be on the shores of the Indian Ocean, where, after a refreshing bathe, they found an onshore breeze that helped to ease the sweaty discomfort of the tropics. Good hotel accommodation was booked and they could now begin to experience the real Africa and its peoples.

Walking in the markets, listening to the laughing, chattering folk, finding that there was a welcome for their white skins, many of the local people offering their hands and exercising their limited command of the English tongue, all were an eye-opener to them both. They spoke gladly of it when relaxing in their room after the day's heat had passed and with a fan circulating the air.

*

Their guide had spoken of entertainments, important

places to visit, the history of the place and warned them to be vigilant and not carry money in any obvious places such as ladies' handbags. It was all so new, so vast a change, so pleasant a relaxation that they almost forgot the affairs of home. However they did manage to remember that Judith was busily arranging her new house and that medical life also went on for Gordon. They succeeded in sending a photo of an African icon showing ancient chiefs in their robes including descriptive letters. John managed to obtain the use of a typewriter from the hotel manager's office and enjoyed himself. He wrote,

'Dear Judith and Gordon,

Here we are after our grand tour of the Med and all its ancient wonders,

I'll tell you all about it on our return. We had a short look at Egypt where we left the Pyramids, Sphinx and Mummies behind and took a plane that has deposited us here in Mombasa, a very busy city rapidly acquiring a semblance of modern 'civilised' life. After a conducted tour through the markets we were conveyed to a pleasant hotel very close to the beautiful beach of the Diani coast. Warm, turquoise waters of the Indian ocean almost lap our bedroom window inviting us to hop into bathing costumes and immerse ourselves So we did. Lovely, not even a hungry shark....

Now we are told to prepare for a journey by wheels into a Safari Park, not the Serengeti, where we shall be accommodated in a pleasant 'lodge', safe from marauding carnivores and even protected from the no less dangerous mosquitoes and malarial parasites of Africa. It will be a long drive, hot and uncomfortable, but a 'bucket' shower will refresh us, we're told, and the food is excellent...

Later, by hand, - we have arrived at the lodge, showered with the bucket and feel better after the many miles of dusty road and the heat. We've just had a meal. It was indeed very good. Shortly it will be time to enjoy a good sleep and we must get up early because there will be a 'game drive' tomorrow, starting very early to see the animals at the break of day before the sun gets hot. Instead of a bedtime story we can hear the buzzing of insects outside our mosquito nets, and was that the distant roar of a lion? I wonder. Just the thing to induce sleep!

A few days after writing this we were encamped in a tent. Here's the transcript of our conversation, written in the third person. --

"John, is that a lion? It sounds ever so close. I'm frightened." Mary moved close to her husband for comfort. They were cosied up within a tent that seemed extremely flimsy when thinking of the massive strength of such a carnivore with its fearful claws and teeth, uttering that dreadful penetrating roar. Could it be roaming around seeking an entry?

"It's all right my Darling", said her husband. "The beast is quite a long way off. A lion's roar carries a long way. Anyway our guide said they are not interested in humans; they just protest about our smell. Also we have a number of fires around the camp which are kept burning, and wild animals won't come anywhere near a place guarded by fires ".

Back on the typewriter again. --

That was our first night in real Lion country following the long hot travel from Mombasa and lectures from the guides and protectors had been quite exhaustive. En route we had seen several full grown female lions with a couple of cubs in attendance and realised the immense power that lay latent in those sleek and beautiful tawny bodies. There was a lot to take in. After a while, the sounds not

314

coming any closer, Mary relaxed and, tired after our full and strenuous day, we lapsed into peaceful sleep.

We were woken just before dawn with mugs of tea from our minders. These faithful chaps informed us that one of their scouts had reached the camp with the news that a herd of elephants had been discovered; it was proposed to get going shortly after breakfast and seek them out for the travellers to watch and photograph. Nothing loath, we readied ourselves, downed our very adequate breakfast of fruit, scrambled eggs on toast and additional toast and marmalade to sustain us on the long trek ahead.

After breakfast we climbed into our sturdy transport and went off on the elephant hunt. After about there hours we espied he massive shoulders of an enormous male pushing through the trees; he was followed by a party of females with, here and there, a small baby elephant toddling along trying to keep up with the herd.

We were warned to keep very quiet and make no sudden movements. Gradually we approached nearer and felt impressed by the colossal size of the big male and by the civilised manner in which the rest of the herd moved peacefully together. They were on their way to a lake of water, we understood. We followed at a respectful distance and watched while on finding the lake they drank, squirting water into their mouths and afterwards giving themselves a refreshing bath and plastering their hides with mud. A fascinating sight.

Later, as we were returning to camp we noted zebra in quite large numbers and even saw a pride of lions in the distance; they sleepily paid no attention either to the zebras or to the smaller antelopes which kept carefully away from the great cats. The latter must have fed well for they were quite uninterested. Anyway it was too hot for chasing about unnecessarily. To us, who were entirely new to the sight of such magnificent creatures, the experience was very captivating. We hope to make the acquaintance of a rhino in the next day or two and to gaze up into the sky to see the head of a long necked giraffe as he nibbles at the luscious leaves of an acacia tree. We are told that if a rhino decides to charge the correct thing is to stand still. On no account should one run away - he can reach 30m.p.h if he wants to. If you stay still he'll give up and turn away. I should hate to meet a charging rhino. The giraffe is a much more peaceable creature. As for crocodiles or hippopotami, chimpanzees or gorillas, I doubt if we shall meet any of those gentle people. We are too far from rivers full of crocs, and the Nngorongoro crater- the enormous volcanic occurrence of long years ago- is also too far from here. The slopes of Mount Kenya are covered, we learn, with trees where the big primates swing to and fro, imitating Tarzan; that also is much too far, so just pictures of them will suffice this time.

I learn that the Shimba Hills National Park is only an hour's drive from the Daini coast and is an excellent area from which to view the animals, but it is not in our itinerary. Nor is the Masai Mara, an extensive savannah also having vast herds of game and home to the Masai people, but a plane flight away. The continent of Africa is very vast indeed.

We feel most privileged to have seen this wonderful Safari park and will hope to show you all our extensive photo record when we return. Time to take a break from this typing, so bye bye, and God bless. "

*

Honeymoon Couple Return.

Their letter re\ached Gordon and Judith not too long afterwards and was soon followed by a message with information about their home arrival time. Again Gerald was determined to meet them and drove to Heathrow. Their arrival in Oxenby was quite dramatic with the streets near the manse once more lined with parishioners waving a welcome and bouquets of flowers were pressed upon them. The manse was warm and tidy. Judith had arranged to be free to greet them and had made all ready for their arrival. The local press, not to be outdone, had sent a reporter to record the event. Pictures of the couple laden with flowers as they entered their gate appeared in the evening paper and John was inveigled to make a suitable comment saying, "It was quite wonderful. We are in perfect health and ready for action."

The children were thrilled to see their Grandparents again and demanded stories about their adventures. Jilly was particularly impressed with accounts of their journey and even more so when seeing the pictures and photos that they had brought. Evening times were often spent listening to wonderful accounts of their African visit and Judith and Gordon were glad to find the dear couple so well and vigorous after their holiday/honeymoon.

Jilly was full of questions.-

"Could you see the stars when you were up above the clouds?"

"Was it really warm in the Arabian sea?"

"It must have been frightening in the tent with lions outside. However did you sleep?"

"Why aren't there tigers in Africa?"

"Would a rhino have charged your 4 by 4? How big was the baby elephant?"

Often Judith had to shoo her away to bed, for the returned couple still felt tired after their plane flight. But it was good to find their little girl taking such an intelligent interest in the trip.

Christmas was rapidly coming now and much preparation was needed. The minister would be greatly sought after to look into problems and make all sorts of arrangements. He and Mary went to it with a will. Telling their people of the enchantments of the classical world and the excitements of close contact with the great animals of Africa could wait. Christmas could not.

A kindly meeting of the congregation demonstrated to the couple the affection in which they were held and a lavish welcome party was arranged with an evening dinner in the church hall. John and Mary were addressed in affectionate terms by the church stewards and then it was necessary to plunge into the sea of problems and ensure that all were dealt with and that everyone was given an appropriate job to do in preparation for celebrating once again the Birth of the Christ Child.

A Saturday visit to Judith and her family in their new home in Bifford renewed the lovely sense of loving kindness that had always existed between them all, and the girls were all agog to talk excitedly about the new baby that would shortly grace the medical household.

"Grandpa, are you going to slap water on the baby's face?"

"Grandpa, make sure you don't drop him."

"Grandpa, would you like me to hold him for you?

And a lot more, but all that was some months away. First there would be the birth of another Baby to celebrate and for that it would be 'all hands on deck'.

Christmas shopping was now on the menu for John and Mary as well as for the young family and that, along with the excitement of the school Christmas plays and occasional pantomime outings, meant weary parents at the end of the day. Their normal work was fitted in somehow Mary vowed that she would provide the Christmas dinner and of course Judith and Gordon shared expenses, while Judith cooked puddings, mince pies and attended to lots of the usual trimmings. The girls were adept at creating decorations and loved the choosing and writing of cards. Stamping of envelopes was fun. John's Christmas Day sermon hit the nail on the head as usual; Santa Claus visited, unseen as was his custom, and Father Christmas managed once again to come and see the family all gathered at the home of Gordon and Judith. What a shame that Daddy had to go out and missed him, again...The girls wondered why...

*

The New Year introduced itself with a party given by Sally and Ronald. Kids came wrapped in pyjamas and blankets and John and Mary arrived after their Watch-night Service Merriment and happiness were the order for Jan 1st;. Good wishes and African stories with hot ginger drinks helped to ease the passage into the cold of the next day when snow had laid a sprinkling of white over the land and ice crystals sparkled and decorated every outside object.. The transition from the heat of Africa made John and Mary shiver but many layers of clothing made for good insulation and if they resembled Christmas parcels when entering the doors of parishioners on return to pastoral work, well, it was just a further measure of Christmas time, and they were persuaded to sit by the fire with a cuppa and tell stories of Africa Recounting the stories, remembering the heat, the wonder of Africa and its people, its animals, its drums, and its roars in the night, all helped the winter to move onwards and encourage spring to come and grace the lighter days, with the promise of Easter not far away.

****

Chapter 7

A FUTURE ASSISTANT?

"Let me carry that case, Missus, you've got enough to carry", said the taxi-driver. He was a kindly chap with a brood of five children and an overworked wife, and felt much sympathy for Judith as she slowly followed him up the steps of the hospital. Gordon had been overstressed with a round of visits; they were in the midst of a 'flu epidemic and his morning round was a long one. When the first pain struck Judith knew that her husband would not be home in time to convey her to the hospital; a phone call to the taxi service was answered most expeditiously by the arrival of the driver with his vehicle. The walk down the corridor to the maternity ward was lengthy and painful. As she entered the door to that busy department, suddenly her waters broke with the start of another pain. She hung on to the door and called to the blue uniformed figure in the nurses' station. "I think it's coming," she shouted breathlessly. In haste Sister grabbed an absorbent cushion and told the nearest nurse to bring a wheel chair. Rapidly they seated Judith and quickly ran her into the labour ward. The taxi driver relinquished her case to a porter muttering to himself 'Coo, that was a narrow squeak', as his mind revered to the cushions of his taxi. A hospital cleaner, aimlessly pushing a vacuuming gadget over the polished floor, hurriedly swapped his suction apparatus for a mop and bucket and began to attack the puddle.

An hour later things had happened. Judith was propped up on pillows sipping a welcome cup of tea while Sister took a face cloth to her sweating face and brow. The midwife on duty wrapped the baby boy, pink and protesting loudly after his bath, in a nice warm towel and offered him to his mother. She told Judith, "He's the most beautiful young fellow in the ward so far on this first day of April. He fooled you all right didn't he?"

"He certainly did", said Judith. "His daddy is going to be delighted. When can I phone him?"

"Let's see if you have any colostrum for your little nipper. Then you can both settle down to sleep. I guess your hubby will need to relax a bit after his busy round this morning. Phone him before his evening surgery and he can come in afterwards with time to enjoy you both."

Judith bared a breast and offered it to her baby, closely cuddled in her arm. He sucked vigorously, giving up when no more fluid was available. "I think we're going to have fun." said his Mum. "I think I'd better speak to Gordon now if you don't mind, or he'll be anxious.

I could only leave him a very brief note." The midwife agreed and brought Judith a phone.

"Hallo, Darling man. A nice surprise for you. Your son has arrived."

"Judith, my Sweetheart, that's marvellous. What a

wonderful girl you are. I hope it wasn't too difficult. Are you all right my Darling? You've done a very quick job this time. I must come and see you right away. What a delight to have a boy to play with. I'll bring a football".

"I'm fine, Gordon, but of course it was quite hard work. I think I would like a bit of sleep now, if you can wait a bit. You put your feet up for a while and come after evening surgery. Then we can have a good 'natter' and you can get acquainted with your little boy. He's quite adorable, you'll love him, so 'bye' for now my Darling, see you later."

"OK. my Sweetie, if you say so. You must be pretty weary so have a good nap. I'll try to be patient. I'm longing to see you. Bye, bye, my Love."

The midwife took the phone and the staff quickly settled mother and baby to have a good rest. Soon both were fast asleep.

Gordon took rather longer to settle. He rang his father who was quite over the moon to hear that he had a grandson, and promised to take out an insurance policy for the education of the 'young man'. He would leave the young folk to enjoy their celebration together and visit tomorrow. Gordon then telephoned to Judith's father and passed on the glad news. Relief and rejoicing were both forthcoming and of course Mary wanted all the details. Equally of course Gordon was unable to satisfy her but promised to ring later after seeing Judith. He then had a short chat with his medical colleague who congratulated him and told him to go and put his feet up.

Eventually he did.

Evening surgery was a long one. Complications from the flu abounded and folk were tired and wanting restoratives to assist them back to health. Explanations and advice to each individual could be a tedious process, but somehow Gordon managed to sift out all the weary folk and make ready to visit his dearly beloved and his much wanted little boy.

Tenderly he greeted Judith and assured himself that all was well with her. Then to pick up his newborn baby, the son whom he had always wanted, the future companion with whom to play football, tennis, and many other sports, as well as teach, hopefully, the rudiments of healthy living. He wondered afresh at the perfection of human anatomy as revealed in a new baby and gently lowered him into his mother's arms for another dose of breast milk.

It was a happy visit full of questions and answers, hopes and plans for the future. The baby's name had been decided long before. "Do we stick to John Leslie for his name Darling? And of course his Grandfather will be called upon to baptise him in his own church. How long before that ceremony? I expect John will tell us tomorrow when he comes to see you".

As Gordon had forecast John and Mary as well as Gordon's father visited the next day and all were delighted to see their new grandson; all holding him in their arms for a short while and John said a little prayer over him. Mary was determined to be his Granny. .

As days went by mother and child performed well with Gordon visiting every day while his colleague looked after the practice during Gordon's visiting times. Judith's discharge was a red letter day for them all, and of course especially for the two little girls who were overjoyed to have their mother at home and made a great fuss of her. They were thrilled to see their baby brother, each begging, "Mummy, can I pick him up and cuddle him?" Jilly especially reminded her Mum that she made a jolly good job of nursing Grace when she was a tiny babe. Judith supervised that exercise carefully, guiding her daughters wisely about it.

Sally continued her care for them all until Judith felt able to cope with her new load of responsibility. Gordon, finding his life remarkably busy, valued all the help that his neighbours gave him. Fortunately the little chap was a good sleeper and with artificial milk to supplement breast supplies he gave little trouble. They copied the habit of the native peoples of Africa in feeding their baby in the vertical position so that as the milk went down any air bubbles in his tummy came up automatically. 'Winding' was seldom needed. After all an African baby slept in an upright position on its mother's back and there was no trouble in 'winding' it by bouncing the baby up and down or patting its back. It was all automatic. "High time" said Gordon, "for so called 'civilised society' to catch up with the ancients. I'll apply for time on the B.B.C. and Inner Wheel to give 'em a heart-felt lecture on the subject. "

The influenza epidemic continued to give trouble and urgent requests for medical attention were often received on their home telephone after the surgery was closed. There were often days when some doctors, despite modern ideas of locums to undertake out-of-hours calls, still felt the urge to give year long care of their patients, day and night. If they wanted time off they arranged with partners or other colleagues, to take over for a few hours at nights or weekends. In due course they would repay the courtesy. Gordon and his colleague, with both their families, were fortunately able to keep free of the virus, and did their best to avoid contact with people in shops, buses, meetings and other places where folk met together and shared each others germs and viruses.

The antibiotics which were useless for 'flu' were invaluable for its serious complications when other germs attacked debilitated tissues and produced a variety of life threatening situations. Many were the occasions when

Gordon's syringe and long needle were called into play, with dramatically beneficial results. He considered that an intramuscular dose of antibiotic would certainly, through the blood circulation, arrive at the required area of trouble in very quick time. The oral route, - a tablet swallowed – faced the uncertainty of passing through the stomach and, finally reaching the intestine, of being absorbed to a greater or lesser degree before circulating to the troubled area. Gordon believed in a needle and syringe as first choice. His results were satisfactory.

A district nurse to continue injections twice daily and the installation of an oxygen cylinder in a patient's bedroom were often measures that could, and did, save both a hospital bed and the life of a patient too. Naturally doctors were often tired, but their wives were towers of strength and attended to their needs faithfully. One just hoped that lady doctors in general practice also benefited from similar help; often they were married of course. Not all medical people escaped the virus. Difficulties were encountered sometimes. A flu epidemic is not funny. Judith and Gordon managed to escape infection, possibly having acquired some immunity from frequent periods of brief contact with their suffering patients.

*

The days of Spring were becoming well advanced and sunshine persuaded folk to venture out into the fresh air rather than 'preserving ' life and health by sitting around the fire in smoky rooms. Baby John was, from the start, wrapped up snugly and placed in his pram outside in the manse garden where he snoozed peacefully, being admired by visitors and passers by. His sisters, especially

Jilly in her rapid growth towards maturity, happily cared for him, delighted to have a real baby instead of dollies for their practising. Even at her tender age, Jilly, in frequent contact with her parents' medical problems, was acquiring valuable knowledge..

While Gordon continued regular work in an organised manner, attending to emergencies promptly and sharing with his colleague the 'stings and arrows' of a doctor's life, the daily things of home life became more ordered and regulated. Judith created a routine that suited the whole family and found much satisfaction in producing a well organised home for husband and children.

As weeks went by she began to wish for the return of at least some of her secretarial work to occupy her occasional spare time. One day she telephoned her employer saying, "I have got this household into order and feel perfectly capable of doing some intelligent work. Looking after babies is nice but not mentally satisfying. Have you a letter or two for me to deal with?"

"That is just what I was wanting, Judith. Thank you very much. I'll bring you a wad of correspondence at once. There are some letters that urgently need your particular brand of secretarial skill. There will be plenty more when you've dealt with these," he assured her.

"I shell be very happy to have a go." she replied. "Kids are lovely but I have got a good routine going now and want something to stimulate my brain." Saying which, she got down to her typewriter with a will, coping with all that Gerald could throw at her.

****

Chapter 8

ACQUIRING FRENCH FRIENDS

An event that would demand the energies of both husband and wife occurred one evening. While Gordon was snoozing quietly after the evening meal and Judith, having washed up and attended to the children's various needs, had just seated herself at her typing, there came a sudden furious scream of tyres tearing up the road followed by the sound of an almighty bang. The blaring of car horns added to the horrid shattering of the evening peace. Husband and wife leapt to their feet and rushed to the door. Outside the garden gate could be seen a couple of cars savagely interlocked, horns blaring, and screams mingled with and almost drowning the horns. Gordon picked up his medical bag, called "Come on, Judy", and rushed to the scene followed by his wife.

The 'how and why' could wait. The immediate question was whether serious injuries had occurred. The larger car was that of their bank manager neighbour. He was seen dragging himself with difficulty out of his car. The smaller, which had smashed head first into his, was obviously badly damaged and its two lady occupants were hopelessly entangled in the wrecked front compartment. The driver, unconscious, was slumped in her seat, one hand still on the horn button. Her lady companion had thrust two hands, both now bleeding profusely, at the front windscreen which was badly smashed. Her forehead was also bleeding messily, a wedge of forehead skin badly torn.

"Wrap up the bleeders, Judith.", callrd Gordon. "Bandages are in my bag. I must get the ignition keys out and look at this unconscious woman." He called, "Are you OK Roland?"

His friend replied shakily, "Yes I think so. Just a bit shaken and my leg feels twisted." He went on to comment, rather rudely perhaps, on people who drove on the wrong side of the road but Gordon wasn't listening. He was using his stethoscope to help him to assess the condition of the unconscious lady's heart. He looked up, saw Sally attending to her husband and shouted to her to phone the ambulance quickly and ask also for the fire brigade and police. She left Gerald, who was able to stand and walk a few steps, and fled into the house to phone.

It was useful that both the front windows of the small car were fully open since the front doors were stuck firmly closed. Judith had staunched the bleeding, hopefully; of the lady passenger's hands, head and face, and was trying to comfort the patient who was now weeping copiously. Calling to Sally who had emerged from her house Judith suggested a little brandy might help and shortly she came with two glasses.. Only one could be used. Gerald asked for the other. Gordon, concerned about his patient, found a heart stimulant in his bag and administered a dose intramuscularly. He pulled a pen torch from his jacket pocket and checked that eye reflexes were present. He held the patient's wrist, feeling the erratic pulse and hoping the ambulance would not be long.

It wasn't. Ambulance and police arrived at the same time and the fire brigade followed very shortly. There was urgent need to extract the unconscious woman as quickly as possible and the fire people rapidly assessed and took control of the situation. Gordon had managed to extract the ignition key as soon as he had reached the car and escape of petrol was minimal. The firemen sprayed with foam the inside of the engine compartment whose lid had been forced up. Then it was a question of where to cut the steel body. They used their wide experience to good effect and ere long the lady driver was lifted out of the car with great care and carried to the ambulance. Gordon collected his bag and hopped in beside her. The other lady, not quite so badly hurt, was still waiting to be released but it was important to move the unconscious lady driver to hospital as quickly as possible and this was done.

.By the time that patient no.2 had been rescued from her position, wedged into the vehicle, another ambulance had arrived and she, with Roland protesting vigorously that he was 'jolly well all right', were both seated carefully into it and taken off to the A and E, Sally of course accompanying them.

Judith, left on her own, was now questioned by the police who were anxious to know how the accident had happened. She could only state that they had heard the scream of tyres and the bang. No, she did not know the women. Yes, the man involved was their neighbour, a bank manager and it was about his usual time for coming home. The only clue to the mystery was, perhaps, that the woman with the bleeding hands spoke French, saying, 'Merci, madame, merci beaucoup'.

"Aha," commented the policeman. "And they were in a French motor car and on the wrong side of the road. That seems to make some sense. The driver made a mistake."

Judith left them to continue theorising and examining the two sad vehicles. She returned to her house where she found Jilly still awake and anxious to know what had happened. She explained that there had been an accident and that two people had been hurt and taken to hospital.

"Will they be all right, Mummy?"

"I hope so my Darling. I don't know any more I'm afraid".

"I hope God will make them better. How does He do it, Mummy?"

"He has given people brains to learn how to be doctors and nurses and also to folk who can build hospitals. After that it is their job to use their hands and their brains to do whatever is necessary".

"I hope He will give me a brain, Mummy".

"He already has, my Darling. Your school teachers tell you how to use it"…

"Well, I've got a nice teacher, Mummy".

"Good, so now you can go to sleep. Good night, my Pet."

Judith sat down at her desk feeling that a lesson had been learned. She found it difficult to settle to writing and went into the kitchen to make salmon sandwiches for Gordon and her neighbours when they got back from the hospital. She felt extremely concerned for the driver of the small car, wondering just how they had come to collide with Roland. If they were French it would be natural to drive on the right and they would veer further right if they noticed a possible emergency. No doubt the policeman was correct.

Half an hour passed. Gordon phoned

"Hallo Judy, everything is under control here. The cardiologist has come to take care of the lady driver. She is now awake and improving. She is being looked after. Sally and Roland and I are coming home in a taxi. See you soon".

"OK my Darling. I'm all ready for you. Salmon sandwiches are waiting your arrival with suitable restoratives. There are plenty of apple pies in the fridge. Would you like anything else? Will salmon sandwiches be enough for the party? Think about it en route. Bye now".

On arrival they were most grateful for Judith's thoughtfulness. She learnt that the patient with damaged head and hands was undergoing surgery to repair matters. The cardiologist had been called in to look after the other patient who had recovered consciousness. The identity of the couple had been established. In fact they were from France, having a holiday in England. They found it difficult to remember the rule of driving on the left in our country. Seeing the opposing motor car the lady driver had promptly turned right and of course Roland had also turned to that side. A head-on collision resulted. Hence the severity of the damage. The ladies had had a lucky escape.

Sally and Roland opted for home and bed very soon, Gordon providing his friend with a mild nerve sedative. Their baby-sitter would be glad to go home too. The evening ended happily all being relieved that apart from Roland's bruises and twisted ankle no serious damage had afflicted him. A night' rest would revive hem all.

The remains of both vehicles had been removed before most of the morning traffic began, thus leaving little trace of the accident to trouble the children on their way to school. Police came in the morning to check that Roland's car papers were in order and he travelled to work by taxi. Judith, after Gordon had departed to his surgery, attended to correspondence for Gerald. A phone call to the hospital brought the news that the two ladies were 'as well as could be expected', so Judith decided to see them at visiting time. 'That was a nasty old emergency' she thought. 'Thank goodness it was no worse.'

The ladies, who were sisters, had both been admitted to the same ward with their beds adjacent so making possible their continued togetherness in a foreign country. Judith found them to be most gracious and grateful for the attention given both in the hospital and at the roadside where she had been much in evidence. They were able to converse very well in English. They told Judith, "Our home is in the Loire valley, very near the river. It is a lovely area.. An aged uncle left us a small legacy which made possible this long desired visit to England and we have enjoyed a quite lengthy tour of the country. It included Cornwall and Devon, south Wales and we went even as far as Edinburgh. We have had a wonderful time."

From Lands End they had gazed over the sea to America; from St Davids they glanced towards Ireland and in Auld Reekie - they loved that name - they cast their minds back to the days of Bonnie Prince Charlie.

Being a little elderly the business of driving on the wrong side of the road was somewhat trying, hence the accident. They hoped the Police and the Insurance people would adopt a lenient attitude towards them.

Judith felt it would be good to cultivate a happy relationship with them and invited them to come and visit when they were discharged from hospital. The ward sister told her, "They are doing well medically and will probably be discharged in two or three days."

Judith replied, "I'll telephone for information later". They parted on a cheerful note.

"Mummy, can they speak French?" inquired Jilly on learning of her mother's visit to them in the hospital. .

"Yes, of course, Jilly, and they were quite pleased when I spoke French to them."

"That's good; I'll be able to practice my French to them when they come." Jilly promptly demonstrated her prowess to her admiring mother who was glad to assist her with pronunciation in advance of the ladies' coming.

The planned visit occurred a few days later when Judith collected them from the hospital. It proved most successful. Both ladies were teachers and quite charmed by Jilly's manners and attitude as well as by her endeavour to master the sounds of the French language. They were going on to Oxford by taxi when well enough and then back across the Channel. They thought that the family might like to visit them when coming for an educational session in France.

The idea was taken up gladly by all the family and, with addresses and phone numbers exchanged and affectionate 'Goodbyes' said, the guests departed by taxi to an hotel in Oxford There they could inspect the famous colleges and 'dreaming spires' of the city.

A few more weeks passed with baby John becoming accustomed to the regular hours of feeding, potty palaver and fresh air outings. It was time for Judith to return to work and baby-sitting arrangements were made,

One day, all snags being resolved, Judith sallied forth and made her long delayed return to her office, welcomed with enthusiasm by the staff. There were fresh flowers, a most pleasant aroma of scent in the office and all looked spic and span. Gerald welcomed her with a kiss on both cheeks and made a charming speech of welcome while the staff happily clapped and gave a little cheer. Judith felt it was quite worth having a baby to be the subject of such fuss. Quickly she settled down to work, 'all systems go'.

One evening Gordon returned from the surgery wearing a cheery smile. He greeted Judith with a hug and a kiss and enquired, "Where would you like to go for a holiday this year, Darling? My boss has fixed the dates, so it's up to us to choose."

. "That will need some thought. We have an added complication this year," said Judith, regarding the new infant in her arms, wide awake after his pram outing and eagerly sucking his bottle.

"OK we can go into consultation after grub. I picked up some travel brochures on the way home."

And after dinner, dishes washed and children peaceful after a bed time story, they conferred together. Judith was well aware that her husband's mind would undoubtedly be moving in the direction of life on the ocean wave, but while sympathetic to this she felt that the waves would be more suitable in the sheltered bays and waters of Cornwall rather than venturing over them in the Bay of Biscay. She steered the talk in that direction and was relieved to find that the idea was most acceptable to Gordon who had remembered well their previous boating expeditions on the gentle waters of Carrick Roads 'twixt St. Mawes and Falmouth.

"Why don't you phone the Portscatho people and see if they have a vacancy in that house in Gerrans that we rented before? It would be ideal for the children and I'm sure we could find a good baby sitter. Jilly loved it and Grace will too I know. Come to think of it, a place in Portscatho would be very suitable for Daddy and Mary next year. He could watch seabirds all day long and the local Anglican Church would be quite a pleasant change from his usual place of worship."

"That's an excellent idea my Sweetheart. Wonderful that our thoughts are so often in accord". Gordon picked up the phone at once. Judith smiled an understanding smile. The two were always close enough to realise each other's hopes and desires. In a very few minutes their holiday was settled.

"I might as well phone our sailor chappie and see if he's still operating his boating business. You liked that yacht didn't you. Even little Johnny could snooze happily, 'rocked on the cradle of the deep'. There's room for a night on board too you know… Suitably moored in the river of course." he added hastily.

The old 'sailor chappie' responded in his delightful Cornish growl and assured them that he still looked after folk trying their luck on the waves. He added, "I'll be very glad to see you all again. Yes, my boats are in good order and need old hands to come and try them out. I've installed a two way radio in the cabin so that there is access to the coastguard if required, so people can always be in touch with help if needed."

It was all very satisfactory and after reading a chapter of their books two weary people were glad to get to bed

At the next weekend Judith mentioned that their friends in Swindon whom they had met on the beach at St. Anthony might like to know about their holiday arrangements. Gordon gladly took up the idea and found their telephone number. The men were enjoying a pleasant conversation when suddenly an interruption occurred, "Sorry, Gordon," said Jeremy. "My wife wants to natter with Judith; talk later, my friend". Gordon too passed the phone to his lady wife who was at once greeted by April almost shrieking into it. "How are you Judith? Last time we saw you an addition was on the cards. Have you had it?"

"I certainly have. He's three months on and yelling for a Cornish holiday. Are you coming too this year?"

"Yes we've just been talking about it. What are your dates?"

And the talk became fast and furious, almost interminable, until both ladies finally gave up quite exhausted. The men resumed their talk, more peaceably. Discussion of sailing technique continued until wifely intervention again threatened.

"My wife's grumbling again, Gordon. How about yours?"

"Mine looks rebellious too," said Gordon, observing Judith's face "I think we'd better bid each other Goodnight. See you in St Mawes." He passed the phone to Judith and retreated to read the B.M.J. The ladies went back to their 'nattering.'.

****

Chapter 9

SEASIDE FUN

"I was wondering when you would wake up. It's twenty past eight. Want a cup of tea?"

"Ooh, yes please. What are we going to do today? It was a long hard night. That young Mabel took a long time producing her first."

"I could tell you something about that too. Go back to sleep. I'll put the tea beside you."

The day was Saturday, Gordon's day off. His wife had already been up feeding the family. The girls were out playing next door; Johnnie was gurgling happily and exercising legs and arms, his fingers catching at the baubles that hung over his cot. Judith had hung up the washing to dry and had breakfast ready for her husband-when he returned to life. She took a mug of tea up to the bedroom and placed it beside him, regarding his sleeping form fondly. She yawned, returned to the kitchen, took up the morning paper and relaxed in a cane chair. Half an hour later she woke to the sound of his footsteps and the scraping of the chair as he sat himself at the table.

"It's a lovely morning, Judy. How about a weekend by the sea? Mablethorpe is within reach. Louth would probably have B.& Bs available. I heard the forecast while shaving. There's a high pressure system over our area for a couple of days."

. "OK I'll do a picnic for lunch on the sands. Is it possible to book a hut on the beach? It makes good protection in case of wind or weather becoming bad. I wonder if Sally and the boys would like to join us? Rollo is away for a few days, so she might be glad to come. Shall I go and ask? I'll tell the girls. They'll be thrilled."

All was efficiently arranged and three quarters of an hour later the two families were packed into their cars and ready for off with suitcases, sun cream, sunshades, deck chairs, cushions and towels all stowed away. Their fridges had been raided. Food was essential. Rollo had gone to his appointment by train so Sally drove the big car.

Judith devised 'I spy' and other games to relieve the tedium of travel while Gordon, efficient as ever at finding his way, chose a route that would take them over the Lincolnshire Wold. As they rose and fell over the rolling hills they could espy the slim, graceful spire of Louth Parish Church appearing and vanishing when the car reached a hill top and dipped into the valley beyond.

"I believe that spire is 296 feet high," said Judith. That is second only to Salisbury Cathedral. Do we pass near by?"

"Yes almost underneath," replied her husband. "Do you fancy stopping to inspect the church?" Judith felt tempted but with a car load of children she knew that sand and waves had priority.

"Sometime later", she responded.

Leaving behind that charming market town they shortly reached the flat section of road leading to the coast. Mablethorpe was only minutes away and soon the car stopped, to the sound of cheers from its young occupants, in a big car park near the beach. Sally with her brood was close behind.

"Right," said Gordon. "You lot buzz off and find the hut I've booked on the phone while Mum and I go and locate a B & B and do a bit of unpacking.

Sally spoke up. "I'll stay with the mob. You can leave wee Johnnie with me and I'll arrange drinks for them all. See you later."

A pot of tea awaited the two parents when they returned, hot and thirsty and well satisfied with their lodgings. Shrieks from the girls greeted them while the boys industriously raised their sand castle to an even greater height.

"Can we bathe, please, please, please?"

"Judith looked at her husband. "How's the tide?" she asked. "Coming in," was the reply. "Over warm sand; let's get it over before our picnic. If you and Sally will do the grub I'll change into bathing togs and keep an eye on them"

In a remarkably short time the children were ready and streaking down the beach to splash delightedly into the small breaking waves. Gordon followed keeping a careful eye on them as they ventured deeper. Soon Jason and Jilly were swimming while Grace and young Tommy contented themselves splashing each other or sitting in the little waves that broke gently over them, to their delight.

"Don't go out deep, stay parallel to the shore," shouted Gordon to the swimmers, and he checked to make sure that they obeyed. Other people were indulging in the fun of course and the water was soon full of folk enjoying the coolness that offset the heat of the midsummer's day. It was a wonderful change for people immured in industrial towns to experience the freedom of the beach and water, all at no cost and with no cares or anxieties..

Gordon simply strolled along in the water at knee level, watching the youngsters as they revelled in the fun. Suddenly there was a different sound. A voice shouting! He thought it cried "Help!" He searched the sea and soon descried a head above the water and arms that flailed about frantically. He also saw young Jaaon swimming strongly with a vigorous crawl stroke towards the person in obvious trouble. He remembered that the boy had been commended for his life-saving prowess, and he too waded into deeper water and then swam, albeit at lesser speed towards the developing emergency. He could no longer see the person's head but spotted Jason who had reached the young man and was pulling his head above the water, assuming the life saving position that he well knew was urgently needed. Jason kicked strongly back towards the shore and ere long Gordon reached the two and was able to assist. His feet touched bottom and they were able more quickly to pull the casualty to the beach and above the tide edge.

The girls had seen the emergency and Jilly had come quickly. "Run to Mum and get my car keys," said Gordon. "My medical bag is in the boot," and with Jason's help he quickly turned the young man over, put his hands under his tummy and pulled him up until water ran from his mouth. He laid his patient down on his back and bent to place an ear on the chest. There was no heart sound. Very rapidly Gordon took up position and with both hands pressing vigorously on the chest he began the urgent 100 per minute pushes needed for artificial restoration of heartbeat. Stopping to blow forcibly into the patient's open mouth he showed Jason how to assist him and between them they continued for several minutes. Jilly returned with the medical bag and stood by, watching the procedure carefully.

Suddenly to their joy there was a response. The patient took a breath, coughed and began to breathe and splutter. Gordon found a pulse at the wrist and stopped pumping, turning the young man over into the recovery position. By this time Judith and Sally had arrived, bringing towels, a rug and a cushion, and between them their patient was made comfortable. The relatives also appeared and there was much talk with fervent expressions of thanks to Jason and Gordon. The latter, seeing that the young man was more stable, announced that he should be taken to hospital for further care and observation. The lad's father and mother agreed and Gordon chased off vigorously to find a telephone. Sally quickly brought a cup of tea, well sugared, and they dressed him in warm clothing after towelling him dry. After a while he was helped to stand up and he managed to walk back to his family's hut to recover further while awaiting the ambulance. Gordon appeared saying that it would soon be there. Correct. It was…

As the sound of the ambulance engine faded in the distance Judith took a deep breath and said firmly, "Now perhaps we can have our picnic."

Later that evening a candle-lit dinner at a local restaurant proved a happy occasion. Gordon told Jason it was just to congratulate him for his very expert life-saving effort He was quite covered with confusion just saying 'Thank you, but I only did what was needed.' They all applauded.

Bedtime was rather late for them and sunburn cream was needed for the children despite precautions. Sally strongly advised using vinegar saying it was better than all the fancy stuff in the chemists' shops. She had brought a bottle and dabbed the many burnt areas.

"How's that?" She enquired, after treating the whole bunch. "Fine, do it again tomorrow please." They replied. Relaxing at last in bed that night Judith said to her husband, between cuddles,

"What a clever boy you are, Darling. They'll be very grateful, I know." Her comment was followed by a rather longer loving session than usual after which he replied, breathlessly, "All in the day's work, Darling." The night was peaceful and prolonged.

After breakfast the young folk toddled off to the beach, Jason having promised to watch them all carefully. The landlady came in to inform the parents that a couple of folk wished to see them. It was the parents of their half drowned patient. The father addressed them, "We have to get off home now but we wanted to see you and say 'Thank you' properly. Our son Roy was discharged from the hospital this morning. His chest is quite clear and the doctor says it was due to your extremely prompt action It is quite impossible to say how grateful we are and we do feel that we shall be for ever in your debt. Gifts are quite inadequate to express our feelings but anyway will you accept this bottle as a memento". And they handed to Gordon a carefully wrapped bottle of rather expensive champagne.

After suitable acknowledgement they exchanged names and addresses. Gordon and Judith were persuaded to pose for photographs, goodbyes were said and they all felt glad to have made a couple of new friends. It had been an event to be remembered. What impression would remain in the minds of the two older children would doubtless be apparent in days to come.

Judith had not forgotten that it was Sunday. She took Gordon's arm and said "Gordon how about going to the service at the Louth parish church? Sally told me yesterday that she would look after the crowd of kids if we'd like to go."

"Right ho, my darling. We'd better get going. Nice to sit underneath that mighty spire. Hope the vicar can match your father's sensible sermons." And off they went.

They enjoyed the service. Even the choir came up to expectations, and afterwards the vicar noticed them as newcomers and singled them out for a special welcome, telling them a little of the history of the old church. They promised to attend again on their next visit.

The remainder of the day was spent with the family on the beach, Gordon indulging in a snooze before the evening drive home. The return journey was in the gloaming after watching the sun as it gradually descended over the rising and falling of the Lincolnshire Wold. The children slept in the back seat and Gordon and Judith talked in whispers occasionally as they sped along. Gordon said, "Do you know Judy, I feel more and more that I've made a wise choice in choosing general practice. The more I work at it the better I like it. There is plenty of scope and no lack of change in the work with emergencies of one sort or another constantly cropping up. It's never dull, always a new excitement."

Judith replied "I'm so glad my Darling. You are just the man for all these odd happenings, and the patients all love you. So do I."

Gordon squeezed her hand, then saying "We must tell Roland just how expertly young Jason rescued that laddie. He performed superbly". Later that night they did.

Roland was most impressed saying a little present would be indicated. He would let Jason choose; either something he wanted or an addition to his savings account in the bank. Next morning after congratulating his son he was equally impressed when Jason chose savings.

The morning surgery was going along nicely in Gordon's consulting room when his door opened to admit his colleague, Dr. King, wearing a big smile, his eyes dancing. ."When you've finished with this patient would you come into the house for a minute", he said. After final advice to the elderly chap with a slightly failing heart condition Gordon rose, wondering what he had done wrong, and found his colleague with his wife waiting for him.

"Really Gordon," said Dr. King, "you are always making the headlines." He held out a morning national paper where a page showed a photograph of Gordon and Judith with the headline –

They Do it On the Beaches'.

A vigorous account of the rescue of their Mablethorpe patient was given with Jason's effective rescue and the resuscitation by Gordon as the young man lay on the sand.

"Very hearty congratulations from both of us," said his colleague. "Keep up the good work. We'll attend when you go to the palace for your M.B.E. You are unaware of course that the gentleman whose son you rescued from death's door is a senior journalist of this newspaper."

"Crikey," said Gordon. "That sounds like trouble from the press. Oh dear! How do I cope with that?"

"You have a problem indeed. Anyway it's all good advertisement for our medical services. Perhaps your lady wife will deal with the mob of reporters before you reach home for lunch. She's pretty competent, I judge. Meanwhile your patients are all agog to offer you their congratulations, so get to it chum."

He did. They were. Morning surgery was longer than usual and by the time Gordon had finished his round of home visits he felt a little tired and was not too pleased on finding a small collection of newsmen still awaiting his arrival.

Judith told him, "They won't go away. They want a photo and a statement. I told them it would cost them, the money to go to our favourite charity. They all agreed." She mentioned a sum and Gordon agreed and posed with his wife for the photographers, making a short statement, and hoping they would remind readers not to venture out of their depth when bathing. People should be aware that on an incoming tide the depth of water beneath them was increasing all the time. He invited them all to attend the palace in due course…All enjoyed a good laugh, professed themselves very grateful and assured Gordon that copies of their newspapers would be forwarded to him. The Louth and Grimsby reporters were much in evidence. .

"Next time we'll go to the zoo", said Judith. "You can try reviving an elephant."

****

Chapter 10

SALLY GETS ONE. ALCOHOL. ROTARY & A NIGHT JOB.

A COUPLE OF years passed with the affairs of home and child education proceeding smoothly and relations with their neighbours better than ever. However after the beach episode there had been a tremendous excitement in the house next door. Sally had mentioned to Judith with a great thrill in her voice that she had missed a couple... Both women went into ecstasy immediately and a visit to Dr. King's surgery brought the glad news that a new baby could be expected. Roland too was very thrilled and pleased, quite over the moon in fact. Like Gerald he promptly arranged a policy for her education, for they were all certain that the expected baby would be a girl. Both families were quite adamant on the matter.

"It's got to be," said Jilly, and Grace and the boys were equally certain that a little sister would be coming to bring joy to that household.

Sally's pregnancy would be the concern of Dr. King in view of the close friendship between the two neighbouring families, so she had attended his surgery regularly. In the later months there was concern about her blood pressure and eventually the birth was arranged three weeks prematurely. Their expectations were gladly realised and in due course Sally gave birth to a lovely baby girl that would bring a wonderful sense of happiness and fulfilment to Sally, Roland, and their two boys.

While Sally and Judith frequently joined in earnest consultation sessions the male side of the family were proud to revert to pram pushing. Roland said that he felt years rolling off himself and declared to friends in Rotary that he had been given a new lease of life In the year following he could often be seen walking with his tiny poppet who insisted on hanging onto one of his fingers even when, later, she was well able to toddle on her own.

The two fathers sometimes joined together for an evening walk after surgery. On one occasion Roland mentioned again the question of Gordon's possible membership of the Rotary Club.

"You remember that I once asked you about this a few years ago. We now have space for another member and I wondered if you would like to join us. May I tell you what it is all about and take you to an evening dinner with the lads one day? I should introduce you as a guest and you would be welcomed in that guise. Later if the club saw fit they could invite you to become a member. This gives you time to consider and decide"

They went into earnest discussion during which Roland enlightened his companion regarding the nature of the club, its aims and objects. Gordon was uncertain whether he could take a Rotarian's duties in view of his commitments as a practising G.P. but agreed to join his friend at an evening meeting.

One evening, at home when the meal was over, games played, and all the lambkins, having heard and commented on the bedtime story were tucked up for the night, Gordon was thoughtful.

"Judy, now that baby palaver is a bit less demanding we have time to chat together while playing scrabble or whatever. What about a serious discussion sometimes in the evening?"

Judith regarded her husband carefully. "Yes," she said. "Have you anything particular in mind?"

"Well subjects are legion. We hear a lot about alcoholic drinks now-a-days. Have you any thoughts on that subject?"

"There is certainly a lot of hot air talked about that, and I hear commentaries on the radio while ironing or washing up quite often Yes, I can add my own comments on the matter."

"Good, go on then," said Gordon.

"Well to start from scratch we have to face fact. Alcohol is a poison, as is strychnine, belladonna from the deadly nightshade plant, digitalis from the foxglove, aconite and so on. It is possible to take such substances in very tiny doses, for medical purposes only, but in excess they can damage your health and even cause death."

"I take your point. But alcohol has been used in drinks timelessly. Have we only recently discovered that it can cause trouble?"

"It must be thousands of years ago that humans began to use it. Maybe the sap from a damaged bark of a palm tree was collected by some thirsty ancient, left to ferment, and later drunk. It made him tipsy and happy and he collected it again and became addicted. He told other people. Or perhaps somebody drank liquid from a pot of barleycorn that had been left in the rain, fermented and built up a level of alcohol. He had a drink of beer and again became addicted. He acquired a beer belly. Now the stuff is widely drunk across the whole world."

"Yes indeed," said Gordon. "And a lot of trouble all this causes. What is the actual damage?"

"You know more about that than I. My understanding is that alcohol causes the synapses of the brain to work inefficiently; the result is that messages from one nerve centre to another are passed on only slowly or even not at all. The messages or instructions from the brain therefore are sent inefficiently to the muscles, or other organs. So muscles don't work or work inefficiently or the wrong way; body organs are affected likewise and the end result can be either just embarrassing or serious or even fatal. Would that be an accurate summary?"

"Yes I think so, Judith. The trouble is that folk don't know how much effect the alcohol is having on them because their brain tissue is not working properly. So they make no response or the wrong response to events or words or people's actions. Instead of talking quietly they shout or laugh loudly. They may do things that would normally be quite contrary to their normal habit. Obviously they are not safe to handle machinery because machines can only obey instructions. If the instructions are wrong there may be havoc and mayhem. They cannot be trusted to say what is right because their normally sensible ideas are out of proper control".

"That's right. For that reason my father and many ministers in his position do not drink alcohol at all, even in small quantities. Doing so may provide an example to other people who may be unable to keep the habit in proper control, and the results can be disastrous. For the same

350

reason doctors, surgeons, nurses, car drivers, aeroplane pilots and so on must all avoid using drinks containing the stuff when they are on duty We are very well aware that even the most responsible people fail to observe that advice. Your A&E department is often overloaded with them."

"Well folk have to drink watery fluid of some sort. What would you recommend?"

"Oh dear, the poor things If they can't drink plain water- and I know it's pretty awful sometimes, tasting of chlorine and such like, there are all kinds of fruity flavourings available. Some of them taste quite excellent, far nicer than wine which always gives me a dry mouth in the morning after indulging the previous night. A lot of people drink in the evening to help them relax after the frantic days when they are trying to earn a living. Of course, the Tele doesn't help much with its tales of woe and wickedness, war and vice all stirring up the nervous system and giving folk bad nights. So they take up drugs to calm their shattered souls, and of course alcohol is most certainly a drug."

"Didn't St Paul advise Timothy to try a little wine for his stomach's sake?"

"So says his epistle. Probably the wine, in reasonable amounts, was safer than the local water. Alcohol can kill germs as well as people (although only in high concentration) and there's no doubt that much of the water in primitive lands is very polluted. Water would be collected in non- sterile pots and stored when travelling in bags made of animal skins, camel perhaps. How safe would that be? It is only comparatively recently that we have learnt of the advantage of boiling our drinking water".

"So we have a problem," said Gordon. With the shelves

of the supermarkets loaded with vast numbers of bottles of potentially dangerous drink, what is the answer?"

"Prohibition did no good in the U.S.A. and Parliament can't help. No government official would dare to ban the bottle. There is plenty of info' about the danger associated with alcohol consumption if only people would read it and act on the advice given. If they don't, well only their relatives can complain when they kill themselves off with cirrhosis of the liver, a drink driving accident or a stroke from high blood pressure. There is no compulsion to be stupid, but if they are they may not get a second chance. 'What, are you answered yet?'"

Gordon accepted his wife's words of wisdom and they settled down to finish their game of Scrabble and listen to the ten o'clock news with a packet of his favourite 'liquorice all sorts' and a drink of cocoa.

*

A few days later Roland invited Gordon to be his guest at the Rotary Club's dinner. This was held at midday so after sprucing themselves up they drove along to the charming old Ballroom for the occasion. Members were gathered round the bar ordering drinks as was the custom. Roland introduced Gordon to two of the men who welcomed him heartily asking if he was proposing to join the Club.

"Well thank you. I've just come along to see what the form is. I don't know anything about Rotary really".

"I've been a member for twenty years," said a hefty chap with a strong handshake. We are, each one, admitted under the classification of our occupations. I'm a builder and my friend here is a solicitor. We look after each other. Are you a G.P. by any chance?"

"Yes, that's right," said Gordon. "Are there any other doctors in the club?"

"Surely," was the reply, "Old sawbones over there swallowing orange juice, is a pathologist. He chops them up. It takes all sorts."

Just then Roland returned to introduce his guest to the President who welcomed him and invited them to join him at the top table. All were shortly seated. The President announced that a member was celebrating his birthday and the company sang the usual 'Happy Birthday'.to him. It was his pleasure, after thanking the club, to present a bottle of wine for each table, - a long established custom for birthday boys.

A very pleasant soup introduced roast beef and Yorkshire and the conversation went along happily. Gordon enquired, "What is the purpose of Rotary Mr. President? Roland has told me that you have a motto, 'Service before Self', but what does this boil down to in practice?"

"Right, Gordon. There is a little booklet available that will provide you with the detail, how it began and where it has spread and its aims and objects. It is really a club with the object of furthering fellowship and friendship between its members and also takes on helpful projects for the benefit of people who need help in one way or another. This obtains both here and overseas. At present we are aiming to collect money to help in the matter of restoring sight to an enormous number of blind people in India. We organise camps for young folk to enjoy a holiday sometimes. At Christmas time we run a caravan to set up shop in a nearby town and supply hot dogs and sausages to tired and hungry shoppers. And a lot more. Roland will tell you of course and the booklet spells it out. And my name is Bill Brotherston.".

"Thank you, Bill. I gather that members have to undertake office in the club at times. I rather wonder whether, with a busy medical life and the liability to be called out urgently in an emergency, I could really manage membership. That is, if I were invited."

"I feel sure that in such a difficulty something could be arranged. Don't worry about it."

After 'The Queen' had been toasted a speaker had been invited to inform the club about the European Common Market... He spoke at great length, bored everybody with incomprehensible verbiage and succeeded in enlightening nobody.

The meeting concluded when all stood for the final toast, 'Rotary the World Over' and members went back to work. Gordon thanked his host and the President, escaping to continue his round of visits to poorly folk in their homes. He finally returned home, thoughtfully, read the B.M.J. until his eyelids drooped and he snoozed until it was time for a cup of tea followed by evening surgery. Later, after supper with Judith and the children, he broached the following subject with his wife.

"If I were a Rotarian you would become a member of the Inner Wheel. How would that strike you? Sally is already a member isn't she? Life would expand with lots of new experiences. You could give them a lecture on Antiques or a dissertation on 'How to get kidnapped.'"

"Gosh," replied Judith. "This opens up possibilities by the score. I must talk to Sally." Their usual game of Scrabble provided more brain teasers and the discussion continued, interrupted by the inevitable array of horrors in the News programme. Bed was a welcome relief.

Gordon was still on call. He was lucky. The telephone was silent. They slept.

*

"Mummy, when are we having our holiday? Jason and Tommy are going to the Canaries. Do we have to go to Cornwall again? I'd love to fly in an aeroplane."

"Well, Jilly Darling, it's all fixed up for this year. It's very expensive to fly you know and I don't think we can manage it just yet. But we will one day. You liked Cornwall last year and the boat is all arranged too. Auntie April and her red setter will love to see you. She doesn't have a little girl. Can you possibly wait till we can afford a holiday overseas? There's a lot in Cornwall that you haven't seen yet. There's a huge cave where they used to mine tin; there's the fishing harbour at Newlyn. We could drive down early in the morning and see the fishing boats coming in, every one surrounded by hosts of seagulls. Boxes of fish are unloaded and put in a huge shed. The auctioneer comes to get them sold. It's all quite fascinating. Then of course you ought to see Lands End and the tall Longships lighthouse out on thr sea; there's also St Ives with its lovely big beach and the wonderful rocky headlands on the north coast. We could even take a boat ride to the Scilly Isles. That would be on quite a big boat going out west about thirty miles over the bouncy waves."

"OK Mummy. It sounds nice. I wonder if Jason and Tommy would like it there one year. I'll ask them tomorrow." The message was not lost on Judith; she told Gordon saying, "Our little Jilly is growing up."

He commented saying, "Yes time certainly moves on. Roland is very thrilled about his little daughter. Next year she will be ready for the Cornish beaches like our young Johnny. It was good that the midwife's wedding ring again proved right."

And they grinned at each other, going on to discuss

the pros and cons of joining Rotary and the Inner Wheel, There was the matter of expense to be considered of course; but after batting ideas to and fro for a couple of hours they decided to go for it, provided Gordon was invited to join of course. There would be snags as they well knew. One of them happened the same night at two a.m. when a midwife demanded Gordon's presence to assist with the arrival of a new baby. It was a sleepy doctor who dragged himself to the breakfast table for his customary spoonfuls of porridge from the Aga next morning.

"Why did I take up general practice?" he moaned to Judith as she passed him a boiled egg. "I could have specialised in skins. They don't have night emergencies I reckon."

"Never mind Darling, you make a lot of people happy. The midwife rang up to thank you very much. The baby is perfect and the parents are very grateful to you."

Gordon polished off his egg, toast and marmalade, rose, stretched, collected his stethoscope and agreed that there were compensations. He hugged and kissed his wife and departed to the surgery. It was another day

****

CHAPTER 11

ROTARY. BAPTISM.
JASON DOES IT AGAIN.

THE EXPECTED LETTER from the Rotary secretary arrived as forecast by Roland. It was the hoped for invitation to become a member of the club under the classification 'General Practitioner'. The secretary mentioned that there were two other doctors present, the pathologist and a G.P. who was also a police surgeon. Gordon found time to write a suitable reply of acceptance and attended at the next meeting. The President welcomed him into membership and he enjoyed the lunch followed again by a speech from a member about his favourite hobby, viz. 'Coleoptera and their Oddities' Gordon had been invited to make an introductory speech by thanking the speaker. Among other remarks he expressed interest that, having used a dictionary to discover the meaning of the lecturer's title, beetles were an extremely useful species. They were adept at disposing of animal remains by burying them, similar to the habit of the Scarab beetles of Africa that rolled a ball of dung into an underground hidey-hole for the benefit of its own progeny. The applause was vigorous and Gordon felt that he had established himself as a reasonably intelligent member. Roland added, "Carry on like that Gordon, and the club will fall for you. I'll bet the speaker finder will be knocking at your door".

That evening Judith enquired, "How did it go, Darling?"

Answering her query with a description of his admission as a member, her husband went on to ask how she would address the Inner Wheel when first admitted and asked to speak.

She replied, "I'll talk about 'My Egyptian Odyssey'. That should shake them."

He agreed, saying that they had a police surgeon member in the club and he wondered what he would think of the sulphur cure for baddies.

Some days later Judith, in her turn, was invited to attend the Inner Wheel and be introduced into membership. She and Sally went along together. The experience proved most encouraging with a kind welcome for the young wife of a well known doctor in the town.

Judith felt that she could happily fit into the cosy fellowship that seemed to promise friendliness and expansion into a slightly different life. At the same time she realised that entry into a world of folk whose object seemed, as she expressed it, to be largely based on 'living it up' would not be entirely acceptable to her. She should, at all costs, keep to the simple kind of life that had been so much a part of her own family happiness. Sally listened to her with interest and told her friend that she heartily agreed. They would go along fervently with voluntary acts of charity and helpfulness but avoid any persuasion to join the 'smart set' of women with little to occupy their time. They agreed that such was the right decision for them.

*

Jilly and Grace were in the habit of pushing the prams containing their young siblings on a Saturday morning. One morning a young lady met and talked to them. She patted her bulging tummy and announced that she would soon be able to meet them pushing her own pram. Jilly's mind began to think. "Mummy how do you know when a baby will be born," she asked on returning from the walk

. "Why do you want to know?" Judith began to think quickly. Her little lady was certainly growing up. Children advanced more quickly these days.

"Oh well, I just thought. How do you work it out anyway?"

This was the crunch point. Judith felt that she should take advantage of the opportunity. She took a deep breath, put down her knitting, pulled her daughter down beside her and began to explain the business of life. It took some time and when finished Jilly just said,

"You tell it much better than our teacher. What's for supper? Afterwards I think I'll start making a shawl for that woman's baby. I've learnt in knitting class."

On his return from evening surgery Gordon was interested to find mother and daughter sitting side by side busily clicking knitting needles in happy companionship. . "Well, what industry," he said, humorously, as he picked up his new B.M.J.

"How you can understand that stuff I can't imagine."

said Judith. "I've looked at it sometimes and find it quite incomprehensible."

"To tell you the truth, so do I very often," replied her husband. "Any grub, or am I too late?" Judith rose, putting aside her work, kissed him and opened the Aga's bottom oven.

"How was the surgery, Darling?"

"Much the same as usual, 'nothing to laugh at at all', as said the poem about young Albert before the lion swallowed him whole. However, apart from that something of interest has come up. The Rotary Club is invited to visit a factory making clothing from Terylene. It should be an instructive hour or two. What are you two making anyway?"

"We've tried to work out when a young lady's baby is due and decided to ensure that he or she will have something to keep it warm, but not Terylene. Here you are, have a hot supper and be thankful."

Gordon thanked his wife and attacked his supper.

Later, with Jilly tucked up and asleep they settled together at the Scrabble board. "So what's the object for discussion tonight then?" asked Judith. The reply came briskly.

"Tobacco should keep us pretty busy."

"Goodness. That's another one the government fight's shy of, though they have tried a little bit with taxes and health warnings. Alright, you can start this time."

"Well it's been going on a long time. If Walter Raleigh first brought it to our country he gave folk a lot of pleasure and now we have discovered that pleasure has a price. I heard a story from an old doctor that he used to go to medical meetings armed with a supply of handkerchiefs for mopping his eyes. The room was full of cigarette smoke. One evening he went as usual and found that he could actually see across the hall to the other side. The news had just been given out that tobacco smoke causes cancer. His hankies stayed dry that night. He informed the club about a patient of his who was a heavy smoker, using about 40 cigs a day. The man suffered from emphysema. His son smoked too but the wife and mother did not. Their home must have been thick with the stuff. It was the wife who caught the lung cancer. She did not survive. He lived longer, finishing off in a nursing home paid for by the state, as were the numerous bottles of oxygen used to keep him alive a bit longer."

"That's a nasty story, Gordon. That's what they call secondary smoking isn't it. I'm glad you don't smoke any more."

"Well the research people are constantly looking at more and more possibilities of the troubles caused by tobacco smoke. The medical journals have got something to say about it every week. It's becoming an important consideration in the cost of the health services."

"That means higher taxes of course whatever the government says to the contrary."

"Yes undoubtedly. M.P.s have got their heads in the sand about that difficult subject. The last thing that their voters want is that taxes may have to go up. But obviously more bad health means more expense trying to cure disease. More cures cost more money. More pharmaceutical firms are going to spend money in researching more effective cures. Research workers command higher salaries. So there are higher prices for drugs and greater health costs for the N.H.S. Inevitably higher taxes result in one way or another. That should give you a choice of bigger and longer words for Scrabble. It's your turn. I wish you the best of luck"

"Thank you, very clever. Here's a word –HORRIBLE

-.See what you can do with that. And while you're thinking about it don't imagine that we've finished with tobacco. There are other considerations. For one thing, what about the matter of addiction? A lot of people who would like to give up smoking find that they can't. They have become addicted. Are they addicted to the taste or smell of the weed, or what?"

"Now my Pet you have hit on the nub of the matter. Our science masters tell us it is due to the sedative effect caused by the nicotine in the tobacco. That opens up the question of how to overcome the sedation or nullify the effect of the nicotine in some way. So far the matter has been approached by offering people tablets of nicotine to take or patches containing the stuff to stick on the arm so that the addict continues to get a steady dose of sedative, and therefore does not need to inhale the harmful tars in the tobacco which seem to be the cause of the cancers. The smoker is now just an addict to a drug."

"That is only one way round the problem, Gordon. It reduces the likelihood of cancer certainly so must improve the health service costs, but the individual then becomes an addict to a chemical. What are the risks of using nicotine? What is the cost of buying the drug? To what extent are the other members of the family influenced by a parent's continued addiction? Will some of them go on to use other drugs, possibly much more harmful and dangerous? There will be lots more questions to be answered."

"I remember that when we first met I thought you would make a good Parliamentarian with all these questions. They are very difficult to answer and some of the answers will not be pleasant. Maybe the psychiatrists will be brought in to give them all a dose of horrible treatment. I don't think that we shall solve this problem tonight. And you have diverted my mind from the Scrabble business. It's all very horrible, so you've been very clever with that word and I can't go. The game is yours."

. And they voted for cocoa, the late night news and bed.

Judith tidied the kitchen; Gordon set the breakfast table and both raised their mugs of cocoa to wish the Minister of Health the best of luck and to the Treasury more tax income and to the P.M. lots of plain commonsense.

*

One morning when all had gone to work or school and Sally was looking after the small kiddies the phone rang. It continued until their answer phone cut in.

"Oh sorry folks, I forgot you would all be out. It's John with a reminder. Your latest little lamb has not yet suffered his baptismal ceremony. Would next Sunday be convenient? I have two others to baptise that day and thought we might just as well fit little James Leslie in as well. Would Sally and Roland wish for their little daughter to join in the water frolic? Will you think it over and give me a ring. Hope you are all well. Love, Dad."

Sally was opening the door to bring some nappies for young James and heard the last words. She played the message back. 'Oh dear, she thought. Roland was going to arrange a boating expedition that day. He'll have to fix a picnic on board instead of a meal at the pub up river. Oh well...

Later she discussed the matter with Judith and between them they sorted out who would do the sandwiches and who the puddings on board. No difficulty. All they needed was transport to the church. The men would do their stuff.

In due course everything went like clockwork. The babies were all named and blessed, their brows crossed by John's wet finger and a little homily delivered for the parents' benefit. Coffee followed the service when Judith proclaimed how she and Gordon had dealt with the business of smoking and its damage to people as well as costs in taxation. John said he would mention the matter at Synod and the families split off to join together later in a quiet boating expedition on the river.

The sun shone, there were no clouds to threaten rain and, with all settled comfortably, they chugged gently upstream with Roland at the wheel. Something was troubling him. He found a knot in his handkerchief and remembered.

"I suppose you are off duty, Gordon. I forgot to ask."

"Yes it's alright, Rollo, I'm off until 6 p.m. Then I take over."

"Oh right ho, I'll have you back before then."

The ladies took over the commissariat and unpacked an excellent lunch to gladden the hearts of both men and kids. At a convenient spot under the shade of a large weeping willow Roland brought the boat to the bank; Jason jumped out and, with extra rope, tied the painter to the trunk of the tree. It was an idyllic scene with much cheerful munching, orange juice for the children and Judith and cider for the rest. Declaring themselves replete the men settled to snooze; the ladies to pack up the picnic bits and pieces. With all tidily packed away Jilly and Jason went off to indulge in a fishing competition. Peace and quiet reigned… Suddenly it didn't.

*

Frantic shouting shattered the quietness of the afternoon. A man was chasing madly along the river bank towards them hopping over the grassy tussocks and flailing his arms and hands distractedly. He yelled to them "Hallo, hallo, have you seen her, my daughter? She went down the river in a boat."

Roland shouted back, "There was a girl in a canoe about half an hour ago."

"Yes that would be her. Just a kid. Long blonde hair; big boobs, only just 15.. She's gone to meet her boy friend. He's 18. I don't trust him an inch. There's a weir down the river. They don't know about weirs. I must go." He ran away downstream, vigorously..

"I'd better go too, Rollo. Can you bring the boat? There may be trouble". And Gordon jumped out onto the bank and ran as fast as he could after the distressed father. The two families packed up and when all was shipshape Jilly untied the painter and took her seat. Jason left his father to start the engine and turn the boat round to follow the men downriver; but he jumped out and ran as fast as he could after Gordon.

Reckoned at his school to be a good half-miler Gordon still failed to overtake the harassed father; who, poor chap, desperate with anxiety and driving himself to the limit, shouted to the man in the boathouse as he passed, "Have you seen my daughter in a canoe?"

"Yessir, she'm gone downstream twenty minutes ago. She'd a young feller with 'er. Snoggin' something awful they was. Ope they remember the weir down river."

The two men increased their pace even more to come within sight of the weir. The youngsters must have stopped somewhere for a short time for the two kids were now to be seen paddling furiously to persuade the canoe to reach the bank before being swept over the weir. But the effect of several days of rain in the previous week had swollen the waters and the current ran strongly carrying the little boat sideways towards the edge. Escape was impossible and the men watched in horror as the canoe was tipped over, ejecting the girl and boy who were carried down into the boiling waters at the bottom of the weir. It seemed an age before the two heads reappeared above water and the two began to cough and splutter, trying to swim towards the bank. But their swimming powers were too feeble to resist the current and the water simply carried them further downstream.

.. At the side of the weir was a sloping cut in the river bank up which boats could be pulled. Gordon and the father skidded down the muddy surface to the water. Gordon quickly shed his shoes and shirt, plunging in to swim strongly after the unfortunate pair. The father, unable to swim, simply regained the bank and ran down stream keeping pace with the youngsters in the water. But more effective help was at hand. Jason had seen the accident too and promptly ran further down the river bank carefully judging the distance. Pulling off shirt and shoes he used a flat racing dive that carried him far across the water. Swimming strongly he reached the spot where, he judged, he would intercept the girl as she was carried down towards him. And thus it was. Adopting his well practised life saving method he raised her head and kicked powerfully for the bank tugging her along. It took Gordon rather longer to reach the boy who was making little progress. He then was helped by Gordon eventually to reach the bank further downstream.

The girl's father helped her to scramble up the river bank assisted by Jason. Turning to the lad he thanked him most effusively for saving his daughter; then, hugging her tightly, wet though she was, he admonished her for her naughtiness. Jason said "I'll see if I can rescue the canoe," and he ran off, embarrassed, glad to leave the two to sort out their differences.

A hundred yards above the weir Roland brought his boat to where several willow trees graced the river bank with boughs that drooped towards the water. He reversed the engine to slow its progress sufficiently to enable Jilly to leap ashore with the painter which she fastened around one of the trees. When all was secure her mother descended to the cabin and lit the gas under the kettle.

"I guess the first thing they will want will be a cup of hot chocolate," she said. "Life saving is a thirsty business," and while waiting the return of the adventurers she with Sally and Roland proceeded to slake with cool drinks the thirst engendered by the excitement. Jilly, having first checked that her Dad was safe ran off down river to join Jason. He, having rescued the canoe was busy paddling it back upstream. Reaching the weir he was glad of Jilly's assistance to pull it up the muddy slope into calm water. Jilly hopped aboard with Jason and together they paddled up the river to join what was now becoming a happy tea party...The wrath of the father, who gave his name as Tony Dugald, was now subsiding, his daughter having promised obedience in future. Even the older boy who had apologised to her father had gained acceptance to the family party. The presence of mortal danger and the successful rescue had brought about awareness of the realities of life and the need to obey rules for human safety.

Names and addresses were exchanged again and Gordon carefully ascertained that Tony had no connections with newspapers. One morning surgery full of inquisitive patients was quite enough to satisfy him. After recovering from their exertions and handing over the canoe to Tony, they said 'Goodbye' and watched as the girl, Alice, and her friend, Alistair, paddled quietly back upstream. The families' home going was rather quiet and thoughtful...

****

Chapter 12

EMERGENCY AGAIN.
HOLIDAY. DR KING 'S IDEA.

ALL WAS GOING smoothly. Gordon found his expertise being well taken up by the poorly folk of his Bifford practise. The summer season was producing the usual crop of mild casualties in the surgery and the advent of new babies was presenting no desperate problems. Jilly was doing nicely at school and teachers were pleased with her progress. The family's two younger children were progressing normally. Judith found her work very satisfying and had attended two meetings of the Inner Wheel when speakers talked of the joys of growing orchids and the importance of keeping children away from the drug habit. She visited her father and Mary occasionally and entertained them for a meal on a Saturday. She felt it was time to give thought to the approaching holiday in Cornwall once again and began making preparations. It could be fun; the children would love sitting in the boat dancing on the little waves.

That tiny beach at St, Anthony's Head dwelt in her mind; a.lovely spot…

But there were still two weeks to go. That evening she must attend an Inner Wheel meeting and listen to someone talking about some abstruse subject. What a bother Judith got to the Church Hall where Inner Wheel held its meetings just in time for the meal. She settled herself beside a lady who confided to her that she was on her own; her husband and younger son of twelve years were having a holiday in Gibraltar.

As they sampled pineapple and Cornish cream a waitress approached Judith's companion and asked if she would go to the phone. Her husband was calling her. The lady returned five minutes later saying that her husband had come back early because the boy had developed a very painful leg and wanted to see Dr. Jenkins, so they caught a plane and had just got home. They would ring the doctor next morning. Judith said,

"Perhaps you should ask for a visit this evening."

"Oh we mustn't bother him tonight. I expect the morning will do."

"Did your husband say how long the leg had been troubling him?"

"Yes, about three or four days, apparently, but he's complained for a week or two."

Judith thought for a minute; then feeling rather concerned she said, "Let me run you back home and see if he needs the doctor now. It could be serious if it's been going on that long without any treatment." The lady agreed and after apologising to the president they drove off and shortly reached her house. They found the child in bed crying with pain, while the father was trying to comfort him with a hot bottle. Judith asked if she might see the leg and the child drew up his trouser to show her. Below the knee the leg was swollen, red and hot, intensely painful to the slightest pressure.

"May I telephone my husband?" Judith asked. They handed her the phone and Gordon answered. Judith reported the findings to him. He said "Oh that sounds very nasty indeed. I'll come right away."

He was received gladly and shown to the child's bedroom. He felt the child's pulse, noted his temperature and confirmed Judith's findings. From his medical bag he extracted a syringe and prepared an injection which he expertly delivered so that the little lad hardly felt it.

"That will make it feel a bit better. I'll talk to your Mum and Dad."

Downstairs he told the parents, "Your little boy has an infection of the leg bone, the tibia. It is most important to send him to hospital immediately. It needs urgent treatment. May I use your phone please?"

"Not tonight surely, Doctor. Can't it wait till morning?" said the mother.

"No my dear, it is extremely important to get treatment going at once. It may require an operation, so don't give him any food, just very small sips of water or weak, sweet tea."

Gordon got on to the ambulance and phoned the duty doctor at the hospital explaining the urgency of the case. After writing a letter to the doctor there he and Judith waited until the little chap was carefully settled into the ambulance with the parents accompanying him, and finally went home together.

"I think you had some inkling about the diagnosis there, Judy my love. You did well to insist on taking the mother home for you to look at the child. It's a good thing his dad brought him home. I hope the hospital gets on with the job quickly. There's probably an abscess in the bone already."

"It makes me think it was worth while joining the Inner Wheel," she replied. Gordon yawned. "It's 10 p.m, lets go and listen to the rest of the horrors," he said, "although a dose of osteomyelitis is quite enough for one evening. Heigh ho, hope it's a quiet night."

It was, and the next morning found them both alert and ready for their day's work. Gordon said he would take the children to school as it was raining and he would have a bite of lunch at the surgery between visits. Judith declared that it would be steak and kidney pie at 7 p.m, she was finding life quite busy. In the evening the family would all meet together. They did.

"Hi, Dad, said Jilly. "What were you doing at Jimmy's neighbour's house last night? Was it Philip with a leg pain again?" She was home from school, and had evidently heard about the episode from her classmate. Her mum was now back from work and Gordon was about to depart for the evening surgery.

"Yes it was, my Darling. What do you know about it? Has he had trouble before?"

"Yes, he complains about it sometimes. His dad thought he had hurt it playing soccer. That's why he took him for a little holiday."

"Thank you Jilly, I'll make a note of that. It's a good job his father brought him home."

"Good thing Mum rang you and got a proper doctor to go and see him. I think you're wonderful. What was the matter with Philip's leg Dad?"

Gordon regarded his daughter. She was developing fast, he thought It could be quite beneficial to offer her an explanation, and he did so in some detail, as much as she could be expected to assimilate. She listened, taking it all in. "They should be very grateful to you, Dad."

"Your Mum did a jolly good job my Pet. They should thank her. But Jilly, Darling, this is confidential medical stuff. You must not mention what I have told you to anyone"

"OK Dad, mum's the word

The front door-bell rang. Judith went to open it and was presented with a huge bunch of roses bearing a little letter of thanks from Philip's parents. "We thank God for such good friends and expert doctoring. Philip had an operation the same night. They found an abscess just as Gordon had said. They needed to open the bone and drain the pus away. Our little boy is beginning to feel a quite a bit better. "

Perhaps the Inner Wheel could be a useful tool for a doctor's wife, thought Judith.

The next two weeks were busy for Gordon, his colleague being away in Greece for his holiday. However all things progressed well and Judith fitted in holiday preparations between her work hours as well as answering calls from patients anxious for her husband's opinion and medical wisdom. Jilly helped to pack and by the time Dr. King had returned they were all ready for off and anxious to get going m the Sunday. Gordon had changed his car for a larger vehicle capable of housing all their luggage and paraphernalia. Amidst much excitement from the children when the holiday morning broke fine and clear, all piled into the car and set forth.

There is no need to spell out again the details of this Cornish experience. The well known village, the narrow lanes, the welcoming neighbours and the lovely vistas both from Portscatho and St Mawes provided as previously good satisfaction and peace to the soul. The rolling hills, green fields, blue sea and white spray when the wind blew, ruffling the water's surface was relaxing and welcome. The sandy beach for building sandcastles and running races with wavelets to wet the feet of the little ones and deeper water for Jilly to practice her swimming provided endless entertainment. Gordon soon arranged his yachting practice with his sailor friend and induced his family to undertake small responsibilities on board ship. Judith was just content to oversee the family's happiness and make provision for their nourishment without undue stress of cooking. There were plenty of eating places where they were remembered and welcomed.

JIlly demanded to see Lands End and the great ancient cavern of a tin mine. Gordon gladly drove them, stopping to inspect the famous old fishing harbour of Newlyn. At Penzance they noted the Helicopter pad for possible future holidays on the Scilly isles. One morning they started early and caught the 'Scillonian' as she sailed on her way from Penzance to those idyllic islands and spent a most pleasant voyage and playtime on the faery-like island of St Mary. From there a fisherman rowed them over to the isle of Annet to observe the vast number of gulls and other birds that nested there and brought up their young fledglings. Ir was a perfect day for looking at nature's loveliness. They enjoyed a picnic sitting on the soft mossy grass and snoozed afterwards under a blue shy with the sound of waves in their ears as a gentle background to the cries and squawking of the birds.

A seal popped up to inspect them, curious about humans. Jilly chased away a large black-backed gull intent on catching a small chick to eat for his supper.

One afternoon, having driven with a picnic away down past Lamorna where they stopped for lunch, they spent a happy time at the remarkable open air Minack theatre of

Porthcurno near Land's End. Built into the side of the cliff with the open sea as a backdrop, it made a superb setting for the performance of plays or musicals. They watched a version of Mole and Ratty, Badger and Toad as they fought and dispersed the Weasels from Toad's Hall. The children were delighted. "I love old Badger with his big stick bashing the naughty weasels and stoats," said Jilly

"I like Ratty chasing them all, and he's ever so clever with his boat," said Grace.

"I like Toady, bet I can drive like him when I'm bigger", said little Johnny.

Refreshed and happy, though sorry to end that holiday, they finally returned home to find that their neighbouring family had just arrived after their time abroad in the Canaries. It was a joyful reunion with both families vying with each other to tell of new scenes, new foods, new fun and their firm desires to repeat it all again. Parents were almost equally inspired to recount stories of their holidays and it was late indeed by the time the little ones were bedded and fast asleep. The older children continued to compete with excited voices until parents suddenly took account of time and shooed all their chickens away to roost.

*

After evening surgery on the following Monday Dr. King asked Gordon to come into the house for a minute. "I have an idea," he said, which I want to put to you and it would be best if Judith were also present. Can you make it convenient to come in for coffee this evening? If it's difficult on account of baby sitting perhaps my wife and

I could come to your house for a chat. Will you speak to Judith and let me know."

Gordon assented and returned home to tell his wife.

"I wonder what this is all about," said she. "What interesting proposition has he thought up? It would be difficult to arrange baby-sitting tonight. I think we must ask them to come here." A telephone call quickly arranged matters and having eaten and washed up the supper things the Kings were welcomed and made comfortable with a coffee table all prepared.

He was a big well muscled man with greying brown hair and twinkling blue eyes. His wife, by comparison was quite a tiny person, extremely neat and tidy in a charming light blue gown, still with lovely auburn hair and green eyes.

After a few preliminary remarks Dr. King began, "First of all may we get down to Christian names. My wife is Jennifer and as you know I am Herbert or Bertie, for short. I'm a bit hesitant about this proposition but feel I must go ahead and make it and hope you will consider it. I have a nephew in Canada who has recently completed his medical studies. He wants to practise in Canada, but wishes to have experience of general practice in England before settling down eventually in Toronto with a friend of his father. When reading the B.M.J. last weekend I came across an advertisement that spoke of a locum doctor needed for a mission hospital in tropical Africa. It sounded most interesting and I took it upon myself to ring up the missionary society concerned and make enquiries. It is a hospital of excellent repute with most modern facilities and good accommodation for its medical staff. The post will offer astonishingly wide experience in all branches of medicine and surgery. I wondered, Gordon, if you would consider adding to your already wide experience by filling this post for six months. I would then offer a temporary assistantship to the young man in Canada.

I enquired further about the hospital, its geographical location, its facilities and what tribes it serves, what language they speak and a lot more and am quite happy to discover all that you might want to know before you make a decision about this idea. It is in southern Nigeria, in what used to be a forest region, although much of the forest has been cleared by the local folk for converting to crop growing areas. It is certainly tropical, pretty warm and moist and malarial mosquitoes are rampant and have to be kept at bay. I asked the mission authorities to send photographs so I can show these to you when they arrive. You would continue to receive your salary from our practice and I expect the mission would augment this with the customary income for their people, possibly enhancing that with an extra payment for a locum tenens.

The medical possibilities are endless involving all kinds of tropical ailments as well as the usual human troubles that we know so well. There would be a lot of surgery and maternity problems in addition. I looked into the local library for a book on the whole subject and will leave this with you to examine. Please don't think that there is any pressure on you to take up this idea. The young Canadian can find other openings, I feel quite sure. Only think of accepting the idea if it appeals to you and if Judith agrees."

Gordon's mouth fell open. He didn't know what to say. He looked at Judith, but she averted her head. She too felt it was impossible to comment At last Gordon took courage and replied to his colleague saying, "This is quite an astonishing notion, doctor. I really have no idea how to respond. It will take a lot of thought and talks with Judith before any decision can be reached. It is a most remarkable thing. May we have some time to think it over please? "

"Yes of course. I am sure it must be something of a shock to you both. Take plenty of time, and I will try to find someone who has been there and bring you together somehow. Then you will be able to find out more than just an advertisement and a letter from the mission authorities can give you. One thing you will find is that the political situation is in a state of flux but at present a reasonably strong government is in place. We'll find out more details of the political situation at the present time and how it looks for the future. As I said there is no pressure on you. It's just an idea."

"Well, thank you for that. We shall have to think hard and discuss a lot of things" replied Gordon. "Naturally," said Dr. King. "I've given you something of a problem, I'm afraid. We had better run along and leave you to recover." Saying which he and his wife rose and after kindly expressions made their exit, leaving the young folk to talk it all over.

"I think another cup of tea would be acceptable," said Judith. "Better that than alcohol. We'll have to keep our brains clear."

"Agreed, what a pile of problems this idea brings up. Separation from me for you and the children. We've never been apart except for the orthopaedic job in Sheffield. This is 3000 miles away in a foreign country. An unknown language. People with ideas quite different from ours. We'll have to think hard."

After their colleague and his wife had returned home the two settled with cups of coffee and Judith suggested that each of them should make a list of thoughts and ideas concerning this most unusual proposal from Dr. King. Pros and cons would be likely to feature prominently. There would be disagreements, and they must be very careful to discuss these calmly and without getting heated.

The decision would not easily be reached, but it needed to be a united decision. Family unity was a most important matter. For the best part of an hour each sat with pen and paper making careful and considered notes while sipping their tea and nibbling some of Judith's much loved flapjacks.

"Shall we discuss now?" said Gordon, "or might it be wiser to let the matter simmer in our brains for a day or two." . "I'd like to have some time to think it over," said Judith. It might be good to have other folks' ideas and opinions to help decision making."

"Yes, Grandpa's thoughts could be useful. Perhaps we might approach Donald and Angela too. They are a wise pair. I imagine that the B.M.A. would be knowledgeable on the subject. We need to do quite a bit of research," added Gordon.

Having decided on that thought they concentrated their minds on a game of Scrabble, after which sleep was a welcome diversion.

For several days they were fully occupied at work, but on the Thursday when Gordon had a half day they went to see Donald and Angela and asked them for their views regarding the proposed locum in Africa, having already informed them of the idea by telephone. Donald had talked to the B.M.A and a friendly West African expert had checked up on the mission hospital as well as on the political situation and the climate. Angela had talked to the Mission headquarters people in London to discover as much as possible concerning living conditions and about fellow workers and staff at the hospital. They were well informed.

Gordon would have a bungalow to himself with an

African cook and a steward to look after him. Furnishing was simple but adequate. A mosquito net was always used over the bed. Electric light was from the town supply but the hospital also had its own generator. A manager looked after this and all other needful household necessities, gardening etc Motor transport was available for shopping and a driver cared for its mechanics... Much of the food supplies were obtained by the steward and there were shops in the town where the doctor could shop on his own account. Great care was taken to ensure that food was well cooked or boiled and sterilised. There was a piped water supply and if that failed each house had a tank full of rainwater. All water was boiled, cooled and filtered. The staff of doctors and nursing sisters often joined together for social occasions, tea parties or sometimes dinners in the evening. Senior African staff joined them by invitation and there was nothing in the way of a colour bar. Nurses in training had their own accommodation and ate separately. Medical lectures to them were given by the doctors and nursing sisters.

Injections for yellow fever, typhoid and tetanus were routine. Anti-malarial precautions were essential as also were anti-polio oral drops and an injection against Hepatitis B. Smallpox was now considered to have been eradicated. Other troubles like dengue and loa-loa worms might occur and must be faced .along with a number of other tropical diseases of various kinds. Tsetse fly bothered cattle but humans rarely suffered.

Attack by animals was almost unknown. Snakes would normally avoid human kind but must be remembered and avoided carefully. The grass of the hospital compound was kept well trimmed providing little shelter for them. The rule was to kill a snake when possible and enquire afterwards whether it was a poisonous type or not. Safety first was essential. Anti snake venom was kept in the hospital.

The weather? Being only a few degrees north of the equator it was hot. The area was in the tropical rain forest and rain was abundant at certain times of the year. Humidity was often very troublesome. Furious storms occurred with lightning and thunder and a rainy season took the place of our summer.

Our winter was their dry season; marked by excessive heat by day; it was cooler by night and prolonged drought was the norm with very occasional storms. Very fine sand from the Sahara made the atmosphere unpleasant to breathe and caused haziness in the air. It was so dry that even table tops of hardwood could develop a slight warp from side to side.

Should the water supply give out and rain be insufficient there were wells that always contained water. Hospital buildings and staff houses had a piped supply of cold water. Every roof supplied rainwater to its own cold water tank; from this water could be pumped up if necessary by a semi-rotary pump to the roof tank. Cooking was by electricity normally but old fashioned stoves were still serviceable and could be used with wood for fuel if necessary.

Gordon and Judith listened carefully, making notes. They spent time in discussion with their hosts until late, finally retiring to their home to rest their minds with sleep. The next day would be a busy one but the weekend would come and they could consider and discuss all that they had learned. A decision could not be long delayed.

Saturday morning dawned fine and clear. The girls wanted to play with their friends next door. Judith asked if Sally could look after their little boy for an hour or two. They put a picnic basket, prepared the night before, into the car and climbed aboard. In the shade of a big oak standing in a new park only a few miles away Gordon switched off the engine.

"I guess we have as much info as we need Judy. Have you any thoughts on the matter?" Gordon wanted to discover what were his wife's deep feelings about this suggestion It had taken them both by surprise. They would need to be very honest with each other.

"Well there are two obvious points that come to mind. Firstly it's a wonderful chance for you to enlarge your experience," said Judith. "Secondly it will be the first time that we have been apart for any real length of time."

"Yes", said Gordon, "and the second point is the more important for both of us. Being apart affects the children too. For me the separation effects are diluted by having an interesting job to keep me busy. For you it means non-sharing with household responsibilities, quite apart from the sad lack of personal contact."

"We can put lots of kisses on letter heads and envelopes, but it's not quite the same as close cuddles," said Judith. She added "The children will be sad. Of course being very young they have their own concerns and playmates and will soon get used to having only one parent with just letters from the other. You'll miss six months of your little boy, but I expect he'll forgive you."

"But what about you my sweetheart? How will you manage with your lover far away for so long?"

The question was debated for quite a long time, with each assuring the other of their undying devotion. At last with coffee cups in their hands Judith said,

"There is one matter that we have not discussed. What about the need for medical help for those poor people whom the mission serves so well. They desperately need a doctor's services. Folk walk for miles and miles to that hospital. There will be fearful disappointment if there is no chance of seeing a doctor, whereas here the doctor is just around the corner, more or less."

Talk on those lines went on over the weekend, often into the small hours. They were tired, but with the decision nearly made. The next day while at work, Judith asked if she might talk to Gordon's father and arrangements were made. She said to him,

"I've thought hard and long over this question. I think it is the wife's job to reach the decision. My decision is made. There is a lot at stake but I think he should go. I'll tell him this evening."

Gerald took a deep breath. "That is a very honourable and self-sacrificing decision, Judith. I believe it will make your marriage even stronger. I know that Gordon would like to go and the experience will not be wasted in his future life."

That evening Judith told Gordon that he ought to go to Africa.

****

CHAPTER 13

SEPARATION. OFF TO AFRICA.

THE NEXT MORNING after surgery had finished Gordon told Dr. King that he was ready to write to the Mission and offer his services. He and Judith had spent a most emotional evening and Gordon was most appreciative of her strength of mind and depth of love in agreeing to let him go. She was well aware of his desire and convinced that such a course would benefit his career while serving to strengthen the bond between them.

At home Judith took Gordon's hand and pressed it to her bosom. "You must go my Darling man. They need you. But I shall miss you and long for your return,"

"Thank you, Darling wife. Thank you very much. It will be wonderful to come home to you. I love you my Precious." The emotion was deep. The embrace was urgent and lasting.

He wrote a courteous letter to the Mission and received a grateful reply with appreciation of his offer and details of business arrangements. It simply remained to acquire appropriate clothing and other items suitable for life in the tropics. Then he must explain to Jilly and Grace. The former soon understood the need of children for a doctor in the wilds of Africa

"I expect they'll be glad to have you to make them better, Daddy. Take lots of photos and send them back to us won't you? I'm glad we don't have to walk lots of miles to see you when we're poorly. It's nice having a doctor in the house," said .Jilly.

Grace said that she'd be happy to wait till he came back, perhaps with some little gift of African origin to decorate her dressing table which she always kept neat and tidy. "Do they make little people and chiefs out of wood in Africa?" she enquired.

Two weeks later all was ready. The young Canadian medico was arriving, but just too late to meet Gordon. A date for Gordon's flight had been arranged .and in due course Gerald drove him to the airport Judith elected to stay with the children after a very affectionate leave-taking. The younger children just hugged him and told him to come back soon. Jilly, with much understanding of what her father was going to do, said, "Make them all better, Dad. Don't work too hard. Remember to take your tablets and shelter from the sun. I'll write you letters." Judith's father and Mary had come over to support her. She was grateful indeed. With the girls at school there remained only her small son, playing and oblivious to the emotional effects of his Daddy's departure. So the momentous day of separation passed; they could only look forward eagerly to the day of reunion. Meanwhile Mary was there to smooth the churned up emotions. She made a pot of tea. "Let's celebrate his triumphant return" she said.

Gordon enjoyed the long flight over France and the Med, watching with interest the peaks of the French Alps peering above the clouds. A short 'put down' at Tunis was followed by the long night hop over the Sahara to land finally in the early morning at Lagos in Nigeria. He stepped out into the hot sunshine and steamy heat of the tropics. After spending some time persuading the immigration officials of his good intentions towards the sick people of their country, he felt glad to meet the Lagos secretary of the Mission who held up a big card bearing Gordon's name. It was a most kindly meeting followed by transport to the Mission headquarters on the Marina where the secretary's wife entertained him to a long cold fruity drink which was very welcome. Gordon soon felt at home and was invited to telephone his wife and inform her of his safe arrival. It took quite a long time to make the contact but they had a very loving chat and felt together again.

Then down to business with information about transport to the hospital where he was keenly awaited by the overworked staff. They will be extremely glad to see you, he was told.

"At 4 p.m. we'll close the shop and go for a sail if that's alright by you," said the secretary. "Are you a good sailor? Sailing is my hobby and fishing comes in very handy both for the table and for selling nice big jack and sometimes barracuda in the market. It helps to pay Boat Club fees."

"I assure you that I'd be delighted. I should add that I have been an enthusiast ever since my father taught me the basic rules of sailing. I can handle a rod too." said Gordon.

After a meal, of fish of course, he was told to put his feet up and enjoy a snooze until it was time for boat palaver. He was very glad to do so; the flight overnight had not been conducive to sleep.

He woke to a gentle tap on his shoulder. "Come on, time for a sail," was his host's command. Within minutes .he felt the warm air rushing past his face as in the secretary's old car they shot off to the Boat Club. On his right was the blue water of Lagos harbour; with a passenger ship anchored in deep water. It was surrounded by small boats whose owners busied themselves selling their wares to passengers and crew. The boat club men had launched the secretary's boat and Gordon assisted his host to raise the mast and fix the stays; then to haul up the mainsail and jib and pull the sheets. A good push and they were sailing, with centreboard down, rudder operative and a steady breeze propelling them along. It was Gordon's job to prepare the rods, arrange the lures with their hooks and start fishing with no time wasted. Soon came a hefty tug on the line and he began to wind it in with a good 8 lb jack struggling on the lure.

Harry said "Jolly good, you're a fisherman alright. We'll go out to the bar; water's a bit rough but it's quite good fishing out there."

He headed for the harbour entrance and beyond it over the bar Gordon certainly found himself well tested, trying to cope with two rods and fish determined to impale themselves on his hooks. With another five good specimens he declared that it would be nice to find calm water. His host agreed, congratulating Gordon, and went about to return into the calmer waters of the harbour. Letting out the mainsail a little he suggested to Gordon that he loosen the jib sheet too and they returned more slowly, with the breeze now lessening, towards the boat club. There it was easy work to heave up the centre board, remove the rudder, tidy all the ropes and stays after lowering the mast, leaving the club's employees to deal with the boat.

Back in the house Harry's wife brought out cool drinks and enquired how Gordon had enjoyed his trip.

"First class, thank you," he replied. "Your fish are a lot bigger than the trout of our small river back home. I hope you'll get a good price for them."

"Well, we leave that to our steward. He palavers with the market traders and charges us a little sum for his services on the deal. It's all good fun."

A quick bath followed in tepid water and Gordon dressed in a long sleeved shirt, long trousers followed by anti-insect cream smeared onto exposed areas of skin to defeat mosquitoes.

He found that the vigorous on-shore breeze of the day had subsided and the humidity of the tropical air was rather trying when dressed with arms and legs so carefully covered. However it was better than a dose of malaria so they all put up with the discomfort. At bedtime thin pyjamas and a thin sheet were quite adequate. The mattress was a bit ancient. He realised that funds of the mission had to be watched with care. Sleeping under a mosquito net was a new experience. . Warmth and humidity made for a somewhat restless night. The return of morning light brought back the daytime breeze making life more pleasant. Grape fruit, guinea corn cereal with tinned milk from the big store in the town preceded toast and marmalade and made for a home experience that he found comforting. To Harry's enquiries about how he felt he replied, "Fit for anything, ready to have a go."

A short journey to a big store on the Marina found Gordon searching for other items of useful equipment for life in the tropics. Another afternoon sail with his host followed ere preparing for the next part of his journey to the upcountry hospital. On the next day the hospital's car arrived with a driver ready to convey him to his home for the next six months. With packing done and Goodbyes said, he began his journey.

Leaving Lagos and the sea behind they passed through groves of coconut, oil palm and banana and cocoa plantations; also small villages where sheep and goats crossed the road in front of them uncaringly. Here and there women sat beside roadside stalls laden with fruit and other edibles. Oranges, bananas, limes, vegetables of various kinds, yam and cassava were prominent among them. Driving was at times hazardous when great lorry loads of timber confronted them and obliged their driver to veer onto the roadside to afford passageway to the heavy vehicles. Seldom was it possible to obtain a view of the surrounding country on account of the thick bushy foliage interspersed with tall trees that lined the road. Passing, after some 60 miles, through Abeokuta with its great upstanding rocky protrusions superheated by the constant sunshine, they reached the huge city of Ibadan at about the 100 mile mark. Here a stop at a missionary teaching college afforded them a chance for rest and refreshment with a chance to meet other mission workers who all welcomed Gordon to the country and wished him well.

After enduring the last and longest lap of some 85 or more miles during the hot and humid afternoon, they finally reached the mission hospital where Gordon was gladly welcomed and would find work for both his hands and his mind. The senior doctor, contacted during an afternoon ward round, gladly hurried to meet his new colleague and led him to his bungalow where he found the doctor's wife overseeing final preparations for his future comfort. They introduced themselves as Joan and

Alfred Patterson and quickly made Gordon feel at home. Afternoon tea brought some relief for the weariness of the drive after which Alfred invited him to view the hospital and its facilities, and also its patients and responsibilities. In the hospital he met another doctor colleague who was busy with an afternoon clinic. He too welcomed Gordon and told him that his wife and two children would try to provide a little entertainment for him sometimes. If they were noisy he apologised in advance.

Gordon's cook, Johnathan, and Joseph the steward, both members of the Ibo tribe, were introduced to him in his bungalow and he was left to use his bathroom where hot water was ready in a large bucket with cold water laid on in the taps. By the time he had unpacked a little, bathed and dressed, the sun had set and the darkness of the tropics rapidly followed. With his steward, he then inspected the house. This was a compact job, cement-block walled, cement coated and painted well with good quality wall paint. Doors and furniture were of solid mahogany, windows glazed but normally left open, shutters available. The roof was of asbestos cement sheets and was supplied with gutters which led rain water into tanks in case of water shortage in the taps. Two bedrooms, a living room stretching from front to back, a small office and a kitchenette completed the facilities, the whole being surrounded by eight ft wide verandas and totally enclosed by fine wire mosquito netting.

Electric light was adequate and pathways outside were lighted also. Oil palms bordered the paths to other staff bungalows and along one of these Gordon made his way to join Alfred and Joan for an evening meal in their domain. Grapefruit from a nearby tree began the meal and was followed by antelope meat, yam, beans, carrots and some green veg, all well cooked by a competent man of the Ibo race. Apple pie and custard was a welcome treat for his first night's introduction to life in the 'bush'. After conversing for an hour or so Gordon bade his hosts 'goodnight' and returned on the lighted paths under the huge palm leaves to his bungalow. He quickly undressed and beat any possible mosquitoes by sliding quickly under his net which he promptly tucked in securely. He noted a few 'mossies' that had somehow bypassed the wire proofing and were searching for entry via his net; he was intrigued to see a number of fireflies flitting about the bedroom their tiny lights switched on. The full moon shone on the grassy lawns and small poinsettia bushes around the bungalow. He could hear the sound of drumming in the distance; he imagined small parties of African folk making merry with their little shuffling dances to the beat of the drums, mysteriously sending out their messages. All was peaceful and he spent a dreamless night.

A knock on the door awoke him. "Come in" he called and Joseph's young assistant entered bearing his morning cup of tea.

"Hot water dae for bathroom, sah," said he and when Gordon asked what time breakfast would be ready he replied, "Breakfast after prayers with nurses, sah." He added that prayers would be in the hospital chapel, so thither Gordon padded his way in his bedroom slippers. Doctors, Nursing Sisters and all the off duty nursing staff made up a small congregation. A Nigerian nurse read a Bible passage, another read a prayer and after singing a hymn they all trooped out leaving Gordon to greet the Nursing Sisters who bade him a hearty welcome.

"We appreciate your coming doctor. We all hope that you will enjoy the work here and have a happy time with us."

. "I'm very glad to be here with you; you are obviously

doing a wonderful job and I am very proud to be of service along with you." he replied.

Then it was breakfast in his bungalow with grapefruit and guinea corn cereal again, toast and good English marmalade. Alfred called on him shortly afterwards and led him to the outpatient department. Gordon was introduced to the senior clerk.

"Welcome to our hospital, doctor," said Zachariah, a tall well made Yoruba with light brown skin and smiling eyes. He shook Gordon's hand firmly.. "We are very glad that you have come so many miles to help us. We hope you will enjoy the work here and we will be happy to help you in any way."

Gordon made a suitable reply and sitting down beside Alfred they started the morning clinic together. Zachariah brought in the first patient and interpreted for the doctors his statement of complaints. It seemed that a worm was troubling him. So it was listen, examine, diagnose, prescribe treatment and move him along to the dispensary. After half a dozen folk had been dealt with Alfred said, "You don't need instructions from me, Gordon. You might note that in describing symptoms the patient always ascribes his trouble as due to a 'worm'. If you can manage, just carry on with Zachariah to assist. I will get along to the ward and do my round."

Gordon agreed to take over and found the clerk most useful in discovering the details of patients' complaints. There were folk with worms, malaria, dysentery, chest infections, abscesses, throat troubles, jiggers under their toenails, the occasional hernia, urinary troubles and a host of complaints some of which Gordon had never met. After coping with about fifteen of such troubles he was aware of a nurse who had quietly entered through the open door behind him. She presented a note from Sister, and then said,

"Please doctor Sister says can you come very soon. The patient is in great pain." Gordon read the note. "Yes, nurse I'll come at once." He asked the clerk to keep the patients until he returned saying, "Sister tells me there is a man with a tense swelling in the groin, present for three days. She has suggested a possible strangulated hernia. She has told the theatre nurse to get things ready for an operation. I'll go and confirm, and come back to see the rest of the folk."

Reaching the male ward he joined Sister at the patient's bedside. The poor man was trying not to groan with pain. It was the work of a moment to see that Sister had been correct in her diagnosis. She was busily preparing for the insertion of a glucose saline drip. Gordon, holding the man's pulse was concerned; he was glad to perform the needful procedure of inserting a needle into an arm vein. The fluid was turned on and the flow adjusted.

"What is your habit regarding premed.injections for such patients, Sister"

"Morphine and atropine, intramuscularly", she replied

"Right, will you give a dose straight away please and I'll come as soon as theatre is ready. Do I have an assistant?"

"Yes certainly, doctor. The chief clerk, Zachariah, will stand opposite you. You will find him an excellent assistant. He always has the correct instrument ready when you want it. He has been well trained. He could probably perform the operation on his own."

Sister grinned happily, knowing well the capability of their excellent clerk, interpreter and operating assistant. Gordon felt most impressed, pleased indeed to find such expertise in the midst of the African bush. He managed to finish his O.P.s just in time when the message came that 'theatre is ready', doctor.' Zachariah guided his steps to the theatre and Gordon was impressed to find a large room, spotlessly clean, white painted and measuring some 20ft square.with a fairly modern operating table in the centre and a large shadow-less lamp hanging over it. Instruments were already laid out on tables and the patient, well sedated, was already in place covered with a blanket to ensure warmth. An old Boyle's anaesthetic machine stood at the head of the table and Sister sat there ready to commence the anaesthetic. .To his enquiry about the manner of sterilising he received the one word reply, 'Steam'.

Gordon felt more impressed and even humbled to think that missionary work could be so very much up-to-date. He hastened to 'scrub up' at the basin filled with warm water, treated with Dettol. A jolly good scrub, a sterile towel, gown, hat and gloves lubricated with sterilised powder, and he and Zachariah were ready. Sister had already rendered the patient asleep under the anaesthetic with halothane, gas and oxygen.

The surgical detail of a major abdominal operation is not for the tender mind of the average reader. It may be found in an expensive textbook of surgery. The incision, the blood vessels severed and sealed off by catgut or cautery, the handling and investigation of the damaged section of intestine may be interesting but is not for the fainthearted. Nor is the matter of deciding on removal of the damaged section of gut and sewing together of the healthy ends of the intestine.

The closing of the wound, the days of worrying about whether the normal function of the intestine would return must be left to the concerns of the surgical team. Let them ponder about it. Just be glad to know that the patient made a good recovery, regained normal intestinal function, began to eat small meals and within a month was well enough to walk to the town and find a lorry or bus going to his village. Did the villagers throw a party to welcome him? Surely there would be rejoicing that he had been rescued from the gates of death. Perhaps a feast would be appropriate with a garland of hibiscus around his neck, drummers and a shuffling dance to celebrate his return. Lots of palm wine no doubt...

Alfred called at Gordon's bungalow to congratulate him on a piece of expert surgery. The nursing staff were pleased that their new colleagues had shown such admirable skill at the operating table, and the patient's relatives were much n evidence with their 'Adupe O' and 'O ti shay dahdah' – (Thank you & he's done a good job'.), whenever he passed them in the corridor. That evening Gordon asked if he might pay for a phone call to his wife. He was told 'yes' but there would probably be a two hour delay ere he could get through. Never mind, persevere.... At last it came through.

"Hallo my Darling, here's your husband sending you lots of love and hoping you are managing to survive the stings and arrows along with our little cherubs. Hope you are all well. I love you."

"Gordon, how wonderful to hear you, where are you Darling? Somewhere in the middle of the rain forests of Africa? Dear man, however did you manage to phone? Yes we're all fine. Missing you but very proud of you doing that job for the poor folk in Nigeria. Would you like to talk to Jilly?"

A loving and lively conversation ensued with the two girls ensued. Afterwards Gordon managed to tell Judith of his first emergency operation and she countered with news that his Dad was shortly going to visit the huge Pyramids and Museums of Cairo, hoping not to be abducted by villains or mesmerised by the Sphinx Gordon told her that he would write a long letter and they just had time to declare their undying affection for each other before the operator cut them off.

Later, having consumed his evening meal of goat's meat, yam, beans and carrots followed by rice pudding made with Klim milk, Gordon walked peacefully across under the huge palm leaves to his colleague's house. They had planned a talk and perhaps some gentle games of Scrabble. He liked the quiet walk under the great palm leaves, in the light of moon and stars with the hospital and compound lights, all against the background of a pitch black sky and innumerable twinkling stars. In the distance the drums of Africa were still spelling out their messages- he wondered what tales were being told.

Alfred's greeting was warm. "Good to see you, Gordon. How has your day gone after that chopping adventure in the theatre this morning?"

"I'm finding Africa very interesting, thank you. Folk always seem to blame their woes on a worm; certainly there is a splendid variety of wrigglers in this country. They insist that it is a 'very bad worm' that troubles them. When one of the garden 'boys' killed a snake this morning he too said it was a very bad snake. How would he know?"

"Well," said Alfred, "it's just as well to despatch them first and ask questions afterwards. Many of the snake varieties here in Nigeria are poisonous, perhaps most varieties are so. One of my predecessors used to pay sixpence for a snake's head. A useful income for the gardeners and it made life a bit safer for everyone."

They chatted while the coffee lasted with Gordon telling them of how things were progressing in England, both politically and in the field of medicine. Heart operations had become more commonplace; coronary occlusions were being better investigated and treated, costs of the N.H.S and manufactured goods were rising. We were becoming a nanny state with people depending on the 'government' to do everything for us. Higher taxation was the result and of course folk would vote, willy-nilly, for the chap who said his government would not raise taxes. He kept his job and the tax was raised on the quiet some other way. Many voters failed to realise that services must be paid for. It was just a matter of simple arithmetic. Heigh ho!

A game of Bridge or Scrabble diverted their minds from veering into politics. Let them get on with it. Hospital life in the African 'bush' was a serious matter and a relaxing game helped greatly to ease the tensions. Later it was time for the night round and, hopefully, bed. It was Gordon's turn to do the hospital night round. Into each ward went he and the charge nurse reported about any patient who was rather ill or needed attention. Each nurse in turn wished him a 'Happy night's rest'. Sometimes that would be his pleasure, often such pleasure was denied.

*

As he became more experienced Gordon would realise that often a patent was kept in the house all day and only brought to the hospital's care after dark when he would be less likely too be observed by neighbours; perhaps because of the fear of 'ill wishing'? Superstition abounded still, despite education. This would sometimes make the late evening very busy, especially if work in the operating theatre was necessary, The Sisters coped with maternity patients in the labour room and only involved the doctor if some emergency threatened. The doctors on the staff were tending to specialise, each in one particular field, but they all took part in the work of the outpatient consultations and large numbers of patients were attended to in that way. At all the evening get-togethers Gordon began to learn much of the local ways of life both in the hospital and among the townsfolk. A good night's sleep afterwards was a bonus much to be welcomed, although the duty doctor might well find his sleep disturbed by serious emergencies.

****

Chapter 14

DAD'S JOB IN DETAIL.
A DISPENSARY TRIP.

"Mummy", said Jilly one day "what does Daddy actually do in Africa? It's a terribly big country isn't it? Are there lots of children for him to look after?"

"Yes, darling, it's huge. It is a continent with many different countries and many thousands of boys and girls. Daddy helps them to get better when they are ill."

"Bur what does he actually do to make them better?

"Well my pet, first of all he has to examine them after listening to what their mummies tell him about their illness. He counts the pulse at the wrist and takes their temperatures with a thermometer; he listens to their breathing in their chests; he hears their heart sounds and feels their tummies. If they need their blood examined he sends them to the laboratory. After all that he has to decide what is wrong and then write a prescription for medicine or tablets for their mummies to give them. Then they will get better."

"He must be pretty busy, Mummy. I wonder if he ever sticks needles into people? Does he Mummy?"

"Sometimes he has to do that darling, especially if they are very ill and need the treatment urgently. Putting medicine into them with a syringe and needle gets it to the source of the trouble more quickly."

"Does he do operations on people Mummy? A little boy in our class called Johnny Wilcox was sent into the hospital to have his appendix out. They put him to sleep and the doctor cut him and found the appendix and took it out. Does Daddy do that too?"

"Yes my sweetie, when it is necessary he does operations. The patient is always very deeply asleep so doesn't feel anything. What a lot of questions."

"Did Daddy ever give me an injection, sticking a needle into me?"

"When you were a tiny girl and we were on holiday you were quite ill one evening; very hot and coughing a lot. Daddy listened to your chest and said, 'This little girl of ours needs help quickly. She has a very bad infection in her chest'. We couldn't find a doctor at the time so Daddy opened his medical bag, got some medicine in a syringe and gave you a needle prick. You didn't like it much and screamed the place down for a couple of minutes. But next morning you were a lot better. So that's enough for now. Go to sleep. Good night, my darling."

After a cuddle and a kiss Jilly clasped her teddy closely and closed her eyes. Judith rang up her friend next door and they had a good laugh over Jilly's medical question and answer session. Sally remembered that she had an appointment to see the midwife next day. Dr. King had surprised her with news that another baby was on the way. She asked if Judith would like to join her and hold her hand and was quite disappointed when told that Judith had a work day. "Oh well", said Sally, "only seven months to go anyway. I guess I can cope with a B.P check... She's a very nice woman. I'll tell her about Jilly and her medical interest."

Judith thought that would be a spicy bit of news for Gordon and took out her writing pad and an envelope. She sighed as she addressed the envelope and whispered "five months to go." She wrote a long loving letter, kissed the signature and placed the letter on her work file for posting in the morning.

*

Gordon placed a big cross on the back of his letter to Judith, kissed it and fixed a stamp on it. Tomorrow the hospital driver would take it to the post office. Tomorrow also he would be introduced to the business of taking medical expertise to the dispensaries in the 'bush' where resident nurses would collect patients for him to see on his round of dispensary visits. These happened once monthly and the doctors took turns to do the visits. These journeys also served as a pleasant change and even relaxation after the previous month's hard grind in the hospital. The dispensary round could be busy but provided a refreshing alternative to the hospital routine. That night was his night on duty but he was lucky; there were no calls.

Having packed quickly to face a night away he attended morning prayers, breakfasted and found the hospital car ready and waiting. It was serviced, fuelled and loaded with medical boxes of drugs and medicines. One of the clerks would join him and the hospital driver would manage the journey driving the heavy car. The three men climbed in along with Gordon's steward who would look after them, waved to Sister and set off. Through the busy streets of the town they drove, threading their way among the crowds of pedestrians, using the horn frequently and trying to avoid goats and sheep that shared the road with the populace. The driver chose a road going northeast, now tar-sealed, but still only wide enough for a single vehicle. When two vehicles met the near wheels must move to the side, off the tarmac hoping it was not too muddy from recent rain.

Very soon they entered the region of tall trees and thick high bushes redolent of the tropical forests of Nigeria, but the road passed efficiently through the area. It had been well cared for by the public works department; there were no trees across the road and potholes had been repaired. Now and then they passed through a roadside village where the market women sat beside stalls laden with fruit and vegetables of various kinds. They stopped to purchase oranges and bananas and were thanked graciously by the ladies.

Twenty miles along the road the driver stopped in a village outside a building bearing the sign 'Dispensary.' The building, mud walled and cement finished with a galvanised iron roof, stood amidst a row of similar houses in a side road leading out to another village. The road was laterite surfaced, dry and dusty, but horribly wet and slippery in the rain. Gordon's first morning job awaited him. A young Yoruba girl in nurses' uniform, looking very neat and tidy, opened the stout iroko door and greeted him politely. She led him into a small consulting room where stood a table and two chairs with a stack of record cards piled up on the table. An examination table stood along one wall. The rear door remained open for ventilation.

Gordon sat at the table and the nurse brought in the first patient and translated.

"He complains of a hernia. It comes out and goes in but he is afraid it will get stuck and strangulate. He has seen other men with such trouble and is much frightened."

Gordon examined the man on the table.

"You are quite right, nurse," he said. "This man needs an operation to cure his hernia. Please tell him to come to the hospital next Monday and we will do the operation next day."

While nurse explained to the patient Gordon wrote up the record card and selected the next one. The man seemed satisfied. He said "Adupe O" - thank you - many times and went his way.

For well over an hour and a half the session continued with many complaints of malaria, diarrhoea, chest troubles, worms of various kinds and leg ulcers and even a case of osteomyelitis with a discharging abscess below the knee. For him an operation at the hospital was essential. There were cataracts needing removal at hospital, vaginal leakage of urine following a difficult childbirth, (another operation needed) and children with measles, whooping cough and the dreaded kwashiorkor. The latter had to be admitted to hospital at once and arrangements were made to send a messenger for the hospital's ambulance to collect child and mother.

Lastly there came a man who looked anxious. Tall and well made he was accompanied by his wife, looking equally fearful. Silently she pointed to three areas on her husband's back. Gordon saw several very pale patches of skin. He glanced enquiringly at the nurse.

"They are terrified of leprosy, doctor," she said.

After examination Gordon concluded that the couple were quite right. Leprosy it was.

"Tell them, nurse that they are right, but the disease is now quite curable. They need not be afraid. It is not likely that the wife will catch the disease. He will need treatment at a different hospital."

Gordon looked at the nurse enquiringly again. She nodded;

"Yes, I know the hospital, doctor. They will need to get a lorry or a bus. I will tell them where to go."

She spoke to the couple for some minutes. The wife replied asking urgently how long the treatment would take and nurse told her it would take three years. He would be taking tablets every day and be looked after at the hospital. .They had a lot to think about but they looked relieved and thanked Gordon and the nurse. She said that she would talk more to them later.

Gordon breathed deeply. He was beginning to realise still more of the great need for medical aid in this huge land. After helping to restock nurse's shelves with supplies from his boxes he joined the others in the car to travel the next thirty miles to find accommodation for the night at a missionary's house. In the compound there a dispensary with another crowd of patients awaited his attention. Gordon enquired, "How long have they been here, nurse?"

"They have been waiting for hours, many since dawn," she replied. "Some of them came several days ago and have taken lodgings in the village." He felt that he must deal with them immediately. The nurse found him a drink of orange, and a couple of biscuits from his bag sustained him for the duration of the consultations that followed.

He found the complaints much the same as before. The malaria and the diarrhoea in children were often serious enough to make him fear for their lives. All he could do was to hope that the nurse would manage to cope with the treatment. The difficulty in persuading folk to take the correct dose of medicine or tablets was very real. If one tablet thrice daily would make them better in a week why not take three instead of one and get better sooner? Explanation was very necessary and could take a long time.

It was with relief that he retreated to the missionary's big double storey house when he felt that he had done his best. That best had ended with an operation under anaesthetic on a very nasty abscess in the hand of a local farmer. Nurse had carefully instructed the man to take no food that morning in view of a probable anaesthetic. Gordon doped the poor man with ethyl chloride and ether (the old fashioned anaesthetic), and used the scalpel to good purpose, cutting into the abscess between the first and second fingers. A generous river of pus streamed out. The condition must have caused the patient real agony and on waking he was glad indeed to find his pain much less. An injection of morphine had helped also, plus penicillin of course.

In the house the clerk was also given a room while the driver stayed in the nearby village with the cook who had come in to prepare meals for them. A warm bath refreshed Gordon and, clothed and protected from mosquitoes in the mossie-proofed lounge-diner, he was served with an excellent meal by the missionary's steward.

His employer had been absent on furlough for some four months but his 'boys' kept everything in good order and coped with visitors by arrangement. There was a generator to provide electric light and this powered a radio that was carefully .wrapped to protect it from the moist air of the tropics. An ancient gramophone with '78 'records was displayed prominently in one corner. Gordon chose a record in which the singer averred that 'Glasgae belangs tae me' and felt as though he was on holiday. After that piece of wisdom he played 'Loch Lomond' which almost brought tears to his eyes. Ending his entertainment with the lovely song about 'Roamin in the Gloamin with a Lassie by my Side' he was inspired to settle with pen and paper and write a long epistle to his beloved wife ere retiring to bed. Finally, unwisely braving the mosquitoes, he stepped outside onto the veranda and inspected the heavens.

The view from the southern aspect showed in the bright moonlight a vast forest of trees and high bush beyond the confines of the large compound. Above, the Southern Cross was visible lying on its side and stars sparkled brilliantly against the enormous blackness of the night sky. It presented a splendid picture to ease his mind as he turned his steps toward bed. He felt a great peace as he tucked himself under his mosquito net and slept soundly until morning light.

He was woken by the steward with a welcome cup of tea and the news that he could expect another fine, hot day. The clerk, Zachariah, joined him for breakfast. Grapefruit, guinea corn cereal and Klim milk followed by a couple of boiled eggs and toast and marmalade made him feel quite at home and he looked round, almost disappointed to find no Aga in the Nigerian bush!

"How far do we go today?" he asked.

"Well, first we attend a clinic at a village 15 miles away," said Zachariah, "and the next stop brings us to the maternity hospital. There will be another outpatients' session in the compound there too. The Sister in charge will be glad to welcome you, doctor. She is a very pleasant lady and is always pleased to see the doctor from our hospital every month."

"What kind of road is it?"

"It used to be a laterite road and very twisty with lots of sharp turns; there is much up and down work, with many sharp corners and wooden bridges over small streams. Now there is asphalt wide enough for a single vehicle, but we cannot go very fast even when the road is dry. It is a hot journey doctor, but the Sister has a fridge and will cool us down when we get there."

"That's nice Zachariah, let's get away on the job and then we can enjoy the icicles."

Their driver was ready and very shortly off they went.

Their road had been well described by Zachariah. It was indeed hot, dry and dusty with short steep hills but the old wooden planked bridges over the little streams had been well modernised. Sometimes the road could present an acute bend just before coming to a bridge over the stream seven or eight feet below. In former days it would have required good judgement to place correctly the car's wheels on the narrow wooden planks. If incorrect – very nasty trouble!

The work at the next dispensary went as already envisaged at the others. During the session a small deputation of local chiefs requested an audience and Gordon broke off to meet them. The spokesman politely addressed him speaking excellent English, saying, "Doctor the maternity problems in our district are very big. We praise the work of the nurse in our midst and we know that she often helps with women who are in labour. We very much appreciate what she is doing for them and for our children who have greatly benefited. However we wish to ask if the hospital would consider stationing a qualified midwife in our village. She could relieve the nurse and bring better health to the women in the village and the tiny settlements around it. We know that this will cost money and the community will be glad to pay for her services."

Gordon replied saying that as he was only a locum doctor and not a real member of the hospital staff he could not make a proper reply to such a request. He would certainly take it to the hospital staff committee and the senior doctor would doubtless write to them. The chiefs communed favourably together and their spokesman expressed their satisfaction. The interview terminated with expressions of goodwill on both sides.

"Phew," said Gordon to his clerk, "does that often happen?"

"Well," replied Zachariah, "they probably feel that the next village with a maternity hospital and a European Sister outranks their own village. They would like to bring their village higher up the social scale and a midwife stationed among them would help to make them feel more important."

"Oh, I see. I'm being educated in African affairs of state am I?"

"That's right, doctor," laughed Zachariah.. "By the end of your six months with us you'll sit an examination and we can mark your exam papers."

Gordon joined in the laughter and called for the next patient.

The clinic ended and the nurse's medicine stocks having been re-supplied, they resumed their somewhat hazardous road journey reaching, after twenty miles, the Maternity hospital where Sister Edith held sway.

The buildings had been established in a pleasant grassy compound with nicely arranged paths well shaded by the huge leaves of oil-palms. Two wards with a labour room and Sister's office between them were supplemented by an outpatient department. This was composed of a waiting-hall, a doctor's consulting room, a small operating theatre and a nurse's room for doing dressings of various kinds. Sanitation and washing facilities were alongside an engine room that provided efficient electric light for this little hospital in the 'bush'.

Sister Edith met them and conducted them to her bungalow a short distance from the wards. She had refreshments all ready and was extremely pleased to welcome the 'new' doctor.

A small wiry lady, full of energy and bubbly conversation, she dominated the meeting, as she did any other meeting where she was present. Fair of face with blonde hair drawn into a tidy 'bun', her hand grip was firm and her voice positive. No fool, this lady. Gordon soon realised when shown around the little hospital that the efficient order which was evident was entirely derived from a woman of determination, courage and ability.

"Eats first and work afterwards," she said. Can you manage antelope meat from the bush and potatoes from the big store in Ibadan, doctor? After that you can have pineapple grown in my little allotment with cream from a tin. Finally there is coffee from a proper coffee apparatus."

"Marvellous, civilisation in the jungle", said Gordon, quite impressed

"Well, I try to keep up to date I haven't 'gone native'… yet" she added.

After a cup of scented Earl Grey tea she commanded Gordon to indulge in half an hour of rest with his feet up and gave him a Readers Digest to look at. Afterwards with undiminished energy Edith took his arm saying, "Come on, I'll show you your patients. They'll be glad to see you."

The waiting room was full. A nurse was present and

showed the folk into the consulting room one by one, each with their minder or even interpreter if they were of a different race. Gordon spent a busy two hours sorting out many troubles and then attended to a couple of infected hands that needed operative care. Sister wielded a bottle of ethyl chloride anaesthetic to good effect and the sufferers awoke from their surgery, bandaged and grateful.

A cup of tea followed and then Sister introduced him to the maternity hospital. This was an eye-opener. In the deep bush this lone Nursing Sister had complete charge of a twelve bed hospital for mothers-to-be. Here she conducted antenatal care and followed this with supervision of the mothers when they went into labour. With the aid of two midwives trained in the base hospital she conducted the delivery of the babies and if the baby was a breech delivery or forceps were required to assist the birth she expertly managed the appropriate manoeuvre, giving anaesthetic as required with a nurse to assist. There were twelve beds and as many cots for the babies. Adjacent to one of the two wards was a labour theatre having a good operating table and an anaesthetic apparatus complete with oxygen and nitrous oxide with halothane as required.

Sister drove a second hand Volvo station wagon and would go out to a patient in a bush village if needed, often bringing the patient back to be dealt with in the hospital.

Gordon was impressed again at the expertise and dedication of such a lady. He asked what happened if Sister felt a Caesarean section was needed.

"I draw the line at that," she said. "I do my best to ensure that such a case is diagnosed in the antenatal sessions and taken to the hospital in good time. Should the emergency occur during labour I drive the patient to the hospital myself."

"Eighty odd miles?" said Gordon.

"It's a big country." she replied.

Sister gave them a meal before they hit the road again. Gordon asked if her car was in good shape and properly serviced.

"Yes, I have a young mechanic type who looks after the lighting engine and deals with the car He is very capable and keeps it all in good order."

"What a wonderful job, Sister. It's been a privilege to meet you Thank you for your help and for showing me round your domain. May I say 'God bless you'.

"Oh yes, He does. He keeps telling people to look after me and that's how I get by."

And they said 'Goodbye'.

Returning in the evening was delightful. The visit and talks with Sister Edith had brought new insight to Gordon's awareness of medical problems in the 'bush'. There would be more to think and write about, giving Judith further knowledge of what this locum job in Africa involved.

They had left while it was still light. Suddenly the quickly lowering sun dropped below the skyline and very rapidly complete darkness enveloped them, necessitating headlights and extra care in negotiating bends and bridges on the road. Travelling in the dark with windows wide open and the sounds of the bush titillating their ears was an experience to be remembered. The chirping of cicadas and the calls of the tree frogs were like music, a balm to the soul. Soon they had passed the missionary's large house and compound and began the journey through the tall trees of the forest. The forest music intensified and continued. .Occasionally a village appeared in the headlights with the lights of lanterns and small fires indicating, with plumes of smoke, the preparation of evening meals. A gentle whiff of scented smoke joined the bush noises that filtered to their senses. The slightly raucous calls of the women as they shouted to each other defined further the existence of humanity far out in the wild regions of Africa.

No other cars, no lorries, buses or local forms of transport were apparent. It was just a smooth rush on an empty road through Nigeria's tropical rain forest. There were no animals, just perhaps the late harsh call of a bird or the sight of a big snake that had been warming itself on the heated road. If the passage of the heavy car ended its life, well, perhaps that might mean another human life saved from a poisonous snake bite and an agonising death. Two big villages with roadside stalls still trading by the light of kerosene lamps or brighter gas lamps powered by kerosene or even petrol under pressure gave way, at last, to the lights of their own township with its lighted shops adding further signs of civilisation A turning off the main road and the gates of the hospital were shown in the headlights. They returned a wave from the watchman at the gate. Gordon felt he had learned a great deal more about Africa from his adventure into the 'bush'. Bed would be welcome. Thoughts could come later.

****

Chapter 15

JILLY WRITES. HAPPENINGS HERE AND THERE.

"Mummy I want to write to Daddy."

"That's a nice idea, Jilly darling," said Judith. "What are you going to tell him?

"There's lots to tell him, Mummy. Tell him I've got full marks for my maths, and am near the top of the class for Geography, and best of all I'm top in English. My French is quite good and I'm best in the form for running and jumping. My swimming is good too, so there lots of success to make him happy."

"That should give him a great thrill, Jilly. And you haven't forgotten that you had top marks for reading and came near the top in singing have you?"

"Gosh, I'd forgotten that. This is going to be a long letter. And there's quite a lot to tell him about my friends and all the fun and games we're going to have on bonfire night."

"Are you going to start now or will you come with Gracie and me to town for a shopping spree? I thought we might ask our neighbour and the two boys and have lunch in the new restaurant above the old cinema."

"OK Mum, you're on. Can I go and ask them?

And it was all arranged one Saturday morning. Roland was quite pleased to be free for a job he had agreed to do for the Rotary Club. Sally was delighted to join them as she had shopping to do for her boys who needed some new shirts and socks.

They were leaving their little brother and Sally's two year old in the charge of the baby sitter who had been commandeered specially on this Saturday to take them out in the park.

It was rather a crush in the car but Judith coped well as always and, after parking it, the shopping was managed (with occasional bother) and all crowded into the nice new restaurant in high spirits. What fun to be presented each with a copy of the menu and told to make a choice; and if they were guided in their selection, well it was all part of the fun. It was a merry meal with Sally and the boys adding their suggestions for Jilly's letter to her Dad. A row on the park's lake followed when the boys displayed their prowess with the oars to the admiration of the girls. They were very happy throwing bits of bread to a pair of beautiful swans who sailed a little too close to their boat for comfort. The two mothers sat on the bank chatting and keeping a close eye on the children's progress. The swans seemed friendly and as their cygnets were securely tucked away in the nest the mothers thought the youngsters were safe enough. There were still scraps of bread for the fish and the girls were fascinated as usual to see them plopping up with a splash to collect them. Eventually all felt weary and elected to return home for tea with toasted muffins covered with raspberry jam and a good slice of Mum's fruit cake.

Evening found the boys watching a Western with their Dad while Judith and Sally relaxed, chatting happily and talking about Sally's much desired second baby girl, due in six months time. Grace lay on the floor colouring a picture book with her Christmas crayons and Jilly sat at the table, most industrious with pen and writing paper and telling her Dad all about everything. It had been a good day.

*

Late in the year the weather in Nigeria veered towards the dry season with very hot days and cooler nights. Gordon was interested to see that the nurses donned woolly cardigans and wrapped them closely around themselves. He felt much more comfortable in the evenings and looked out a pair of grey flannels. One of the Sisters advised him, "Make sure that you keep covered at night. No throwing off the bedclothes. Keep covered."

Gordon had found her in the Sisters' office when he did his night round. She was busy completing clerical work that had been neglected owing to more work than usual on the wards. Though off duty, she had returned to the hospital after her evening meal to ensure that her work was finished properly. Gordon felt impressed; much of the duties of the staff were carried out so faithfully that he felt obliged to mention it

"But it's all part of the missionary's job, doctor. It's no good telling a nurse to make sure her work is properly done unless you're prepared to show yourself willing to do it as well. You will remember the story of how Jesus washed the disciples' feet?"

"Tell me. Sister," he said. And she did.

That night he found a Bible in the drawer beside his bed. Safely ensconced inside his mosquito net he found the relevant chapter and verse. He read into the small hours.

While coping with his outpatient crowd next morning Alfred came in through the back door. After the patient had gone he asked Gordon if he could do a little job in the town. The hospital's diesel supply was in need of replenishment.

"Will you kindly visit the U.A.C.. store in town and order a supply of 44 gallon drums. Of course we have electric supply from the town but should it fail we use our own Lister engine and generator. The driver always keeps it in good order, just in case. Just order six drums. I've written a cheque because they like it in advance and anyway it saves clerical work and postage. I normally go myself but I have a Caesarean section needing urgent attention."

Later when driving out of the hospital gate he noted a man and woman rushing into the compound in an agitated state. One of the clerks followed waving a record card calling them to wait. Gordon stopped the car and enquired saying, "What's the matter? Why the hurry?"

The man replied in English of sorts,

"She get worm for eye Sah, make you take him out now, now, I beg you." Gordon climbed out and went to look at the woman's eye. He was surprised indeed. "Good gracious," he said to the clerk, "he's right. There is a worm squiggling about under the conjunctiva. Will you send them to the outpatient theatre and I'll go along and deal with it."

The nurse in charge of the O.P. theatre told Gordon

"We always keep a small tray of instruments already

sterilised for these little emergencies. I'll set it out at once; then you can catch the worm before it hides itself away."

Nurse quickly explained the procedure to the woman, laid her on the table and put cocaine drops in her eye. With a tiny pair of forceps Gordon picked up the conjunctival membrane, snipped a little hole in it and, with a small pair of forceps delicately collected the pale, inch long wriggling offender. He consigned it to the rubbish bin. A pad over the eye to keep out dust until the wee snip had healed and the job was done.

The gratitude of the woman and her husband was most touching. The little worm struggling and unable to escape from the enclosing membrane must have been intensely irritating. Gordon felt as pleased as if he had performed a major operation. He returned to the car and departed to the U.A.C. under the direction of the driver.

*

The telephone had been ringing for some time. Judith stopped her autumn gardening and rose, took off her rubber gloves and went in to answer it.

"Hallo, Judith Jenkins here….Oh hallo Jenny, what can I do for you?

There was a pause while Jenny replied, at some length.

"Good gracious, you say the Rotary lot want us to go and hold their hands while they entertain a camp of kids. Whatever next? They probably want us to do the washing up too. We have a clever crowd of cute husbands haven't we?" A further comment from Jenny confirmed that the occasion would be on the same afternoon and that Sally, Judith's neighbour, would be going to the field where the

Rotary Club would be giving a little holiday to children who lacked parental support for such luxuries.

"Well I'm sorry Jenny, but I simply cannot manage it this time. I have no baby sitter now because she has elected to have a baby herself. Isn't life complicated?"

"Mummy, I can look after the family while you go," said Jilly

"Hush dear, don't interrupt. I'm sorry, Jenny, Jilly is being helpful. Anyway have a good time and I'll get all the news from Sally."

Jilly looked rebellious, insisting that she was quite capable of looking after the house and her sister and baby brother.

"I know you are most efficient, but it needs an adult to be responsible in matters such as this. I know Daddy would agree with me," said her mother.

"Oh well, perhaps I could go with Aunty Sally and give a hand."

"That is an excellent idea. I'll arrange it with Sally," said Judith. And she did so straight away. Sally said "I should be delighted to have Jilly to he[p. She will be useful indeed keeping the kids in order."

The year was moving on and the autumn term was near. They had spent a short holiday by the sea and Jilly had written again to her father putting her letter in Judith's envelope. He would be delighted to have a note from his daughter. It was more an epistle than a note. That little lady would be going up into the next form when school began and her spirits rose to match such an advance. Judith noticed this and commented about it in her latter to Gordon.

"Our young lady is progressing well and actually looks forward to harder work next term. Where does she get this from? I was always looking back over the good things of the past. I notice that you are enjoying facing up to more difficult surgery now. Hope that you are taking your anti-malarial pills faithfully. You are a very faithful hubby".

*

The 'faithful hubby' emerged from the operating theatre to receive the morning post from the driver and retreated to Sister's office to imbibe a cup of coffee while reading Judith's letter. He had been performing a vaginal repair to cure the awful leakage of urine for a woman from the 'bush' who had suffered a long labour and a difficult delivery of her baby miles away in her village With a successful operation she would be a much happier woman in the future. This was his first such procedure on his own and he was quite pleased that all had gone well. Letters from his darlings at home would really make his day. He read on, his mind far away until Sister reminded him that the next patient would now be under the anaesthetic and awaiting his ministrations. The rest of the letter must wait. Hospital life tended to be busy. That cannot be said too often.

His evening meal was taken with Alfred and his wife. There were comments on the day's work and discussion of the request from the village chiefs for a midwife. The staff meting had been very sympathetic, noting the comments from Zachariah, but felt that the needs of the hospital must come first. Since the Sister at the maternity hospital had reliable transport and was known to be extremely efficient in maternity matters that particular region was as well served as possible until more trained staff were available.

Gordon was interested in the pictures and decorations in his colleague's bungalow. Two water colours of Cornish seaside villages appealed to him. Alfred and his wife were lovers of the southwest and its proximity to the Atlantic waves, whether calm in days of summer sunshine or furious with equinoctial gales. Her people were Cornish from Sennen Cove and her childhood had often been spent watching the vast clouds of spray thrown up as huge waves crashed thunderously on the rocky coast of the Lizard or Land's end , Cape Cornwall and the rocks of the Longships lighthouse. She could tell stories of the fishing boats that never returned and of the bands of mourners walking behind a hearse on its way to a cemetery by the sea. Her family owned such a boat and had experienced the grief and pain of losing a son when his fishing expedition had met with a tragic end. They found stories of Cornwall a source of endless interest and chatted late into the night. Sometimes the night round of the hospital on such occasions was a little late.

Sister Jasmine approached Gordon one day and asked, "Dr.Gordon, would you be prepared to give lectures to the nurses on medical subjects. One of the nursing staff is due for furlough and it would be very helpful if you could do the lectures on, say, anatomy and minor surgery." Gordon replied

"Yes, I should be very pleased to help but it would take quite some time to prepare the lectures and hospital emergencies might make this rather difficult". Sister explained,

"The lectures have all been typed out and are ready for you to use. You could just explain difficult areas as you go along."

"Ah, that makes it much more feasible," said Gordon. "I shall be happy to have a go. Can we start on the anatomy?"

"That is just what I thought. I'll tell the girls to come

to the lecture theatre at 4 p.m. if that's all right for you. I'll give you all the relevant notes."

Gordon felt pleased to be allowed to involve himself in the training of the staff and vowed to do his best. That evening he took down a book on applied anatomy from his bookshelf. It was up to a teacher to make his subject come to life. That would enable students to store the information in their minds. There was much more to this missionary business than he had supposed. Tucked up within his mosquito net the same night he took out the Bible and read again chapters from the 'Greatest Story on earth'.

At 4 p.m. the next day while Alfred attended to the afternoon outpatient clinic Gordon repaired to the nurses' lecture room. A big room with some twenty desks similar to the desks of a schoolroom at home, it was well lit by open windows and supplied with a teacher's desk in front of the class with, behind it on the wall, a big rectangle of slate. Beside this stood an easel with a smaller slate. Chalk was used for writing.

Twenty junior nurses assembled quietly and sat at the desks. Gordon quickly introduced himself as a G.P. from England, coming as a locum while one of the mission doctors was back on holiday in his home land. He told them the subject for the day was anatomy.

"Do any of you know about this word?" he asked. There was no reply.

"It is made from two old Greek words. *ana* meaning up, and *temnein* meaning cut. So the meaning of the word is -- cut up. We are studying the human body and to find out what it is made of when we need to cut into it to do operations. We'll only pretend to do it of course.

First we'll talk about the body's muscles. What are they used for?"

Several nurses raised their hands. "Yes nurse" said Gordon, pointing to one of them.

"Please doctor they are used to move us about and to pick things up."

"That's right. Let's demonstrate. Will you all put your right forearms on your desks. Now l et the hand hang quite loosely over the edge. Good.. Now place the fingers of your left hand on the front of your upper right arm so that you can feel what happens. OK.? Now slowly turn your right hand to face upwards. You will feel the muscle in your right upper arm move a little. Right? Do it again to make sure you can feel it. OK? Now bend the arm upwards until your fingers touch your shoulders. What do you feel?"

They all spoke at once. "A big swelling comes up. It gets very tight and quite hard."

"Yes indeed. That is the big muscle that bends the elbow joint. First it turns the hand around, then it brings it right up to touch your shoulder. It has a name. Does anybody know it?" An answer came fast. -

"Yes doctor. It's called the biceps. I know because my big brother is always showing off and boasting to us about what big muscles he has, especially his biceps." The nurses laughed happily.

"Quite right, nurse. When muscles are often used they become big and strong. Every time you lift food to put it into your mouth you use your biceps. What else do you do with it?"

Suddenly the class came alive with loud talk and shouts; the number of uses for the biceps had become legion.

"Right, that's your introduction to anatomy. Interesting isn't it?" And they all agreed.

"Now let's look at the hand. How many fingers have you? Yes, five. OK. Each one has its own muscle to move it. The muscles that close the hand are on the front of the forearm. Those that open it are on the back. Put your left fingers on the front of your right forearm and then close each finger of the right hand separately. Can you feel the separate movements in the arm?"

"Yes doctor, this is fun."

"Some of you may find it difficult to feel the movement. It depends how much fatty stuff you have in your arms. Try the back of your hand and raise each finger separately while feeling the back of your forearm. It's easier if you feel the tendons on the back of the hand. .. Well, are you learning anything?" Nods were plentiful.

"Yes I see that you are becoming interested. Well every bit of the human body has muscles to move it. Every muscle is attached at both ends; one is attached to the thing in the body that it has to move while the other end is attached to a bone that stays in one place."

Having captured the girls' interest Gordon found it easy to continue with the lesson, explaining how muscles move and how so many of them had different names and uses.

"We are just going to start with the muscles, but there are very many other things in the human body and we have a lot to learn, so let's begin…"

On their way back to the Nurses' Home after the class there was much noise and chatter with everyone telling their neighbour all about how things happened in their bodies. Gordon listened to them, pleased, and felt that he had learned something too. He went to Sister's office and they joined together for a round of his patients in the wards, after which he told her of the enjoyable hour he had spent with the junior nurses.

"I expect we shall hear all about your lecture tomorrow. They will chat happily about their new doctor, I'm quite sure," said Sister.

Two new patients whom he had admitted that morning, one with malignant tertian malaria and the other very ill with pneumonia, were holding their own. Sister made several useful suggestions and after discussion he returned to his bungalow. He wrote several letters ordering drugs and supplies and hoped that was the end of his duties for the day - apart from the night round of course. In the meantime what about food?

Meals tended to be standardised and not very inspiring. His cook had no qualifications and less imagination, but even so Gordon survived and maintained his energy. Selecting a large writing pad he settled to his favourite occupation and, with many endearments wrote happily to his darling wife and daughters. There was much to tell them and much to comment on from their letters to him. He found Jilly's letter very absorbing. The wording was good, the spelling excellent and her phraseology left nothing to be desired. Congratulations were in order and Gordon made his reply quite flowery. He tried to describe his dispensary journey in glowing terms and commented particularly on the lonely Sister far off in the bush with the lives of so many people in her hands. He gladly recorded that she had a competent driver to care for her transport. There were times when she was obliged to bring a patient to the hospital for a Caesarean section. Other difficulties she managed herself, even to giving the necessary anaesthetics. When he returned home he would be glad to address the Inner Wheel and his Rotary Club, bringing them up to date on how medical services were managed by the Missions. He was rather late to bed that night.

****

CHAPTER 16

GORDON LEARNS. STORM.
SALLY REPRODUCES. MALARIA.

As TIME PASSED Gordon became well inured to the solitary life, but greatly enjoyed contact with the staff of Sisters and the other doctors. . He found the African nurses in training to be a happy bunch, willing to learn and acquiring expertise that astonished him. He mentioned this to Alfred. The reply was firm indeed, "You must realise that their development is accounted for by the wonderful dedication of the missionary Sisters. They regard it as their first responsibility to ensure proper training and a Christian attitude in their nursing staff. It is truly amazing what they have accomplished. Our nurses are eagerly snapped up by hospitals and health authorities all over the country."

The lives of African people Gordon found most interesting. He wrote to Judith at length. "It's quite entertaining to note the way in which things are carried upon the head, leaving the hands free. Not only bowls of food, baskets of produce from the farm, four gallon kerosene tins of water, (very heavy - a gallon of water weighs ten pounds), bundles of cloth, but even items such as books and umbrellas are all beautifully balanced on the head. The bearer is thus able to walk upright with a lovely carriage, the hands free. They can turn their heads smoothly without disturbing the balance and never do any items fall off their heads.

It's just as interesting to see how children are carried. A small child or baby, carefully supported with a strong piece of cloth, is carried on the mother's back, the cloth coming round her body and fixed above her breasts. This enables her to carry extra loads on her head. A family will travel along a road with the man carrying a stick in his hand and the woman carrying the heavy loads, accompanied by children all carrying loads of wood or baskets of produce in similar fashion. I notice that when crossing a road, having looked for possible vehicles, a mother with a baby on her back walks across, not pushing a pram in front of her into the traffic, but herself facing any possible danger with the child safely behind on her back. I wonder perhaps if the 'primitive native' has got a point. The 'civilised' modern mother might learn some useful ideas from her African sisters who use traditional methods, rather than modern, expensive and probably more dangerous 'up to date' ways of coping with children facing the bright new world with its speed and its horribly lethal vehicles. How civilised is civilisation?"

Another intriguing point that gave him thought was the manner of breast feeding a baby. The little one was not taken in its mother's arms, laid almost flat with a bottle's teat pushed into its mouth. That way milk and air were taken in together; the stomach, filling with more air than milk would need relief and mother is obliged to raise up the wee mite for 'burping' to give relief. That was 'civilised' palaver. The African mother slung the baby round to sit astride her hip. She supported it from underneath while it stretched up to reach her nipple and sucked. Down went the milk and any air could come up automatically; just plain common sense.

When sated the baby was returned to her back sitting upright with the usual support. Baby slept peacefully, wind came up without trouble and Mum could carry on with her work, pounding yam, spreading mushrooms out to dry in the sun, carrying farm produce home and all the thousand and one jobs that are a woman's lot. One gets the feeling that 'civilised' methods of 'burping' are really rather stupid…

Gordon's brain cells absorbed all this and much more of the old African ways of doing things. He recorded faithfully the facts and his thoughts to Judith in his many letters. The hours spent in writing to her were very precious. Interruptions caused him twinges of regret. Often they were emergencies that required surgery in the theatre; sometimes just a call to the ward to examine and prescribe or undertake some essential doctor's job. The Nigerian weather was, as mentioned, moving on towards the dry season when it would be very hot and exhausting by day but cooler after the sun had set. There were more cases of pneumonia and the air, being laden with extremely fine sand from the Sahara, made breathing unpleasant and gave the appearance of being fog filled.

Often the eyes of the townsfolk would turn eastwards seeking a possible cloud that might presage a storm. They knew that an electrical storm was quite possible and longed for it to cool skins tired of hot sunshine, moisten throats parched with the dry air and help to fill water tanks long emptied and waiting for drenching rain to refill them. Joy filled their hearts when a little cloud appeared in just the right position for a soaking. The cloud rose in the east, enlarging, spreading right and left, promising, darkening, covering the bright sky. Higher and higher it rose and spread, blotting out the distant view, giving welcome shade to people and houses. Like a fortress it appeared to be built of great castles as the cloudlets that composed its whole developed, appearing like mighty battlements surrounding the furious lightning strikes within its walls. Expanding widely, it began to rush forward, blotting out the sun, darkening the land.

Huge, jagged sparks of lightning flashed within it from side to side. The distant buildings of the town began to disappear, hidden by intense rainfall. A raging wind struck Gordon's bungalow. His steward and 'small boy' rushed round the house closing shutters. Suddenly the lightning struck somewhere among the compound's buildings accompanied by a fearsome crack of thunder that rolled, seeming to rebound from cloud to cloud across the sky. Another flash, another fearful explosive crash and the storm enveloped them with all its might. The rain fell. At first a few drops, stirring the dusty ground. Then suddenly a veritable flood of water streaked out of the threatening cloud, down, ever down, turning the paths to mud, soaking the grass, bending the flowers, shrubs and huge palm leaves, draining river-like through the down-pipes from the roofs into the tanks and poring down the compound's gutters towards the distant swamp.

Foot deep ditches beside the paths rapidly filled to overflowing with water running noisily away down any sloping ground. Constantly, lightning strikes with thunder crashes smote the ear drums while the furious rainstorm filled the air.

Slowly, very slowly the storm passed onward. The flashes became less frequent. Thunder lessened and rain changed from its awful intensity to a steady downpour. The cloud began to pass on, clearing from the east. Perhaps a nurse would shortly arrive under an umbrella. Perhaps she would carry a note from Sister saying, 'Doctor there is a new patient. He has a severe pain and a swelling in the groin. .I've ordered the theatre nurse to prepare for an operation."

Gordon would say "I'm coming nurse," and he would seek for his umbrella and his stethoscope. Urgent need would again demand his skill. There was a life to be saved.

*

While Gordon continued to busy himself in wards and theatre, his family at home were looking forward to the fun of November 5th and the delightful lighting of the streets with elegant Christmas decorations overhead and in shops as well as those seen through the windows of houses. Judith found herself involved as of yore in preparation for forthcoming festivities both at work with her colleagues in Antiques and with the more imaginative members of the Inner Wheel. The latter seemed to be constantly vying with each other to invent new forms of entertainment. She found that her time was taken up needlessly in such frivolity and rather resented this type of fun when it interfered with her writing of letters to her dear husband far away.

However other matters came to the fore. After a particularly busy day in the office and attending to Inner Wheel demands she was relaxing with a cuppa while the girls earnestly applied themselves to homework. Their adored their little brother, John,, who played happily with a pile of wooden bricks, piling one upon another, clapped his hands in delight when his building crashed down. The telephone rang.

"Judith, I've started," said Sally. "Roland isn't home yet and I can't reach him anywhere. Can you possibly get me to the hospital? The boys would come in and baby sit, I know. You wouldn't be away for long."

"Of course, Sally. I'm coming at once". And Judith snatched up her coat explaining hurriedly to Jilly and Grace that things were happening next door and the boys would come in and join them. She had warned her daughters of such a possibility and they accepted it as just part of life and were not alarmed.

"OK..Mummy, we'll play a game of monopoly with the boys. Give Aunty Sally our love. Bye."

Very quickly Judith had the car out and, with Sally and her suitcase settled she drove off in the evening traffic, using Gordon's doctor's warning sign to obtain urgent priority if traffic were difficult. In the middle of the monopoly game Roland, home from the bank, walked in demanding to know what was happening. Jilly told him in quite straightforward fashion.

Alarmed, he asked where the brandy was kept, took a dose and flung out of the door saying, "I must go to the hospital. I'll be back sometime. Bye". And off he went without even saying 'Hallo' to his boys. Half an hour passed and the game of monopoly had become quite exciting with money passing and hotels rising and falling when Judith appeared and asked if she could join the game. One of the boys promptly placed a chair for her and dealt out a ration of cards. Jilly asked her mother if she had seen Uncle Roland.

"No my Pet, do you mean he has gone to the hospital?"

"Yes Mummy, he was in quite a hurry, but had a spot of brandy when we told him about Aunty."

"Oh dear, the poor man! He hasn't had any food. I'll give the ward Sister a ring and ask if she can arrange something for him".

She did so and the Sister was concerned, saying that Roland refused to leave his wife and go to the restaurant. He seemed to be 'in quite a state'. Judith replied saying, "He has been worried about Sally all through the pregnancy; no wonder that he's a bit frantic now she's started in labour. I'll make a plate of salmon sandwiches and a big slice of apple pie and bring it back to the hospital for him. Could you make him a cup of tea Sister?" Leaving the children to enjoy their monopoly she went to work in the kitchen and shortly afterwards drove back to the hospital.

It was late ere the family were finally bedded with the boys camped down in the Jenkins' sitting room. Judith told them that their father was spending the night at the hospital until the baby was born.

At 5 a.m. she was woken by the telephone. Sister told her that all had gone well and a lovely little girl was being happily cuddled by her father. She would persuade him to go home and rest. Sally was 'fine'.

"That's wonderful, Sister. Thank you for telling me. Will you tell Roland that I'll go and warm up his bedroom and put a hot bottle in his bed please.."

"Right-ho, Mrs Jenkins. He and his wife are just going to have a cup of tea and then I'll shoo him away."

By 6 a.m,, with the boys in their own beds and Roland

settled down after telling Judith the whole saga, she was at last able to lie down, thankfully, for an hour's sleep before the day demanded her attention.

*

Five days later furious banging on the front door interrupted the family breakfast. Judith opened it to allow entry for a near neighbour, Marion Wingfield, breathless and clad only in pyjamas and dressing gown.

"The people next door are having a fearful row," declared Marion. "You can hear them yelling and there are bangs and crashes in the house as if furniture or pottery is being thrown. I'm frightened in case he will hurt her. Can you phone the police?"

"Well, yes", said Judith. "But they are not very responsive to domestic arguments you know. Would it help if I come over to try talking to them?. Perhaps Roland from next door would come too."

She rang Roland who was busy looking after the family and his wife and new baby. He grumbled that it was a police job and why not ring them anyway. But he said he would come.

Judith heaved a sigh and rang the police putting the case as strongly as possible. They suggested that neighbourly help might be a better idea. So, after pulling on her coat she and Marion sallied forth to try and quell the row.

She knocked vigorously on the door of the house where frantic yells and curses were still continuing and shouted loudly, "Police, police!" She repeated knocking and shouting several times until at length the door opened and the young husband, dabbing scratches on his face with a handkerchief, roughly asked what they wanted.

"Tell him to stop it", screamed his wife from the top of the stairs. "He's taken all my money and he's going to bet it at the races."

The appearance of Roland, tall and competent with the look of authority, then persuaded the householder to open the door wider and allow them to enter.

"We were all worried, in view of the noise and screaming that somebody was in danger of being hurt," said Roland. We are all neighbours of yours and would like to help if you will allow us. Perhaps the ladies could go upstairs and assist your wife," he added.

The presence of the local bank manager seemed to calm things down a little. Judith and Marion climbed the stairs and went in to the young wife. Roland was invited to sit down and the young man began to explain.

As usual the matter turned out to be simply a 'storm in a teacup'.

"I was just going to use a fiver for betting on the races and put the rest in her account in your bank, Mr Wainwright. My wife thought I intended to take it all. I never meant that at all, but she didn't believe me. I love her very much.." And he broke down in tears.

Upstairs Judith and Marion persuaded the wife, little more than a girl, to calm down and give her version of the affair. Obviously a simple misunderstanding had occurred with tempers flying and harsh words being flung at each other. It seemed that her husband rather enjoyed a bet at the races. He was temporarily out of work and hoped to improve their finances.

"I think you should get dressed quickly and then listen to what Mr. Wainwright can tell you about money matters. Do you love your husband?" enquired Judith.

"Oh yes, yes, I do, I do. We adore each other," was the emphatic reply. "Then you can both make it up and we'll go and see to our families".

Not many minutes later Ruby, the girl, rushed down the stairs and flung herself into the outstretched arms of the husband, crying "I'm so sorry Ronnie, I'm very sorry." He clasped her closely saying, "I'm sorry too my darling. I love you. I'll stop betting for ever."

After a while Roland rose saying "That looks a lot better. If you would like to come in to the bank this morning I shall be happy to give you some useful ideas about money matters If you will give me a ring on this number I shall be able to give you a definite appointment".

After handing Ronnie his card he returned home to his wife and new baby, leaving the pair still closely cuddling.

Sally, wiping sleep from her eyes asked,

"Whatever have you been up to, Darling? I thought you might like to feed the new arrival today."

"Just money palaver my Precious. Anyway I haven't got the right anatomy. Can you produce yet?" And, picking up their baby girl, he handed her to his wife.

*

The Nigerian sun beat down mercilessly. After completing a morning clinic and a ward round Gordon agreed to assist the hospital engineer to perform an electric lighting job in the roof of the operating theatre. The heat under the roofing sheets was quite appalling and they were glad to climb down after an hour and partake of a cold drink in Sister's office.

"What was it all about?" enquired Gordon.

"Well the shadow-less lamp was only operating intermittently and there was difficulty at the emergency Caesarean section last night. I promised immediate attention to the matter. Hospital engineers have to be on the ball, our doctors insist on perfection," was the reply.

"I hope there won't be too many sessions like that again," commented Gordon. "It was abominably hot under that theatre roof."

The sun disappeared one evening a week later in a ball of flame. When eating his evening meal Gordon began to shiver. He felt cold. The shivering rapidly increased to severe rigor; he was shaking from head to foot. Very quickly he changed into pyjamas and slipped into bed picking up a couple of blankets for extra covering. He picked up the phone beside the bed. With shaking fingers he dialled Alfred's number.

"Hallo, who is it?"

"Al-Alfred, it's m-me, G-Gordon", he said with difficulty. "I th-think I've g-got m-malaria. I'm sh-shivering from t- top to toe."

"All right, Gordon. Get to bed and wrap up warm. We'll be with you right away."

A few minutes later Alfred and his wife arrived, laden with extra blankets and two hot water bottles. A rubber sheet to spread under the bed linen would help and this was quickly tucked under Gordon's sheets. His kettle was boiled and the bottles filled with hot water. Alfred's wife tucked one at his feet and the other behind his back. The rigors continued.

"Now here are your anti-malarials, just swallow them with this drink," and Alfred handed him two tablets. Gordon took them shakily and managed to get them down.

"Now a pill to help you sleep. The rigor stops when you

reach the highest temperature point and then you'll drop off, I'll come over in the morning and see to you. We've put a jug of water beside you. You're going to sweat quite a lot and afterwards you'll feel better but don't get up in the morning. I'll get night nurse to look in on you. You'll need a few days off duty."

They stayed in his sitting room until the rigors had stopped and Gordon was fast asleep. When doing his night round of the hospital Alfred instructed a senior nurse to look in on Gordon several times during the night and attend to any of his needs.

He woke when the nurse looked in on him at 2 a.m. and she rubbed him down and found him a fresh pair of pyjamas. He had been sweating profusely.

"Now I know what malaria is all about. I shall be able to sympathise better with the patients" he told the nurse.

"You should be free of parasites, doctor," she said. "You have a mosquito proofed house. I wonder how you got bitten."

"Maybe when doing emergency ops in the evening, if I was caught before I had changed into long trousers. Perhaps the nasty little mossies sit under the operating table and just wait for some unsuspecting doctor to bring them a meal," he replied.

Alfred and his wife visited him in the morning, gave him further tablets and changed his sheets and pyjamas. They instructed his steward to provide a light breakfast and insisted that he remain resting.

"Your temperature has dropped to normal but it may go up again. You'll have o take life quietly for several days." said Alfred and, leaving a supply of tablets he returned to duty in the hospital.

Gordon, feeling distinctly better but rather feeble, asked his steward to brink his writing pad. He must tell

Judith all about malaria. For an hour after breakfast he wrote, telling the story with a dramatic quality that he felt sure the family would appreciate. Then, his energy having drained away, he fell asleep and dreamed of home and his lovely wife and enchanting children.

He woke to the sound of his steward's voice as he stood holding a mug and a bottle of tablets.

"Time for coffee Sah. Time for medicine too, Sah."

A very faithful chap was his steward. He received the mug of coffee with a biscuit and after downing the tablets and his drink he fell asleep again. A couple of hours later he woke to find Alfred sitting beside him and his steward holding a tray with a dish of rice pudding on it.

"You look a lot better" said his colleague. "Now you know what malaria is all about."

"Yes, it isn't at all nice" said Gordon. "No wonder people lose energy after that. When can I get up?"

"You can get up and sit in a chair. But go to bed early and remember your tablets".

*

Several days passed before Gordon felt able to return to the consulting room. He still felt very shaky but succeeded in attending to the patients in the waiting room. Two men with hand infections he left for his colleagues to manage. The laboratory called him about his blood check. No malarial parasites were discovered and his haemoglobin level was satisfactory.

Sister came to see him; "You must be a good boy and have an afternoon sleep. You have to treat malaria seriously. I have a special little candle to light in your house to produce a gas that will deal with any mossies. Like the stuff they pump into aeroplanes"

So, obediently and gladly, he retreated to his bed and slept.

****

CHAPTER 17

BACK to BLISS

THE WEEKS WENT by quickly. Mail to and from Nigeria was read avidly. Judith and family in England and Gordon, 3000 miles away, never stopped counting the days for Gordon's return to complete family togetherness that would bring normality back to all their lives.

At home the Nov 5 fireworks and Christmas celebrations had gone along as usual but it wasn't the same without Daddy. At the hospital in the tropics anti-mosquito precautions had been stepped up and the usual clinics with ward rounds and emergencies in the operating theatre had all provided experience and sometimes even entertainment. The sight of a hospital porter standing in attendance late at night when a new patient was being admitted to the female ward was not unusual, but when one of his ilk stood trembling, mesmerised by the threatening head of a black mamba entwined among the rafters above the door of that ward, this was a rarity not be missed, the fear and terror only eclipsed by the violent action of junior nurse who snatched the man's cutlass and struck a lightning blow that sliced off the snake's head in a trice, well that was a picture for Metro Goldwyn Mayer to boast of for years…. Gordon's next letter home revelled in hyperbole on the episode.

The New Year had brought snow and ice, snowballs and skating at home, while the Nigerian hot, dry season had its share of occasional violent electrical storms as well as, after the rain, blue and golden crocuses lifting their heads to the brilliant sunshine, brining an uplift to the heart.

At last there broke the news that the missionary on furlough had his flight booked to return to his post. Alfred brought the news to Gordon one morning.

"This is what you've been hoping for," he said. "Now you can get your skids on and book a flight home to your *'never, never land'*. I'll bet your kids will be delighted. Even your wife might be glad to have someone else reluctantly to wash nappies sometimes".

'And there was joy in the house' that morning, only equalled or exceeded by the reaction in Gordon's home next day when a telegram revealed the date of his return to the fold. Judith promptly rang Gordon's G.P. colleague.

"Dr. King, Bertie, hooray. He's coming home". Judith was almost dancing with excitement when she told him the date.

"That will make your day", was the comment. "You have been wonderfully patient all these months without your nappy washer. It must have been good to get letters telling of all his adventures, both in the theatre and elsewhere, but a homecoming will bring quite a different flush to your cheeks. I must thank you, Judith, for letting him go. My nephew has been a great help and the experience has done him good, but I too will be very glad to have Gordon back in harness He must have a holiday before he starts work here again. What about that skiing trip you never had? Can you get him on the phone? Snow and ice might be good refreshment after the tropics. A couple of weeks would do him good."

Judith thanked him profusely and rang off. Then she thought. Perhaps a week at home and then a week in the snows. What a lovely idea. She booked a telephone call to coincide with his evening meal and went about her work with renewed vigour.

The call came through, amazingly at about the right time, and was answered by her beloved. After some minutes of endearments she put the proposition to him. Gordon was thrilled. "Just the job" he said. "I could do with cooling down. Off on our own for a holiday, all by ourselves. We shan't need a chaperone either. Hooray! Go for it my Darling, and get your Dad to give you time off".

Judith set to with a will, gathered her wits together and made a list of things to do. First she mentioned the idea to Gerald so that he would have time to arrange for a temporary girl to do the secretarial work. Following Gerald's agreement she phoned his brother who years before had booked the holiday which was cancelled due to the interfering appendix. Suitable clothing, boots, gloves, hat and scarf, not to mention an appointment at her hairdresser's salon were all attended to, as well as a few cheap decorative items to complete the ensemble. Jilly and Grace were most intrigued, asking countless questions and pleased that their parents were going to have a holiday together.

"Mummy, you'll have to cross the channel. Will Daddy take the car on the boat? How far is it to the French Alps?

Will Mary be coming to look after us? Oh goody, we like Mary. She always cooks us special treats."

And a lot more, finishing with the question,

"Mummy, can we go to the airport to bring Daddy back home?"

That was crucial to the whole matter and Judith, for the sake of peace, was obliged to contact Gerald.

"The kids are almost demanding to go to Heathrow for their Daddy".

"Of course they are" was Gerald's immediate reply. "And so they should. Yes, certainly they must come. It's on a Saturday so they won't miss school. It will be lovely to have them."

A week of interminably long days passed agonisingly slowly until on the Saturday, very early, John and Mary arrived to look after the baby boy. Gerald's car, loaded with Judith and two excited little girls, set forth to reach the airport.

"Will we able to see the plane coming down, Grandpa?"

"How long before it comes?"

"How does it stop?"

"Has it got brakes?"

"Questions, questions, questions", said Gerald. "We are half an hour early so we can see planes coming down from the viewing balcony. You'll see them coming in one by one. We shan't know which is which but we'll go down to welcome him at the appointed time. It it's going to be late there will be an announcement on the loud speaker."

With the car parked the girls danced happily along and up the stairs to watch the huge planes going up or landing with no fuss or hindrance. All progressed with the smooth efficiency of a well organised programme. It was the first time they had been to an airport and admiration and wonderment were boundless as they watched the huge machines descend to roll smoothly along the runway and turn off to their appointed gates. A further barrage of questions was interrupted by a voice announcing the flight number of their Daddy's plane.

"Come on kids, hurry up, that's his plane number," called Judith, and they scampered ahead down the stairs, eyes and faces shining with anticipation. Joining the waiting throng they hopped from one foot to the other, Gerald meanwhile holding up a placard with the name

'Dr.Gordon', written on it in large letters. Suddenly Jilly saw him and, "Daddy, Daddy" they both yelled with all their might. Unrestrained they threw themselves into his arms while Gerald collected the luggage and Judith waited patiently. Gordon gave way to emotion with tears in his eyes for a minute or two. Then he said,

"I love you both very much my darlings, but please let me go and say 'Hallo' to Mummy" Reluctantly they released him and then he was able to wrap his arms around Judith in an ecstatic embrace. It was a homecoming that they would remember for a long, long time.

The walk to the car was a pleasant exercise after the cramped conditions of the aircraft and the feel of the children's hands in Gordon's was magical.

"Which of you will sit in front with Grandpa while I hold hands with Mummy in the back?" was his question answered joyfully by Jilly who enjoyed watching traffic on the roads, estimating speeds and distances while observing other drivers' care and attitudes.

The welcome home from John and Mary made Gordon's day complete while he found that the sight of his home, so loved and in such splendid condition, just filled his heart with happiness. To get down on his knees and play with his little boy, to have his hair pulled by infant fingers gleefully tugging was the final accolade. Gordon was home.

At the dining table, where Mary had performed superbly to present, instead of the never ending goat's meat, lamb chops with mint sauce, real English vegetables and roast potatoes followed by her own cooking of apple pie and proper custard, the home feeling intensified. With a child clinging to each side of him Gordon was bombarded with questions shot at him as if from a machine gun.

"How hot was it, daddy?"............................"Pretty hot."

"Could you fry eggs on your car bonnet? "I expect so"

"Did you have to mop your face all the time?..........."Quite a lot."

"How did you mop it in the theatre?".................. "Sister mopped it for me."

"Did it rain every day?"............"No, it was mostly sunny."

"What was the lightning like?"…Huge sparks, miles long".

"Were all the people quite black? "Most were dark brown."

"Were they black inside when you operated on them?"

Gordon laughed. "I'm trying to eat my dinner" he said. "Tell you all about it tomorrow." Judith put in an oar, "Peace for Daddy," she said. "Poor Daddy, this is getting like Prime minister's question time. He's not a P.M. and you're not the opposition Quiet, both of you. There will be lots of time for questions. Belt up and eat up."

"Well", said Gerald, "that last one was quite an astute question. At least they show an intelligent interest. I can see you're going to have fun this next week my son. I guess we'll all have lots of talks together. Your letters were pretty descriptive, so we have a good idea of much of your life there. You'll be able to fill in the cracks."

Later, nursing s cup of Mary's milky coffee, Gordon continued a soliloquy until bedtime finally claimed the children. Even then he was commandeered for a 'story please', Daddy." Being well prepared he commenced a saga that would keep his little beauties enthralled for weeks to come. Little Hezekiah tickling his tiny squirrel and his sister Comfort fondling her Goliath beetle would be Nigerian hero and heroine for his own young lambs to fantasise about every night.

Not until the guests had all departed, the house tidied and set in order, breakfast prepared and baths taken did Judith and her husband find time lovingly to greet each other with actions rather than words. Gordon emerged from the bathroom clad in a towel around his waist to find his lovely wife similarly attired, a big bathrobe fastened above her breasts; she was just brushing her hair in expectation of his coming. In two strides he reached her, dropped his towel on the floor, unfastened her bathrobe and pulled her to him. They were as one, each clasping other with all their strength. Gently they backed to the bed. Wonderfully they made love. Then lying gently side by side, hand holding hand, they stayed quietly gazing into each other's eyes.

"It's been a long, long time, my Darling," she said.

"Far too long, my Sweetheart," was the reply.

Silently they waited while pulses settled, emotions quietened and sweet reality replaced the ardour of reunion. The long, tender loving session served to bind them together again in the firm single unit that they had always been. They were again the essential, central figure for their family's confident regard; the reliable, loving, parental model so greatly needed by growing children for guarding and guiding their developing lives. .The family was whole again. They gazed into each other's eyes, content.

"Letters can't take the place of love my Treasure," said Gordon.

She nodded, her eyes moist with tears. "Love always wins, my Gordon," she said.

She kissed him and turned on her side. He drew close, curled an arm around her and together they drifted off to sleep.

*

Attending Grandpa's church next morning little John mixed it with a dozen other small poppets under the watchful eye of a competent carer. Judith's hand sought Gordon's as they sang old favourite hymns with their two daughters closely snuggling beside their parents. Grace coloured a picture book during the address while Jilly gave close attention to her Grandfather's exposition of the Sermon on the Mount. Many folk wanted to welcome back the young doctor at coffee time and to speak again to their long lost friendly medical adviser.

Returning to the manse they all rapidly changed into clothes for a boating excursion, having made due preparation, because, for a welcoming treat Roland planned a boat ride on the river to his favourite pub. There he had ordered a slap up meal for the two families and Gerald to celebrate Gordon's return from *darkest Africa*. In his speech of welcome he alluded to Gordon's fortunate avoidance of the wicked wars in Africa, although Gordon privately thought that for him any way to escape the little winged devilish mosquitoes was probably more worthy of note.

The party went down well. After Roland's speech of welcome the ladies contributed little speeches quite charmingly and great was the applause when Jason and Jilly rose to have their say. At last it was Gordon's turn to respond.

"Thank you for enduring my absence and for this wonderful welcome back to the fold. During my six months locum work I have had a remarkable time in the company of the medical missionaries and nurses among whom I've been serving. I've learnt a lot medically. I have discovered how the other half lives and how great is the suffering they endure in that difficult climate, far from what we call civilisation. In particular I have found something of the meaning of service when watching how the Doctors and Sisters view their work in the mission hospital and attend to human need at all hours of day and night. Their watchword was not 'Who is On Duty?' but rather 'What is the Need?' At any time that need was to be satisfied.

I have learnt a lot, not only medically. I hope that what I have learnt will appear in practice during my future years while trying to provide for the needs of the people of Bifford."

. There was an accolade of a five full seconds silence before applause broke out. The landlord of the inn and head waiter and waitresses had also been listening and joined that applause heartily. Roland asked for questions and for another half hour Gordon was bombarded by questions and comments from them all including the staff of the inn. To end it all the landlord asked for hands up for wine or otherwise, 'on the house' and opened a bottle of champagne. At Gordon's suggestion the toast was –

The Mission Hospital and Long Live Medical Romance.

A happy party returned to their own house where Roland, Sally and the boys left their friends to enjoy their own family cosiness. After a frugal supper – they were all well filled – family games occupied them until bed called. Then it was time for Gordon's new series of African stories to relax the sleepy minds and bring refreshing sleep.

Two weary parents joined each other on the settee, drowsily holding hands. The joy of being together again precluded any requirement for speech and for a while they gave in to their need for the quiet relaxation of lovers... But Judith, with a woman's intuition, felt the urgency to arrange their time-off-work-schedule so, nudging her beloved gently asked,

"And now that you're back in the land of the living what adventures have you planned for tomorrow? You will remember that your Dad has given me a fortnight off work."

"Good old Dad, has he got the usual temp. to take up the cudgels?"

"Yes, all fixed. Now all we need is to get fit for activity on the snow slopes. It occurred to me that you might need some physiotherapy to improve your muscles after standing so long in an African operating theatre. You know that we have a very useful gymnasium here in town. What about a session there every day this week? Are you game?

Gordon groaned. "I was hoping for peace and quiet," he protested

"You can have a Jacuzzi session afterwards. They have a masseur too. OK?"

"I give in. Let's forget the agony and try a dose of Scrabble, first time for ages."

And they fought each other gently on the Scrabble board, talking and occasionally cuddling while making the letters combine into cute and clever words. At last the letters gave up the struggle and it was time to seek rest. Gordon emerged from the shower as before draped in a towel around his waist and arranged a book tidily on his bedside table. Behind him Judith appeared from the bathroom, a large bath towel wrapped around her and tied loosely.

"And is romance still alive?" enquired Gprdon.

"You won't need that book my Darling," she replied shedding her bath towel. He did likewise and in a trice they were in each others arms, again collapsing gently onto the bed behind them. Again the wonder of love renewed never failed to astonish them Later Judith murmured,

"Whatever could you do without that in darkest Africa, after banishing the mossies and tucking yourself under your net?"

"Just listened to the far away drums and drowsed off, waiting for the nurse's footfall and gentle knock on my door, with her shy little voice saying, "There is a new patient, doctor."

And dreamland came to bring refreshment to them both.

****

CHAPTER 18

HOLIDAY JUST FOR TWO

How MARVELLOUS IS home life. How could I ever have left it, thought Gordon as the Aga did his toast to a T and the girls rushed through their breakfast to pull on shoes and pick up satchels for the jaunt to their morning school.

"How would you like to run them to school in the car?" said his wife. "I'm busy with your son."

"I'd love to," he replied, remembering that home life brought responsibilities, but it was nice when some responsibilities also brought happiness.

On his return Judith advised him of an appointment at the gymnasium and thither in due course they went complete with towels and pumps. The very competent masseur in charge carefully questioned them about their needs, noting that Gordon's exercise for the last six months had consisted largely of sitting in the consulting room, standing beside the table in the operating theatre , or driving the hospital car to outlying villages. He would certainly need to encourage muscles and ligaments to be strong and fit for the more strenuous skiing palaver in the Alps. He had the impression that Judith, coping with house, children, getting to work, shopping and carrying supplies for the home, might well be the fitter of the two. He cleverly devised a suitable exercise programme for each.

"You will need every muscle of your bodies to be as fit as possible for the holiday you have in mind. So here goes. I'll deal with you, Gordon, and give Judith to the care of our lady physiotherapist."

After an hour's session both were very glad to relax in the Jacuzzi and let the water jets warmly massage their tired muscles. Their limbs were only too glad to give way to the luxury. Weariness seemed to shed away like magic and they returned home with lightness in their steps and lists of home exercises in their pockets. As the children were fed at school it simply remained to pick up little Johnny and find a café that could cope with the demands of such a youngster. Judith had one in mind.

Nourished and relaxed they repaired to the town's large park where Gordon decided to encourage watery frolic for his youngest. The lake was well supplied with canoes and small boats and soon the three were parked comfortably on the cushions of a pleasant rowing boat. Gordon took the oars to encourage his muscles and tried to instil into the head of his little son the language of a seagoing mariner.

"Don't be silly, he can't possibly understand what port and starboard mean. Wait till he has learnt basic English. Just teach him about little fish and dickybirds. I brought some bread for him to feed the pond life." Judith's admonishment was taken in good part.

The little chap quickly picked up the idea and began

to throw bits of bread for the denizens of the lake. He chuckled with laughter as ducks jostled each other and small fish rose with a splash to snaffle small morsels from under their beaks. When a pair of large swans smoothly breasted the water to join in the largesse the parents thought it wise to move their precious youngster away from those powerful beaks and Gordon took up the oars again. The afternoon was a delightful start to their holiday together, but schools were closing and mums and dads should be at home for children's return.

Jilly and Grace arrived in good time, eager to see their Mum and Dad together as in old times. Tea and homework, games and bath time all occupied the evening cheerfully. At bedtime Gordon's story found willing ears as he told of further mild adventures in the African bush.

Thus passed the days of their first holiday week; sometimes evening entertainments included a cinema programme and a night at the theatre, thanks to Sally who brought her sleeping infant and sat in for them. On the Saturday Roland insisted on a boating trip up river to his favourite restaurant and both families wrapped up well and enjoyed the water and the feeding of fish and any coots, water fowl, or water rats and voles prepared to venture out onto water in the presence of humans. It was a happy occasion with crackers and candles, paper hats, speeches in which all the children were invited to take part, each one making a little speech applauded by the staff and the proprietor who were very pleased to have the families back again. It was a fitting farewell party for the coming skiing trip.

A Different Holiday.

Weekend packing and car preparations followed and on a Sunday morning loving farewells were said to their darling children who bravely waved them Goodbye. It was an emotional few minutes but Sally was there to take them to Sunday school and the younger poppets were easily cheered and helped smoothly over the separation.

Gordon and Judith travelled south on the Sunday afternoon to catch an early evening ferry from Dover to Calais. They had chosen a hotel a few miles south of that port at Abbeville. They were made most welcome for the night with a candle light dinner that tickled their appetites and brought with it a wonderful sense of freedom and new adventure. On the Monday morning Gordon pointed the nose of his car towards the high mountains and snows of the French Alps.

Some twelve years had passed since their earlier holiday had been postponed on account of Gordon's episode in the operating theatre when his appendix was persuaded to see the light of day. He had on that occasion carefully mapped out his route and since his uncle had again booked them in at the same hotel, (one bedroom only this time), he had fished out the old road map and compared it to a more modern Michelin that Judith had purchased for this adventure. The highway had greatly improved and would be easy to follow. After filling the petrol tank and carefully choosing the right hand side of the road they drove away to their chosen *Shangri-la*.

Gordon had little difficulty in remembering to drive on the right. He had been warned that following a stop somewhere he should be extra careful to keep right, not left. Far south in the Rhone valley lay the city of Lyons,

France's second city. Having left Abeville quite early it would still be five o'clock when they reached the city, even on the fast motorways.

Judith, knowing that concentration could lapse when driving fast on motorways, had come prepared. After they had settled to the drive she said, "Gordon, would you like me to read you my notes about the Vercors region? While you've been prodding people's tummies and jabbing children's little arms to protect them from tetanus and whatever, I went to the library and got a book on the area around our hotel. So here goes with my digest of it all.

"The Vercors is a very large region and is designated a National Park. It is one of the most splendid of such parks in France, There are mountains covered to their summits with trees and great pine forest areas. It is triangular in shape, and is about 60 or 70 miles from base to apex while from one side to the other it will be about 50 miles. You can reach it by coming out of Grenoble on a road to the southwest. You can also come off the motorway on a road that goes right through the middle of the region. Somewhere in this maze, and the book calls it a wilderness of pine forests, mountains, waterfalls, caves and deep, narrow gorges, we shall find our hotel. From there no doubt somebody will guide us to a slope covered in snow. What fun it's all going to be Darling, I can hardly wait.

"We should look out for Mont Aiguille which is a mountain peak soaring to 6,842 ft. We could have a good climb one day if we're tired of skidding down the snow slopes.

"Apparently the area was a centre for the French Resistance movement during the war. German planes punished it by destroying several villages. Museums are there demonstrating artefacts from those old days.

I suspect that we are going to have lots to think and talk about.

"I thought we ought to have some information on the subject of skiing, so the library obliged again. Of course you've done it before but a reminder is always useful. According to the book there's more in it than meets the eye. You start with the ski-boots. They have to be absolutely spot-on with an accurate fit and no tight painful places anywhere. Then there are the fastenings that attach boots to skis. There's a lot of information about that subject; it's very important. We shall need a good fitter to ensure our safety."

Driving south on the motorway they talked interminably, Judith bringing up numerous items of information from her reading and Gordon referring to his memories of experiences when disporting himself in the snows with his uncle. It passed the time well and served to keep Gordon awake and able to concentrate on his driving. The hours went by and notices to Lyons appeared while they were still chatting and laughing over occurrences that had illumined their lives; all of it eased the passage of time.

They decided to find the old part of the city, '*vieux Lyons*' and seek a night's accommodation. From there they phoned their host in Grosse en Vercors to advise him of their change of plan. In the charming old region of cobbled streets and ancient buildings they found a real thrill. It would be good to halt there for a night's rest and, using the Michelin map, they discovered a suitable spot not very far from one of the two old Roman amphitheatres, built to accommodate 30,000 people. On a warm, sunny evening they sat at a table outside a café, relaxing and admiring the citizens of France as they busied themselves and talked volubly about prices and politics.

The waitress appreciated Judith's command of French and was helpful in directing them to a small hotel where they booked in for the night. After a cosy night and excellent breakfast, (English of course), Gordon used his camera to obtain views of the very large amphitheatre of Roman times, as well as ensuring a photographic record of Lyons' ancient city...With lots of photos recording their stay they set forth again.

Judith had remembered to look out Jack Jenkins' original letter and now turned to it as they drove south. Perusing it along with the volume on France culled from their local library, she told Gordon "Grosse- en-Vercors is south of Grenoble and should not be too difficult to find. It is stated to be very quaint and the ibex come into the village and toddle along the roads in the evenings. The guide book speaks of small ski runs and also hiking trails for walkers that might appeal to us.. A brochure mentions marvellous natural caves in the Grenoble area. Crowds of students are frequent visitors. It will be quite cosmopolitan".

"It all sounds lovely" she added, "and you'll be encouraged to practise your French. I can help you there of course. I repeat, I just can't wait...,but it's all right Gordon, you can keep to the speed limit."

It was not such a long haul this time but the journey was uneventful and they arrived in Grenoble for late tea *a l'angleterre*. There was just time to admire a few dwellings of the great, and then on to their booked hotel further south in Grosse-en-Vercors where they were welcomed with true Gallic enthusiasm and hospitality. They were too tired to notice the quaintness or the patrolling ibex, but enjoyed the excellent meal later put before them.

Monsieur was most attentive, wishing them a night of

happiness and free from trouble. In a cosy bedroom that was just what they found.

"Goodnight Judy, more fun tomorrow."

"Sleep well, Gordon, my Darling. This is all quite marvellous."

****

CHAPTER 19

LE SKIING

THE HOTEL WAS small with just twelve bedrooms, a very lovely old fashioned building and nicely furnished, standing in a valley between huge pine woods on either side A good sized dining room was tastefully arranged with polished tables, tidily laid out with white embroidered table cloths and gleaming cutlery.

Monsieur greeted them in English, Judith replying in French. He served breakfast and later said, "I understand M'sieu and Madame, that you desire to have some lessons in Skiing, according to the instructions given by the gentlemen who booked your accommodation".

"Yes that is correct." said Gordon. "My wife has no experience of skiing. I learnt to ski about 15 years ago, but have forgotten most of it. We would like to be regarded as novices and given all proper instruction, including rental of the necessary equipment My uncle who arranged the accommodation told me that you, M'sieu, would be willing to make the needful contacts for instruction and hire of equipment, We should be very thankful to be helped in this way".

"That is good. In that case I will at once telephone to an excellent instructor, if you will excuse me sir, and all shall be done as you desire."

Nor very long afterwards a young lady appeared and introduced herself, speaking excellent English. She was the instructor, specially chosen on account of Judith's presence and her ignorance of the art. Flaxen haired and blue eyed she appeared to be of Nordic extraction and quickly gained Gordon's admiration while being most attentive to Judith. "I will take you," she said, "to a supply institution where boots, bindings, skis and all necessary items can be hired or even bought. I will make all the preparation for fitting boots, binding them onto skis of the right length and attend to proper clothing, gloves, and glasses to protect the eyes. I will attend to any needful advice and then we can begin instruction at a suitable site for beginners."

Proceedings began when she guided them to the rental shop in the village. She approached a senior assistant in the shop and demanded his personal attention to her charges- a very important doctor and his wife from England- she explained. Particular attention was paid to the choice of boots, the correct type with the proper kind of toes; skis of the right length which should reach when stood up to the level approximately of the wearer's chin; the careful matter of bindings to attach the boots to the skis by the toes only and the choice of several pairs of thin knee length socks, and of course lined gloves being as waterproof as possible. They spent well over an hour very usefully and Gordon was pleased to rent boots and skis and bindings, while purchasing other items.

Judith found all this extremely interesting and did her best to understand and absorb the advice and information, while co-operating with their instructor who was obviously experienced in caring for foreigners and well able to converse in English.

With boots well fitted, comfortable and securely bound onto a suitable pair of skis, they were not long in commencing the slippery business of moving with care on the level area of snow chosen for them. Poles for hand use provided support and gave Judith courage as she slid gently over the cold, white surface. They kept the skis parallel for ordinary straight and forward movement and were shown how to point the toes of the skis towards each other for slowing and stopping. The morning was spent in practising such gentle movement, and they were advised to eat and rest for a while before attempting the next session .That would involve the art of turning and it was important to be wide awake to ensure understanding of the manoeuvres involved. It was in turning, their teacher said, that possible danger could occur when skiers could encounter each other in collisions, and falls with injuries might happen.

As they practised a few falls did occur, but very gently and with no damage to either of them. They were shown the methods that might be used in getting up from a fall; prone and pushing up with hands for a woman while the angle of spread of the feet was important, and more a sideways roll for a man and use of his probably more powerful arm and shoulder muscles to raise him to the vertical using his pole suitably. The instructor assured them that if there were any risk of skis becoming entangled the boots would promptly separate from the skis and all would be well. "That is why they are attached by the toes only", she said. This they found was their experience. There was no trouble. Thus the time was spent, with frequent stops for coffee and talk and meeting other novices with whom they joined merrily chatting in different languages.. If such folk were French Judith was in her element and Gordon found them only too willing to interpret and help him to understand the language. They were also very willing to practise their English. Altogether it was a happy and appreciative crowd of skiers who gathered at the day's end to eat, drink and chat merrily together before retiring to a well earned rest.

"What did you think of today's adventure then, and are you rarin' to meet the snowy slopes of tomorrow?" asked Gordon as they retired to their room.

"It was all very interesting, Gordon. I felt like a knight in armour with all that array of merchandise fitted around my body. What are we going to do tomorrow?"

"That's where the skiing palaver really hits us," he replied. We shall be taken to the piste and taught how to slide safely on slippery skis down slopes of snow and ice. Not too much ice of course, preferably none at all; it's far too dangerous."

"And what exactly is a piste?"

"It is a carefully prepared slope covered in snow where skiers may ski in reasonable safety. It is away from the threat of avalanches, with no crevasses, rocky protuberances or other hazards. Beginners start on a quiet area and are taught the basic arts of skiing; how to slide straight, how to turn, how to fall when it's unavoidable, and all the little extras, like avoiding collisions with other skiers. It's great fun. You are going to enjoy this. Skiers are strongly advised to use only the piste. You start by moving across the piste; only when fairly competent do you go up the little hill and point your skis downward. Straying away from it may land people in trouble, so the piste will be our homeland for the rest of the week. Of course we can do other things as well...

"As a point of interest, how do you stop?" asked his lady, rather anxiously.

"No problem, the bottom of the hill will begin to slope up and stopping will be quite automatic." replied her beloved. "If you point your toes together just a little you will begin to slow down. It's all quite safe, my Darling."

"It all sounds fascinating, Gordon."

"Do you feel that it will be worth while my Sweetie?" enquired Gordon, sliding an arm around her as they snuggled into bed.

"Very much worthwhile, my Darling. I could do with a month or too of this. Sleep well, chum."

And in due course they did...

Morning brought clear skies and a good English breakfast. Their instructor joined them for the meal and continued her instruction while they ate. "You will meet the piste to-day" she said. Very soon she took them along and showed it to them.

"There is something else you must remember. After exertion do not retire and curl up like a teddy bear or a dormouse. You should stretch all your muscles and do gentle exercises; that will prevent them from becoming stiff. That is quite important."

. Such were her words of wisdom before starting their exertions. "The first thing is to get your stance right," she said. "Stand with skis pointing forwards, lightly bend your knees and flex your ankles a little"

For a couple of hours they followed her instructions carefully, concentrating with minds as well as movements. Gradually fear was banished and the pleasure of movement began to take hold. They mounted the little hill and, with skis pointing downwards and toes very slightly approximating, Judith experienced the pull of gravity and proceeded down the slope in a straight line stopping at the bottom as the ground began to rise. Gordon was beside her.

"That was wonderful," she said.

"Good" said the instructor. "Do it a few more times and then we'll practice the turn, first one way and when you're OK with that we'll do it the other way. Later we'll do one after the other, making a kind of S shape. There's no need to hurry; we do it all very gently and slowly until you are quite au fait with the manoeuvre"..

This they did and when their fair instructor felt that they had learnt and practised enough she declared "It's time to call a halt. Hot chocolate drinks and nourishment are good for body and soul Come on." She led the way to the appropriate bar. They were soon seated and enjoying chats with folk of different nations, all beginners and elated at their first attempt at the gentle art of skiing.

Having warmed up a little, stretched all muscles and done a few quiet exercises they trooped out for a further session. Returning to the piste Gordon began to look round. He noticed an area of snow where, on the hillside away from the piste some separation of the smooth snow line had occurred. "Has there been a small avalanche there?" he asked the instructor, "and look, there is a dark object sticking out of the pile of snow at the bottom. I believe it's the toe of a boot."

"You are quite right" said the lady, after pulling out her binoculars and viewing the area. "Oh dear, that looks like a very nasty incident. It must have happened last evening when we had all gone off for the night. Someone must have strayed off piste." She extracted her mobile phone and quickly dialled the number of the emergency team.

"Can't we go over and try to help?" asked Gordon, his doctor's mind being instantly in the mode for life saving.

"No, it's far too late." she replied. It's also far too dangerous. You can see the huge thickness of snow above just waiting to come down and trap the unwary. We shall have to wait for the expert team. They are always on the alert and very efficient. They won't be long. I fear they have a body to dig out".

And so it proved. Some beginners returned to their exercises in skiing practice but most stood by, with sad and concerned faces, watching as the team of life savers moved in carefully to retrieve the body of a skier from the huge pile of snow at the bottom of the mountain. Their lady instructor said she must speak to the team leader and went across to him. She mentioned the mass pf snow that was poised ready to bring down a second avalanche.

"Yes, we have taken note of that," he replied. "In fact when we heard about the missing man we came out yesterday evening and had a good look with torch lights but failed to spot the boot. Perhaps it was still covered with snow at the time. However we shall be arranging to bring down that mass of snow and it will be necessary to close this piste in case a really massive avalanche occurs nearby. So your customers will need to move away to another, safer area. She then told him of the presence of an English doctor on the scene.

"That could be very useful" he said, and he came across and asked if Gordon would be willing to certify death.

"Certainly", said Gordon," if it is legal for me to do so in France. I shall be glad to help." The team leader conferred with his fellows and told Gordon that such a proceeding had occurred a few months previously when an Austrian doctor had helped them in that way, so Gordon went along

464

and after viewing and briefly examining the unfortunate man's body confirmed that life was extinct.

The necessary form was produced which he duly signed. The body was removed on a stretcher that conveyed it to a waiting ambulance. .

"Somebody is going to be very sad." said Judith.

"Yes, I am afraid so" said the instructor. "There was a flash on the news last night that a man had gone missing. There was no mention of an avalanche, but of course that is always a possibility. Unwisely he moved off the piste, not knowing of the danger which now seems obvious to us."

Most of the beginners began to move slowly into position for renewed skiing ventures on the piste. Some of them decided to end their day's sport in view of the tragedy and returned to their lodgings. Gordon and Judith felt that they must continue to practise. Their lady instructor approved and attended them. She also notified everyone that the piste would be closed next day, mentioning the words of the team leader.

"I wonder why it is," said Judith, "that whenever you and I, Gordon, attempt some form of holiday adventure we always become involved in a medical emergency."

"It's just one of the hazards of a doctor's life, Darling. Equally a Cairo kidnap might be said to be a hazard of a beautiful secretary's existence."

"Ha ha!. Who was the funny poet, psychiatrist or whatever who averred that pain wasn't real, only to be answered by some wise guy who declared that 'although my pain isn't real, none the less , tra la la, tra la la, tra la la, I don't like what I fancy I feel.?' In other words it would be nice to enjoy our pleasures minus medical bother, or perhaps that isn't a proper simile"

"I agree my Darling. We will stop registering as

'Doctor' and Mrs. and stick to Mr. and Mrs. in future. That might do the trick."

"I doubt it dear man. You'll still be a doctor. What are we going to do tomorrow?"

"What about a potter over to Grenoble? There are lots of Museums there, and after a culture shock we could just sit beside tables on the pavements and watch the world go by."

"Lovely. It's a date."

Again the morning dawned bright and clear. After a leisurely breakfast Gordon brought the car round and they moved off together in a northeast direction to find Grenoble. Judith read from her library book, using also the Michelin map to guide Gordon towards that city which was, of course, well sign posted.

"This is a very ancient city." she read. "It used to be the capital of the Dauphine region of France, .standing at the confluence of the Isere and Drae rivers. At its heart are the 13th century Collegiale St Andre and the 16th century Palais de Justice. There are quite a number of Museums, including one about the French Resistance during the '39 to '45 war. It's quite big with getting on for 100,000 people and has a University that is science oriented, including the study of nuclear physics. You could advance your education here, my lad. By the way there is also a cable car from near the city centre up to the 10th century Fort de la Bastille. It must be quite high up; you get a wonderful view of the countryside with the huge massifs of Vercors to the south west and the Chartreuse to the north. Let's take a ride and have a look at la France."

Gordon was impressed and eventually found a parking place in the city among vehicles and their occupants from many countries all agog to view the old city and sample its culture.

A good walk through Grenoble, using the Michelin map, brought them to the Stephanie-Jay quay and here they indulged in a pavement style coffee with pancakes while watching the populace and the visitors ambling peacefully along.

Refreshed, they addressed their steps to the cable car near by and joined the mob all eager to sample the air beside the Fort de la Bastille. An excellent ride with views of the city, the rivers and the city's environs brought them to an elevated position beside that Fort. The guide book was right. The view before their eyes was magnificent, with mighty mountains, forests and gorges; snow capped summits stretching far into the distance, brilliant in the morning sun. This was a thrill for everyone. Cameras clicked incessantly.

After photographing, chatting to other visitors, French (very few), British (more, all eager to absorb culture), Scandinavians and Germans (busy making comparisons), and others, they found a light lunch in a fashionable restaurant near the Fort, still looking out at the vast geographical vista that surrounded and enthralled them. Eventually, leaving their pinnacle of enchantment behind reluctantly, they entered the unique gondola cable car and enjoyed the smooth ride of the downward return to base.

In the city there was time to visit the Musee de Grenoble where art of all periods educated them; then they felt it impossible to leave before spending some minutes, or even an hour or more, in the Musee de Resistance. Here they rediscovered heroic acts of determination by faithful French folk who were determined to prevent further occupation of their homeland by the Nazis with their brutal regime.

Impressed by all they had seen and learned they found

that the hours had slipped by and they pointed their wheels towards the Vercors. It was too late to inspect the huge new avalanche but they were in time for their meal with the lady guide who excitedly told them all about it.

The next two days were spent on the slopes, gradually gaining in confidence for Judith who was beginning to enjoy the sensation of sliding with increasing control down the piste. She could ski from a straight line to a curve one way, then the other, and managed to perform without colliding with other beginners, even able to manage the necessary avoiding manoeuvres when some beginner was bent on a collision course with her. She became quite thrilled with her new dexterity and often turned with shining eyes to Gordon to thank him for persuading her to 'have a go', laughing and, after removing her woolly hat, tossing her hair like a teenager.

But the end of holiday must be faced. A last meal was spent with their lady guide, chatting like old friends and vowing to meet up at 'another time'. Thanks said and kisses exchanged they made ready with final packing. The next morning after thanking their host and waving 'goodbye' they snuggled into the car and faced the long journey home. Reaching Lyons at last they looked at each other.

"I can see a travel agent," said Gordon.

"Just what I was thinking" said his wife.

They kissed and vowed with one accord that it would be easier by plane.

"It will be more expensive certainly, but so what? It's only money. That travel agent is advertising cheap flights; lets pop in and try our luck", said Gordon.

"Oui M'sieu, Madame, c'est possible," was the response. Yes there were two seats next morning and he could arrange for their car to be delivered to Oxford. There was no problem. He also knew of a reasonably inexpensive B&B where they could spend the night. In an absurdly short time it was all arranged, paid for in franks and they were free to enjoy Lyons and visit the Cathedral. This they felt was 'Expertise a la France' at its best. They spent a wonderful day viewing everything that could be seen. They also telephoned Gerald to inform him of the change of plan.

"That's excellent" said Gordon's father. "It will be Saturday and I can collect your little lambs; they will be quite over the moon on meeting you at Heathrow. I will tell John and Mary. They will be very pleased too and will have everything ready for you. Perhaps I could manage a small transfusion to your bank account as well. Don't worry about a thing, as the anaesthetist said to – who was it?" On that they put down the phone, thrilled. They had a good night in the neat and comfortable B&B. The morning afterwards a pretty air hostess was asking them as they rubbed shoulders comfortably in a 747 if they would like a cup of tea *a l'Angleterre.*

*

"Wakey wakey, rise and shine. Everybody out. Breakfast's ready". So the merry voice of Mary smote the children's ears on a fine Saturday morning

"Oh Granny, it's Saturday, we have a lie-in on Saturday. Can't we get up later?" Jilly's reply to her granny's emphatic call was slightly mournful

"Not this Saturday. It's a special one," said Mary. "Come on, rout out all of you."

"Why special Granny?" asked Jilly.

"Ooh I know," cried her sister, Grace. "I saw Granny

cooking like mad yesterday. Someone must be coming. Who is it Granny?" And they shouted with one accord, "Yes, tell us, Granny. Tell, tell, tell,"

"Guess," said Mary.

"It could be Uncle Gerald Is it him Granny?"

Well, yes he is going to be here, but he drops in anyway sometimes".

"What about Uncle Jack? Oh no, he and auntie are in Majorca."

"I guess we give up. Come on Granny, tell…please."

"OK. only it's a bit cool after all that excitement. What about your Mum and Dad?"

"Really? We thought it was next week" they shrieked in unison. "Hooray, hooray, hooray!" and in a trice they were out of bed, into the bathroom, washed, dressed and down the stairs in record time to spoon porridge into their mouths, followed by a boiled egg and toast with honey. All were ready betimes for the arrival of Uncle Gerald.

"Your Mum and Dad are flying home, so Heathrow is waiting for them", said Mary.

"Are we going to the airport?" said Jilly. "That will be wonderful".

"Can I go too?" shouted Johnny. "I want to go and find Mummy and Daddy".

"Yes, that's what it's all about. Yes Johnny darling, you're going too. They have changed their plans and are coming by air. The car will come over later. Your Mum and Dad will be thrilled to see you all. As soon as you've finished clean your shoes, put your coats on and Uncle Gerald will be here. Have a wonderful day. I'll have a special kind of pasta for you when you get back. And, remember to be very good in the car. No quarrelling. If you do Uncle will turn round and bring you straight back. OK?"

There was a ring on the door bell and Gerald came in, greeted vociferously by all three children who flung their arms round him and shouted their heads off.

"You'd better loose me or we shall miss the plane," he said. "Everybody into the car, Jilly in the front passenger seat; you are to help me find the airport. Hallo Mary, what a furious tribe of creatures you have got here."

"They are a bit excited Gerald. We had a game of guessing who's coming today. Will you give me a ring when you leave the airport and I'll have dinner ready."

"Right ho, the time of arrival depends on weather and traffic, of course."

With all children quietly ensconced in the capacious Volvo, Gerald put the car into drive and they slid smoothly away, hands waving to Mary who waved back happily. .

*

"Uncle Gerald, what's that?" said Johnny, rather to everybody's surprise. He wasn't one for asking questions, accepting things as they were and putting up with them. He went on, "It's got something on top of it whizzing round and round, what is it Uncle?"

They had reached the airport at Heathrow and after parking the car were now upstairs on the viewing balcony watching planes coming down and others zooming up into the sky. But Johnny had spotted another plane, smaller than the mighty 747s and their competitors, and the whizzing propeller intrigued him.

"That's a helicopter" replied Gerald "It is only a little chap compared to those huge things that go off to Africa, America or France and Europe. It's used to ferry people around our country from town to town and is very useful.

Sometimes it is used to collect people from a road accident and take them to hospital. It can rise straight up into the air without a long run along the ground. The thing whizzing round on top of it is a propeller and as it pushes air downwards the little plane rises up. It has another propeller at the back which pushes it forward when it wants to go somewhere."

"Well are Mummy and Daddy coming home in one of those little ones?" He was quite anxious.

"No, Johnny. They will be in a great big 747 plane. It's one of those that flies in almost every minute. You can see them over there," and he pointed, "appearing out of the cloud and making straight for the landing strip. Then they land and run very fast along the strip. The captain puts the brakes on and soon the plane will stop and the passengers will all get out. I think I hear the number of their plane being called now, so off you go, everyone downstairs and we'll wait at the barriers until they come along"..

Judith and the children lost no time in lining up at the barriers. Impatience was very evident. Time was passing and the children became a little restless.

"Why are they so long Uncle Gerald?" Johnny was anxious again.

"It's because they have to wait for their big suitcases to be unloaded off the plane and then they have to go through Customs. The luggage is put onto a moving platform called a carousel. That goes round and round with the suitcases on them and the passengers wait till they see their own. They pick the cases off the carousel, put them on a trolley with wheels and you'll see Daddy pushing it along very soon."

And all of a sudden they did. With a yell of welcome Johnny skirted the barriers and rushed to meet his Mum and Dad, hugging them madly. As happened the last time when John and Mary arrived the parents had to beg for release in order to greet their daughters who were equally loving and enthusiastic. Everywhere around them there was the joy of reunion. For Gerald the greeting of his son and secretary was a real thrill and he kissed her on both cheeks, while gripping Gordon's hand with the strong handclasp of a father's genuine love.

What a wonderful moment when, later, they stepped through the door of their home to the loving greeting of John and Mary. Holidays were a delight and a refreshing change of scene, but to return to the unfailing love of children and parents was a boon without compare. Gordon remembered that responsibility was also to be considered and was relieved, when reporting to Bertie, that no desperate maternity emergencies awaited his arrival. Bertie however welcomed him effusively and offered him plenty of work on Monday. Meanwhile Mary had performed with delightful efficiency on the Aga. They set to with a will, after the minister had said grace that offered thanks for their safe return.

. Questions by the dozen demanded answers with details of snow and skids, falls and flailing skis, boots and gloves lost and retrieved and all the fun relived of playtime among the snows and the ski lifts of the French Alps. .All stories were illustrated with photos of mountains and forests, the lovely architecture of old France, the modern gear and apparel of enthusiastic people of different countries all happily enjoying life among the snows. Gordon and Judith carefully kept off the subject of bodies in avalanches while in the children's presence

Later there was little chance of snoozing when children persisted in asking questions. They called on their neighbours, Roland and Sally, to thank them for their help with the children. Then, all wrapped up against the cold, they sallied forth in the chill February air for a brisk walk in the lanes and fields of dear old England.

Finally unpacked, preparations made for the morrow and the porridge in the bottom oven they were cosily bedded and ready for sleep. "So what about that for a morsel of drama in our dull unromantic lives, my Darling?" said Gordon.

"Quite enough drama for me, and while you're around there's no lack of romance either, so I'm a very satisfied wife and I love you. Thank you, my dear man for a lovely holiday."

"Love is a nice idea, my Treasure. Let's leave further drama till tomorrow. They did.

****

Chapter 20

DOING WELL. WHAT NEXT?

AFTER THE WEEKEND the morning drama involved a wife poring over the Aga, porridge being spooned into hungry tummies, boiled eggs, toast and marmalade followed by the donning of coats, hats and gloves. Then with satchels, brief case, or stethoscope, to school, antique shop or morning surgery, as each formed the backdrop to the serious business of life in the small town of Bifford. The family waved goodbye to each other, the girls walking to school, Judith taking her small car while Gordon dropped his son at the infant school ere facing his patients in the surgery. Gone were the days of crowds of snivelling, coughing folk sharing germs together in a busy waiting room. Appointments were beginning to be the norm and only a few folk seated themselves in that tidy area. While the receptionist, carefully protected behind armour plate glass, sorted out the phone calls and hoped she was doing folk justice.

Gordon entered his consulting room and, changing his coat for a white one, checked the list of appointments, turned on his light and pressed the button. In the waiting room a request sounded for the first patient to go to his room. All was most efficient. When it worked... The aim was to give the patient seven and a half minutes with the doctor (in some instances even a little more). Listen to the complaint, peruse the history as revealed in the patient's records, examine the patient, decide on a diagnosis having considered the various alternatives, think about treatment or further investigation, complete laboratory forms, write a prescription, not forgetting to write down all necessary findings, hope that your decision is correct and tell the patient to make another appointment if no better. Then wonder by how many minutes the norm had been exceeded. The drama of the morning surgery would fill a book. Gordon managed to wonder how his wife's morning drama was proceeding... he pressed the button for the next patient.

*

Perhaps now is the time to indulge in a revision of this family saga and assess the progress of the individuals. For each an illuminating little bit of history is developing.

Gordon, now a husband and father of a growing family, has become established in general practice with prospects of a partnership in a few years. He works hard and conscientiously, endeavouring to render good and proper service to every patient, taking little account of extra time spent in the process. He takes a keen interest in each of his children and wishes it were possible to allow more time to get to know them. He tries to pay attention to the demands of his Rotary club while assuring that they do not interfere unduly with family responsibilities. He is highly regarded by patients and friends.

Judith, a successful and greatly appreciated secretary in Gerald's business, has created for herself an extremely useful niche there and is a valuable member of the staff. She sorts out problems both in relations with clients and in any staff difficulties and behaves as if she were almost a partner in the business. At the same time she is the mainstay of the home and her wisdom and commonsense are the first ports of call for the young people when they need support or have problems of one sort or another, requiring solutions. Helping to organise their work and play, often providing transport as well as making nourishing meals and ensuring that their clothes are in good order, such matters are always the most important of her duties. Membership of the Inner Wheel, while interesting and sometimes entertaining, is of secondary importance. Support for her husband and a genuine interest in his work figures very largely in her daily life. What a busy woman she has become. What a real mother.

The children are developing rapidly and showing promise.

Jilly, nearly fourteen, has become a useful family member, often assuming responsibility in helping her younger siblings to solve minor problems. A hard worker at school, she performs well in class, winning the approval of her teachers and often the admiration of her classmates. A prize for English composition is greatly treasured. On the playing field she performs well also and is adept in swimming, learning the crawl stroke to good effect. She attends church with her mother and listens to her Gandpa's sermons intently. Generally her progress is considered very satisfactory.

Grace may fall a little behind in view of her sister's prowess but is also quite a valued member of her school society. Her work is good in all subjects and especially in art and design when she pleases her mentor and gains his commendation at the end of term. Nearly ten years of age she has fun in writing poetry for small children and, when encouraged, will even write little tunes to accompany their dancing. She reads a lot, largely fiction but also follows the adventures of Captain Scott and his fellow adventurers in their tragic Antarctic journey. Running is not her strong point but she will cycle miles on a bicycle at weekends with a cycling group. She loves cooking and is quite expert on the Aga.

As for little Johnny, he shines brightly in his class at infant school and is preparing to enter the primary school next autumn. He likes sea stories and is always happy when the family goes to the seaside for a day out. On a little bicycle he has become quite proficient. He cleans and polishes it to perfection. He draws pictures, tackles puzzles and reads stories with real interest

Thus the family group goes forward in learning and experience. To follow their adventures in the awkward years of teenage development, bodily and mental growth with all its difficulties, occasional rebelliousness and even tantrums is not the aim of this saga. Rather let us leap forward to more stable years when Jilly is looking out to the wider world of further education, hoping to enter a university and trying to decide in what particular discipline she should study…

She was helping to dry the dishes after taking them out of the dishwasher one evening. "Mum", she said, "my exam results were good enough for a university place, but what subject should I read, isn't that the word?

"Yes Darling, that's the word used. It all depends what you want to do with your life. Have you begun to think about that yet? What ideas have you developed?"

"Oh well, I should like to find a nice boy to marry and have a family like you and Dad. But I would like something else too. You have a wonderful secretarial job and Dad is a jolly good doctor. I'm pretty good with letters and articles but don't really want to spend years typing letters to people....I wonder, Mum, do you think I could manage a doctor's job?"

Judith rapidly oriented her thoughts. It sounded as if this was another crunch time. She must be careful.

"My Darling, that needs a lot of thought. You need to know quite a lot about what such a job involves. It is not all fun and medical drama you know. Not all just listening with a stethoscope or looking through a microscope. It means listening to patients' complaints, sorting out what is important and being very helpful to them. You have to find out what is the cause of their symptoms and recommend treatment. It involves a lot of quite serious medical and surgical work, even collecting babies and resuscitating them, cutting into live flesh and stitching it up again, all under anaesthetic of course".

"I've chopped up worms in the Biology lab of course. Anyway how many years does it take to qualify?"

"It takes at least five. Then you have to do several hospital jobs under supervision before you are let loose on the public. That takes another two years. Some people get married before they finish. There's a lot to think about."

"Yes, I see. I thin k I'll go to bed. I have an Agatha Christie to concentrate on. That should get my brain in order. Goodnight, Mum. Thanks for the chat."

To Gordon a little later Judith said "I think our oldest fledgling is thinking of leaving the nest, Darling. She may decide to follow in your footsteps."

"Really, have you been having a talk?"

"Yes, it looks as if being just a housewife will not satisfy her. It certainly looks as if something professional is in her sights; medicine is her idea at the moment. She's bright enough anyway."

"That is very interesting," said Gordon. "I had better prepare myself with information for answering intelligent questions. Our young lady will require something very precise to bite on. How does one apply for a university place now-a-days? Perhaps the B.M.A. can help. Let's see what they have to say. I had better write for information."

When the reply came it provided Gordon with enough information to occupy their thoughts for weeks on end.

"Hallo Pop. You're back early. Of course it's your half day isn't it. I'm off this afternoon too."

"Nice to see you Jilly. How come that school has let you out?"

"We had a lecture from some big wig about drugs and he asked the head teacher if we could have an afternoon off. He was quite a pleasant person. When question time came I was very forward and rather cheekily mentioned to him that the glass in front of him looked like wine. I said. "If that contains alcohol, isn't that a dangerous drug too?" He was a bit taken aback but answered very nicely thanking me for my contribution and saying that this was something everyone should think about very seriously. We didn't take it any further."

"Good for you my Darling. What about a walk and talk in the good fresh air before Mum comes home?"

They were soon out in country lanes and conversing freely. Gordon had been distressed that a pigeon and a couple of blackbirds had been killed in their garden and wondered if a sparrow hawk was the murderer. Jilly commented that she presumed the hawk had a family to feed. "That seems to be Nature's way of maintaining life for the fittest. Didn't Darwin have something to say about it?" she asked.

"Yes, indeed he did. But I love the sound of the blackbird's contralto song and feel sad that two nests of fledglings may die if their fathers are not there to feed them. The mother birds will try of course. That reminds me. You have a lovely voice, but you are a soprano aren't you. Is your choir doing any end of term concerts?"

"Yes Dad. We're doing Gilbert and Sullivan's works this year. I'm singing 'Tit willow, and Jason is the 'Lord high Executioner.' We're also practising Handel's Messiah for a pre- Christmas production.. The choirmaster hopes I'll be able to take part, although I may have left school by then."

"That's a solemn thought my Precious. Mum tells me that you have some ideas about professional work."

"That's right Dad. I asked her if she thought I could manage doctoring. I have thought a lot about it and over the years that I've watched you at work. I think I would like to follow your example."

"I take that as a great compliment my lovey. I believe you could certainly manage the work. You would make a fine doctor, I feel quite sure. There's a lot to think about. You have to write applying to the Central Committee and give reasons and lots of detail. Also you have to make a list of medical schools in order of preference, and that needs thinking about."

"I'm going to be busy, I can see. I thought I might have a talk with our biology teacher and ask his opinion too."

The walk and talk continued with Gordon giving his daughter lots of useful information and gentle advice. This was going to draw them even closer in the future. After their evening meal while Grace applied herself to home work and Johnny played with his car racing set the home was quiet. Jilly, with her parents, went into quite serious discussion. It would be advisable to acquire information regarding future studies. How much chemistry had she done? Had she a good grasp of physics? What would be her attitude if faced with the body bits of corpses to dissect? Jilly began to understand that answers to such questions and others of even more import were not easy but must be faced. After a couple of hours' session it was a most grateful young lady who said 'Goodnight' to her parents.

"That was a useful talk Gordon, Darling", said Judith. She is lucky to have a doctor for a father. You will be a real asset in her future life."

"I'm glad to be of some use, my Pet, but it's the mother who is the leading light in a girl's development you know. I think you're marvellous, Darling. Come on, bedtime."

Settling back on her pillow while Gordon nuzzled her ear lobe she needed further chat. "Gordon", she said, "I have been asked to talk to the Inner Wheel next week and am not quite sure what story to tell them and how to approach it."

He considered, then "I think it would be best if you simply recount your kidnapping experience just as it happened, with chloroform and all the trimmings. It will all be quite new to them and should stir their emotions and even educate any of their police friends when you relate to them the gaseous details of your release. Just have a go my Darling and '*damned be him/her that first cries, 'Hold enough'*. Of course it's the District Meeting isn't it? That's good. Your fame will be spread even further abroad. It might help to boost esteem for our medical practice too."

And the night and morning were yet another day.

****

Chapter 21

SUCCESS AND A REWARDING SAIL

THE MONTHS AND years passed by with all the family working well and Jilly in particular tackling her 'A' levels to try to gain the highest possible passes to ensure entrance to the University of her choice.

On a bright clear morning a south- east wind blew gently, cooling the little town of Bifford. The family were at the breakfast table preparing for whatever the day might bring in terms of further education; thinking too of work in the Antiques business or the moans and groans, real or only imaginary, of Gordon's patients in his surgery.

Jily was restless, glancing frequently out of the window. Suddenly the rattle of the letter box startled her to her feet and she sped to the front door. A short pause gave way to a shriek of delight. "Dad, they want to see me. I've got an appointment next week. Isn't it marvellous!"

She came back, eyes shining with excitement and threw her arms around her Mum and Dad.

"That's lovely, my Pet. Now you'll be able to wear that party dress and necklace that uncle Gerald gave you for Christmas," said her father. Judith clasped her daughter closely, too delighted to speak. It looked as if a place for Jilly was assured.

"Where will it be, Darling?" enquired her mother.

"Southampton I hope Mum. That was my first choice."

"I hope you'll be lucky my Darling. Not everybody gets their first choice."

"Maybe it's something to do with all your 'A's and 'A plus' results," said her father. "You certainly worked hard for it. Congratulations, Jilly."

"I suppose school calls today, but we'll have all the weekend to make you beautiful to please the interviewing people. Not that that will take much doing; you look lovely anywhere."

"Perhaps a new pair of jeans, Mum. My old ones are wearing out."

"Very suitable for an interview, I don't think! But something for a boating excursion would be nice," commented Judith,

"Shall we have a day on the boat and go round the Isle of Wight from Southampton? Is that why you chose that city for your medical course? Five years of living near grandpa's yacht?"

"It had occurred to me, Dad, I confess."

"Spending weekends snoozing on the foredeck in a bikini,-clever girl. Well thought out. It must come from all the 'A'levels. After to-day's work we'll begin to make plans."

*

Gordon phoned his father with the suggestion of a weekend family boating excursion. It was taken up with enthusiasm, Gerald being very pleased with the news about Jilly's interview. He felt sure that the child would be accepted and said so in no uncertain terms.

"I think a fresh sail around Wight Island would be a very nice idea to celebrate young Jilly's success" said Gerald. "She has worked very hard and deserves recognition. Maybe she would like to take the helm for a bit. OK. Saturday morning as before; hope it doesn't rain."

On the Saturday morning Jilly and her mother spent an hour in Southampton shopping while the men prepared the boat, and joined them later by taxi.

After coffee on board Gerald started the engine and reversed out of his berth in the marina. With everyone wearing safety harness Gerald steered out into the Southampton water and made for the open water of the Solent. He had purchased a thirty five footer, replacing the smaller yacht, and was glad to have some practice in sailing it. There was more room for the growing family and sometimes guests could be invited as well.

Passing near Ryde he felt confident enough to raise the sails; Gordon and Jilly assisted most competently and they sailed on towards Sandown where he planned to drop anchor and eat lunch on board. The wind was now south-westerly, standing at force 4, and they were all comfortable. When Gerald decided to go about, both for practice as well as from necessity, the manoeuvre was accomplished expertly by all, sheets being hauled and heads ducked as necessary.

Approaching Sandown Judith and Jilly climbed down into the cabin to prepare a meal for them all. The younger children amused themselves with a portable T.V. on the cabin table.

"It's going to be bacon and eggs all round; if that'll do," shouted Judith, and assent was given willingly.

The anchor was dropped and Gerald checked for possible dragging. It had a firm hold. A good inspection of the sky westwards to check for weather seemed satisfactory and all sat comfortably in the cockpit to taste the ladies' offering. They pronounced it excellent and the meal was finished off with peaches and Cornish cream from tins. Gordon and Grace offered to wash up while Gerald did a radio check on the weather. He pronounced that the low pressure system was advancing a little more quickly than anticipated and decided to return to spend the night in Ryde rather than continue round the island. However the family could go ashore for a short time in Sandown if they wished. After dropping the dinghy into the water from its yacht fixings all except Gerald went ashore for an inspection of the town, its shops and its picture post cards.

They regretted that time was lacking for a visit to the dinosaur museum, where, it was said that the roaring of the monsters was most realistic. Postcards would content them meanwhile; perhaps a holiday there would attract in later years. Then it was up anchor and up with the sails. Gordon was invited to take the helm and did so with alacrity and expertise. Jilly, interested, came to stand beside him. The breeze remained steady meantime although it was forecast to rise by evening. Gerald noticed her absorption and asked, "Would you like to steer, Jilly?" The reply came promptly, "Oh yes please, if you think I can manage without upsetting the boat."

"I'm sure you can Jilly; perhaps Dad will hand over the wheel."

"Here you are" said her father, relinquishing the wheel. "You will also have control of the mainsail; the sheet for that is fixed in the cleat. With this steady breeze it probably won't need alteration. If it does Gerald or I can help. Just keep half an eye on the compass in front of you. Now that we have passed Culver Cliff you can adjust the wheel so that the needle stays on 45 degrees. That will take us to the Foreland Point off Bembridge. Then Gerald or I will adjust the sail and we'll go round towards Ryde. Jilly loved it, having little difficulty in making any adjustments to the steering and noting several big vessels including ferries from Portsmouth and Southampton moving quickly off towards Cherbourg or Le Havre. More distantly she spotted a huge liner moving southwards from its dock in Southampton, and thought that although sail had the right of way over engine power, to insist on her rights would be disastrous. She steered appropriately avoiding it without difficulty.

"This is fun Dad" she said. "What about a sailing dinghy for me to play with when I'm not immersed in books on anatomy or physiology?"

"What makes you think you'll have any spare time my Darling. Medical studies keep you busy day and night".

"Oh dear, is life as bad as that?"

"Well, you could try sweeping the streets, I suppose."

"Thank you, Dad. I think I'd rather chop out appendices."

And with banter and laughing they made quite swift progress until Gerald mentioned that the Foreland Point was on their port bow;

"Well done, Jilly. Now I think we'll alter course and try north-west, looking for Ryde"

Taking the wheel, hauling in the sail in the freshening wind and rounding the shore off Bembridge, he drove the boat hard for the harbour of Ryde where they would spend the night. Eventually, tied up in the harbour, and having reported to the Harbourmaster, the family went ashore for an evening meal with all the trimmings, romantically by candlelight. There were toasts to Jilly's future and she made a little speech.

Back on board there was just room for them all in the two cabins. Snuggling down under a duvet Jilly thanked Gerald and her Mum and Dad, saying "That was a wonderful celebration; thank you all very much. Now I shall be quite happy to work day and night as long as they'll take me."

Judith and Gordon replied, "Sure they will Darling. Sleep on it."

*

Motoring in the yacht from Ryde to Southampton was a cinch. It was simply a matter of sailing near enough to the massive cruise liners to be able to wave to the passengers lining the decks while feeling smug that yachting types could be happy on sandwiches from their little fridge, unlike the liners' guests whose retirement-golden-handshakes had been damaged beyond repair by the swollen costs of their ocean voyages.

Return home was always a joy as well as a relief for folk to whom that word meant a happy haven away from the uncertainties of modern life.

For Jilly it involved the provision to prepare in every way for her coming interview.

Her parents helped in all ways from the caring for her appearance to the answers that might be desired to likely questions from the board of interviewers.

"You see Jilly," said her mother, "when you are asked why you want to be a doctor don't just say that it is to help people. It's more than that. Surely it is both to satisfy an urge to assist the sick or injured and also to give you a purpose in life that will satisfy your own desire to make your life worth while."

"Yes, Mum, I see what you man. I'll spend time this evening preparing a little speeeh."

*

The anteroom outside the interviewers' sanctum left much to be desired. A desk and chair for the receptionist, a low table on which sat a vase of wilting flowers and four or five upright chairs against the walls were all that relieved the bareness of the room. No pictures on walls, no stacks of reading material on the table. Three other students were present when Jilly entered. She sat in silence for an hour while all of them were seen. At last the bell on the desk rang briefly and the receptionist told Jilly that it was her turn. Nervously and perhaps a little shakily she opened the door and went in.

"Good morning, Miss Jenkins, please sit down," was the invitation from one of the two interviewers who were seated facing her over a long mahogany table. He was a big man, clean shaven with dark-framed spectacles. A pleasant smile lightened a slightly severe face.

His companion was an elderly lady with bright, intelligent eyes and a welcoming smile.

"We notice that you wish to study medicine. Please tell us about your motivation".

Jilly told them Other very pertinent questions followed to which she answered as well as she could. After she had left the room the two were silent for a minute. Suddenly man and woman both broke into speech together, one saying,

"That is a very interesting young lady," the other observing,

"I think that perhaps we have just met a new kind of doctor."

*

A week went by during which Jilly's eyes constantly swept the road for a sight of the postman approaching their house. One day brought the welcome news of examination successes. She revelled in the letter telling of GCSE passes, four A's and three A plus results. With a couple of B's.it was a thrill indeed.

The next day, after slitting open another letter she once again shrieked with joy.—

"I've got a place, and it's in Southampton," she declared loudly to her Mum and Dad who had been waiting with equal excitement for that letter "Hooray, hooray, hooray." She wrapped her arms around them both in ecstasy.

"Well done darling "said her Mum and,

"I told you so. Best congrats" was her father's response.

Her parents were both somewhat late for their work that morning. The celebration was quite overpowering and took some time to settle down.

****

CHAPTER 22

HELPINGS HANDS

JIILLY'S TRAIN ARRIVED in busy Southampton on time. Her father had insisted that she take a taxi from the station since she had quite strongly declined his offer to take a day off and drive her down. Three young men in the waiting queue heard her mention the medical school to the driver and asked if they might join her. Arriving there they all shared the expense. Jilly stopped to adjust her coat and sling over her shoulder a bag containing handbag, a mac, and sandwiches while the students went on in front of her.

Taking a deep breath she followed them through the door of the medical school and entered the institution where, she hoped, in five years time, that she would qualify as a doctor. She walked forward over the carpeted passage way. Approaching her, a middle aged man suddenly put his hand to his chest, swayed, crumpled at the knees and collapsed on the floor striking his head with a gentle thud on the carpet. While the other students just stood, shocked and feeling helpless, ,Jilly rushed to him, knelt, took a wrist in her hand feeling for a pulse and noted his greying colour. He was not breathing. There was no pulse. Quickly shedding her bag she placed two hands on his chest and commenced cardio-pulmonary resuscitation at about 100 pushes to the minute. Every fifteen pushes she bent, placed her mouth over the patient's, held the nostrils closed and blew. The chest rose in response. The young students gathered round in admiration. A white-coated man approached the group, saying, "I'm a doctor; what's happened?"

Pushing through the ring of students, he knelt beside the patient on the floor saying, "Why, it's Dr. Williams." Speaking to Jilly, who continued her task, he asked her for information and rapidly understood the situation. He immediately asked her to continue blowing air into the patient's lungs while he would compress the man's chest. Then he said, "There's a phone just along the passage. Will one of you please phone 999 and ask for an ambulance. Tell them it is a suspected heart attack and urgency is needed." One of them quickly ran to find the instrument, made contact with the ambulance people, and gave the message.

"They're on their way, sir", he said. Two warm coats were offered, and a woollen scarf was folded to place under the patient's head. Shortly the ambulance sirens were heard and the vehicle drew up outside the main entrance. A pair of efficient paramedics entered, bearing the tools of their trade, one being a defibrillator to restart the heart's beating. The examination was very rapid and soon electrodes were in place.

"Right, contact please" said one of the men. Immediately the patient's body jerked and a stethoscope was applied.

"Again please," said the operator. Again the jerk and this time the paramedic smiled and after listening to the heart beat said, "Good we're in business." The doctor checked the pulse that was now palpable and, on a stretcher, the patient was lifted into the ambulance. This all happened most expeditiously. Warm blankets were wrapped around Dr. Williams and the paramedics applied the contacts for an electrocardiogram.

Jilly felt in her handbag. "Would they like an aspirin?" she enquired of the doctor.

"My word, you think of everything" he replied. "I think they will have all that's necessary in the ambulance, dear. Thank you very much for your wonderful and efficient action. Are you people wanting to get to your class? If this is your first day I'll show you how to get there." Tsking Jilly by the arm he led the little troupe along to the correct door, thanking the girl again most fervently for her help. He added, "When it's lunchtime get the receptionist to find me. I think you deserve some small reward for your useful effort. My name is Dr. Roberts. Bye bye, and enjoy your first lecture. I think Dr. Williams will have a good chance of recovery, and we must leave that to the hospital."

"Gosh you've made an impression," said the young man sitting beside her in the classroom. "Where did you learn your expertise?"

"Well my dad's a G.P. and I've watched him performing at emergencies several times," she replied. Several of the other students offered her their congratulations, and Jilly began to blush a little and was glad when the lecturer commenced his introductory speech.

When the morning ended she found that Dr. Roberts had left a message for her and she was taken to a dining room where several senor staff members were sitting round a big table. They rose and welcomed her, thanking her for the help rendered to their colleague, Dr. Williams.

Jilly was seated between Dr. Roberts and a female tutor who expressed her pleasure at meeting her. They all made her feel very welcome and she quite enjoyed chatting with the lady and Dr. Roberts, both of whom made helpful hints about how she should approach her future work. She appreciated the meal which was certainly an improvement on sandwiches. Afterwards she hurriedly excused herself to ensure her punctuality at the afternoon session. She would have an interesting story to relate to her parents that night.

*

Her introduction to medicine was followed by four years of work, unrelenting and hard on mind and body. Jilly, surviving well, felt tired and in need of some relaxation.

She stood, beside her sailing dinghy looking out at the bouncing waves, stirred up by a rising wind. Into her mind stole words quoted by her English tutor when, after stimulating the mental powers of his class to imagine the little English trawler with 'salt-caked smokestack, butting up the Channel in the mad March days' he changed happily from Masefield's lovely description of the seaways and merchant vessel venturing through them to Walter-de-la-Mare, quoting,

'Bunches of Grapes, said Timothy,

Pomegranites pink, said Elaine,

A Junket of Cream and a Cranberry Tart for Me,

Leading later to… A Bumpity Ride on a Wagon of Hay for Me, said Jane.

That last line had certainly topped all the thoughts in

Jilly's mind as she watched the waters facing her outside the harbour. It had been quite calm in the morning when she thought that a quiet sail in Southampton water would be just the thing for a mild celebration at the end of her fourth year of study. Now the wind had risen and a little white froth curled over some of the small waves. A bumpitty ride it would surely be, but she thought that her sailing practice over the last four years would be sufficient to cope with that. She made ready the dinghy with sure hands and pushed the little vessel into the water. Hopping in she lowered the centreboard, fixed the rudder and grasped the tiller and sheet; then, as the wind took the sail she sat, tiller in one hand and sheet in the other. Soon the little dinghy heeled over in the wind and, leaving the harbour behind, she fixed the sheet in the cleat and made out to sea.

The four long years behind her had indeed been hard work, beset with a constant stream of unknown facts to remember, new instruments and electronic gadgets to master, and of course exams to cope with, all under the watchful eye of her tutors Most of all she had enjoyed the clinical work in the wards, examining patients, talking to them, trying to calm their fears and, when a diagnosis had been made, assessing whether they were fit for operations, germ killing antibiotics, or chemotherapy and all their likely side effects. Reporting her conclusions to her tutors and listening to their comments were salutary, but she had succeeded in acquiring a great deal of knowledge and in demonstrating her ability to use it. .

Put that behind her and concentrate on the sailing, she thought. The wind was still rising, and the boat heeled over further needing all her attention. It had picked up speed and was slicing through the water, rising and falling with a hefty slap into the troughs between the waves. She was in an area largely frequented by yachts and needed care to avoid being on a collision course. After an hour of vigorous boat handling in the midst of wind and wave she considered that to return to shore might be a wise plan. She looked around. There was plenty of room. She put the helm hard over, hopping over to the other side of the dinghy with head well bent down to avoid the swinging boom. But her foot skidded on a slippery patch and, losing her balance she fell, releasing her hold on the tiller at the same time. A strong gust of wind took the sail, the sheet flew out of her hand and in a second the dinghy was laid flat in the water with JIlly overboard struggling frantically to keep her head above water. An efficient life jacket helped while the boat was blown out of her reach and she found herself alone in the sea being pounded by small but vigorous waves.

But not quite alone. She heard the sound of an outboard engine; looking around she saw, coming towards her, a small motor cruiser. Help was at hand. A young man at the wheel deftly steered close to her, stopped his engine and threw a rope . Jilly clutched the rope and pulled as did her rescuer. She grasped the gunwale and was helped over the side into the cockpit.

"Thank you very much", she said, when she could get back her breath. "That was absolutely wonderful; it would have been a long hard swim back to shore. I'm lucky".

"Always pleased to rescue damsels in distress" he said. "I think I know you. I was sitting near you the day you rescued Dr. Williams with his coronary a few years ago. That was an expert piece of work for an up and coming first year medical student. You're Jilly Jenkins aren't you? You must be in fourth year now, am I right?" He put a towel around her shoulders and pulled the engine rope.

"Yes that's correct. I've just finished it. Thank you for

the towel, much warmer. .You must be qualified now. Are you working in Southampton?"

"I graduated last year and they gave me a job in the hospital, houseman in medicine. My name is Ben Bradshaw."

"Nice to meet you Ben, and I'm very grateful indeed for the rescue. By the way where is my boat? It was getting blown away. Oh look there it is," and she pointed.

Ben revved the outboard and shortly drew alongside the dinghy. Jilly reached over the gunwale and managed to grasp the sheet that was trailing in the water. The dinghy was on its side with the mast and sails lying flat. Ben gave her a hand in pulling it alongside and then, reaching for the stays they succeeded in pulling the boat up. While Jilly kept a tight hold on her dinghy Ben stepped into it and lowered the sail, fixing it on the boom He returned to the motor boat and suggested tying the dinghy to a rear cleat by its painter.

"It's half full of water; so could you manage first to empty some of it out with this polythene bucket, Jilly? We can tow it then, but it's a bit heavy at present."

So leaning over the side Jilly scooped bucketfuls of water out of her little boat until Ben said, "That's fine, I think we can get going now. I'll just attach it behind us with the painter fixed in a cleat I'll apply a stronger rope as well and we'll motor along slowly. Tell me where you keep the dinghy," It was certainly a bumpy passage over the bouncing waves, but at last they reached Ben's mooring in the harbour and made the motor boat fast. Ben then attached Jilly's boat to his own small dinghy and used its paddles to row to the shore where they pulled them both up on their trolleys and tied them up, stowing mast, sails, rudder, centreboard and paddles under the boat covers.

"What about a spot of supper somewhere. There's a

convenient small restaurant nearby which does quite a nice meal," said Ben. "You could dry off in their bathroom and eat in the warm. I have a set of dry clothes that are kept in the motor boat, if you don't mind male trousers" Jilly thanked him. She would be glad to dry off and warm up.

Some time later, showered, dried and dressed in Ben's spare set of shirt, jeans and woolly pullover, JIlly joined him in a cosy corner of the restaurant. Ben had ordered dinner, being the roast of the day – roast pork, roast spuds and hot veg – and very shortly this was brought in by a young Polish girl speaking good English and anxious to please. Jilly politely declined the offered wine asking for tomato juice with Worcester and they set to hungrily.

After settling the first pangs of hunger they began to talk. Ben told her of his work as a houseman, describing some of the staff with whom he worked, tall or short, thick or thin, serious and earnest or cheery and happy-go-lucky. The senior consultant and sisters were accorded his respect however and he learned much from them all.

"I suppose you have finished your fourth year now, so are you taking a break before sitting down to the finals next year?" he enquired.

"Yes I'm going home for a couple of weeks and then coming back to share digs with two other girls and working in M & S until the term starts. I'll be doing a bit in the wards sometimes too. I might learn about the electrocardiogram business."

"Well if you are not desperately busy perhaps I could detach you from your electronic wizardry with patients and we could join together for a spot of sailing sometimes before the weather becomes too bad. I'd like to learn how to handle a dinghy. The motor boat is just loaned to me by my father."

"Yes, OK. That would be very nice at a weekend sometimes. All work and no play make Jack a dull boy, or so says the ditty. I'm quite sure it applies to girls too".

The meal was enlightened by stories of hospital life, serious, funny and sometimes quite merry. Ben, a muscular, athletic looking six footer with a twinkle in his eyes and a ready laugh, wore his dark brown curly hair rather long, often stroking it backwards with his right hand. He regaled Jilly with accounts of his days as a student in the operating theatre, picking out the odd mannerisms of the surgeons and the apparent absent mindedness of the anaesthetist who, in fact, was extremely expert in his work but often pretended to be far away in a never, never land of make believe. To an anxious surgeon who suggested that he might check sometimes to ensure that the subject was still alive, he would reply that since severed arterioles in the wound still spouted bright red blood he thought there was no need for concern. Jilly found Ben delightful company, enjoying his stories and countering sometimes by relating stories of her younger days on holiday in the faery land of Cornwall, where mighty seas thundered relentlessly against the age old rocks of the promontories.

"Surely" said Jilly, thinking of westerly gales that battered that county, "Tennyson must have stood upon the beach below Tintagel on a stormy day with lowering clouds and angry sea, when he was inspired to write of 'wave on advancing wave, each mightier than the last'". Cornwall had always been her favourite *Shangri la*. Their time together was well spent but at last she felt obliged to say that it was time for her to return and pack her things ready for travelling home next day. Ben offered to run her back to her digs, an offer that she gladly accepted, thanking him when they separated with a quick kiss on his cheek.

The next morning a taxi conveyed her and her heavy suitcase to the station and Jilly sighed with satisfaction as the train slid quietly from the station towards her home.

*

"I'll pick her up, Judy"; said Gordon. "I have the time of her train's arrival. I told the receptionist yesterday to leave me an un-booked space of twenty minutes. That should be adequate for reaching the station, collecting Jilly and her luggage and getting her back home. Then back to the surgery again and I'll do an extra half hour."

"Good, and I shall be able to come home for lunch today. I have got it all ready in the bottom oven," replied Judith. "It will be lovely to see her again. Only one more year to go and she will be spreading her wings and leaving the nest for good."

"I suppose so, unless she acquires a hospital job locally. Then she could live at home sometimes. How would you cope with two doctors in the house?"

"That could be a problem; do doctors always 'think the same and cordially agree'?" And they agreed that with the advancement of medical knowledge younger medics might well possess ideas unknown to the older stagers. Time would doubtless reveal all. They separated to their respective work places.

Jilly's train swept into the station on time and she jumped out to be hugged in a joyful welcome by her father. Securing her heavy suitcase he led her to the car and soon afterwards was escorting her to her dearly-loved home. Sally from next door stood at the door to welcome her with a hug and assured her that her room was all ready and her mother would be joining them for lunch.

"Wonderful," said Jilly. "Home looks lovely as always, and how are your little nippers, and have they had all their injections, or am I completely out of date?"

"All in good order, darling Jilly. No need to practice your medicine here. We're well served by your Dad," laughed Sally. "You are indeed hopelessly out of date. My two little nestlings that were have grown like you. They are important members of Senior school now so I have to mind my p's and q's.. Coffee is all waiting for you, so we can have a chat when you're ready. Your Dad will be going back to his surgery."

Gordon returned downstairs after lugging the suitcase up to Jilly's bedroom. "By the weight of that object I surmise that you propose to be busy with homework. Is it full 0f medical textbooks? Perhaps I could borrow one sometimes and get up to date on a few items. Meantime my patients are waiting so bye-bye, my Jilly darling, and I'll be back for lunch."

An hour later Judith's car entered the drive and Jilly rushed to throw her arms around her Mum. As always it was a rapturous reunion. Sally left them to enjoy their privacy together.

"Absolutely super to be back, Mum, and you look wonderful." Jilly was always in finely tuned accord with her mother and appreciated her progress in the work of the Antiques business where she had become almost a partner to Gerald.

"Lovely to see you my Precious; have you had a good term? Now for the final push; decorating your shoulders with a stethoscope and walking tall among the hospital corridors. Come and let's have a chat."

Joining her mother with a cuppa Jilly mentioned that her holiday would involve some working time with books and invited her to view the selection brought in her suitcase.

"Good gracious JIlly, that's a massive weight of literature. How did you carry all that to the station?"

"No problem, Mum. Ben couldn't help this morning but the taxi driver was most efficient and helpful and put it in the train for me."

"That was nice darling. Who is Ben may I ask?"

"Oh, when I was out in the dinghy yesterday a gust of wind knocked me flat with the boat overturned. Ben was nearby in a motor boat and rescued me. He's really nice. We had a meal later at a restaurant where I dried out and wore his spare shirt and jeans He qualified last year and has a medical job in the hospital at Southampton."

"I see" said Judith, visualising rather a lot, but adroitly moving the conversation to more homely topics. These occupied them until it was time to prepare for lunch. Jilly unpacked and inspected the garden

"Autumn is nearly here Mum. Are you planting any more exotic offerings this year? What happened to that pineapple plant that Dad wanted planted last spring in the greenhouse?"

"It was the plant base from which a pineapple had grown. Dad had brought it back from Africa, wrapped in polythene. It escaped the customs somehow, very naughty. He was convinced that when planted in warm soil it would grow another pineapple. Alas, the poor thing had other ideas and quietly faded away. So no, I think we're well established now. Exercise with Dad and fun with the Inner Wheel keep me out of mischief. Help me to plant spring bulbs my Darling. The garden can look after itself once we've cleared up the fallen leaves of summer and autumn."

The scrunch of tyres was heard as Gordon pulled up

in the drive. A family lunch was on the menu and a merry time it was with just the three of them. Dad wanted the textbook of medicine. Jilly said he'd have to join the queue; there were four people after it and their names were all Jilly. So Dad recalled a case that was puzzling him in the surgery and recounted to his daughter all the symptoms, asking for a consultation, if she could spare the time. Jilly thought, then, "Have you considered the possibility of a psychological problem resulting in a succession of well considered symptoms designed to attract the attention of the doctor?"

"Golly" said her Dad. "What medical language. Maybe you've hit the nail on the head. It's all emotion now-a-days. You mean of course 'How are her marital relations?' I think I'll leave you and Mum to sort out that little job. How about it Judith?"

She screwed up her face replying, "My appointment book is rather over full at present. Would a month on Monday be OK?"

The suggestion fell on stony ground, giving way to all the fun and banter of former years and returning to the happy family life that had always been theirs. The return of Johnny from senior school and his sister Grace from the college where she was studying science and art completed their cheerful assembly, giving rise to questions and comment that would keep their minds active for the two weeks that was all Jilly could spare before settling to a job in a big city store, with minor hospital jobs to assist her intensive study after work in the evening. .

Twice her father invited her, with his patients' agreement to accompany him on house visits when she acquired instruction from him in listening to the complaint, examining the patient and, when possible, reaching a diagnosis. The first episode involved differential diagnosis between an 'acute gall ladder', a coronary attack, pneumonia or simply indigestion. She declared for a coronary and phoned the ambulance whose E.C.G confirmed her diagnosis. The second gave her practice in discovering 'a probable retrocaecal appendicitis'. Again she cleverly decided on the appendix and the hospital agreed with her. On the morning of her return to take up her store job, Dad told her of another important diagnostic opportunity. She promptly went for it and chose a later train. Examination for 'a ruptured ectopic gestation' was her useful experience on this occasion. Once again having correctly diagnosed the trouble she arranged hospital admission under her father's guidance and felt very pleased with herself.

*

The taxi driver at Southampton grumbled gently at the weight of her suitcase, but kindly conveyed her from the station to digs already arranged, courtesy of the university's staffing arrangements. The next morning found her on a bus for the city centre where she donned suitable wear for selling cosmetics to customers. The same evening there came a phone call from Ben. He expressed himself vigorously, "I'm thoroughly fed up with the eternal moans and groans of folk in the medical wards. Is there any hope of fun on the water?"

"Ditto," said Jilly. "What's the point of selling face cream to people who have already washed their faces and whose skin can cope with the ravages of time and weather better than the expensive face cosmetics. I have a day off on Thursday. Let's go. Two o'clock at the boat house."

It became a weekly adventure to the satisfaction of

them both. When at last the autumn term approached Jilly knew that such fun would have to be sacrificed for intensive study. Perhaps just an occasional jaunt should suffice, weather permitting. Maybe an evening meal of fish and chips or beans on toast would keep the friendship going.

Then the lectures, the tutorials, the instruction in modern methods with all the business of coping with electronics, making and writing up notes and keeping abreast with the expert teachers who valiantly sought to instil good medical practice into their students' minds. There was little let up. Christmas was celebrated at home happily, but soon she would start work again and continue throughout the New Year towards the finals in midsummer.

Jilly coped with it all, tired often, working till late at night and even till one or two in the morning sometimes. Then, struggling with winter weather to boot, she was thankful to live in the south of the country without the threat of skidding on the ice and the inches of snow that afflicted northern climes.

Easter brought a week's relief and a welcome short holiday at Bifford where her parents provided refreshment and sympathy. Attendance at her Grandfather's church with her mother and Dad was also a delightful experience where some of his parishioners congratulated her on all her work and success News of her clever work in suggesting to her father the possible diagnosis of several of his patients had reached them in roundabout ways and was still remembered. They were impressed. So was Jilly. So were her parents.

The final term. There was no relief from constant study, but an occasional outing on the water for Jilly and Ben proved a useful means of relaxation. Sitting at the helm, rowing home when the wind dropped, wrapping up the sails, setting up the dinghy on its trolley, - all these routines of a different nature followed by a simple meal in a café provided excellent refreshment of body and mind. Then came the final tests, the exam papers, the oral interviews and the anxieties, the waiting for results; the thoughts of how a better answer might have secured a higher mark and all the worries of young folk facing the stressful news of failure or triumph.

****

CHAPTER 23

A̲T̲ ̲L̲A̲S̲T̲ ̲C̲A̲M̲E̲ the great day. The results were published. Jilly had passed. She was, at last, a doctor.

It only remained to announce the result to her parents, attend her graduation, receive her Diploma with her shoulders adorned by the elaborate tribal gown, and she would be ready to face the world.

But first the all important telephone call to her Mum who was at work in her office…

"Hallo Mum, guess what. Your daughter is sporting a stethoscope around her neck".

"Oh, that is wonderful my Darling. Warmest congratulations. With two doctors in the family we shall have to mind our 'p's and 'q's like Sally said. What fun! I'll ring Dad on his surgery number, or perhaps you had better do that. . I'll give you his number. I'll ring you back when I'm free."

"That's all right Mum, I know his number; it's in my

head.. I'll get onto him right away." And she did. Gordon was in the middle of his morning surgery when his receptionist told him that his daughter was on the line. He asked the girl to get Jilly's number and, having finished writing his patient's prescription and said 'goodbye', he promptly phoned back. The voice of his dear daughter was thrilling with excitement.

"Dad, guess what". She gave him no time to reply. "I've done it. I'm through. I'm a doctor. I told you I would pass."

"That's marvellous my Darling. Welcome to the club. Congrats and when do we come to that most important ceremony, your graduation?"

But Jilly was far too full of excitement to register the information about that great day. She simply nattered to her father about exams, orals, friends and their joys and disappointments until her Dad said, "What about Grandpa? Are you going to ring him now?"

She took the hint and rang John. Mary took the call saying that her husband was out visiting some parishioners. Suddenly the penny dropped. "Oh, Jilly, have you got news?" The excitement began again and the phone line grew warm with the wild thrill in Jilly's voice. Eventually Mary broke in saying, "I'll tell John as soon as he comes in. He will be delighted. What about Gerald? Are you going to ring him too?"

Judith, while madly happy for her precious Jilly, had been in her office when told the news of her success. She finished typing her last letter and took the little pile to her employer for him to sign.. She managed to control herself with a carefully modulated voice when requesting signatures. As she left the room the phone on Gerald's desk was ringing. He idly stretched out as hand and picked it up. "Hallo, Gerald Jenkins speaking."

"Grandpa, it's me. What do you think?"

"I've no idea, Jilly. It's too early in the morning for an old man to think. You tell me."

"I've passed, Grandpa. Aren't I a clever girl?"

Gerald slapped the desk in exultation. "That's marvellous my pet. I knew you would." And he joined in wild jubilation until Jilly's mother re-entered with his cup of coffee. Taking the cup he said to Jilly, "When you've found out the day for the graduation ceremony you can look in the Telegraph and see what's showing in the Drury Lane theatre that evening. I've got a box booked for everyone to share. We'll celebrate with dinner at the Ritz, and I know a young lady who likes parties.

"Grandpa! You knew the date all along. What a clever old bird you are, Grandpa. Thank you, thank you, ever so much."

Gerald surrendered the phone to Judith who reckoned that he had had enough excitement and, after a while, she ended the talk, telling Jilly to go off and celebrate with her friends. "Come and see us tomorrow Darling. I'll have steak and kidney pie especially for you."

Then she added to Gerald, "I'll bet she will take Ben out for a sail in her dinghy, just to celebrate. Clever of you to find out the date and book a box, and very kind too. I guess you know what that evening show is as well. Jilly was right about the clever old bird, very clever!" And Judith bent down and gently kissed his cheek.

"Thank you, my dear" he said. "Of course I had found out the graduation arrangements before booking the theatre and the dinner. In addition we have a hotel night booked for all of us. It should be a happy evening for our clever young lady. Bless the child; she will make a fine doctor."

On the great day the family, including John and Mary were all ensconced in their booked seats in the Nuffield hall, among many other families all desirous of seeing their young people receiving the Diplomas that would entitle them to work as doctors. One by one they approached the dais and shook the hands of the Chancellor and the Minister of Health who had been persuaded to present them. Rapturous applause greeted each young doctor as they returned to their seats. There were speeches. There were loving congratulations. There were no strokes, no coronaries, no hysteria, just great joy. At last, with their admiring relatives and friends, the young men and women walked out through the doors of their university to commence their new lives in the outside world. .

Drury Lane welcomed the family along with a large crowd of folk all anxious to see what would happen when the 'Lord High Executioner' pronounced the inevitable sentence. Equally thrilled and with tears in many eyes the audience listened, rapt with emotion when 'Tit Willow' was sweetly sung of a little bird's impending doom in the waters of fate. The box was much appreciated. It was a great thrill to the young folk who had never imagined such luxury. To crown it all the late dinner at the hotel served by gloved waiters and seated among the great and good of London made it a red letter day to shine in their memory for ever. As for the late breakfast following the comfortable night in the gorgeous bedrooms, well… Jilly wondered if she could ever take to the simple things of life again.

*

But more excitement awaited the new doctor. Two letters were on the doormat on reaching home in Bifford after the weekend. Both were addressed to Dr Jilly Jenkins.. Quickly she sat to open them with fingers trembling with excitement.

Grandpa Gerald wrote "Darling Jilly, after your hard grind of five years work you deserve some reward. I remember that you longed to see the 'Glory that was Greece'. I hope you and your Mum will enjoy the cruise that I have arranged for you before you start your real work session in the hospital where you will actually learn to cure the sick. The other letter explains all. With much love from Grandpa Gerald," She could hardly wait to open the other letter. On doing so, out tumbled two tickets for a cruise to Corfu, Athens, Rhodes, Crete and Santorini, following a flight from Heathrow to Venice.

Jilly was utterly overwhelmed. Seeking her mother she flung her arms around her and burst into tears.

"Is it a bit much my Precious?" said her mother, understanding the emotions felt by her dearly loved daughter.

"It's too wonderful for words, Mum Dear Grandpa. I never thought he would realise how I've felt It is quite amazing".

"Yes, he is a remarkable man and his son takes after him. They both have depths of understanding that are not easily observed. We are very lucky to have them to care for us."

"What are the dates on the tickets Mum?"

"Let's have a look. A week today, my Darling. The holiday is for two weeks. We shall be back just in time for you to start your hospital job. He told me all about this of course."

"It's just marvellous. I shall love delving into the old

Classical times of Greece. No wonder Grandpa runs an Antiques shop. You must love it too."

"I certainly do. Now we must begin packing. We'll need to go shopping next week. There will still be plenty of sunshine in the Med. so you can pack a bikini or two."

Jilly accepted her Mum's advice and added her tiny modern camera with built-in telephone. "Just for Ben's benefit." she said.

****

Chapter 24

CLASSIC ENDING.
NEW BEGINNING.

"This is the stuff, life on the ocean wave, frantic indeed." shouted the young maiden, balancing herself. as she held tightly onto the deck furniture of their lovely big vessel ploughing through the stormy waters of the Med. "I'm glad our ship is a bit bigger than St.Paul's little boat. That must have been terrifying". Her voice only just reached her mother's ears.

"Have you learnt the geography of the Med?." shouted her Mum in reply. "Crete will be our next port of call. After that we shall bypass Malta to go north via the Adriatic again. We'll hope the storm will be over and St, Paul can have Malta all to himself."

They had enjoyed the flight to Venice and boarded their fine modern liner to sail south to Corfu. Remembering Grandpa's description of the donkeys garlanded with flowers and his account of seeing the temple of Achilles.

Jilly thrilled to see from the high cliff the view of tiny Mouse Island far below. They too loved the ride up there in the donkey powered carriage and photographing the beautiful interior of the temple of Achilles as well as the little island. Then after passing the great promontories of Greece they had docked at the Piraeus to visit the Parthenon, wondering at the marvels of ancient architecture, noting the absence of the 'marbles' removed by Lord Elgin, ostensibly to preserve them. The famous account of St.Paul's speech to the Athenians so long ago came vividly to their minds. It was all quite new and wonderful to Jilly.

Rhodes and its equally famous Colossus, now sadly disappeared beneath the waves, the walls and the feats of the Knights Templar, all were notably fed into their memories during a 'Sound and ' Light' programme during their quiet evening there. Then, on the way to Crete, the storm zoomed in from the Atlantic to provide a change from the glory of autumn sunshine and a chance to exercise their limbs in maintaining their balance on the deck while battling against the violent figure of eight movement that tormented the big vessel. An announcement had warned them all of the approaching bad weather and sandwiches had been prepared for folk to eat in their cabins if they couldn't manage the dining area They had acquired a pack of those edibles but enjoyed their time on deck hanging on to any solid and immovable objects and managing to stagger round the deck with reasonable safety. Very few others risked such a balancing exercise. Jilly felt it was an excellent introduction to the storms of winter. In hospital she would be ensconced in consulting rooms, beside patients' beds, in the operating theatre maybe, or even the post-mortem room. The fresh air, violent winds and heaving seas provided an exercise 'much to be desired', as she quoted to her Mum who did her best to enjoy her daughter's obvious pleasure in defying the fury of Nature.. So Jilly struggled and tottered round the deck and her Mum followed in a desperate attempt to emulate her daughter's physical prowess.

When she had breath to speak Jilly yelled against the noise of the storm, "Mum where do we put in to harbour on Crete?" Her mother shouted back,

"I think we go in to Iraklion on the north coast, Jilly. After that it's a coach ride to the Palace of Knossos. I don't think we shall be meeting the Minotaur, but of course you never know…."

Breathless from such an exchange they found a door and slipped inside, glad to find shelter from the ferocity of the storm that was sweeping the deck.

Judith continued, "In the Isle of Wight they have a dinosaur roaring at you. Maybe the Cretans have .thought up a nice civilised Minotaur to terrify us. You could be Ariadne with a ball of string. If Ben were here I'm sure he would make a good Theseus to go and slay the beast."

"When do we go to see Santorini Mum? " Jilly skated over the subject of Ben. Perhaps we'll sail over there first and look at the remains of the island. Then we'll cross over to Crete; the storm might be quieter by then and we shall be able to get into the harbour."

"You seem to have got your geography right. Perhaps you would like to pop up to the bridge and tell the captain which way to steer,Darling. I'm sure he would listen to wisdom from such a knowledgeable young female doctor".

Giving up the exchange they opted to retreat to their bunks.

The .next day brought some quietening of the weather and breakfast was possible in the dining area. Afterwards an announcement on the Tannoy suggested that passengers might like to view the remains of the island of Santorini, now visible as they passed by. Since the previous evening had not been suitable for the usual lecture a short account was added about the fearful explosion that had occurred thousands of years ago, when nearly the whole island had been blown up in a catastrophic volcanic upheaval that must have caused havoc throughout the Mediterranean. It had particularly affected the nearby island of Crete. After reaching Iraklion they would have the opportunity of going to see the devastation that had afflicted the Palace of Knossos.

*

The coach for Knossos was packed. Lively conversation about volcanoes, tsunamis and the terrifying effects of Nature kept passengers occupied in noisy converse. Jilly felt she had much to learn and asked their guide questions concerning the geography and also the history of Greece. She asked "What about the Minotaur? Where does that monster come in? Who was Theseus exactly, and did he and Ariadne go to Athens and live happily ever after?"

The guide listened solemnly, hiding his amusement, and tried to keep Jilly happy.

Examining the palace remains kept them all busy. The archaeologist's reconstruction of part of the palace was carefully noted and comments were passed, some approving, some suggesting that things should have been left in their devastated state. At any rate they could walk down repaired steps to the four thousand years old Queen's bathroom and view the painting of dolphins on the wall, the colours still vivid and thrilling the astonished viewers.

Also they could admire the piping, constructed thousands of years ago providing water supplies and drainage. Jilly vowed, "I must certainly visit the library and read all about Knossos when we get home. I suppose they have a library in the hospital."

"You are going to be a busy doctor my girl", said her mother. "I guess that textbooks of medical reference will be your main reading for quite some time." Her daughter, thinking, felt brought down to earth and agreed. "Yeah I guess so" she admitted..

The Adriatic proved fairly calm and they reached Venice in time to take a boat ride from the array of boats outside St. Mark's Square, going from the Grand Canal on a trip around a number of smaller canals. They observed how the canals acted as streets between the well constructed houses; and how little bridges connected them. They noted the Doge's palace, the Bridge of Sighs and finally after their boat trip they inspected carefully the Famous Church of St Mark's in the Square, and admired the gondoliers who blew kisses to them from their gondolas in the nearby waters of the Grand Canal. It was all in Judith's story. Romance was in the air as some sang songs of love, seeking to vie with the finest of Italian tenors.

"Well there you are my darling daughter. Out time is up and the plane calls. Perhaps you will come for a holiday here some day and discover much more to satisfy your mind. A family holiday in Venice could be quite instructive don't you think?"

"I guess so Mum. Meanwhile there's always the library for information, and, thanks to you and Dad, I'm quite good at delving into encyclopaedias."

*

At Heathrow, Gordon, being off duty for the week-end, was there to meet them with Grace and Johnny, all thrilled to hear about their trip in the Med. Questions were unending; Gordon begged for quiet while seeking his route out of the London area. On the motorway Jilly and her Mum tried to satisfy the enquirers until reaching home. They had a busy time.

Time indeed was of the essence for Jilly needed to be installed in her room at the hospital by Sunday evening. It was fortunate that she had had the forethought to pack all her things before the holiday. She, with the family, would even be able to attend her Grandpa's church for the morning service before leaving for London.

Gerald took them all to their favourite restaurant for dinner on the Saturday evening.

Jilly made a little speech thanking Gerald for the wonderful holiday enabling her to realise a long and earnestly desired journey backwards through time. She also thanked her Dad and Mum for all their loving care of her over the years of childhood and growing up. She thanked John and Mary for their help and influence and advised her sister and brother, saying, "You jolly well listen to your Gran. and Grandpa. They may be ancient but they're wise". (Applause!) She went on, "Finally I shall be very glad to provide knowledge and advice about modern medicine when necessary, and I wish all my family everything your hearts desire". Laughter and uproarious applause greeted her

Tales and events without number bounced to each other from all sides. It was indeed a very happy evening before the eldest bird left the parental nest to spread her wings in the outside world. Next morning Grandpa's Sunday sermon was most appropriate for a young person leaving home. Mary had provided a dinner for the family, including Gerald, and Grandpa said a little prayer committing their grand daughter to their Father's care. Then it remained only to pack all Jilly's luggage in the big car and take the road to the hospital in Southanpton. The journey was quiet. They didn't talk much.

Gordon and Judith, helped by Grace and Johnny, assisted the new doctor to take her possessions to her room in the doctors' quarters of the hospital. After a light supper in the restaurant when no one ate very much they returned to the exit and Jilly saw them to their car. It was not a time for overlong leave taking. All advice, words of wisdom, hopes of good success and future meetings had long been said. Hugs, kisses and a tear or two were exchanged with just a few words of well wishing as the family prepared to return home. Before closing her car window Judith said to her daughter as she fastened her seat belt, "We haven't met your Ben yet. I hope we shall be introduced to him some day. What's he like, Jilly?"

Jilly's eyes sparkled and a lovely smile spread across her face as she thought how to reply. …Then it came, emphatic, in no uncertain terms,. "He's absolutely gorgeous Mum". She waved them off, brushing away a tear. Turning, she braced her shoulders. Erect, with stethoscope slung around her neck, she marched firmly to the door of the hospital, took a deep breath, and entered.

Inside, waiting patiently stood Ben. "Come on, have a cuppa", he said.

THE END